DOUBLE CLUTCH

www.totallyrandombooks.co.uk

DOUBLE CLUTCH

LIZ REINHARDT

Definitions

DOUBLE CLUTCH
A DEFINITIONS BOOK 978 1 782 95124 7

First published in Great Britain by RHCP Digital,
an imprint of Random House Children's Publishers UK
A Random House Group Company

CreateSpace Independent Publishing Platform edition published 2011
RHCP Digital edition published 2012
Definitions edition published 2013

1 3 5 7 9 10 8 6 4 2

MIX
Paper from
responsible sources
FSC® C016897

Set in Palatino

Definitions are published by Random House Children's Publishers UK
61–63 Uxbridge Road, London W5 5SA

www.**randomhousechildrens**.co.uk
www.**totallyrandombooks**.co.uk
www.**randomhouse**.co.uk

Addresses for companies within The Random House Group Limited
can be found at: www.randomhouse.co.uk/offices.htm

THE RANDOM HOUSE GROUP Limited Reg. No. 954009

A CIP catalogue record for this book is available from the British Library.

Printed and bound in Great Britain by CPI Group (UK) Ltd, Croydon CR0 4YY

This book is dedicated with my whole heart to my loves, Frank and Amelia.

To the person I love to laugh with every day, my best friend and the love of my life, Frank. Being with you has challenged me to write a guy even fractionally as amazing as you are . . . and I'm very happy to report that I'll probably never do it, because you just keep getting more awesome. I love you.

To my soul, my deepest love, my brilliant Amelia. I can't even begin to imagine the millions of ways I'll keep falling in love with you over the years. Know that I love you with every fiber of my being, forever.

Double Clutch: a pattern of breathing in which a runner inhales two breaths for every one breath exhaled.

Chapter 1

My mom waltzed into my room on the morning of my first day back at high school in Sussex County, New Jersey, after a year in Denmark. I breathed a sigh of relief that she kissed my forehead like it was my first day of kindergarten instead. It was nice to have that familiar comfort on a day I knew would be full of change.

'Good morning, Brenna.' She sat on my bed and smoothed back my short, blunt fringe, which had been very cool in Denmark. I hadn't seen one on anyone here when we were shopping at Walmart and Target for back-to-school stuff. I shuddered a little when I noticed a lot of the girls had big bows tied around their high ponytails, like they should have been wearing poodle skirts and saddle shoes too. My fringe might as well have been a neon Mohawk based on the open-mouthed stares I got.

'Morning, Mom.' I slid a look at her out of the

corner of my eye. People always talked about how they thought their mother was the most beautiful woman in the world when they were little kids, but I still felt that way. My mom wasn't beautiful in a lots-of-hairspray, full-of-herself way, like women were when they regretted having kids and wound up trying hard to stay looking young. My mom had soft, freckled skin, a cleft in her chin and blue-gray eyes, like the sky in summertime when thunderclouds roll in. She had the most delicate hands, and any perfume smelled incredible on her skin. I loved her fiercely, and to protect her, I swallowed around the lump of pure, raw nerves that was growing by the second in my throat.

'Don't be nervous.' When it came to reading my thoughts, my mom was a fortune teller.

'I'm not.' I raised my eyebrows, mostly to keep the tears from spilling from my eyes. 'I am *world traveled*.' Funny how glamorous our little joke still sounded. Like we sunbathed on the Riviera or strolled through Paris modeling the latest fashions. In fact, we spent most of our year abroad holed up in a quaint old dairy farm reading books. A lot of books.

'Don't I know it.' Her eyes crinkled at the corners when she smiled.

I smiled back. 'We already conquered *The Scarlet Letter*. What more can they throw at me?'

Mom guided me through a home-school program in Denmark, because there was no way I could curl my tongue around Danish fast enough to be eligible for even elementary school. Since I breezed through the thin ninth-grade pack and moved on to devour the tenth just to do something other than stare at the fields around our house, I was technically ahead of my class. But being ahead didn't mean school would be a breeze because this year I would be attending two schools.

I was going to have the world's weirdest schedule. Because I'd been able to do what I wanted while we home-schooled, I flew through my math and science requirements, and now I was loaded up with English and American government. I also had to take crafts, just to fill out my early day. In the afternoon, I'd head to trade school. I didn't know anyone who'd taken a schedule quite like mine before, but the guidance counselors said I would be on track to graduate with my class in twelfth grade, even with my dual schedule, so I figured it was all OK. No matter how weird my year might be, it couldn't be any stranger than doing classes all alone in a foreign country and only talking to tutors over email, so I figured I'd probably be fine.

Mom pursed her lips and squinted at me a little. 'Are you sure tech school is a good idea?'

'It's Share Time, Mom,' I pointed out.

This meant I would be spending half my day at the regular academic high school and half my day at the vocational technical school down the road, which Mom wasn't thrilled about. Share Time students, or Techies, as they're called, graduate with a regular diploma. But Techies might as well wear a big scarlet 'T' on their shirts as far as academic high-schoolers are concerned, and I was trying not to dwell on the whole outcast thing any more than I had to.

'It's *tech school*.' Mom rolled it off her tongue like she was trying to get a bad taste out of her mouth.

She graduated, six months pregnant with me, from an academic high school. She should have gone to university, but she had to raise me. My mom has always been one of the most brilliant people I'd ever met, degree or no.

'Don't say it like that.' I tugged on her little hand. I didn't get my hands from her. Mine are long and bony with short, thin nails and bumpy knuckles. 'It's only half the day,' I argued. 'I still get a good academic thing in the morning. When we did all that photography and silk-screen printing in Denmark, I was really interested. Technical art gives you skills you can keep forever. And it will help when I want to get a job, much more than throwing pots and making macramé will, but you never get upset when I take an art class. Haven't you always taught me to be self-sufficient?'

'Yes, yes, yes.' She closed her eyes and kissed me by my ear, hard. 'You want breakfast?' I let out a small sigh of relief; the tech conversation was over for the day.

'How about porridge?' I'd acquired a taste for porridge in Denmark and couldn't shake it now.

I rolled out of bed and stood like a dazed alien in my own room. On one hand it was so familiar, I could see every detail when I closed my eyes. On the other, it was another world. It was exactly the same as the day Mom decorated it when I was nine, the year Mom married Thorsten. Every detail was how I remembered it, right down to the lace-edged gingham curtains. I always felt comfortable in it, like it was a part of me, until the day we got back from Denmark and I opened the door and stood, shocked, looking at my private space with new eyes. Really new eyes.

Lilac walls complemented a patchwork bedspread. Over the bed hung three pictures of cats doing cute, silly things, like batting at butterflies. The wooden floor was covered by a black-and-white checked rug. There was a tall, white chest of drawers filled with clothes I hadn't worn for over a year. I pulled open the creaky drawers and took out piece after piece slowly, surprised by how little sense they made. When did I ever like clothes like this? They were mostly plain crewnecks and polos and unflattering jeans with glitter and heavily stitched logos on them. In the closet were two pairs of boring, white Keds sneakers and a pair of penny loafers. I picked up one of the shiny loafers, which seemed like they were the kind of shoe a young child would wear, and it was strange they were something I loved only a year ago. These clothes were so unlike who I was this morning, a girl about to go to her first real day of high school, I felt like I was looking through a little kid's dressing-up box.

I pulled my suitcase from under the bed, and vowed that I really would unpack. Soon.

The clothes in my suitcase were the only part of the room that felt real to me, and my stomach clenched with excitement as I dug through for the perfect first-day-of-school outfit for a new year and a new me. I took out my slim midnight-black jeans, a pair of black Converse, my favorite black-and-purple striped sweater, and a tight black V-neck T-shirt to go under-neath.

I yanked a brush through my long, light-brown hair, and imagined it dyed a come-hither red or a daring black. Mom cut my fringe herself, but told me hair-dye was a mistake that could wait until I was older. I ran the toothbrush in slow circles around my teeth and tried to swallow back the acidic churning in my gut.

As I smoothed my make-up on, I thanked Odin for all that time in the Danish countryside with Mom's *Cosmopolitan* magazines and no soda. My skin, which had been spotty and gross in middle school, had cleared up and become the perfect canvas for hours of cosmetic experiments in Denmark. If the retro-disco look ever caught on like *Cosmopolitan* promised it would, I would have hours of practise with metallic eye shadow and false eyelashes under my belt.

When I came out to the kitchen, my stepfather was putting a bowl of porridge on the table. 'Hey, Fa.' I kissed him on the cheek. 'Fa' is what kids in Denmark call their dads, and since Thorsten is from Denmark and not quite my dad, 'Fa' seemed like a good alternative.

'Ready for the new day, Brenna?' Thorsten smiled. He had straight, white teeth. He'd never even had to see an orthodontist. They sometimes made me wish I was his biological kid, just so I could have avoided my painful face-off with braces.

'I think I am.' The force of my lie made my porridge sit heavy in my gut.

'Do you want a ride in?' he offered.

'No, Fa, it's cool. You have a long drive to work. Anyway, the bus is OK with me.' I pushed my congealing porridge around in the bowl. 'I wish we were close enough to ride my bike in.' I shot a pleading look at Thorsten, who looked at my mother expectantly.

'You know I don't like it.' She sighed. 'Danish people are used to cyclists, Brenna. This isn't Denmark. Cars aren't going to be expecting you. What if you get hit? What if someone grabs you and takes you?'

I said what I knew was the only thing that might possibly work. 'That's cool.' I made sure to keep my voice only very slightly depressed. 'I'll miss the exercise, but I'll get over it.'

I could feel her wavering, but I didn't look up. I couldn't blow it now.

'Brenna, you would only be able to do it for a few weeks. Soon it will be freezing and then it will start to snow.' Her voice was full of worry.

Then she was quiet, waiting for me to beg or plead or cry, but there was no chance of that. My mom was a master at persuasion and getting what she wanted, and I learned my techniques from the master herself. Finally, she gave a loud sigh.

'Fine. But you need to leave now, so you have plenty of time. No riding with your iPod in. And keep your phone in your pocket.'

I squeezed her shoulders tight and smacked a kiss on her cheek. 'Love you!' My jacket and backpack already in hand, I breezed a kiss on Thorsten's face and beat it before Mom had a change of heart. 'Have a good day, Fa!'

'You too!' He focused his conspirator's smile on his iPad, but I caught it.

'Be good! Be safe! Love you!' Mom followed me to the garage, where I unlocked my bike and grabbed my helmet. My iPod was safely hidden in my pocket. I needed my music, but didn't need Mom to worry. As if she knew my intent to break the rules, she grabbed me and kissed me again.

'I'll be fine,' I reassured her. 'I'll call you before I leave school.'

Mom looked like she might cry, just like she had on the first day of school every year of my life. For the first time, I felt like crying, too, so I knew I had better hit the road fast if I wanted to make it to school without puffy, red-rimmed eyes.

I got on my bike and started pedaling. I was going to have to ride close to five miles, but I was up for it. I loved the freedom of it. I liked being able to get myself places. My sixteenth birthday was October 11th, so even though I'd be eligible for my permit to learn to drive, my license was far away. Until I got it, my bike was the best chance I had for freedom.

I pedaled hard; I didn't want to be late on my first day. I gulped down the clean, cool air mixed with the sweet, rotten smell of dead leaves and the acrid smoke from burn piles. I focused on the pumping of my legs and the strong beat of my heart. I had been fairly sedentary before the big Denmark adventure, and the further I got from that kid, the more I wanted to leave behind her old, lazy habits.

Before I knew it, I reached the high school, all three stories of sandy-colored stone with wide front steps and a patio with trees and bushes and benches. There was a completely empty bike rack, where I parked and chained my bike. Then I walked up the front steps and into the reception with my eyes trained straight ahead of me.

The school had the same weird familiar yet un-familiar feeling that my room had. I had toured it and the tech school back in eighth grade, when I was so excited about starting high school I could hardly con-tain it. I didn't know then that within a few months I would be leaving for an entire year. Only a few of my friends even knew where I went because it had all come together so quickly and we were all separated during summer vacation.

I wondered if anyone would recognize me. I was so nervous, I couldn't look at anyone.

'Brenna? Brenna Blixen? Is that you?'

I turned and saw a fairly heavy-set girl with a large nose, bright-red lipstick and curly black hair with a big bow in it. But she was cheerful and smiley so I tried not to hold the bow against her.

'Meg Yakovy?' I was suddenly folded in an excited hug.

'Yeah! You look great! Did you really go to Germany with your parents and the Peace Corps?' Her curls shook around her excited face.

'No. I went to Denmark. My stepdad inherited some land and a house, and we went there so we could fix it up.' I wriggled in her firm grip and she let me go.

'Oh.' Her face fell, apparently disappointed that it hadn't been the Peace Corps and Germany. 'So, did you, like, meet some hot Dutch boys?'

'Danish,' I corrected. 'Um, no. I was in Jutland. It's a lot of farms and stuff. We didn't have any neighbors my age, and my mom home-schooled me, so I didn't go to school.'

Her eyes shimmered with agonized, sympathetic

tears. 'That must have been so, so terrible. Just you and your parents.' She shivered and closed her eyes. 'I would have killed myself.'

'Uh, it wasn't so bad.' I hadn't been in the company of someone my age for months, but she seemed weirdly dramatic.

'Well, you look really pretty! You should try out for the drama production. It's *The Miracle Worker*. It's going to be amazing.' Only she said it *ah-MAYZ-ing*. And shivered again. She was making me kind of cold.

Aha. Meg and drama club. How could I forget her belting out 'Tomorrow' all through seventh grade when she landed the lead in *Annie*?

'I will, uh, think about it.' The idea of getting on stage and performing sounded almost as appealing as hot pokers in my eyeballs, but I didn't want the first person who talked to me to hate my guts right away. 'So, it was good seeing you, but I have to check in at the office.'

'All right!' She hugged me again and shook me back and forth a few times. 'It was so, so good to see you, Brenna. I am so, so glad you're back.' Another warm, perfume-dense hug.

Meg was a nice girl. She signed 'HAGS' in my yearbook at the end of eighth grade, short for 'have a great summer', and added the obligatory, 'See you in high school!' But, other than that, I could hardly remember her talking to me. Maybe high school just made her even friendlier?

I made it to the office unrecognized by anyone else and waited behind kids who didn't like their schedules and were pretty much being told to deal with it and get to class. Harsh, but it made the line move really quickly.

'Hello.' I put my hands on the counter and unpacked my biggest smile. I'd worked on my smile a lot in Denmark because, since I had never learned more than a few basic sentences of Danish, I found that a big friendly smile (besides marking me out as an American) was appreciated as an attempt at communication. 'My name is Brenna Blixen, and today is my first day.' I handed the lady behind the counter my registration forms.

'Brenna Blixen.' The secretary had curly red hair and kind eyes that soothed my anxious nerves. 'I heard about you. Didn't your family take off and go to Austria for a while?'

'Denmark.' I sighed. Why did Thorsten have to be from the least recognized of all of the European nations?

'Well, welcome to Frankford High.' She smiled wide. 'I'm Mrs Post, and you can come here if you need anything. Wow, you have a crazy schedule,' she added, suddenly noticing what was on the paper she held out to me. 'You're going to do Share Time?'

I tried to guess what her tone of voice implied, but I had no idea, so I decided to pretend it was just curiosity, even if it wasn't. 'Yes. Graphic design.'

'You didn't strike me as a hair and beauty type.' She handed me the paper.

I wasn't sure how to respond, so I just shrugged. 'Thanks.' I gave her a little wave and walked out.

'Brenna! Brenna!'

My heart lifted a little. A voice I knew.

'Kelsie!' I cried and we embraced, a real hug this time. Kelsie Jordan was still petite and still had dark, shiny hair and pretty eyes. She also had a plump butt, something she had always hated, but I thought it made her look curvy and sexy.

'You look incredible. Not that you didn't look great in eighth, but you look really cool now.' She swept her hair behind her ear and a pair of silvery bell earrings chimed sweetly.

Kelsie had changed her style, too. I had a flashback to both of us in polo necks, shiny jeans, and Keds. Today she wore a hippie-type peasant shirt and dark jeans with sandals and a flowery bandana in her long, dark hair. My mom always said Kelsie's hairline was too low to make her truly pretty, but I think that was just because my mom didn't like Kelsie. Because looking at her glowing right in front of my eyes, there was no denying how beautiful she was.

'You do, too. Look cool, I mean. It's weird to be back.' I shifted my backpack and tugged on the edge of my sweater. 'It's like I know everyone, but I don't, you know?'

'It must be crazy. Let's see your schedule.' She snatched it out of my hands. 'Hey, we've got crafts together!' Her head snapped up. 'Brenna, they have you down for Share Time!' Her voice didn't leave me wondering. She was clearly horrified.

'Yeah, graphic design.' I took the schedule back and folded it into a tiny rectangle that I turned over and over in my fingers.

'But you were always so smart.' She held up her hands, at a loss. 'Why would you go to tech?'

'It's just Share Time.' I could feel the scarlet 'T' glowing on my forehead and a little nagging voice in my head wondered if I should have listened to my mother. 'I gotta go. I'm gonna be late for English. Do you know where 204 is?'

Kelsie pointed down the hall, her hand glittering with silver and amber rings, rows of beaded bracelets swishing on her wrist. 'Go to the end of the hall, turn left. It's on the left, the English side. Right side is the art room, so I'll meet you there third?' We didn't say anything for a minute, then she pulled me into another quick hug, but this one was a little awkward.

I ran down the emptying hall, determined not to be late for class, and I sat down as the bell rang. Mr Dawes, the tutor, walked in. He was a fat, squat man with a ready scowl and a syllabus designed to knock us out from day one. There was a lot I had read last year, and a lot I hadn't. Vonnegut stood out like an old, familiar friend, and the plays by O'Neill sent a shiver down my spine based on title alone. Who wouldn't fall instantly in love with *Mourning Becomes Electra*? I saw Jane Austen's name and had the funny feeling we were going to be good friends, and I sighed with relief when I saw *The Grapes of Wrath*. It had collected dust on my shelf for two years, spine uncracked, but I felt like it was something every American had to read.

A quick glance around the room told me that I was in foreign territory. Frankford High pulled from four districts, and my middle school was one of the smallest, so I wasn't going to see too many kids from there.

Mr Dawes took attendance rapidly, glancing up with narrowed eyes after each name. 'This is honors English, kids.' His growl made me sit up straighter and click my pen with purpose. 'I don't accept late work. At all. And I don't announce every quiz and in-class writing. Stay on your toes.'

He looked a bit like one of Santa's jolly old elves, just in a really scowly, pissed-off mood. He tossed us copies of *Lord of the Flies* by William Golding and we passed around the sheet where we put our names and how beat up our book was, probably so he could fine us accordingly when we handed them back in. I thumbed through the book, which I'd read before. Even though it was about a bunch of killer schoolboys, I'd never managed to get into it. But I decided it was a fresh year, and the best tactic was to give everything an equal chance, even if it had disappointed me before. The boy in front of me turned around and stared at me like I was a fish in an aquarium.

'You need something?' I asked. His direct gaze made me squirm.

'Who are you?' His social graces were so awful they were almost funny.

'Brenna Blixen. Who are you?'

'Devon Conner.' He shuffled his big feet and blinked hard. 'Are you new?'

'Kind of.' I watched him bite the inside of his cheek.

'Mr Conner, Ms Blixen, why don't you join your classmates in silent reading?' Mr Dawes scowled.

I ducked my head over my book quickly and

Devon followed my lead. Pissed off a teacher on day one, first period. Great.

I focused on the story, the boys on the mysterious island, lost and confused and clinging to the order that had dictated their lives in their schools back in England. I felt like I had the sacred conch shell in my hand, my feet on the white sand beaches, Jack and Ralph glaring on either side of me, when the bell jarred me back into the noisy classroom where Mr Dawes waved a hand, dismissing us.

I had to race across the school, stopping a few times to ask directions, before I found my next classroom. I got there last, again, just slipping into the chair at the bell. The teacher barely looked up.

This was my AP class in American government, where I'd be at least a year younger than every other student. I was very nervous to take an advanced placement class, but it fit my weird schedule, I had the prerequisites for it, and my guidance counselor said universities were looking for lots of AP courses on transcripts. It was never too early to plot life after Sussex County. My classmates checked me out coolly, like a group of sharks.

A total of eight students and our teacher, a graying hulk of a man in a too-tight shirt, sat in an ante-chamber around a u-shaped table. The teacher took names with impersonal speed in his plan book with a ruler underneath his pen at all times. It struck me as weird, but the other students were paying no attention, busy organizing notebooks, laying out pens, examining textbooks with sharp, eager eyes. Whoa, alpha class.

There was one exception.

He had inky black hair that managed to look both perfectly styled and like he'd just crawled out of bed at the same time. His dark brown, almond-shaped eyes flicked slowly around the room, clearly unimpressed with everyone and everything. His olive skin was smooth except for a prickle of five o'clock shadow already darkening his jaw. Those eyes settled on me and his lips curved into a taunting grin that tugged at me and made me fight not to grin right back. He didn't have a backpack, didn't have any papers out, and didn't seem the least bit interested in his textbook. He was calm amid all the busy chaos, leaning back in his chair with a sleepy, bored look in his eyes.

'Sit up before you break your neck, Saxon!' the teacher barked. The dark-eyed boy gave him a sharp salute and banged the chair down on all four legs, never taking his eyes off of me. My mouth dried up and my heart hammered fast and erratic.

'I'm Mr Sanotoni, for whoever's new. Who's new?'

The teacher looked down at the roll book and up. 'Blixen? Like the reindeer?' The class chuckled with him.

I cleared my throat. 'I think you might be thinking of Blitzen? My last name is Blixen, like the Danish author. Pen name Isak Dinesen.'

'I like this one.' Mr Sanotoni pointed at me with his ruler and laughed a strange sound that was something between a bark and a howl. Everyone else joined in except Saxon.

Sanotoni stood up and snapped down a map of the United States. 'We're dividing into parties and setting up a mini caucus,' he ordered. 'Let's make it a three-party system in honor of the kooks who think that might ever work.' He barked/laughed again, handed out pamphlets and instructed us to move into groups to start answering the campaign sign-in questions using the textbooks he gave out. A petite girl looked at Saxon then me, rolled her eyes, and headed over with lots of huffing and sighing.

Saxon sauntered over, plopped his textbook down on the table and fell into the chair with a lazy smile just for me.

For some reason, that smile made me think of a predator. I shivered suddenly. Meg Yakovy's dramatics had definitely rubbed off on me.

'I'm Brenna Blixen.' Kind of unnecessary since Sanotoni just mocked my name, but between Saxon's sexy stare and the girl's pronounced scowl, I felt like someone needed to make normal introductions.

'I'm Lynn Orr,' snapped the girl, shooting at me out of her eyes. 'This is Saxon Maclean. Are you planning on actually working this term, Saxon?'

'Why should I bother? Don't you already know all the answers, Lynn?' His words stretched out slow and sweet as warm taffy. He turned the wattage of his lazy smile on Lynn, and that smile only widened when she snarled in his direction.

'You're such a stoner. I don't even know how you got into this class,' she pouted, flinging her textbook open.

Saxon uncrossed his long arms and leaned close to her, his words sliding out with lazy glee. 'Well, it wasn't based on the fact that my mommy's the big, fat mayor. Isn't that how you got in?'

'Screw you, loser,' she hissed, her hands clawed around the edges of her book, her teeth bared.

'Um, so I think the answers to questions one to three are on page eighteen,' I announced a little loudly. 'About registration requirements. Here, on page eighteen,' I repeated, thumping my index finger on the page, hoping to distract them from jumping across the table and ripping each other's throats out.

'You're right,' Lynn sneered at me, her glare fixed on Saxon. He crossed his arms and flexed his muscles, the biceps bulging under the sleeves of his T-shirt, clearly enjoying Lynn's simmering temper. 'Aren't you going to write this down, Saxon?'

He flipped her a smile and shrugged.

'Why don't we all just do our thing and not worry about anyone else?' I suggested desperately.

'Yeah, and what if we get a group grade, genius?' Lynn turned her malice on me. 'Are you willing for your GPA to take a nosedive for this idiot?'

I blinked in the face of her open hostility. 'Well, if we get a group grade, it will probably be based on one paper,' I pointed out. 'So, let's get one done, and we'll save all our grade point averages. OK?'

'This is bullshit,' Lynn muttered, but she began filling her questions in with angry slashes of her pen.

Saxon winked at me and pulled his chair over so our shoulders bumped. He wore cologne. I had smelled guys' cologne a million times before, but whatever he wore made me want to bury my head in his chest and take long, deep breaths until my lungs couldn't take it any more. My pen wobbled in my shaky fingers. Saxon leaned over my open book, his warm arm pressed against mine, his cheek inches from my face, and acted as if he were innocently checking the pages. 'You rode a bike in.' His voice was low, so low that Lynn didn't even look up.

He noticed I rode a bike in? How? When? My head swam. Words. I needed words. 'Yeah,' I finally managed. 'I ride my bike to school.'

'You won't be able to do that for long. New Jersey winters are long and cold. Lots of snow.' His voice had a vibration to it that I felt right in the pit of my stomach. It was almost like he was this big, purring jungle cat.

Ugh, what was I thinking? Who was I, Mowgli? I had to focus on government, on not failing, not on some good-smelling, purring jungle boy. I brushed my fringe back, sat up straighter, and decided to focus on breathing, do my work, and stop my brain from curling around this guy who was making my heart thump.

'I know. I've lived in New Jersey for most of my life. Listen, I had this speech from my mom this morning. But I haven't figured out what the average percentage of incumbent wins over a five-year period in the Northeast is, so can we get back to that?' I gave him my best all-work, no-messing-around, strictly-school face and prayed he couldn't tell how much I wanted to smell him and stare at his lips all day long.

There were little gold flecks floating in Saxon's irises, but mostly they were the same inky black as his pupils. He leaned close to me, licked his lips and whispered, 'Bottom of page twenty-one.'

It took a second for me to shake myself out of his hypnotic stare. I looked down frantically at page twenty-one, seeing the numbers but not processing. I felt hot. Fever hot.

'Thanks,' I managed to mumble, and wrote down the answer. 'Do you want to fill your sheet in?' I offered, hoping that he would look at something other than me.

'No thanks.' His eyes never wavered; the gold flecks shivered. 'I have a photographic memory,' he said with a smug smile.

I narrowed my eyes at him and tilted my head. 'Really?' I stretched the word out. 'How exactly does that work?'

I swear his incisors gleamed like the Big Bad Wolf's when he smiled at me. 'I look at a page.' He traced one finger down a page in my book. 'I look for like twenty seconds. Then it's here.' He tapped his head. 'And it doesn't leave. At all.'

'Lucky you,' I croaked, shaking off images of Saxon tracing one finger down me. What was wrong with my brain today?

He shook his head. 'It's a curse. It feels like my brain won't turn off.'

I raised one skeptical eyebrow, and he snatched the book out of my hands. He flicked his eyes up and down the page and then snapped the book shut. 'An incumbent's chances for success are magnified by three important factors. The first is . . .'

Saxon kept talking, his voice smooth and fluid. I grabbed the book and flipped it open to the page. He was reciting it word for word. I stared at him and he stopped mid-sentence. I glanced down – that was how the page ended.

'So that page from our government book is in your head forever?' I flicked from his gorgeous face to the boring black-and-white print.

'Yep.' His mouth was set in a grim, unhappy line.

'So if we meet up in an old people's home in seventy years and I say, "Saxon, tell me about page twenty-one in our high school government book," you'll be able to?'

He laughed at my old lady voice and nodded. 'Sure will.'

'I guess I wouldn't pay attention to much then either. I'd want to have some say over what stuck in my head.' I traced my finger down the same path his had traveled on the page.

He looked at me like I was an algebra problem with no solution for x. 'Exactly.'

'What about things you listen to or hear? Are you a lyrics brainiac too?' I joked to clear the air that had gotten serious and intense fast.

He smiled, but this time his smile was different. It was happy, not made to provoke anyone or mask anything. And it was so beautiful my breath caught in my throat. 'No. I'm really bad with lyrics. You know that band from Ireland, The Cranberries?' he asked.

'Love 'em.' I did love The Cranberries. They were amazing, and I had deep respect for post-grunge female-led bands on principle.

'They had this song, "Zombie", right? And when I was a kid, I thought it was "Tommy". So, I'm belting it out, eyes closed, all serious and deep, when my dad stops me and says, "Idiot! You're singing the whole thing wrong!"' He laughed.

It was the kind of laugh that tugged at my lips and coaxed my own laugh up and out of my mouth. 'Funny.'

Our eyes locked, really locked, like they talk about in books and movies. I had a fluttery feeling in my stomach, like I was going to chuck up all of that porridge I had been so hungry for. The screech of the school bell shocked me out of my trance.

'Tomorrow!' Sanotoni bellowed. 'We finish to-morrow!'

Everyone groaned, and I saw Lynn march up to the teacher with lots of hissing and hand-waving. Sanotoni listened with half an ear, and then finally barked, 'So go with the Independents, but it's up to you to catch up.'

'Looks like the bitch ditched us.' Saxon picked up my book and handed it to me. 'Just me and you, Blixen.'

I had never been on a date, and it's not like I considered AP American government class the definition of one, but something like anticipation rippled through me, exactly the way I imagined it would if I was going on a date.

'Yeah, OK. Tomorrow. Um, try not to intentionally suck something useless into your brain.'

He stopped in his tracks and looked at me from head to toe, so I looked right back at him. He was wearing a slim black T-shirt, dark wash jeans with just a tiny bit of wear that actually looked genuine, and some kind of color-block Nikes that were so obnoxious they were cool. He didn't have a backpack. He had one notebook rolled up with a single pen stuck in it.

'Like what?' His voice clicked me out of my eyeball assault.

'Like the ingredient list on a cereal box. Or the instructions on a conditioner bottle.' I bumped my shoulder against his and we grinned like two grinning fools. Was this flirting? Was I, Brenna Blixen, flirting?

I stressed over our goodbye, but managed to hijack a few more seconds when Saxon walked backwards the same direction I was headed.

'Going this way, Blix?' He crooked his finger at me and smiled at my eye-roll.

'Yep. Crafts.' I knew I should walk away from that crooked finger, but I wanted one more look at the gold flecks in his eyes.

'Oh, good. I have to meet someone over there any-way. I'll walk you.' He waved to a few guys down the hall and when his arm dropped, he skimmed his hand over my hip. A thousand electric jolts ran straight up my side and left my skin tingling.

'So you really think I'll never need to know every single chemical in my Cocoa Puffs?' His hand closed over my elbow as he steered me around a herd of chattering girls, and I leaned closer to drag the moment out as long as possible.

'Is that what you eat?' I scrunched my nose in disgust. 'That's a nasty breakfast.'

'What do you have? Half a grapefruit? Isn't that the official girl breakfast?'

'Not this girl.' I jabbed a thumb in my chest. 'I have a bowl of porridge.'

His dark eyes gleamed with interest. 'What are you, a girl guide?'

'What are you? A third grader? Cocoa Puffs,' I sneered.

He was still laughing when we turned the corner to the art rooms. 'Man, I haven't laughed that hard in a while, Blix. You're a good sort, for a trailblazer.'

'Yeah, OK, and I hope you enjoy *SpongeBob* with your cereal tomorrow.' I rolled my eyes.

I could feel it the minute his attention dropped from me. It was like he was a dog that had caught the scent of something it wanted, and that was all it could focus on. I looked in the direction his eyes were turned.

'Kelsie,' he said in a gravelly voice.

I don't care what my mom said, that butt of hers attracted guys like a magnet. She smiled warmly and gave him a careless hug, her bracelets clicking together softly. 'Oh, hey, Saxon,' she said, then turned to me. 'Brenna! I'm so excited we have crafts together. I hope we start with clay.'

'You know each other?' Saxon's eyebrows knitted together in the center of his forehead.

I looked at his face, and it felt like infinitesimal

cracks were spreading through my heart. As soon as I had that thought I shook my head. My heart! What was I thinking? I didn't *love* this guy! More like my ego was getting a beating. Because somehow I knew that he was concerned that I knew Kelsie. I realized with a jolt that he liked to keep girls he flirted with separate. I read it clear as day in his expression.

'Brenna and I went through school together.' Kelsie swung an arm around my waist and squeezed, her rings biting into my side before she let go. 'Then she moved to Sweden for a year and now she's back.'

'Denmark,' I corrected, pasting a smile on my face. 'I went to Denmark.'

Saxon looked at me with those almost-black eyes. I was so close I could see every gold fleck, but I took two very deliberate steps back.

'You went to Denmark?' he repeated, a little dumbly.

'Yes. Denmark.'

'Class is going to start,' Kelsie breezed, pulling me by the hand. 'Bye, Saxon. See you later.'

'Oh, I was going to see if tonight at seven was cool?' His eyes darted to me for a split second and were back on Kelsie so fast I wondered if I had imagined all the chemistry earlier.

'That sounds great. Pick me up, OK?' Kelsie yanked

me through the door, away from Saxon. She giggled and stamped her feet. 'He's so hot, isn't he?' she gushed, leaning her head on me.

I liked her head leaning on me, but I felt a need to put Saxon into perspective. 'He's all right,' I managed. 'I think he has a good idea of how hot girls think he is.'

'Yeah,' she giggled and waved her hand around. 'But I like him anyway. Ooh, they have glass, Brenna! I can't wait.'

I followed Kelsie to a display of glass crafts, but I couldn't really pay much attention to them. Kelsie and Saxon were going out tonight. That was fine. I had known him for almost exactly forty-five minutes. It wasn't real, what I felt. It was just a crush, an infatuation. Something I could very easily put out of my mind.

I half listened to the lecture on crafts. We would be doing some pottery, some macramé and working with copper and glass. I suppressed a groan. Maybe this had been a mistake. I just had a hard time picturing myself doing any kind of weaving. Most of the class I spent looking over at Kelsie. She was very pretty. And she was artistic. I heard her tell another girl about the beaded necklace and earrings she was wearing: she had made them herself. They were a complicated design and it was obvious you needed a good dose of talent to make them.

So I knew this wasn't going to be one of those things where I liked a guy and then this awful girl liked him, but I got the guy in the end because I was so wholesome and right and good. This was real life.

And in real life Kelsie was awesome and gorgeous, and Saxon would be lucky to have her and they would be great together. In real life, I had to get a serious grip.

When the bell rang, I headed to the only thing on my schedule I was truly nervous about.

I had to take a PE class – it was compulsory.

A total lack of coordination, poor reflexes, and difficulty understanding the rules of games in general combined to make me one of the suckiest PE students in middle school, and I was pretty sure all my hours on a bike hadn't managed to blot out the rest of my deficiencies.

Besides my natural suckiness, I had registered late, and since everyone picked their PE units at the end of the previous year, I got stuck with running and jogging. I had to assume that was the only class lame enough to not have anyone willingly opt to take it, since it was a pretty sparse group gathered on the track.

Coach Dunn was a tanned, muscular woman with a long, shiny, blonde ponytail and a killer stare. There was a huge track. She gave each of us a numbered placard to pin to our PE shirts. Each time we went around the track, she made a mark by our number. She was fairly quiet, as PE teachers go. No shouts of encouragement, no hoots, no fist-pumping or clapping. I was glad about that. I was just thinking cross country might actually go fairly well when I looked to my right and saw a soccer game going on.

One of the guys was awesome, kicking the ball with incredible speed and agility. He was quick and arrogant, doing a back-flip when he scored a goal. He looked over at the track, and even across that distance, we made eye contact, and I nearly tripped over my feet.

Saxon.

He gave me a wave, acknowledging that he had seen me. I waved back and my heart pounded in my chest. I ran faster, concentrating on the rhythm of my breathing and the burn of my muscles. The cool air stung my lungs, and I gulped it down and ran harder. I ran to forget those mesmerizing eyes and his incredible laugh that twined right around my gut and pulled me in.

I wondered if Kelsie would make him laugh like I had, and right away I felt like a traitor. Kelsie was funny and smart, and if Saxon didn't laugh with her, he was the idiot. I gritted my teeth and ran harder, and I didn't look back at the field, no matter how much yelling and cheering I heard. I didn't want to think about him, I didn't want to meet eyes again. My entire body focused on running; my arms pumped, my feet moved in time, my breath tore down my scratchy throat and filled my lungs while I ran away from all the confusion of my first day back at school.

'Number twelve!' Coach Dunn bellowed. 'Number twelve!'

I looked around and realized the track was empty. I was the last one on.

'Sorry, coach!' I jogged to her and gasped. 'I was in a zone or something.'

'Twelve, you did fourteen laps in one period,' Coach Dunn said, her arms crossed. I couldn't tell if she wanted to congratulate me or spit on my shoes. 'The best cross-country student I've ever seen only did thirteen. What do you think of that?'

'Good?' I ventured, unsure what to say.

'I'll say. I want you to consider trying out for the cross-country team.' She glowered at me when she said it, but I felt like it was probably as friendly a look as she gave.

'I'll consider it.'

She nodded, and I went to change. Afterwards, we all collected outside the gym until the bell rang to release us.

I sensed him before I saw him. The smell of his cologne slid into my nostrils and made my head spin.

'I heard you ran like Forrest Gump.' I could hear the smile in his voice.

'Fourteen laps.' I crossed my arms and glowered. 'What do you think of that?'

'Holy crap.' Saxon laughed. 'You look just like old Dunn. That's a damn good impression and a really decent run.' He punched my arm softly, a kind of manly congratulations. 'So, you gonna do cross country or what?'

'I don't know. I'm not here in the afternoons.' I opened and closed the zipper on my backpack nervously, waiting for the scarlet 'T' to appear on my forehead.

'Do you have one of those get-out-after-lunch schedules? You're not even a junior yet.' He reached out and yanked the zipper shut, stopping the grate of the teeth opening and closing.

'No. I do Share Time.' The way everyone balked when I announced it made me dread this afternoon. What had I gotten myself into?

Even Saxon, resident Frankford High bad boy,

looked just the tiniest bit shocked. 'Share Time? You wanna give me a haircut?'

'Not hairdressing. Believe it or not, that isn't the only trade a poor female can wrap her mind around.'

'What then?' He closed the space between us, boxing me near the wall. I felt the whole world melt into just the two of us.

'Graphic design.' I dropped my voice like we were in a church.

'Why? You missed a year. They won't let you finish.' He moved a piece of my hair back off of my shoulder and to my back, and my eyes followed his hand.

'There are two summer workshops I can take.' I was relieved to hear my voice didn't sound shaky.

'You're smart.' His hand fell and grabbed mine lazily. 'I can tell.'

'One government class and you have me figured out?' I wondered if he could see my heart pounding through my shirt.

'Nope. It wasn't the class. It was you. You figuring me out.' His black eyes searched my face, the gold flecks like tiny fires. 'I see something; I never forget it. You see something, and you cut right through it, don't you, Blix? Right through the crap to what's really there.'

I tried to swallow, but my throat was very, very dry.

'I didn't figure you out, Saxon. There's a lot more to you. And to me.' His hand felt so good holding mine. It was warm, smooth, long-fingered. I liked the way his skin and mine contrasted. I was pale as a ghost, but that looked shocking and right against his darker complexion. We complemented one another. I knew deep in me that we were somehow linked.

My mind instantly conjured an image of Kelsie. I snatched my hand out of his grasp.

'What else is there about you?' He looked down at our hands, now pulled apart.

'I'm a good friend,' I said firmly. 'Like to Kelsie. I really like her. She's very pretty and sweet, isn't she?'

I said the magic words that smashed our bubble. Saxon backed away from me and his eyes were guarded again, mocking me. 'Kelsie's the best,' he agreed, his voice edged with sexy innuendo.

The bell rang. 'Well, I have to go to lunch,' I said.

'I'm headed there.' He looked left, then right. 'Should I walk with someone else?'

He was challenging me, trying to see if I would react to him. 'Why would you walk with someone else when you have my awesomeness right here?' I asked, my voice sunny and light. 'Here's something else about me: I'm always hungry. I'm going to eat you under the table.'

'You're on.' He flashed me a joking smile, not the soul-searching smile he'd given me earlier. I told myself I preferred this one, and I hoped I was right.

He led me to the cafeteria, into the annex reserved for upperclassmen to a table in the corner. We sat with a large group of Saxon's friends, who accepted me immediately. I liked listening to them argue and tease each other. Saxon was pretty quiet, but at the end of lunch he did look at my empty tray and torn wrappers and say, 'I have to admit, I'm pretty impressed by how much you ate.'

'I've always been a big eater.' I shrugged, twisting a sandwich wrapper in my hands.

'That's why you can run like Gump.' He tossed his soda can on my tray. 'Maybe I'll switch to porridge like you, Grandma.'

I emptied the tray and we walked into the hall. 'I know the other kids in preschool don't eat it, but it might work for you.' We were about to pass the doors to the outside. I put my jacket on, zipped it up, then pointed to the door. 'That's me.'

Saxon pushed the door open and walked out with me. He watched me undo my bike lock and put on my helmet. I would never not wear it, but I didn't necessarily want Saxon to watch me put it on.

'It's cold.' He stuffed his hands in his pockets and

pressed his arms close to his body. The biting wind made his eyes tear. 'Tech is about three miles down the road.'

'It's chilly,' I countered. 'And Tech is two and a half miles.'

'You're going to freeze to death in the winter.' He stooped down to pick up a mitten I dropped and handed it to me.

I pulled the mitten on. 'We're just spoiled here. Danish people cycle everywhere in all kinds of weather. I can do it.'

'They don't have this kind of terrain, and they don't get loads of snow, Blix.' I thought this weird abbreviation nickname was kind of endearing. 'When it gets bad, I'll come by your place to pick you up.'

My heart thrilled in my chest. Yes, yes, yes! It screamed. 'No way,' I said. 'I'll take the bus. Plus, you don't know where I live.'

'No.' The wolf's smile was back. 'You won't. And I'll find you.' He reached out and took the end of my hair in his fingers. 'Be safe.' He let go reluctantly, my hair fell back over my shoulder, and he turned without another word and went back into school.

I rode slowly down the steps, bumping along until I came to the road, then I pedaled hard. I was at the school in just a few minutes, and I decided to let myself believe that my thumping heart really had something to do with my ride instead of Saxon. I found an old, rusty bike rack round the back and chained my bike. The Tech building was low and squat with no plants around the rear entrance; though I was sure there were some by the front. I went in; the hallways were narrow and dark, and all of the lights seemed to flicker.

I found a map on the wall and followed it to the front office. A nice older lady smiled at me. 'Hello, dear. What can I do for you?'

It was really weird to be doing this twice in one day, but it was what I had decided I wanted. 'Hello.' I made my smile wide and appreciative. 'My name is Brenna Blixen. I'm new at this school.'

'Well, I'm Mrs Olsen.' She winked. 'My, you're a pretty one. Hair and beauty?'

'No.' I forced the smile to stay exactly where it was. 'I'm in graphic design.'

'Oh.' Mrs Olsen gave me another wink. 'Artsy. Gotcha.' She handed me a thick packet. 'Here's your information and class list. Mr Giles is down the hall and to your right. He's your teacher for your first session.'

'Thank you, Mrs Olsen.' I backed out of the room. I was a little more nervous than I had been at Frankford.

Maybe because there were people I knew at Frankford, and here there was no one at all.

I made my way down the hall and to the right, and I checked every sign until I saw Mr Giles's room. The other students were sitting at tables, already quietly drawing.

Mr Giles waved me in with a kind smile and explained what was going on. 'We're talking about perspective. I had this group last year, so they know the drill, but I'll have you start where they are and we'll catch you up as needed.' He had a big beard and round cheeks, like a garden gnome. 'And your name is . . . ?'

'Brenna Blixen.'

'Brenna Blixen.' He scanned his list. 'You can sit with . . . Jake Kelly. He's one of my best, and he's in an advanced section, so he's done this all before. If you have any questions, I'm sure he can help you out, or just give a holler in my direction.' He pointed to a table in the back.

I grabbed paper and a pencil from the pile Mr Giles showed me and went to the table. The boy sitting there smiled sweetly and I felt my heart thump in a wild staccato.

What kind of shameless hussy was I? I had just calmed down after riding away from Saxon, and this boy gives me one smile and I fall to pieces?

'Hey. I'm Jake.' His voice was so nice, deep but gentle. He held out his hand and I shook it. It was rough to my touch, like I could feel the work he did through all his calluses. 'You're Brenna?'

I smiled back at him. 'Yep. Brenna Blixen.'

'Nice to meet you, Brenna.' He had light brown hair and nice gray eyes, so shiny they were almost silver. Although he was sitting down, I could tell he was tall – and wiry: I could see the definition of his muscles. He pointed to a group of wooden shapes in the center of the table. 'Just doing some perspective drawing. You OK to start?' he checked.

His gaze roamed up and down my body. Not in a bad way; it was just like Jake was taking stock of me, getting a good look so he could reference for later.

'Yeah, thanks. Sorry I ruined your peace and quiet.'

He smiled down at his paper. One of his front teeth had a tiny chip and his left eyetooth was a little crooked. He had a great, warm, slow smile. 'No need to apologize. You're a lot nicer to look at than these wooden blocks.' His eyes flickered over me. They looked just like liquid silver.

'Yeah,' I shot back breezily. 'I get that all the time. If I had a nickel for every time someone told me I was prettier than a hunk of wood, I'd be a rich, rich woman.'

His laugh was an easy sound that welled up from deep in his throat. 'Pretty and funny. I'm in big trouble. I'd better watch out, or I'll be completely in love before the day is out.'

'Line up, then,' I joked, but my voice was a little rushed this time because I felt like all the blood was rushing from my head. 'I get that a lot, too.'

I had to remind myself to breathe over and over. It was like Jake was sucking the oxygen out of the room.

'Yeah, but you never got it from anyone as persistent as me.' He pointed at me with his pencil and smiled. 'When I see the perfect girl sitting across from me, I'm not about to let a couple of thousand suitors just whisk her away.'

'Like Penelope,' I said, without thinking. He wasn't going to get a reference to *The Odyssey*. It wasn't exactly Tech reading.

'Do you think I'm the one who can pull the bow back?' He made a muscle out of his bicep.

I laughed and inwardly salivated over his bicep and the fact that he did know *The Odyssey* after all. 'I love that book.'

'Me too.'

And once again, I found myself taking a good hard look at a very attractive guy and feeling the prick of pins and needles all over my body.

Focus, I told myself. I was here to learn, not to drool over yet another guy. As if Saxon didn't make things complicated enough, I now had Jake to contend with.

Jake and I drew and erased and looked at each other now and then in friendly silence until the bell rang. I didn't have Jake in my next two classes, which were drafting and still-life drawing, but the last class of the day was a project block. In this session we were supposed to come up with an independent design project and work on it for several weeks. I walked into the room and there he was, leaning back at a computer desk, his eyes following me when I came in.

It wasn't even like I was really thinking about it. I just followed my feet and wound up sitting next to him.

'Hey.' He radiated happiness. 'How were the other two classes?'

'Good.' I basked in his glow. 'So do you do Share Time or do you stay at Tech all day?'

'I'm a full-day Techie.' He drummed his fingers on the desk. 'My grades were pretty crappy in middle school.'

'Really?' If someone asked me to describe Jake in a few words I would say ... well, *hot* and *sweet*. But *focused* and *hardworking* would make the top five, no doubt.

'Yeah. I have dyslexia.' Jake moved his hand to the back of his neck and rubbed self-consciously. 'I know a lot of people say that they have it, but it's actually pretty rare.'

'Did you get help for it?'

'Oh yeah. My teachers were really good. But it's just a huge struggle for me to read. I kind of hate it.' He bumped the toe of his boot on the table leg absently.

'But *The Odyssey*?' I asked, confused.

He smiled a crooked smile. I loved it. 'Some books on tape are really good. That one was.'

'That's the same as reading,' I protested.

He looked at me and his crooked smile stretched out over his whole face. 'Yeah, OK. Like drafting is the same as carpentry. I'm a dumbass, Brenna, whether you want to admit it or not.'

It took a minute for it to sink in that he was serious. 'A dumbass doesn't speak the way you do. I can tell just from talking to you that you're smart.'

He blushed a little and we smiled shyly. The teacher finished taking attendance and passing out forms, so we had to settle back and get ready for her to explain our project for the rest of the period. I felt warm from the inside out every time I looked his way. When the bell rang, Jake followed me down the long hall and finally put a hand on my shoulder.

'Where are you going?' he asked. 'The parking lot is over here.'

'I rode my bike in.'

He didn't bat an eyelid. 'Cool. Where do you live?'

'Augusta. I live on Dickerson. Off of Plains Road.'

'Oh. I live in The Lake.'

'The Lake' was Lake Neapolin, the butt of most jokes about Sussex County. It was rumored to be the dirtiest lake in the county, and no one ever swam there. Houses around the lake were typically dilapidated. Back in the 'fifties they had been sweet little summer homes, but in the 'eighties people started buying them to live in permanently. So they were kind of summery and cute, but also prone to being kind of run-down and neglected.

'Well, I'll see you tomorrow.' I gave him a friendly wave. Jake smiled his crooked smile and I felt my heart thud faster in my chest.

I couldn't wipe the smile from my face.

Chapter 2

I remembered to call my mom before I rode home, and thought about stopping at Frankford to talk to Coach Dunn, but I changed my mind at the last minute. I wanted to ride as fast as possible because I knew Mom was timing me down to the second. If I took too long, she would make me get the bus tomorrow. By the time I rode into the driveway, she was peering out of the kitchen window.

Our kitchen was awesomely designed. It was open, with the kitchen and dining room connected, and the entire front wall had nice big windows so you could see our wide front yard and the thick tree line that bordered the edge of our property. Our house was on a tiny, quiet back road. Only half of our road was even metalled; the top half of it was still dirt and loose gravel. It always cracked people up that we lived on a dirt road, but I liked it that way. It meant that not many people chose to use our road, and that was fine by me. I loved living in a cozy, tucked-away place.

I came in through the garage, kicking off my Converse at the door.

'Hey, Mom!' I pretended that I was surprised to see her standing there. 'Oh, were you waiting for me?'

She didn't say a word, just came over and grabbed my face and pinched my ears.

'Ow!' I squeaked. 'Mom, what are you doing?'

'You're frozen.' She shook her head. 'You're going to get frostbite. This isn't going to work, Brenna. I can't believe it's this damn cold and we're only in September. Winter is going to be miserable this year.'

'I just need to wear a hat, Mom. I like riding my bike. You should be happy. At least I'm not some obese lazy teenager. Imagine if I weighed four hundred pounds and you had to home-school me because I couldn't fit through doorways at school.' I grabbed an apple from a bowl on the table and crunched down on it. 'You'd be sad,' I said around the bite.

'I'll be sad when you're hit by a car or your ears turn black and fall off from frostbite. Do you want a sandwich?'

Mom wasn't big into cooking, and since we'd moved back to the States, she'd been even worse. In Denmark, I'd been around all day to help with cooking and cleaning, but now it all fell to her. It wasn't that my mom was lazy or anything like that. She just got bored doing things all by herself.

'Yeah. I'll make them. You go relax,' I offered.

'That's OK, baby. I've been relaxing all day. Thorsten switched schedules with another guy today, so he ran some errands and I had time to myself. He's got to go back in tomorrow, though.'

Thorsten worked on the show *Saturday Night Live* and was on the overnight shift at NBC, so he had to commute to New York City and stay overnight. I only ever saw him in the morning most of the time, and sometimes on Sunday. I had been really worried about living with him for a whole year in Denmark, but he's a laid-back guy, and we got along really well.

'So, how was it, honey?' Mum smiled encouragingly.

'I had a good day. Some of the girls from elementary school saw me, and they were nice. Do you remember Meg and Kelsie?'

'The girl who was Annie in your school play?' she asked, and I nodded. 'And of course I know Kelsie. It's too bad she has such a low hairline. She could be very pretty.'

I rolled my eyes, but she didn't see me. 'My classes seem pretty good. I'm reading *Lord of the Flies* now.'

Mom groaned. 'Didn't you already read that one?'

'Yeah. It's not so bad. It's always cool to see what a

new teacher says about things. And I ran cross country today. Apparently I beat some unofficial school record for most laps in a period.'

'Wow.' Mom raised her eyebrows. 'I didn't know you were such a fast runner.'

'I'm not.' I examined my apple quizzically. 'I think I have endurance. I mean, I wasn't sprinting. Coach Dunn wants me to try out for the cross-country team.'

'That might be fun.' Mom looked at me from the corner of her eye to see if I would agree.

I took everything out for the sandwiches and set it all on the counter. We got a plate each and started to make our sandwiches, picking through tomato and lettuce and various cold meats.

'It might be.' I shrugged. 'As long as they don't want me to live at the track or whatever.'

'I guess they think practise is important.' She shook a finger at me. 'You don't have to, Bren. You need to develop your ability to say no.'

This was another of my mom's favorite lecture topics. She was always reminding me that it was my right to say no whenever I didn't want something. Not in a corny 'say no to drugs' way, or even 'say no to sex', just no in general. Like 'no' when someone offers you food you don't want, or 'no' when your friends want you to go get your nose pierced with them, or 'no' to a teacher who asks you to be her assistant if you don't want to be. Saying no was actually pretty hard to get a handle on, especially with someone like Coach Dunn willing you to say yes.

'So.' Mom took a bite out of her turkey and Swiss with extra tomato. 'Any boys hanging around?'

I shrugged, praying that my cheeks didn't get red. 'I guess. You know, I'm the new girl, so there's always that.'

'Just remember, it's better to date lots of guys without getting too serious. Just have fun for now. Don't get yourself hooked up with one person. There's plenty of time for that later on.'

Mom had been madly in love with her high-school sweetheart, who got her pregnant and then acted like a jerk. Mom severed contact with him, gave me her last name, and didn't even acknowledge him on my birth certificate. She raised me alone until she met Thorsten, and I think she'd stuck with him mostly because on their first date, when she told him about me, he asked her to bring me on the second date.

He took us to a great pizza place and then we saw a kids' movie at the drive-in. I sat tucked between the two of them like I was their daughter already. Mom had stars in her eyes from that day on. Thorsten was in, and he knew it, but I know that's not why he did it.

He just thought families were nice and important and we made a good instant one.

'I'm not even interested, Mom. School is going to be crazy enough without it. But I think Kelsie and I might start hanging out again.'

'Good girl.' Mom smiled. 'You always had a good head on your shoulders.'

After we finished, I helped Mom clean up the kitchen and then went to my very purple room to think for a while. I thought about Saxon's incredible eyes and his brilliance and the way he could match every joke I made. I thought about Jake and how humble and cute and sweet he was. It was a little embarrassing that I couldn't think a little more about my classes and schedule, but how could they hold a candle?

I got out my binders and put everything in order. I hole-punched my worksheets and put those little color-coded tabs on my folder partitions. In short, I reveled in my dorky love of organizing my school supplies. I did my homework pretty quickly and was in the process of taking notes on *Lord of the Flies* when I heard a light knock at the door. I expected Mom, but it was Thorsten, looking uncomfortable. He didn't really hang out in my room much, so it was always a little weird when he appeared out of nowhere.

'Hey, Brenna.' He couldn't hide his eager grin. 'I know your birthday isn't for a few weeks, but I wanted to give you this so you could start the school year right.' He handed me a messenger bag.

'Thanks, Fa.' I reached for it, but when I went to take it, my arm almost gave out – it was that heavy! 'What's in here?'

'Open it up.' Thorsten tended to be a pretty calm guy, so it was strange to see this much anticipation on his face.

'Oh my God,' I breathed. 'You got me a laptop? Really?'

'I thought you would need it for school. And I know you fill your journals up pretty quickly, so now you can have it all in one place. If you don't like this model, we can switch it, but I did some research and I think it's pretty good.'

'Pretty good? Fa, this is top of the line. Thank you. So much.' I got up and we made our way toward one another awkwardly. I put my arms around him and hugged him hard. 'Thank you. I'm going to use this so much.'

'Well, I know it couldn't have been easy for you to leave all of your friends and your school to come to Denmark.' Thorsten's eyes are very light blue and his hair is very blond, so he always looks kind of young and uncertain, but now he looked even more so than usual. 'I just want you to know that I appreciate you doing it for me, and you didn't whine or anything.'

'Fa, you're good to us. I love you. I wouldn't whine. Thank you so much.' For a second I thought about my biological father and was glad that he and Mom hadn't wound up together just because of me. Because there couldn't be a better guy than Thorsten to have as a dad.

Mom was right behind him and we took a few minutes to ogle over the new machine and all of the cool software that Thorsten had installed. I didn't know much about computers, but I knew for a fact that this cost a huge chunk. Mom petted my hair and kissed my cheeks, and then she stopped suddenly.

'Look at this room, Brenna!' she cried.

'I'll clean it up in a little bit.' I was surprised that she was so upset about my school stuff. Mom was usually pretty laid back.

'No, Brenna, *look at this room*!' She put her hands up and shook them dramatically. 'This is a little girl's room. This is not the room of a world-traveled teen. That's it!'

'What's it?' I asked, but I felt energetic suddenly. Mom's enthusiasm was always infectious.

'My birthday gift to you. We're going to redo your

room.' She framed it out with her hands and moved them around like she was checking camera angles for the before and after pictures I knew she'd want to take. 'Whatever you like. Whatever you want.'

'Even if I want black walls?' I tested.

'Even if you want to paint blood dripping down them,' Mom said calmly. She knew I would never paint my room black, but even if I wanted to, she would find a way to make it look awesome. My mom could take the ugliest thing and make it amazing.

'Thank you, guys.' I was looking forward to re-decorating my room with them. Maybe it was because I was an only child, but I'd actually always liked being with Mom and Thorsten. We had fun together, but they weren't always into my business. I could do things without having them breathing down my neck.

'I took this weekend off to use some of my vacation time before the end of the year. We'll go to IKEA,' Thorsten suggested.

'I've got a catalog!' Mom gushed. 'You can look through it tonight, sweetie, then we'll go pick every-thing up. This will be so fun! We can look at paint samples at that little store by the mall.'

'Sounds good.' I smiled when Thorsten winked at me. Mom brought the catalog in and measured the room and windows before she kissed me goodnight.

When I was alone, I was psyched to find out that I had Wi-Fi, and that it actually worked. I had set up my Facebook page in Denmark, but I hadn't looked for many of my American friends. I just felt like it was odd to send friend requests to people I hadn't seen in months and who might not even remember me. Most of my friends were cousins and other family, but tonight I did some searching. I sent a request to Kelsie, Saxon and Jake.

All three of their profiles were set to private. Kelsie's profile picture was really pretty. Unlike a lot of Facebook girl pictures, she wasn't making a duck face at the camera or pouting. She was smiling, and her smile was real and gorgeous. Saxon's picture was just his silhouette, and he was wearing a hoodie, so I could barely make out his face. Jake's picture was of him leaning against a dirt bike, his arms crossed. He was smiling and there were flecks of mud all over his face. Since I would have to wait for them to accept my requests before I could see their pages, I logged off and went to bed.

That night, I dreamed about Jake and Saxon. In the dream they were racing dirt bikes. We were in an arena that looked medieval, and I realized that they were racing for Kelsie. She was the princess, and the winner of the race would get her hand in marriage. I was really mad, watching them, but I didn't want to show it.

The next morning I was in a crappy mood before my feet even hit the floor. I took a shower and got ready for school with a dark cloud over my head I just couldn't shake. Mom was waiting with porridge and ideas for my room. We chatted for a while, and she clicked her tongue when I went to get my bike.

'It's good for me,' I said. 'I like it.'

'It's freezing. They're saying this cold snap is breaking records.' She shivered for effect and hugged her body.

'I'll keep my hat and scarf on. I promise.'

'Wear your helmet,' she sulked.

'I always do.' I kissed her, then started out, and if I was a little bit excited to see Saxon, I didn't admit it. First of all, he was seeing Kelsie, and she was pretty much the only friend I had. Secondly, he was trouble. You just got this sense about him, like no matter how into you he pretended to be, he would be kissing you with his eyes on the next pretty girl he noticed. I pedaled harder, building a really solid case against him. By the time I made it to school, I was pretty sure I could look him in the eye and hate him.

Then I saw him leaned against the bike rack and all those little fragments of carefully built-up hate slid out of my head and got replaced by a warm, happy excitement I couldn't stamp out. I popped my iPod earphones into my pocket and tried not to look like a complete fumbling dork while I locked up my bike.

'Hey, Saxon.' I wasn't going to ignore him. I wasn't going to be rude.

'I want to take you out,' he announced out of the blue. His dark eyes focused on me with wolfish interest.

'I thought you were taking Kelsie out.' I pulled off my hat and smoothed my flyaway hair.

'It's just a date, Blixen. It's not like we're going to get married.' There was a razor edge to his voice.

'Would you tell Kelsie that you were taking me on a date?' I challenged.

'What you and I do has nothing to do with anyone else.' His voice was a little snarly. I tucked my hair behind my ears and looked at him for a long time.

'No thanks.' I whirled on my heel and started toward the front door.

'Wait up!' He had to chase me up the steps, and I could tell he didn't like it at all. I don't think Saxon ever had to chase anyone anywhere. 'We could just hang out then, right?' he said, following me into the hallway. 'As friends?' He gritted his teeth over the word.

'Why?' I asked, hurrying down the corridor. 'You don't really seem all that friendly.'

'I'm friendly when I want to be.' He ran a hand through his hair in frustration, like I was really irritating him. We stopped outside my locker and he pressed one hand on the metal of the top compartment.

'I need to get in there.' I pointed to his hand.

'Say yes to one friendly date.' He dropped his voice to a whisper. 'I couldn't stop thinking about you last night.'

My heart rocketed into my throat. I didn't want to admit that I'd been thinking about him, too, though it would have been fun to tell him that I was thinking about him *and* another boy.

'Maybe you need a hobby,' I suggested, widening my eyes. 'Model planes? Skateboarding? How about music? You could take up the guitar.'

'You're funny,' he muttered. 'I need to get you out of my system.'

I knew in that moment that Saxon felt way more for me than he wanted to or than he was willing to admit. He didn't like that he felt this way about me, so he was going to get rid of me. Well, he could screw off for all I cared. I wasn't about to let him use me for entertainment then dump me when he was done.

'That must suck for you, but I'm not available, and

I'm not interested. So go bother someone else.' Even while I was saying those words to him, part of me wanted him to grab me and kiss me right there. He looked angry and hungry at the same time, and I didn't want him to stop looking at me like that.

'Fine.' His voice was low again. 'But I'm not an idiot, Brenna. This isn't a one-sided thing. I know you feel something about me. We're going to end up together eventually. If you're too chicken to face it, that's your thing.'

He stalked away like he owned the whole hallway, and I went to class so mad I could feel my face flaming. Who did he think he was? Obviously God's gift to women. I had never met anyone so arrogant, so completely full of himself. I marched into English and plopped down in my seat. Mr Dawes was already filling up the chalkboard with notes about Golding's life and career. I took out my blue notebook and binder (everything for English was blue. I know: color-coding is dork central), when Devon Conner turned around.

'You're in Tech?' He blinked like there was something in his eye.

'Yes,' I hissed. 'What's it to you?'

'Well, this is honors English,' he said matter-of-factly. 'I didn't think Tech kids were allowed in honors classes.' He had a big nose. It crossed my mind that it would make an excellent target for my fist.

'Look, jerkoff, maybe you should turn around and take the freaking notes before they ship you off to Tech with all the other dirty lowlifes like me.'

'I was just asking a question,' Devon whined.

'A pretty damn stupid one,' I muttered.

'Is there a problem, Mr Conner? Ms Blixen?' Mr Dawes asked.

'No.' I gave him my most angelic face. 'Devon can't see the board. He was asking to copy my notes after class.'

Butter couldn't have melted in my mouth, I was that good.

Mr Dawes nodded. 'Mr Conner, front and center. Ms Blixen isn't your personal transcriber. If you need a seat adjustment, bring a note from your eye doctor,' he barked. I smirked when Mr Dawes's back was turned.

'Geez, I was just asking a question,' Devon sulked childishly.

Right.

The rest of the day went just as badly. In American government I had to sit right next to Saxon and work through the problems that were on our sheet. He didn't lift a finger to help, which annoyed me.

'We're supposed to be partners.' I scribbled on my

paper with furious frustration when my pen ran dry.

'Not all partnerships are equal.' He smiled meanly, plucked the pen out of my hand, wet the tip on his tongue, and handed it back to me. 'Maybe we don't have a symbiotic relationship.'

'So instead of you being the little bird eating meat out of my crocodile jaws, you're the big, fat tapeworm killing me slowly?' I spat, ultra-annoyed when the ink flowed smoothly on the paper.

'You taking biology?'

'My mom and I did a home-school program in Denmark last year, and we liked the earth science part so much we did biology as well.' I kept my voice monotone on purpose.

'So you were a supergeek, working round the clock on science hypotheses?' He jiggled his leg so the desk moved and made my sentence scrawl sideways down the page. I glared at him.

'Actually, when you cut out the textbook bull and don't have twenty-five other apes to deal with, a lesson that takes forty-five minutes in school can take a fraction of the time at home.' My voice grew louder against my will. 'For example, a government sheet that would normally take me half an hour can take three times longer to do when I have an irritating partner asking me idiotic questions every few minutes.'

He snatched his paper off of the table, dug in his pocket for a pen, and nodded at me. 'Ready?' he asked 'For what?'

'You did pages four to six. I'll do seven to nine.' He raised his eyebrows, at me. 'Ready?' he repeated.

I couldn't help but like the dark gleam in his eye, and if I said I didn't like the way his muscles pushed through his *Black Lips* T-shirt, I'd be lying. I couldn't stop looking at the tears in his gray work pants, where the dark, hairy skin of his legs showed through.

'I'm ready when you are.' I held my pen up expectantly.

'Page seven, question thirty-one. Write this: *The judicial system allows for state governments to decide for themselves whether elected officials should . . .*' His voice droned on and on. He answered every question, not pausing, not looking through the book to double check. And I was willing to bet my life that his answers were absolutely right. It was especially sickening to realize that I was more than happy to listen to Saxon's voice recite government facts all period long. What was wrong with me?

'Done.' He flipped his half-filled-in worksheet on the table.

My hand cramped with pain. I shook it out. 'Thanks,' I muttered.

'You did the rest of the work.' I knew he was trying to be fair.

'Yeah, I bet that really helped you.' My voice dripped with sarcasm. 'I mean, someone with a photographic memory really needs to rely on his underclassman partner to pull him through a set of answers he already had memorized.'

'So maybe *you're* the big, fat tapeworm.' He puffed his cheeks out at me, and I smiled in spite of my resolution not to.

'Call me a parasite and we're even.'

He flicked my sleeve. 'I like your T-shirt.' He took a moment to look at it. I rolled my eyes, fairly sure he was looking at what was contained in the shirt, but did I really have a leg to stand on there? I'd been checking him out all morning.

'Thanks. I made it.' It took me a week to get the picture just right before I silk-screened it. It was a picture of my mom dancing at Thorsten's birthday. I think she had tipped a bit too much vodka into the birthday punch, and it made for a crazy picture. I used the digital program on Thorsten's computer to fade the image, filled it in with swirls of black and red, made a pink halo around it, then printed it, ironed it on a black shirt and flecked white paint on with a toothbrush. Mom cracked up when she saw it.

'Brenna, you made me look like some punk rocker! I was dancing to the Beatles, for heaven's sake!' she had laughed.

'You're kidding.' He looked more closely. 'Like, you added the paint?'

'No,' I said slowly. 'If all I did was flick some paint on it, would I say that I'd made it?' I shook my head. 'I took a picture, morphed it, made it an iron-on. Oh yeah, then I flicked some paint on it.'

'Wow.' Saxon was clearly impressed. 'Really, wow. I love it.'

'Thanks. It was originally a picture of my mom dancing to "Yellow Submarine",' I admitted, even though I didn't really want to share the story with Saxon. I felt like he might think it was ridiculous.

'Your mom? Really?' His grin was completely confident. 'I can't wait to meet her.'

'She'd hate you.' I was surprised by how totally sure I was about it.

'No mom hates me.' His face radiated arrogance.

'My mom likes no boy,' I returned. 'She's very protective.'

'Yeah, well, I'm sure she's no dummy. If I had a daughter like you, I'd lock her in a closet and never let her out.' His voice pitched a few octaves deeper.

'I'm a trustworthy kid.' I ignored his innuendo. 'My parents know that about me.'

'It isn't you I'd worry about.' Saxon burned me with a long, obvious look. 'It's any guy with eyes in his head that would worry me.'

'Yeah.' I kept my voice light even though my heart pounded so hard I was sure it would rip through my super-cool shirt. 'I guess I *am* pretty ridiculously gorgeous.'

He tugged on the end of my hair. 'You're joking. I'm being serious. You're damn gorgeous. It's actually distracting.'

And I wanted to spar back so badly, but there was no way on this earth that I could force words to come out of my mouth, and, thankfully, I didn't have to because the bell rang and everyone started gathering their things together.

'Hand them in! I don't care if you aren't done! That was plenty of time!' Sanotoni yelled. 'In-class writing tomorrow. This is AP, kids, get used to it!'

Saxon walked with me to crafts class, and I felt a wave of relief when I spotted Kelsie. She was the wedge between us, and I needed a living, breathing, physical reminder of why I would be smart to stay far away from Saxon Maclean.

'Brenna!' Kelsie bounced over and gave me a quick

hug. 'I looked for you before the bell this morning!'

'I was a little late this morning.' I traced a finger over her intricately beaded necklace. 'I love this.' It was layers of minute glass beads threaded and twirled together.

'Thank you!' She touched it proudly. 'I made it! Do you want one?'

'Really? But, Kelsie, you shouldn't give them away. Seriously, sell these and you'll have enough money to retire before the year is out.'

She grabbed my hand and squeezed it. 'You're the best, Brenna. I'm so glad you're not in Dutchland this year.'

I didn't bother to correct her this time.

'I love your shirt, by the way. Is it Urban Outfitters?'

'Brenna made it,' Saxon interjected.

I almost forgot that he was there. Almost.

'You have to make me one,' she ordered.

'We'll barter,' I agreed.

Saxon and Kelsie eyed each other. Kelsie raised her eyebrows at him and looked coolly away.

'I am going to class.' I back-stepped away, my voice awkward and stilted in my own ears.

'I'll see you in a minute.' Kelsie never took her eyes off Saxon.

I'm sure they didn't know that their voices would carry from the hall. Although actually, it might have been because I was consciously eavesdropping that I heard their conversation, because no one else in the class seemed to notice.

Kelsie's voice was tight and mean. 'That was a pretty lame date, Saxon. Half an hour at a crappy Chinese place? What's up?'

'I told you, I was just feeling a little weird.' There was a defensive edge to his words. 'Give me a break.'

'Look, this was supposed to be fun, Saxon. If it's going to be all this drama, let's just stop. I don't have the time for this.' Kelsie's voice was definitely that of a woman delivering an ultimatum.

'If that's how you feel, fine.' Saxon's words clinked like ice in a glass.

A second later Kelsie marched into the room.

We sat at the table next to one another, a ball of clay in front of each of us. Kelsie kneaded it violently.

'He's such an asshole.' She punched rhythmically at the clay.

I made a sympathetic face.

'Last night, we go on a date, and this has been, like, a month in the works. Half an hour, Brenna! It was like he couldn't even hear what I was saying, like he couldn't pay any attention to me at all. I am so not going to be that desperate younger girl chasing the older brooding guy.' She scrunched her nose up. 'He's not worth it. There's nothing behind all of that mystery bullshit anyway.'

Kelsie's hands shaped the clay into symmetrical, even pieces and she built them up absentmindedly into something beautiful. I couldn't do what she was doing if I gave it my full attention and effort.

She grumbled and moaned about Saxon, and I sat and made noises of agreement with her sentiments without ever actually saying anything about him. I was ashamed to feel a sense of relief, like Saxon was free for me to pursue now. Because it was dangerously tempting to think of him that way.

And I knew that Kelsie was right; there wasn't anything behind all of his mystery except a bunch of bullshit.

Hadn't Saxon said that I could see clearly through everything?

Though if I agreed with the theory that he was full of bull, then his assessment of me kind of went out the window too.

'Ugh!' Kelsie grunted and smashed her clay into a heap.

'Kelsie!' I yelled. 'Are you insane? That was beautiful.'

'I'll make another one.' She rolled her head back on

her shoulders. 'I so need a girls' night. Are you up for hanging out tonight, Brenna? It would be so fun. We can get a movie and paint each other's toenails,' she pleaded.

And the truth was, I didn't have to think about it too much, because I really liked Kelsie, and I really wanted a girl to hang out with. Plus, if we got closer, Saxon got pushed farther out by default.

And that left Jake Kelly. I felt a little flutter in my heart when I thought about him and his crooked smile and silvery eyes, quoting *The Odyssey* to me. Well, at least referencing it to me. I liked the rough, calloused feel of his hands and the quiet depth of his voice. He was no show-off. He didn't brood.

'I'd love to hang. What movie? Mom will probably be happy to swing by Castle Video and pick something up.'

'How about a really cheesy girly movie? One that will make us cry? Like *The Notebook*,' she sighed.

'Let's make it an awful, cheese-fest Nicholas Sparks tribute night. Let's get *A Walk to Remember* and *Dear John*, too.'

'Love it!' Kelsie gushed. 'And we'll never tell a soul.'

'Never.' I drew an X over my heart with my finger.

The bell rang and I rushed to PE, excited that I had

plans on a Friday night that involved something other than Danish television, my parents, and a good book.

I caught sight of him as I sprinted out of the locker room, late to the track.

'Run, Forrest, run!' he called. A group of guys with him laughed and jostled. I wasn't sure in what spirit he had said it. Was he joking with me or mocking me? I decided that my mom's advice was the best: just ignore them and they'd go away.

Apparently, my mother never tested her theory on high-school track fans. Word had gotten around that I was a decent runner and now I had a little cheering section. At the top of the hill, where the soccer game was in play, I heard hoots every time I rounded a lap.

I put them out of my mind. Students weren't technically allowed to have iPods during PE, but I flipped up the hood on my sweatshirt and put my earphones in. I turned up the music and kept running, loving the feel as my muscles expanded and contracted, loving the cold air that blasted in and out of my lungs.

When I was in middle school I wasn't fat or thin. I was average, but I was soft, undefined, and easily winded. My body felt like some awkward giant robot someone dropped a brain into. It was difficult to navigate. When I got to Denmark there wasn't a ton to do, and everyone rode bikes everywhere, so I did, too.

My bike was my freedom, and soon Mom and Thorsten were sending me to the grocery store, the post office, the bakery and the butcher on errands and trips. It broke up the monotony of the day. After a while, they let me take my bike to the station, where I could get on the train with it, and go all over: sometimes to the beach, sometimes to the bigger cities to see a movie or do some shopping. I guess all the cycling firmed up my muscles, toned my body.

That wasn't the only physical change. Thorsten encouraged me to buy a lot of clothes when I was there. 'I don't want to brag,' he would brag, 'but Denmark is known for the excellent quality of its clothing. You can't find things made this well back in the States. You should stock up, Brenna.'

He was right, and I did. Which explained my eclectic wardrobe. I knew kids checked it out now that I was back in the States, but I was still too new for anybody to say anything to me. I started to think there was a downside to being a little cooler than I was before I left. Maybe people felt that, because I dressed better, I had got all up myself.

In reality, I felt so out of place, and I had this sinking feeling like there was really never going to be much of a niche for me in high school, especially since I'd chosen to do Share Time.

In the midst of all of my memories and thoughts, I smashed into Coach Dunn on the track.

'Hello?' she bellowed as I almost knocked her over. 'Are you blind? Do you have potatoes in your ears, Blixen?'

Luckily, my ear buds had popped out and fallen into the depths of my sweatshirt when I ran into her. 'Sorry, Coach Dunn.' I noticed I had moved up in her esteem; I had gone from a number to a last name.

'Try-outs are in two weeks. I'd better see you there,' she glowered.

'I'm thinking about it seriously,' I called as I jogged back toward the locker room.

'Blixen!'

I looked back.

'You broke yesterday's record!' She shook her head like she couldn't believe it.

I think I was suddenly good at running because I had got to zone out and obsess over something. Once my blood got pumping, I just went to that place in my head, and let my mind wander anywhere it needed to go. I'd be awful at any sport that required me to pay attention or actually think, but give me something on a track where I can just wind up and go, and I'm golden.

Saxon was waiting for me in the hall.

'Why don't you wear those tiny shorts when you run, like they do in the movies?' His voice was low and sexy, and he knew it.

'Because I'm not in a movie. I know it's confusing, since you obviously live *The Saxon Show* day and night, but some of us just want to live a boring old normal, high-school life, you know?'

'You're the furthest thing from boring I can imagine.' He reached out and tucked a piece of hair behind my ear. I actually felt all of those little hairs on my arms stand up when his fingertips brushed my ear.

The bell rang, and he put his hand back where it belonged. It didn't even surprise me when the urge to grab it and lick it ran through my mind. I'd been thinking such weird things the past few days, I didn't even acknowledge half of what passed through my brain anymore. We started walking down the hallway. 'So, let's hang out tonight.' His invitation sent a shiver down my spine.

'No,' I said simply. It was best not to let my traitorous brain think about this one too much.

'Jesus, just as friends, Brenna!' he snapped.

'Wow, as sweet as that sounds, I'll have to pass,' I snapped. 'I have plans.'

'With who?' he asked, his voice tight.

'None of your business, Saxon.' The fact that he was

acting so possessive really irritated me. 'You know what, you're not my boyfriend, and even if you were, I'm not a person who likes to be questioned about my every free moment. You need to find someone else to irritate.'

'But the thought of irritating you is literally what made me want to get out of bed this morning.' He gave me his best charming smile, but I kept my mouth in a straight line. He grunted. 'Fine. Go out with who-ever you want. It's not like I'm going anywhere.'

'I can keep hoping.' I punched his arm lightly. 'If you want, I'll let you buy me an extra ice cream. I was still pretty hungry after lunch yesterday.'

'It's a date, Blixen. I've seen guys on the football team eat half of what you ate yesterday at lunch.'

'I've got a healthy appetite.'

'So, how did you like Tech?' he asked as we made our way into the crowded lunchroom and lined up at the counter.

'I loved it. I met some really nice people, and the work we're doing is interesting.' My mind went right to Jake's face, and I felt a dizzy rush.

'I thought it was pretty crazy when you first told me you were going,' he admitted. 'I've never known anyone with more than a double digit IQ who went to Tech.'

'That's a stupid thing to say,' I said calmly, thinking, again, about Jake. 'People who go to Tech learn to do things that we take for granted. I mean, you laugh about the girls who cut your hair, but if you had to do it yourself, that would suck, wouldn't it?'

'I could just let it grow.' He refused to give me an inch.

He could, sadly. And would probably look completely sexy. 'OK. What about the students who are in the electrical program? Carpentry? Cooking? Car mechanics? Where would you be without them?'

'Maybe I'll convert and become Amish.' He raised an eyebrow.

'Yeah, that makes sense.' I put two yogurts and a banana next to my turkey sandwich and limp-looking salad. 'Leave the modern world to join a sect of people who end formal education in eighth grade to basically learn a technical skill really well.' I gave him my best sarcastic/surprised look. 'Hey wait! That sounds like a whole group of Techies, doesn't it? Only you'd have to also grow a beard, wear a funny hat and pray. A lot.'

'All right, Blix.' He grabbed two ice-cream sundaes. 'No one likes a show-off.' He grinned at me, and I couldn't help feeling proud and happy that I'd managed to impress him.

'You love a show-off, as long as that show-off is you

and everyone is cheering you on,' I said as we sat at his usual table. He tossed me a sundae cup, and I just caught it.

'I thought you were a wonder athlete,' he chuckled.

'I'm a runner, Saxon. I never made any claim to hand–eye coordination. Thanks,' I added, holding up the cup. I plowed through lunch, excited about the ride to Tech and my afternoon classes. And, yes, I was very excited to see Jake Kelly again.

It was weird to think about one guy when the other one sat right there, entertaining a group of cool upperclassmen, looking over at me once in a while as if he was making sure I was paying attention. And no matter how much I tried to train my eyes on anything else, it seemed like he caught me every time I looked his way. Maybe it was just that I looked his way a lot. Or maybe it was that he looked my way a lot.

When the bell rang, Saxon walked me to the doors, then outside. I pulled my jacket on and zipped it, then put my hat on. I promised mom I would wear that and a scarf, which I wound around my neck.

He reached out and tucked the ends of the scarf into my jacket. 'You look crazy.' The way he said it made me think that wasn't quite what he was thinking when he looked at me.

'Feel free to look away,' I offered.

'Nah. I like a little crazy now and then. It's chilly as hell out here. This is freaky weather. Soon I'll be driving you to school.'

'Saxon, I already told you that isn't cool. I like my bike, and when it's too cold to cycle, I'm going to take the bus.' I tried to give him a good serious look, but that's kind of hard when you have on a hat with tiny moose all over it and a matching scarf.

'Listen. My date with Kelsie . . .' He paused and pushed a hand through his hair. 'I don't think there's going to be another one.'

'Great.' I saw a look of hope flash in his eyes and felt good crushing it. 'Great for Kelsie.' I put one foot on the pedal. 'She can do a lot better. I have to go, Saxon. I'm late.'

And I took off, not really wanting to see his face, and not really wanting to stay and talk anymore, because I might say what I really wanted to say. That I wanted to go on a date, just me and Saxon in the dark at a theater or in a restaurant, trading stories and jokes and touching now and then. Being around Saxon was like drinking my one allotted glass of Thanksgiving wine: completely intoxicating to someone who had never had alcohol.

I knew the best way to get Saxon totally out of my system was to pedal as fast as I could to Tech. And Jake.

Chapter 3

When I got there, I was pleasantly surprised to see Jake standing in front of the bike rack. He wore a sturdy workman's Carhartt jacket and a ski hat pulled on over a baseball cap. His jeans were clean, but really old and faded – not like the old and faded you could buy at the store; he had worn them so much the fabric was giving way. He wore work boots that were splattered with mud. I wondered if that was because of the dirt biking.

'Hey!' he called.

I locked my bike up. 'Hey, yourself.' I smiled. 'Why are you waiting out here?'

He shrugged. 'Maybe I was excited to see you,' he said, his voice a little shy. His words sent a thrill of warmth through me. He looked at me quickly from under lashes that were lovely, long and silky. I wondered if boys ever noticed their own lashes.

'You don't have to freeze. I'll come and meet you in class.'

'Then how could I offer to carry your books?'

I laughed. 'You're crazy, I carry a backpack,'

'Good, 'cos I don't. Come on, before some better-looking guy tries to pick you up, and I have to get in a serious fight.' He held out his hand and, even though I thought he was weird for wanting to, I gave him my backpack. He put it on and pretended to stagger under the weight. 'Wow! Frankford must actually make you read and stuff.'

'Don't you have to read at Tech?'

'Nope. Haven't you heard? We're all dirtbags here. We don't need to read.'

He was mostly teasing, but I could tell he partially believed what he said, too.

'That's not funny, Jake. You're smart. If you don't move your brain a little it's going to slide out of your ear.'

He made a gross slurping sound and tilted his head over. I laughed.

'So what books are in here?' he asked as we walked down the hall.

'I've got an American government textbook and *Lord of the Flies* for English. And that's all I'm doing academically. Oh, and my new laptop is in there. That's why it's so heavy.'

'Show it to me later?' he requested.

'Sure.' The laptop hadn't even come up with Saxon. He wasn't really the kind of guy who you could talk to about everyday stuff. It was always exciting with Saxon, and sometimes that was strangely disappointing.

'Was it your birthday or something?' Jake asked. We were in the classroom, and he put my bag down carefully on the table. I liked how respectful he was with my things.

'No. It will be in a few weeks, on October eleventh, but my dad wanted to give me the laptop for school.'

'Nice dad,' he said.

'When is your birthday?'

'November third. I'll be seventeen.'

'Really?' I said, surprised. I'd just assumed he was my age.

'Yeah. Do I seem immature? I stayed back in kindergarten.'

'Kindergarten? What can they hold you back for in kindergarten?'

'I was "unsociable",' he recited.

'Like you wouldn't play with anyone else in the block area?' I asked.

He shrugged. 'I don't really know. I've been a

dumbass for so long, it's hard to remember all the specifics.'

I clucked my tongue at him. 'You're not a dumbass, Jake.'

He just avoided my eye contact. I had never met anyone who was so comfortable thinking so little of himself. I didn't like it at all. Jake was way smarter than he gave himself credit for, and I hated that he was so blasé about brushing off compliments he totally deserved.

We took out our paper and started sketching. I loved how independent the work in this class was, and was determined to master every complicated assignment we were given. His was much more precise than mine, much more detailed. I'd like to think I had a better handle on the subtle aspects, the shading and play of light and dark, but I think it was pretty clear that Jake was just plain better.

We didn't talk much all period. Jake was a really hard worker, and very focused. He took his time and evaluated his work over and over. A couple of times, our hands brushed as we reached for the same eraser or fresh sheet of paper. When they did, he looked at me and smiled his crooked smile, but that was as far as it went.

When we got to last period, he was way more

relaxed. It was another project period. The first assignment was a business card. I already had several sketched out.

'Those are great,' Jake observed when I pulled my designs out of my folder. I flipped them over so he could get a better look at the new tweaks on my project. His eyebrows furrowed as he studied the card sketches for my fictitious T-shirt design company. 'Mine are a lot more boring.'

'Let me see.' I'd watched him sketch out concepts upside down the day before, but hadn't been able to get a good look.

He slid his sketch pad across the table and I flipped through his neat, symmetrical, smart prototypes. 'Jake, these are awesome. Simple isn't boring.'

He brushed the compliment off. 'So how about you show me this new laptop?'

I was so excited to show him I could hardly unfasten the catch on my bag. 'It's pretty cool, right?'

He let out a low whistle. 'This is nice.' He ran his hands over the cover and turned it over, checking the underside, his voice excited. 'Go Dad.' He flipped open the lid, then looked at me, startled. 'Sorry. Is it cool if I take a look?'

'Of course.' There was something about Jake I couldn't quite put my finger on. He was hesitant, and

I didn't know why he would be. We had been comfortable with each other from the minute I met him, but he was always so careful. He was respectful towards me, but there was also a nervous, self-deprecating quality to him that never really went away.

'It's pretty jacked.' I leaned in and showed him a few of the applications on it.

'Awesome.' He finally closed the lid. 'I'm glad you have this. It's going to make this class so much easier.'

'Do we have to do a lot of computer stuff?'

'Yeah,' he said. 'There's a lab though. That's where I go to get my stuff done.'

'Sometimes it's easier to work at school.' I slid my laptop back into my bag.

'Yeah, especially compared to my house.' He grimaced. 'So, I got a truck from my grandpa a few months ago.' It seemed like he wanted to say more.

'That's great. I can't think about driving anything but my bike until I'm sixteen.'

'You're only fifteen?' he said, his eyes wide.

'I'm a fall baby, I turn sixteen in October. It just seems like I'm super young, but I'm totally normal for a sophomore.'

'Oh yeah,' he said, then licked his lips nervously. 'Right. So, not that you have to, but since I'm driving anyway, I wouldn't mind giving you a lift home when it starts getting icy.'

'Jake, you live, like, half an hour from my house. I'm over in Augusta.'

'Oh. Augusta? Well, I work near there, and I'm pretty constantly at work.'

'You do? Where?' The thought of having a job right now was so foreign to me. Mom wanted me to spend my time studying, and we vacationed a lot in the summer. Plus, I had no skills.

'I work at Zinga's Farm.' He pulled his wallet from his back pocket and showed me his ID card. The picture caught his half-smile. I pressed my finger to his smile on the card before he put it back.

'So, what do you do?' I asked, intrigued by this information.

'I run the tractors and help fix them. I load fruit and package it for shipping. I help in the shop. In the fall I work the pumpkin patch and tractor rides and the apple orchard. At Christmas I work the tree farm. Spring we do mulch and flowers. Summer is berry picking. Boring stuff.'

'Sounds pretty good to me,' I said, completely impressed. 'Are you saving the money up for something?'

'Uh, yeah, some. I had to buy a lot of new parts

for the truck. And I want to get a new dirt bike.'

'Yeah, I saw your picture on Facebook.'

His face brightened. 'You saw me on Facebook?'

'Yeah. I asked to be your friend. Don't you check?'

'Hell, I'm gonna check now.' He smiled and leaned his chair back.

'Don't lean back like that,' I warned. 'You're going to flip the chair back and smash your skull in.'

'There's nothing in there to hurt anyway,' he said, wryly. But he let his chair fall back down with a thud. 'So what are you reading for English again?'

'*Lord of the Flies* by William Golding. Have you ever read it?' I doubted he would have, and I could only imagine how painful that particular book on tape would be to listen to. The dry language in the book could knock you unconscious if the plot didn't revolve around savage English kids.

'Is it worth reading?'

'Yeah. I mean, I think so. It's about some English boys who go nuts and turn into delinquents after a plane crash strands them on this island. No adults.'

'Sounds cool. *Lord of the Flies*. Why is that the title?'

'Can't tell.' I gave him my best sidelong glance. 'You're just going to have to read it.'

He didn't say anything, but when he ducked his

head to work on his designs, I saw his mouth curve into a smile. I loved that he took my opinions seriously; that he wanted to read what I read and that he was open about being excited I had sent him a friend request.

'So, are you going on a date or something tonight?' He kept concentrated focus on the careful lines he sketched.

'Are you trying to ask if I'm single, Jake Kelly?' I teased, flicking the corner of his paper.

He laughed sheepishly, but still didn't look up. 'Maybe.' His mouth moved back and forth like he was debating saying something else. 'You don't have to answer.' Again, his voice went to that guarded place I wondered about.

'I'm not FBI, Jake.' I doodled a tiny star on his paper, then flipped my eraser around and rubbed it out. He trailed the tip of his finger through the eraser shavings. 'You can ask me things. I do have plans tonight.' I felt a wicked kick of glee when I watched his face fall a little, knowing that it was all because he thought I was going on a hot date. 'With my friend Kelsie. We're going to paint our nails and watch sappy girl movies.'

'I like the sound of that.' He reached out with a jerky motion and caught my hand. I felt the breath catch in my throat and hold. He examined my nails. 'They look nice like this.'

I realized that they still had the remnants of slightly chipped blue polish on them. 'They look terrible. You don't have to lie to me to be nice, Jake. You can just say, "Wow, your nails look crappy."' I did my best boy voice.

'Well, I will tell you that's a crappy imitation of my voice.' He smiled so wide I could see his eyeteeth. 'But you've got to know you're totally hot, chipped nails and all.' He burned beet red all the way to the roots of his hair. 'Man, you get me to say some embarrassing stuff, Brenna.' He rubbed his hand on the back of his neck.

'Hey, don't blame me when you feel moved to make strange declarations.' I bit the inside of my cheek to keep the giggles back. Then, feeling flattered and very brave, I added, 'And you've got to know you're totally hot, Jake.'

The blush that had been wearing away flamed bright red again. 'Thanks,' he said, not meeting my eyes, but smiling and shaking his head.

'Is this weirding you out?' I nudged his arm with my elbow.

'No.' Then his voice got very serious. 'Just giving me a lot to think about.'

I leaned so close I could smell his crisp aftershave. 'I knew I smelled something burning.' I tapped my head suggestively.

This time when he laughed the teacher looked up at us with a warning glint in her eyes, and we both ducked our heads and got back to work.

A few minutes later, I passed him a note.

Where do you ride your dirt bike? I wrote. I did it without thinking, the way I had done with classmates a thousand times before. As soon as I turned the sheet and saw the nervous flicker in his eyes, I felt like a huge ass. He was dyslexic, for God's sake.

He took out a pen and licked his lips nervously. *Vernon.* He wrote it very carefully and slowly.

Do you compete? I wrote. I did it because I didn't want him to think that I thought he was stupid or that there was anything he couldn't do.

He read it carefully, moving his lips around the words. He picked the pen up again. *Yes. And I win.*

I wrinkled my nose and wrote, *So you're a big shot? Maybe I'll come and see you sometime.*

I slid the paper to him and looked away while he read it. I didn't want him to feel pressured, but I watched out of the corner of my eye as he moved his mouth and squinted. It reminded me of the few times I'd struck up a conversation with kids in Denmark.

A lot of people in Denmark take years of English, but they don't always get to use it, especially in Jutland, which is the countryside. So I'd be rattling away, so excited to have anyone to talk to, and the kid would be working overtime trying to keep up and string together an answer that made some kind of sense. For me, it was all fun and then guilt. For them, it was just exhausting work.

You better. I have a race in 3 weeks. He wrote in neat, blocky writing, like a very textbook version of little kid print.

I'll be there. Where? I asked.

The track at Vernon Valley.

With the snow? As far as I knew, they covered it with snow for skiing.

Not in . . . He stopped and I saw him write an 'a' and a 't' before he stopped again, erased and wrote, finally, *fall.*

I just nodded, and his shoulders actually sagged with relief when I didn't write more. I noticed that when he thought I wasn't looking, he slid the paper off the edge of the table and put it into his jeans pocket.

We worked in companionable silence until the final bell startled us out of our peaceful little world.

I don't think I have ever, in my entire life as a student, felt sad to hear the final bell ring on a Friday afternoon, but I definitely felt it that afternoon. My time with Jake was over, and I wouldn't see him again until Monday.

He grabbed my backpack and we walked down the long hallway full of jostling people.

'Will you stop by my locker with me?' He nodded a few rows down and I followed, weaving out of the way of the pushing crowds.

We stopped and he opened the locker door so I could see binders stacked neatly on top of one another and covered with doodles. He pulled some books out and then grabbed his coat and two hats.

'I like your hat combo.' I smacked the brim of his base-ball cap when he got it on.

He pulled the ski hat over it. 'Good for sun, good for snow.'

We walked outside and he waited while I undid the chain on my bike. 'I guess I'll see you around.' I fiddled with the handlebars and kicked at my front tire.

'Yeah.' He adjusted his ski hat and pulled his brim lower. Neither of us wanted to leave, but what were we going to do, stand there shivering? 'Man, it's cold. This weather is crazy. I hear we might get flurries next week,' he said, blowing out hard. 'I would kill for a license right now.'

'Did you ever notice that old trucks always have the best heaters?' Thorsten's truck made me sweat buckets when he cranked up the heat in the winter.

'There's a technical reason.' He winked at me. 'Someday I'll explain it all to you.'

And then, because he was just the best guy and I loved how he always smiled when he talked to me, and because I was missing him a little already, I leaned over and kissed him right next to his mouth, but not on it. He smelled minty and the corner of his mouth was dry and warm with just a little scratchy facial hair.

'Oh man,' he said as I pulled back. He blinked hard and turned red again. I got on my bike.

'You better be my Facebook friend when I check.'

'I'm gonna be your Facebook stalker.' The chip in his tooth glinted a little as he smiled lopsidedly at me. Then his face fell suddenly. 'I'm actually a little bummed we won't be in school on Monday.'

'We won't?' I asked, puzzled and deflated. No school meant no Jake.

'It's Labor Day.' He ran his fingers along my handlebar, just around my mittened hands. 'With this beautiful weather you didn't realize? Aren't you all ready for a nice picnic?'

'Seriously? I think my brain has frostbite. But that's good news now that I know.' I inched one yarn-covered finger toward his hand, and he brushed his fingers over mine.

'I guess it depends on how much you're looking forward to school. I might just get the perfect attendance award this year.' His fingers crept to the sliver of skin between my mitten and my jacket sleeve and brushed lightly, giving me goosebumps.

'Don't bother on my behalf. I always skip a few days a year.' I bit my bottom lip and gave him my best rebel face.

'Call me before you do. School will be extra depressing when you're absent.' He slid his hands off mine, then off the handlebars, then backed away a few reluctant steps so I had space to pedal.

'Bye, Jake,' I called over my shoulder as I rode away.

'Be careful, Brenna!' he shouted.

When I looked back, he was still watching me, all the way down the road.

Chapter 4

The wind was cold, but I felt so good I didn't mind. My cheeks ached from smiling. Saxon was intriguing, but there was something so real and decent about Jake. I pedaled faster, thinking about Mom waiting at the window, and then coasted for a minute, so I could pull my scarf up over my nose. She would probably grab it today to see if it was cold. I was happy that I was going to be able to tell her that I had plans with Kelsie tonight. She wanted me to hang out with kids my own age a little more.

But I didn't want to tell her about Jake. She had some of the same prejudices about Tech kids that the rest of the county seemed to have, and I felt a little protective of him. I didn't want to hear anyone say the things that seemed to define him: that he wasn't very good at school, that he would probably end up laboring for the rest of his life, that he didn't value academic subjects the way I did. It might all be true about Jake, but that didn't really define him. There was so much more to him than met the eye. He was humble and hardworking and determined. He wasn't full of himself, but he had passion and he had good ideas and he was focused. I liked him.

I really liked him.

Which made the way I acted around Saxon all the more confusing. Why couldn't I get him out of my system? Especially when I had the promise of some-one as good as Jake to care about? Even if my mind wanted to reject Saxon, my body didn't. Something about the way he looked and moved and talked made me feel a warm rush that shook me to the core.

I hated it, but I couldn't stop it any more than I could stop a blush or a shiver. It was automatic. I pedaled faster, harder, focusing on my breathing as I moved quickly along the roads, sending vibrant red and orange and yellow leaves swirling up under my tires. I enjoyed the rolling hills, which forced me to work hard on the uphill, but let me relax as I coasted down. Hills were not part of the terrain where we had been in Denmark, so I was still getting used to the difficulty of pedaling up them.

I turned onto my road and almost slammed into a car parked in the middle of the road.

It was a Dodge Charger, one of the new models that

took up too much road and roared around like big hulking predators, but I liked them anyway. Or maybe I liked them because of those facts.

'Watch it!' I yelled, hopping off of my bike as I skidded to a stop.

That's when I saw the driver's tinted window roll down. 'Watch yourself, Blixen,' Saxon said coolly. 'In case you didn't notice, I'm driving a car. You're on a bike. I don't care who has the right of way, you're not winning that one.' He lit a cigarette. I backed up.

'Get in the car.' He didn't ask or plead. He just told me like I'd instantly obey.

'No way.' I got back on my bike.

'Your nose is red,' he said casually.

'So what?'

'So, your mom is gonna be pissed off. Get in and warm up. We don't need to go anywhere. We'll just talk.' He held his arms out innocently. His face was so handsome, and his eyes were dark and devilish.

'I can't. Mom will kill me if I smell like smoke.' I put one foot on the pedal.

He took the cigarette out of his mouth and flicked it out of the window into the gutter. 'Now c'mon. I'm trying to help you out with this whole ridiculous bike-riding fiasco.'

I laid my bike on the uneven side of the road and

climbed into the car, one hundred percent against my better judgment.

'Don't wait for me like this,' I said, even as my body rejoiced at the warm air blowing from the vents. He had music on, some kind of neopunk. 'What are you listening to?'

'Folly.' He turned the volume up a little. 'Do you know them?'

I shook my head.

'The drummer is a senior at Frankford. They have a gig next week. Here.' He popped the CD out of the player. 'I've got another copy. Listen to it. If you like it, we can go see them.'

He didn't ask if I wanted to go; he just assumed that I'd take him up on it. I shook my head.

'No thanks.'

'What? You don't like music?' he asked, his voice low and mocking.

'I like music. I've . . . I've never been to a concert.' I flipped the vents open wider and basked in the heat, hoping I could store it up until I got home.

'Are you kidding?' He raised his eyebrows incredulously. 'Tell me you're not serious. Never?'

'No. Not with, like, a whole audience.' By now I had started to thaw out. I should get out and go home. But I couldn't do it. Not yet.

'What does that mean?' He stretched back in his seat and gave me his total attention.

'It means that I did see a band once, but by myself.' I pulled off my mittens and loosened my scarf. The air was getting extremely hot, and it wasn't only because of the vents.

Saxon turned the heat down without glancing at the controls and rubbed his fingers against his thumb. 'Like your parents came up with a cool mil and you got Beyoncé to dance for you in your bedroom?'

I clucked my tongue. 'Beyoncé isn't going to shake it in your bedroom for a mil. She's not some cheap lap dancer. My dad works for *Saturday Night Live*, and once Green Day was on. I got to go to the rehearsal. My dad is a really huge fan, and he got me into them. But it wasn't just me. It was me and my dad and the camera crew and sound guys.'

'Wow.' He shook his box of cigarettes, then did that annoying tapping on the box that apparently 'packed the tobacco'.

It was incredibly annoying. I wanted to say, *If you're going to smoke just do it. Don't make it some big show.* But even so, I couldn't stop myself from watching him do it. And even though I hated smoking, I could sort of see how some people might be able to give it that old Hollywood, James Dean cool look. Sort of.

'So you met the boys from Green Day? Unreal. Did you talk to them?' He peeled back the foil paper inside the carton.

I wished I had a more impressive story, but I didn't. I'd been young and completely, dorkishly star struck at the time. 'No. Not really. I told them I was a fan, you know, cheesy stuff like that. They were super nice to me, though, and gave me autographs and all that.'

'Cool.' Saxon nodded. 'Hey,' he said, and his voice completely lacked the excitement that Jake's voice would have had if he was about to tell me something. 'I talked to the guy from Folly about your T-shirt.'

'My T-shirt?' I repeated.

'Yeah.' He put a cigarette to his lips without lighting it. When he spoke, he moved his lips around the cigarette, which was obnoxious, especially because of how much I liked watching him do it. 'He noticed it. He's in your crafts class. Anyway, he was wondering if you'd be able to come up with something for Folly. So, whatever. If you don't want to, don't worry about it.'

'OK,' I said, still in shock. 'Why didn't this guy just talk to me?'

He took the cigarette out from between his lips for a minute. 'His name's Chris Holcomb. Because he thinks you're my girlfriend, so he thought I'd be able to get you to say yes.' Saxon put the cigarette back in his mouth and shrugged as if his words were no big deal. My heart was thudding in my chest.

'Why would he think we're boyfriend and girl-friend?' I glared at him.

'Maybe because of the adoring way you're always staring at me,' he said, his grin purposefully annoying. 'C'mon. Really? He saw us after PE the last two days. What can I say, Blix? We have an attraction that's noticeable.' He leaned over me, his arm sliding past my stomach, and popped open my door. 'All right, I've held you captive long enough,' he said, but he didn't lean back.

So quickly I had no time to react, he pulled the cigarette out of his mouth, pulled me toward him, and pressed his lips on mine. His lips were soft at first, then firmer, then his tongue pressed into my mouth, gently. I opened my mouth, tasting the stale flavor of cigarette smoke and the crisp tang of orange Tic Tac. His hand slid to my jaw and it felt so great, big and warm and strong. Suddenly the entire world narrowed down to me and Saxon and our lips and tongues in that big shark of a car. My body felt warm and ready for something that I couldn't put my finger on. I melted into him, pressed harder to his mouth and even moaned just a little bit.

Then I remembered Jake and our chaste kiss

outside the school. I remembered Kelsie and our plans for the night. I pulled away with a start.

'No!' I grabbed my bag. 'I don't want you, Saxon,' I insisted, and my voice sounded wild in my own ears.

'I would say that's not entirely accurate, Brenna.' He picked up the cigarette and lit it nonchalantly. The smoke began to furl from the end. 'Now run along before Mommy smells smoke and you get in trouble.' He exhaled wide Os from his open mouth and waved me away lazily.

I was so mad I slammed the car door as hard as humanly possible. I hated him! I hated his arrogance and his persistence. I hated that he could make me feel things for him when all I wanted to do was avoid him. I hated that being around him could threaten two friendships that were important to me. And I hated that I got in his car and kissed him back when he had told me with his own mouth that all he wanted was to get me out of his system. What was I doing?

I told myself I was just trying to get him out of my system, but that made me feel like just as much of a jerk as him.

When I got to the house, I saw the curtains flick and knew Mom had been wondering where I was. She did pull on my nose when I got in, and pinched my ears, but they were warm after all that hot air pouring out of Saxon's vents . . . and mouth.

'Kelsie asked me to spend the night at her place. I told her you might be able to take me to Castle Video and pick up some chick flicks. Is that OK?'

She kissed my forehead hard. 'Of course. I'm so glad you're getting back together with your old girlfriends. It's good for you to be around some nice girls your own age.'

I felt a wave of shame sweep through me. How could I have done this to Kelsie? The feel of Saxon's mouth on mine was still vibrating through me, and, embarrassingly, it had made me feel a little wet and warm. I sighed, ashamed, wondering how I had become such a degenerate over the past few days.

'I'll go pack a bag for overnight. Maybe when you and Thorsten come to get me tomorrow, we can go to IKEA?' It would be cool to have Kelsie come to my place, but it might be a little weird if my room was still lavender. Then again, I had never been in Kelsie's room. It could be Barbie pink for all I knew.

'That would be fun. Pack the IKEA catalog in case you want to look through it tonight.'

I stuffed a change of clothes for the next day, pajamas and a toothbrush and toothpaste in a bag with some nail polish and my iPod and pillow. I met

Mom in the kitchen and we got in the car, ready to go to Castle Video.

'So, how was school?' My mom had a serious lead foot, and I watched the speedometer so I could warn her if she did more than ten over.

'Good. My classes are all really decent. I even like PE this year,' I admitted.

'I always had a feeling you might be a closet athlete. Good for you, Bren. It's about time you started to really let yourself shine.'

I smiled wanly. If only she knew that what I seemed to be excelling at was kissing multiple boys in a single day.

We went in and I grabbed the Nicholas Sparks movies. I convinced Mom to rent a couple of movies for herself and Thorsten, and then she bought two big tubs of microwave popcorn and some soda for Kelsie and me.

She dropped me at Kelsie's with a quick kiss. 'Keep your cell on. Love you, baby.'

'Love you!' I called, and she waited until I was in the door and Kelsie's mom waved before she pulled away.

'It's so nice to see you again, Brenna,' Kelsie's mom said.

'It's nice to see you, too, Mrs Jordan.' I liked Kelsie's

warm, sweet mom. Unlike my mother, Kelsie's mom gave her plenty of space and didn't ask too many questions.

Kelsie crashed down the stairs. 'Hey, Brenna! C'mon up!'

I smiled at her mom and followed Kelsie to her bedroom, which was definitely not Barbie pink. It was a deep purple and covered with copies of Salvador Dali paintings, Janis Joplin posters, and black-and-white photos of local wildlife that I was pretty sure Kelsie had taken. The carpet was covered with rugs that looked Indian, and there was a silky sari-like covering on the bed. Kelsie had plants everywhere and white twinkle lights around her windows and ceiling. They made the room seem warm and cozy.

'I love your room.' I stood in the middle and spun slowly, taking it all in.

'Thanks. Look.' She pointed to a picture stuck in the corner of her dressing-table mirror. It was Kelsie and me in eighth grade at our dinner dance. I was wearing a short black dress with a metallic net overlay and my hair was curled. Kelsie was wearing a short purple halter-neck dress and her hair was in a fancy updo. I had my arm around her and we were smiling big, cheesy smiles.

'Wow,' I laughed. 'We were big-time dorks.'

'Oh yeah,' she agreed. 'What's that?' She pointed to the popcorn tub I still clutched in my hands.

'Mom thought we'd want snacks.'

'Your mom is the best,' Kelsie gushed, and I felt another layer of guilt, thinking of all the times my mom criticized Kelsie's butt or hairline. 'So how's it going riding your bike to school? It's been weirdly cold lately, right?'

'Yeah, but, um, it's been OK.' I so didn't want my thoughts going anywhere that had anything to do with Saxon or his stupid ideas about us. I decided the best way to put him entirely out of my head was to talk about someone who was so much better. 'There's this guy in my Tech class.'

At the word 'guy' Kelsie's eyes lit up. 'Yeah?' she asked eagerly.

I felt the giddiness and excitement well up in me. 'He's so cute. His eyes are gorgeous. They're the weirdest color, like silver. Anyway, he's getting his license in November and he offered to drive me home when the weather gets colder.'

'That's so cute,' Kelsie squealed. 'He's making plans for you in November? That's adorable! What's his name?'

'Jake Kelly.' My heart fell into my stomach when I saw Kelsie's face. 'What? Do you know him?'

'No. Not really. I mean, he had a reputation last year as kind of . . . it's not even important. A year can be a long time, and it was rumors.' She suddenly became transfixed with the throw pillows on her bed.

'Kelsie.' I looked her in the face. 'It's, like, your duty as a friend to tell me what you know about this guy. I've only known him for two days. If he's shady, I need to know so I can stay away from him.' But I hoped I would be cool with whatever Kelsie told me, because I knew I was kidding myself if I thought I could just drop Jake with no problem.

'No! I'll tell you what I've heard, but I want you to know, I don't know this guy and it could all be totally exaggerated, rumor-mill type stuff.' She took a deep breath, then dived in. 'I heard that he has been with a lot of girls. Like, everyone. And that he is supposed to be some big conquest. Apparently, girls in Tech rip each other apart to get him to take them out. And he's supposed to be, you know . . .' Kelsie looked uncomfortable.

'What?' I sat on the edge of my seat.

'Good. Like, sexually good. Really good.' She raised her eyebrows up high.

'Oh.'

One piece of me was devastated by the idea of Jake with so many other girls, having sex with them. It made him seem kind of cheap and gross. Another part of me was confused and wanted to talk to him about it. It just didn't make sense. The Jake I knew was definitely really good looking, but he seemed kind of shy and not at all like what Kelsie was describing. But I didn't know. And a third part of me, the part I was pretty embarrassed about, was completely curious. What had he done? How many girls? Did he want me that way? It was exhilarating and humiliating at the same time.

'Don't make that face, Brenna. It's a rumor. And a totally exaggerated one for all we know. Don't take it too seriously, OK? Just, maybe talk to him before you . . . you know.' She nudged me with her elbow.

'No.' I shook my head. 'I've known him for two days, Kelsie. I'm not even sure he likes me.'

She snorted. 'Please. Are you for real? You're all every guy at Frankford can talk about.'

'What? Seriously, this is one sad little farm town if I'm the hot news.'

Kelsie rolled her eyes. 'C'mon, Brenna. You're hot.' She giggled at my blush. 'You're a sexy, sexy mama and you know it! And you're smart. And you're a mystery, with your trip to Europe for a year and your cool wardrobe and your Share Time thing.' Kelsie waved her hands around and popped her eyes out, then whispered, 'Mysterious Brenna Blixen.'

I waved my hands around, too. 'Dork,' I whispered back, and we both fell on the bed laughing. Then we watched the movies and talked about celebrity couples who just did not make sense and the fact that the couple in *The Notebook* should totally get together again in real life.

'I don't care if they've been apart for a million years. They're so perfect,' Kelsie sighed, applying thin coats of black paint to my toenails. I was OK at toenail painting, but Kelsie was an artist. She could paint all sorts of tiny things that look just like decals. She was doing tiny pink skulls on my nails, and they were intricately detailed and assembly-line identical. It was a little creepy how good she was.

'They are really cute together. So, do you have anyone in mind in the love arena, Ms Sex Goddess?' It seemed like it was all done with Saxon, and Kelsie always had insta-crushes in middle school, so I hoped there was already someone new who caught her eye.

'Yes! Do you know Chris Holcomb? He's in our crafts class.'

'Yeah.' I tried to keep my voice even. 'Isn't he in that band Folly?'

'Yes! Do you like Folly?' She bounced up and down on the bed, making all the nail-polish bottles clack and threatening to spill hot-pink polish all over her bed-spread.

I grabbed the pink polish and twisted the cap on it. 'Um, I just got a CD of theirs, but I haven't listened to it. Do you like them?'

'I love them. And Chris is so cute. Have you noticed him?' She shook me by the shoulders and bounced again.

'Someone at lunch mentioned that he noticed my shirt. He was asking about getting something made for Folly.' I wasn't positive how Kelsie would react to my news, but, in typical Kelsie fashion, she was thrilled.

'This is so perfect! I'll go up to Chris on Monday and tell him how you're my good friend, and he'll ask me if I can talk to you about shirts, and that's it. History will be made!' She flopped back on the bed and squealed.

We cracked up, and Kelsie yelled at me for messing up her paint job. I was glad to hear that things between her and Saxon had cooled down in a way that left me feeling less guilty about my kiss.

Not that I was OK-ing the fact that I'd kissed Saxon. It was most of all a betrayal of the unspoken thing that Jake Kelly and I had. But Kelsie had planted some serious seeds of doubt about Jake. Maybe I was taking his interest in me way too seriously. He was, after all, just another guy in my class. Maybe he simply wanted to talk to me while I was in class with him.

When Kelsie went to the bathroom to get ready for bed, I slid my laptop out of my bag. I got an internet signal and went online, logging onto my Facebook page. Jake's picture was there in my very small friend list, and when I clicked on it, I picked up a pretty standard guy's site. His wall was filled with YouTube videos of dirt-bike races and screaming bands mixed with lots of gangster game invites. I went to his pics. He had four up. The first, his profile picture, was him standing in front of his dirt bike. There was one of a big blue truck that looked like it belonged in a junk-yard and one of Jake on a tractor, a piece of straw hanging out of his mouth, his eyes squinty in the too-bright sun. Both were pretty much exactly what I expected.

There was one tagged picture. It was Jake, and he looked like he might be drunk. He was sitting between two girls, his arms around them. They were wearing a lot of black eye make-up and were both tilting their heads down and making kissing faces at the camera. Underneath the picture, one of the girls had written, *Good times, J! Call me when yur around again! XOXO.*

I was looking at the picture when Kelsie walked back in. My instinct was to click the laptop shut, but that always made people totally curious about whatever you were looking at. Unfortunately, Kelsie was curious anyway.

'Let me see,' she demanded. I turned the screen and she looked at the pic with narrowed eyes. 'The hottie is Jake?'

I nodded. She grabbed the laptop and flipped through his four pics over and over again. 'Why is it that boys always only have, like, two pictures?' she grumbled.

'I don't know.' My problem wasn't the lack of pictures; it was the people in them. Who were those girls to Jake? And was that picture an inside look at the real Jake? Or was the real Jake the guy I shared smiles and stares with in class?

'You have picture comments.' She clicked without asking me. I guess I should have been annoyed, but there was something so likeable about Kelsie that I just let her do what she wanted. Her eyebrows went up high. 'Hello, Jake,' she muttered.

'What is it?' I almost didn't want to look, but my curiosity got the better of me.

There were a few pictures of me from Jutland. The one Kelsie had clicked on was a beach scene, and

I was wearing a bikini. I know most girls are freaked out about that kind of stuff, but I thought I looked good in it, so I put it up. There was a comment from Jake. *Hottt!!!!* it said. I felt a weird heat low in my belly.

'He can't spell,' I said lamely.

'Yeah, I don't think it was a misspelling,' she giggled. 'You do look hot, Ms Brenna Sexy Mama. Hot with three Ts.'

She clicked on one of me standing in front of a castle in Denmark that was supposed to be the one that *Hamlet* took place in. It was just me, nothing really special. He had written, *Yur sexy.*

'Um, he's not like this in class.' I felt embarrassed by his openly flirty comments and even more embarrassed by his atrocious spelling. Ugh! I was a prude and a grammar snob all at the same time!

'Boys are always braver online,' Kelsie said knowingly. 'There's one more.'

It was a picture of me reading a book. It had also been taken in Denmark. I was reading *Catcher in the Rye*, which is one of my favorites of all time. When I realized I'd left my copy in the States, Thorsten went out and hunted one down for me one in an all-English book store. I'd read it in one day, and he and Mom thought it was so funny that they'd taken a picture of me curled up in the chair for my reading marathon. Jake had written, *smart gurls rock* under it.

'Woman, he likes you! A lot!' Kelsie gushed.

I shrugged. 'If he lives up to his reputation, he probably writes stuff like this under every picture of every girl who's his friend.'

'We could check any profiles that aren't private,' she suggested.

'Kelsie,' I groaned. 'That's so pathetic. Besides, most of them will be private.'

'You never know,' she sing-songed.

So we tried, and most were private, but Kelsie was friends with four girls from his enormous friend section.

'Let's look,' she said happily, logging me out and logging herself in. 'Oh, a friend request from Brenna Blixen.' She looked at me with wide eyes. 'Should I accept?'

'No way. That's girl's a fruitcake.' My heart was settled right in the pit of my stomach. Saxon might be a jerk, but at least he put it right out there for everyone to see. Jake, it seemed, had this secret other life that I didn't know anything about. I hated it.

'Mmmm.' Kelsie clicked the 'Accept' button. 'I love fruitcake. OK, here is the first girl. Ugh, why am I her friend? She's like a valley girl clone.'

'We live in north Jersey. How is she a valley girl?' I said in defense of the girl.

'She's blonde and she's an airhead,' Kelsie said absently. 'Ooh, here's a picture of her and Jake.'

I didn't want to look, but I was right there at Kelsie's side in a second. How was I supposed to not look? Realistically, there was no way I could resist the temptation.

He gazed at the camera totally bleary-eyed, just like in his other picture. He had definitely been drinking or worse, and his arm was around her in this really lazy way, like he was super-comfortable with her. Her caption was, *Me and 1 of my Boyzzzz!*

'What does that mean?' I asked. 'And why so many zees?'

'It means she's a super skank with a harem of "boyzzz",' Kelsie buzzed, 'and Jake is one of them. Brenna, don't sweat it, this picture is from last spring.'

There were random comments under the picture about how cute the girl looked and what a good couple she and Jake would make written by other fish-faced girls with no grammar skills and way too much eye make-up. It made my stomach churn. I started to really, really wish that I had never checked the stupid page.

But Kelsie was totally enjoying herself. There were

similar pictures of Jake on two of the other girls' pages and it made me similarly upset. How was this happening? How was my Jake also this half-drunk man-whore? They were like two pieces from different puzzles; no matter how I tried, I couldn't fit them together.

Kelsie yawned. 'You like a bad, bad boy.' She poked me with her toe as she stretched. 'I'll go get you the air mattress.' She went to get it and I went back to Jake's profile, to the first picture, the one of Jake with his gray eyes and crooked smile, leaning on his dirt bike. This was the picture that made sense to me. Was I stupid to think this was the real Jake?

We set up my bed, and Kelsie collapsed and was out like a light in no time. I tossed a little. I had gone from feeling like a loose woman to an oblivious loser. What was it I had done with Saxon? One kiss? What had Jake done? What was he doing right now? What was Saxon doing? It was Friday night. Where were they? Those were my last thoughts before I fell into a deep sleep.

I thought I'd have crazy dreams all night, but there was nothing. I was totally at peace until the morning. When I got up, I asked Kelsie if I could use her shower and she rolled her eyes and waved me away. 'Of course. Let me sleep.'

I showered, did my hair, put on make-up and got dressed for my day. IKEA was a good forty minutes away, so Mom and Thorsten were coming early.

'Don't get out of bed. My mom just called, and she'll be here in five minutes.' Kelsie smiled and asked if I was sure. I kissed her forehead. 'I'm sure. Let's do it again soon.' She gave me a sleepy thumbs-up, and I went downstairs and sat on her porch to wait.

Sussex County was made up of rolling hills and lots of big, old trees. It used to all be farmland, mainly dairy, and was still really beautiful. A lot of the population had jobs in New York City, like Thorsten, so there was an abundance of money here, and the people with money bought these old farms and made them look authentic, except really well maintained and with only a few horses for riding. It was like those modern art pictures of cities where they take out the garbage and neaten everything up: hyperrealism.

I sat on the steps waiting for Mom and Thorsten. The wind was cool on my face and smelled really crisp. I loved autumn in New Jersey. Kelsie's mom was in the kitchen; I had said a quick goodbye and thank you and turned down her offer of breakfast. It would have broken Thorsten's heart if I'd eaten on a Saturday morning without him. I knew he would want us to have breakfast together on the way someplace. I could hear Kelsie's mom pottering about in the kitchen through the open window, but other than that I felt alone in the world, which was one of my favorite feelings.

Sitting there on the steps, enjoying the peace, I wondered if I should think about becoming a hermit. Or a nun. Cutting guys out of my life would pretty much slice through all of my current problems.

Chapter 5

When Thorsten's truck pulled up, I was so happy to see them my heart leaped. Mom and Thorsten waved out the windows. It felt good to be loved.

'How was it?' Mom asked as I slid in next to her.

'So fun.' I pulled off my shoe and sock and wiggled my toes, showing off my new pedicure.

Mom shook her head in admiration. 'Kelsie is a true artist.'

'How do you know I didn't do it?'

'Because the skin around your toes isn't painted.' She ruffled my hair.

'I'm starving,' Thorsten said. 'Your mother wouldn't let me eat, Brenna. Is it OK if we stop and grab a bite?'

'Yeah, that's fine.' I laughed; I had Thorsten so pegged it was ridiculous.

My good mood bubbled on and on, and even had me singing along to the classic rock station Mom and

Thorsten love. No one with a soul can resist John Cougar Mellencamp's classic, 'Jack and Diane', even on a bad day. But of course, it was too good to be true. I tried not to let them see my panic when we pulled into Zinga's.

'We're stopping here?' I pressed my forehead to the window and groaned.

'Is this OK?' Thorsten asked. 'I've been craving their apple tarts. Do you want to go somewhere else?'

'No.' I forced a smile and peeled my head off the glass. 'This is great.'

I couldn't live my life avoiding him. Besides, with any luck he'd be out hoeing some pumpkins or whatever they do on a farm, and I wouldn't even see him. Mom was already exclaiming over all the stuff there was to buy.

'Look, honey!' she called to Thorsten, and I could see him struggling between being good to his wife and being good to his stomach. Luckily, he didn't have to decide, because Mom had already bounded away from a stone fountain shaped like a boy peeing into a shell to a huge Virgin Mary standing on a mirrored glass ball.

I wandered toward the mounds of bumpy gourds in huge crates and looked through them absently.

'Hey,' said a voice so achingly familiar it made my head light.

If I said that I wasn't happy to see him, it would be

a bald-faced lie. I was almost sad that I had seen everything I had seen on the computer the night before. But I guessed it was better to find out about him earlier than later, before my heart got completely lost.

'Hey.' I smiled half-heartedly. I couldn't help it. I'd always kind of sucked at pretending that I wasn't feeling something.

He squinted at me with concern. It was the same Jake, complete with his chipped tooth and bashful smile. 'Are you OK? You look kind of tired or something.'

'I checked your Facebook page.' I picked up a bumpy green gourd and turned it in my hand slowly.

His eyes widened and he swallowed twice. 'Oh.' He shifted from one mud-caked boot to the other. He wore almost exactly the same outfit he'd been wearing on Friday. I thought it was weird that he didn't have a separate set of clothes for work and school. 'That picture, with the girls, they weren't my girlfriends. Aren't my girlfriends. I mean, neither of them was a girl I dated.'

'Yeah, I didn't think so.' I arched my eyebrow, and when his face fell, I knew I didn't have to finish with, *And that's exactly the point.*

He pulled his work gloves off and glanced around, then grabbed my hand and dragged me to the greenhouse a few feet away. He closed the door behind us so we were completely alone in the bright, warm space.

'It's not what you think.' He ducked his head to catch my lowered gaze. 'Brenna, it isn't.'

'What do you think I think?' My voice cracked around the words.

'That I'm . . .' Jake was at a loss. 'A party guy, I guess. That I'm a player?' He seemed embarrassed to say the words.

'What is it, then?' I felt so much more hurt than I had any right to feel. I hardly knew him. We weren't boyfriend and girlfriend. I'd made out with Saxon half an hour after leaving Jake at school. I hadn't heard his side of the story. But no matter how much logic I piled on the situation, I still felt hurt.

He swallowed so hard I could see all the muscles in his throat stand out. 'I'm no angel. And I made my mistakes, but trust me, I learned from them. What I feel about you, Brenna . . .' He stopped and took a deep breath. 'I've never felt like this before. Like I've known you my whole life. But also like I'll never know everything about you. Please, don't judge me before I explain.'

How could I say no to him? It was fair. What he was asking me was totally fair.

'That's fair,' I said out loud. 'I can't really talk now. My parents are probably already wondering where I am.'

'Do you have a cell?' He slid his out of his pocket.

I nodded.

'Can I have your number?' His words were slow and cautious, like he expected a 'no'.

I said each digit slowly, and made him read it back to me.

'Can I call you tonight?' Hope made all the muscles in his jaw tense.

'Sure.' My voice wobbled.

'Can I . . .' He stopped and his jaw relaxed. 'Can I kiss you?'

I didn't answer, and he didn't wait for me to. His hands caught me gently behind the neck and he pressed his mouth to mine, softly but firmly. Then he moved one arm around my waist and pulled me closer to him. As the space between us disappeared completely, he deepened the kiss, urging my mouth open and sliding his tongue in. He tasted like clean, cold autumn air and mint gum. I slid my arms around him and kissed him back. The warm, slow spread of his kiss melted my muscles and made my knees knock. He pulled away just an inch or two and left his eyes closed for a few seconds. My heart thundered back into motion, and all that blood rushing back at once made me see little firework-like bursts of light in front of my eyelids.

'Whoa.' He rocked back on his heels, laughed, and turned a little red again. 'I can't wait to talk to you tonight.'

I nodded my dizzy head, but his words floated into my ears and clattered around my head without sinking in.

I wanted him to kiss me again, but he was already leading me to the doors.

'Jake! C'mon, man, the tractor's running!' A man in a flannel jacket standing next to a large green tractor squinted through the greenhouse glass at Jake and waved him over.

Jake grabbed me and kissed me lightly on the lips, then smiled as he pulled open the door, jogged over to the tractor and jumped on. He shifted it into gear and started driving it away. I followed him out of the greenhouse.

'Brenna,' Thorsten called, coming into view just as Jake pulled away on the tractor. 'I got you an apple tart and some cider.' He pressed the bag and cup into my hands. 'Your mom is already filling the truck bed with crazy things for the garden. We won't have room for your stuff if we don't stop her!'

'Thanks, Fa.' I willed myself not to look over at Jake expertly driving the tractor. 'Our garden is going to look like it belongs to an Italian palace,' I joked.

We chuckled all the way back to the truck. I knew Jake wouldn't call until that night, but I turned my phone to vibrate anyway. It was just better not to bring any attention to the whole thing.

Mom and Thorsten spent the ride discussing where they would put Mom's new fountain and birdbath and statues, and I had time to think.

Mostly about Jake's kiss.

He definitely kissed like a guy who had kissed a lot and knew he was great at it. I'm not saying it wasn't toe-curlingly amazing to be on the receiving end of a kiss like that. It just didn't help his 'man-whore' dilemma. After all, if he had that much experience, was it even safe to think about being with him? Would he expect me to sleep with him if we dated? I didn't know if I was ready for that.

But I also knew I was jumping way, way ahead of myself.

We parked at IKEA, and I was relieved to totally devote my entire mind to something other than a guy. Or two.

Mom and I looked through duvets, lamps, rugs, beds, dressers, closet organizers, and knick-knacks. I picked things at random and Thorsten lugged them around, then we put it all together and took it all apart again, not stopping until all the pieces made sense to Mom. My mother just had that kind of eye, and once she'd given it all the Mom seal of approval, I knew it would look great. We got some frames and hit the poster store at the mall to get prints. Then we stopped at the paint store and argued about paint colors. Finally, we stopped at Thorsten's favorite hotdog place and had dinner.

'This room is going to be amazing.' Mom covered her eyes with her hand like it was too much for her to visually imagine. 'Don't freak, Brenna, but Thorsten and I moved your stuff out of your room last night.'

'That's cool. Where am I sleeping?'

'We left the mattress on the floor,' Mom said.

And I was so relieved, because I'd inwardly panicked that I wouldn't have anywhere to talk to Jake in private. I depressed myself with my pathetic boy obsessions.

We made plans to get up crack-of-dawn early and start work on my room. By the time we got home, it was late and everyone was totally wiped out. I had that irrational desire to start working on my room right away, but I curbed it because I knew it was crazy, and that I'd wind up doing a crappy job if I rushed it.

Mom and Thorsten went to their room upstairs after we said goodnight. I thanked them both and we joked about how awful the next day would be, and then, at last, it was just me on a mattress on the floor of my lavender room, where Mom had dusted and swept and washed the walls, so there weren't any creepy cobwebs or gross dirt patches like I was expecting. I didn't know when exactly Jake would call, so I pulled my laptop out, even though I had a feeling it might be a really bad idea.

I opened my Facebook page. Kelsie had left a message. *Hey, girl, keep me updated on the bad boy!!! Last night was supa fun. Get ready to make me some shirts and snag me a boyfriend all at once. Love and kisses, Kelsie.* I had nothing to write back, so I just clicked on my friend page and saw Saxon had accepted my friend request. The red notification bubble told me there was a message waiting for me. I clicked on it.

Hey,
Thanks for the make-out session in the car. Don't sweat it, Blix. I won't tell a soul. Did you listen to the CD? I didn't think so. Do yourself a favor. Folly's cool, and you're about to clothe their groupies.
Later, friend,
Saxon

His note was, of course, designed to make me sweat it. How could it not? It was like he had something to hold over me, and, boy, was he ever going to. I thought about writing back when my phone vibrated. I didn't recognize the number, but it wasn't like I was expecting another call.

'Hello?'

'Hey,' Jake said, and I felt a little tightening in my stomach, but in a good way, hearing his voice again.

'How was work today?' I lay back on my mattress and wondered where he was. If he was in his room, I wondered what it looked like.

'It sucked. Especially after I saw you.'

'Gee, thanks.'

His laugh was hushed. 'It sucked because it was like a tease, Brenna. I spent the rest of the day wishing I could hang out with you.'

My heart picked up, beating hard and fast. 'Sorry. I was busy today anyway.'

'How did your shopping go?' His voice was warm, kind. It was easy to drift away on it and forget all of the things I'd seen on the internet and Kelsie's rumor-telling.

'I think it was good. My mom is going to help me redo my room as a birthday gift, so I have all the raw stuff, and we just have to put it all together tomorrow and see how it goes.' As quiet as I tried to keep my voice, it bounced off the stark walls in a series of echoes.

'I bet it will look great. I wish I could come over and help you. I'm a really decent painter.' I felt a stab of panic. I didn't really want to let Mom and Thorsten know anything about any boys at all. But he wasn't really asking, because he said, 'But I have work this Sunday.'

I clapped my hand over my mouth to stifle my sigh of relief. 'That's OK. I'm sure we'll be fine. There are three of us and my room isn't very big.'

There was a fairly long stretch of silence. I could hear Jake lean back and get comfortable, and it was weirdly intimate to hear it all but not see it.

'So I guess I have some explaining to do,' he finally said.

'Not really,' I returned, and even I could hear that my voice was a little prim and prudish. 'If you don't want to tell me about the pictures, you don't have to.'

I could hear him draw his breath in and push it out slowly, like he was preparing himself for something difficult. 'Even if you didn't see something that made you suspicious, I would have eventually told you all about myself. It's just not the first thing I like to talk about. Like . . .' He stopped for a minute. 'It sucks to say, "Hey, I'm Jake and I've screwed up a lot."'

'Everybody's screwed up,' I said diplomatically. I waited a few long seconds.

'Maybe not like me.' His words had a dark, ominous ring to them, and I forced my mind to shut down and stop imagining the possible extent of his screw-ups. 'I'm not going to cry on your shoulder, but I've had a weird upbringing.' He paused. When I didn't say anything, he went on, 'My mom died when I was seven and my dad started to drink. A lot.'

'I'm sorry.' Sympathy radiated out of me and I willed him to feel it across the distance between us.

'That's OK,' he said automatically. 'My dad totally stopped drinking a few years ago. And even though I hated when he did it and hated how it made him act, I started to drink when I got into high school. As much as Dad ever did, and maybe more.'

'Oh.'

'I was really messed up. I was running around with some wild kids, a lot of them already out of high school, and we were just getting smashed every weekend.' His breathing was unsteady. 'Sorry. This is just really weird. I've never talked to anyone about this, and I really didn't want this to be one of the first things we ever talked about.'

'I'm glad you're telling me,' I reassured him,

though I wasn't sure if I was. A voice in my head kept telling me to tell him to stop. I didn't want to hear anything else that would make me feel bad for him or regret liking him. But it was brave of him to tell me, so, against all better judgment, I said, 'You should tell me everything.'

He let out a long whoosh of air, like he'd been holding his breath, waiting for my answer. 'All right. I, um, I don't know how else to say this, so I'll just say it. I've slept with a lot of girls. I was always drunk. Not even one was, like, a girlfriend or anything. A lot of the time it was older girls I met at parties. I had, kind of, a reputation?' he said uncertainly. 'I'm really not proud of this,' he added.

'It's OK.' My entire body trembled, but I managed to keep my voice perfectly steady. 'Just tell me the rest.'

'One weekend I got really, really drunk.' His voice pitched hollowly. 'I woke up in some girl's bed. I couldn't find my shoes. I didn't know where I was. And my tooth was chipped. I had no idea why. And that was it. I was done with it. I stopped drinking that weekend. That was a year and four months ago.'

Even his adorably chipped tooth was part of this mess. I felt like all of the energy had run out of my body, like my muscles and bones were just congealed mush that left me limp and powerless. I couldn't think of a single thing to say.

'Please,' he begged in a ragged whisper, 'say *something*, Brenna.'

I managed to piece together something neutral and not nearly strong enough to convey all the words and emotions that crashed and exploded in my brain. 'Thank you for telling me.' My voice was as hollow as his had been.

He cleared his throat. 'I pretty much screwed up any chance of us . . . you know . . .'

'What?' I was going to make him say it. I knew it was torturous even as the word left my mouth. He obviously felt like crap and I wasn't helping. But suddenly, I didn't want to. In a sick way I liked hearing him suffer; it let me know he really felt terrible about all those girls.

'For us to go out. Man, this blows.' He laughed, but there wasn't an ounce of happiness in that laugh.

'You didn't lie to me. And I would never blame you for something that you did way before we met.' Or even many, many someones he did. He was right. This blew.

'God, Brenna.' His voice was cracked and raw. 'I feel like I had this one bad year and that's my real life. I can try as hard as I want, but that terrible year is what's in store for me. I won't be able to do better.'

'Jake, that's the dumbest thing I've ever heard. You made some mistakes. So? Big deal. Of course I would still be willing to date you.' The words popped out of my mouth, mixed in the tumult of anger and frustration and attraction that swirled like a whirlpool in my head.

'You would?' His voice brightened. 'I'm not asking you now. I mean, I wouldn't be that much of a loser. But you're serious? You would consider dating me?'

I thought about kissing him and knowing always, in the back of my head, that there had been so many more before me. Would I be able to get over it?

And then I thought about Jake. And his crinkly eyes and his sweetness and the really, really mind-blowing kisses that I knew were all about him and me only, no matter who else there had been before.

I took a huge, deep breath. 'Yes. I would consider it. Definitely.' I felt some of the old giddiness tickle to life somewhere low in my stomach.

He laughed, and it still wasn't a happy sound. This time it sounded like relief. 'That's the best news I've heard all day.'

I wanted to tease him, to tell him not to get his hopes up, but it felt like we were in deep waters and that kind of joking wouldn't fly. But then, I didn't know what to say.

He cleared his throat. 'I guess I dropped a lot on you tonight.'

'Yeah.' It sounded annoyed, even though that's not really how I felt. I curled on my side and cradled the phone next to my ear, blinking in the dim light of my empty room.

'You don't know how sorry I am. You have a lot to do tomorrow. I should let you go.'

And I knew that he was really asking if I wanted to get off of the phone with him, and I also knew that if I said yes, it would break his heart a little. And as much as Jake Kelly had made me crazy, I still felt protective of his heart, like it was an egg I held in my hand that could be crushed without much force at all.

'Not yet. What's up with your comments on my photos?' I knew I managed to make my voice sound almost exactly the way it had sounded on Friday just after I kissed him.

His laugh was so sheepish I could practically see him blush. 'I was feeling brave. It's what I'm thinking. You're just . . .' He stopped again. 'You're like the kind of girl I've only ever imagined meeting, and then you just show up one day across the table from me in school, and I know this is my one chance and I'd better not screw it up. I don't know how to say it. You're gorgeous and smart and funny. And you're not judgmental. You know, I feel like I could tell you all of the crazy stuff I've been through, and you would still see the real Jake under all the bull.'

It was essentially what Saxon had told me about myself, and I felt ashamed that Jake had given me so much credit when I didn't really deserve it at all.

'Jake, you make me sound like some perfect girl, but—'

'But you are,' he interrupted. 'My idea of perfect, anyway.'

'I'm far from perfect.' I pushed my fringe back with the heel of my hand.

'I know I'm not really in your league,' he said matter-of-factly.

'Yes you are.' I laughed and sat up, cross-legged on my mattress. 'I think you're just fishing for compliments.'

'No. Seriously, I'm not.'

'I actually believe you,' I admitted and leaned forward, the phone pressed hard to my ear, my voice low. 'So I'll give you some anyway. No interrupting or being all humble. You are very good looking.' I heard him make a noise, but I rushed on to stop him. 'You are a very hard worker. You're smart – don't even say you aren't. I don't waste time on dumb people, Jake. And, this one is important . . .' I paused for dramatic effect.

He laughed shyly. 'Lay it on me.'

'You are an awesome kisser,' I whispered.

He laughed loud and long. 'Here I was, thinking you were going to get all deep on me.' When he was done with his laughing, his voice got deeper and very sexy. 'So you think I'm a good kisser?'

'You've had enough practise!' I joked. The memory of kissing him made my breath come fast and my lips tingle.

His voice got really serious all of a sudden. 'Not really, Brenna,' he admitted. 'It was . . . kind of heartless. It wasn't . . .' He didn't speak for a few seconds. 'It wasn't good,' he said finally. 'At all. But if you and I were, um, together, it would be different.'

My traitorous body shivered and squirmed with a need that I didn't really know how to respond to. 'I don't have any plans to do much more than kissing for a while,' I said carefully, even as I fought waves of something hot and hungry crashing over me.

'I didn't mean *that*,' he rushed, and his voice was so sexy I got goosebumps. 'I meant kissing. The way it felt with you today was ten times better than all of the sex I've had put together, and that was just one kiss.'

He took a breath, and it sounded jagged and unsteady. 'Or maybe I felt something you didn't?'

'No.' I smiled so wide my cheeks ached. 'I felt it, Jake. I've felt a lot for you. Since the minute we met.'

'I have a feeling we're going to be crazy happy together, Brenna Blixen.' The naked optimism in his voice stung my conscience.

If I decided to move forward with Jake Kelly, I had better be positive that it was all through with Saxon Maclean. If not, I was going to have one hell of a nightmare on my hands.

'I . . . want to see you again. Soon.' I only realized how much I felt the words as they came out of my mouth.

'You will. Now I'm going to go ogle your Facebook pictures and let you get some sleep. Sweet dreams, Brenna.'

'You too,' I said, and we clicked off.

The feeling of aloneness that swelled around me once we disconnected was overwhelming. I usually liked being alone, especially late at night when I could think on my own. But this was different. This time I wanted Jake's voice back next to me. For the first time I tried to imagine what it would be like to sleep next to someone, to have Jake lying in the bed next to me. Just thinking it made me smooth my hand over the empty bed. I was always the only one in bed, and had a hard time imagining it otherwise.

I believed Jake when he told me things that sounded crazy, like that kissing me was better than sex had been. But my belief had more to do with my feelings for him than any type of real knowledge, because I had almost nothing to go on physically. I just had to take Jake's word for it and hope he wasn't saying what he thought I wanted to hear.

It took a long time to fall asleep in my empty, echoey room, and I even considered calling Jake back, but squashed the thought before it could really take root. I was happy enough in my own company.

Chapter 6

The next day dawned brighter than I expected, and Mom and Thorsten already had my window cranked open and were opening paint tins before I rolled off my mattress. I put on old clothes and pulled my hair up in a messy ponytail, then got to work.

Mom and I had picked a duck-egg blue for the accent wall behind my new bed, which was a dark wood frame with a high headboard that had a deep shelf on the top. The bedclothes were cream with bright red poppies and brown pillows. The other three walls were painted a caramel color. There was a large blue and brown rug with swirling flowers. I had a new rolltop desk and a set of hung shelves with glass doors. There was also a tall bookshelf with glass doors on it and shelves underneath. We fitted a new organizing system into my closet and moved all of my new clothes into it. The old clothes that had clogged up my closet got put in a pile for charity. Thorsten hooked up a chandelier hung with long swathes of red crystals. I put together several paper lamps, a few oblong and a few spheres, and hung them from the ceiling, where they cast a soft glow. We put up the paintings: Cassatt's *Little Girl in a Blue Armchair* and Chagall's *Wedding Portrait*. Mom had helped me pick the prints based on color and what I liked. We hung bamboo blinds and curtains with huge red and cream flowers.

By early evening we were finally finished and stood in the middle of the room admiring our work.

'Thank you, Mom.' I laid the hugs on thick. 'Thank you, Fa.'

'Let's take a picture!' Mom grabbed her camera and analyzed angles. We snapped a few shots, and I asked if I could borrow the camera. 'Sure, honey. What for?'

'I told some of the people at school that we were doing this, and they were curious about what it would look like. I just wanted to post them.' I flipped through the shots on the screen.

'Is that safe, all that picture posting?' She had a mom's neurosis about the internet, basically seeing it as a huge pool where pedophiles swam and lured unsuspecting children into the scary deep end.

'It's just pictures of the room, Mom.' I tried to sound comforting. 'I would never give out my address or anything.'

'OK.' She looked a little guilty. 'Honey, Thorsten and I were thinking of going on a date tonight. Would it be too much to leave you to hang here?'

'No! I just got those new books I ordered, and look at this room.' I gestured around. 'Go out. Have fun. It will be totally fine. And remember, tomorrow is a day off, so you can stay out late.'

Thorsten smiled and gave me the thumbs-up behind Mom's back. I gave him a conspirator's thumbs-up back. She was a worrier, and we both loved her for it, but it made life difficult sometimes. Poor Thorsten! Mom still acted like I was in elementary school. The man could hardly ever persuade her to go out and leave me on my own.

I sat in my room and uploaded pictures to Facebook. There was nothing interesting going on online, so I clicked my laptop off and grabbed a new book. A big, thick Barbara Kingsolver was waiting for me. I also promised myself I would reread the assigned *Lord of the Flies* chapters by Monday morning at the latest.

Mom ordered me a pizza and fretted over me before she and Thorsten left, but they finally did go, and I was happy to watch them pull out of the driveway. They were good together: loving, respectful, kind. It gave me hope that people could get married and still be in love years later.

I tried to turn my mind off love! The conversation I'd had with Jake the night before had left me feeling dizzy, but I couldn't think about it too much or my mind would go crazy obsessing. I lay on my bed, and the delicious new décor made the room feel so much more my own. I turned my attention to the book and had got completely dragged into Kingsolver's world when I heard the whine of an engine outside my window. It sounded almost like a weed whacker, but those weren't used much in New Jersey in the autumn.

For a split second I experienced the kind of panic that comes from being a gullible weenie about horror movies. I've told myself a thousand times that the point of a horror movie is to scare the person watching it. I've watched the behind-the-scenes stuff and read interviews the actors gave about their gory on-screen death scenes, but they still scared the crap out of me and there was no getting around that.

So for a long, cringe-worthy minute, I was sure the whine I heard was a chainsaw and a thousand blood-splattered images flew through my mind.

Then I saw a dirt bike. It came out of the woods behind my house and pulled up neatly in my back garden. The driver parked under my window and pulled his helmet off.

Jake!

I opened the window and stuck my head out. My bedroom was on the ground floor, but the sill was still a good five feet off the ground.

'What are you doing here?' I gasped. 'You didn't ride that all the way here from The Lake, did you?'

He smiled at me, and my heart melted into a puddle inside my chest. I loved his sweet smile, his never-neat hair, and the rough skin on his hands. I wasn't going to go so far as to say I loved Jake, but put together everything about him that I loved and you got a pretty intense emotion.

'I finished work and thought I'd come over. I don't want to bother you. Or your parents.' He looked from side to side, and chewed the inside of his cheek, obviously nervous about getting caught here.

'My parents aren't home.' I realized once the words fell from my mouth that in the realm of teenage romance they pretty much meant 'Come in and have your way with me,' but I didn't mean it like that.

Something flashed in Jake's eyes, but I couldn't tell what it was.

'I just wanted to say hello.' He offered me his crooked smile.

'Wait here.' I went to the hall, my heart thudding like mad, positive my mother and Thorsten would absolutely in no way approve of this, and I promised myself that I would make sure Jake only stayed for a little while. I opened the front door and waved him in.

He stood in the front hall and looked around. 'Nice house.' His eyes took it all in slowly.

While he looked around, I took the opportunity to look at him. I could see his muscles under his clothes. I noticed he had kicked the dirt off his boots before he came in, and I could tell from the way he shuffled his feet nervously that he wanted me to ask him to take them off so he didn't have to track mud through my house, but I didn't. Just in case Mom and Thorsten came home early, Jake was going out of my window, no booted evidence remaining.

'Mom ordered me a pizza before they left,' I said. 'You want some?'

'If you were going to eat alone, I'll have some with you. You know, to keep you company.'

I grabbed the box of pizza, the soda, and two glasses and led him to my room.

'Wow. This is your room?' It was a simple fact, but the way Jake said it, it sounded more like, *Here I am, finally in your room, which I've been wondering about for a while.*

'We just finished making it over a few hours ago. That's why it still smells a little of paint. Nice, right?'

'Yeah,' he agreed and we plopped down on the

floor. He poured me a glass of soda first and then poured one for himself, which I thought was really sweet. Then we started to eat, and Jake wolfed down the pizza so fast I had to check my urge to laugh. I was glad Mom had bought a large size. She and Thorsten knew that when I wanted to, I could eat most of a pizza on my own. They would never even ask if they came home and there was nothing left but some grease and crumbs in the bottom of the box.

'Do you like Folly?' I asked. Jake nodded, his mouth full.

I got up and put my iPod in its base and pushed play on the album that Saxon gave me. It was a little weird to listen to Saxon's mix with Jake, but it also felt disloyal to Saxon, which was a big bonus as far as I was concerned.

We ate in happy silence, and when I couldn't force any more pizza on him, I put the rest in the fridge and left him in my room for a few minutes. I thought that was particularly considerate of me. I always loved to poke a little in a person's room, just to get a feel for what they liked. Of course, Jake had the disadvantage of my room having been just redone and perfectly neat and bare, but he could still look at my books and check out my photos.

When I came back, sure enough, he was looking at

my bookshelf, his hands crammed self-consciously in the front pockets of his faded jeans.

'You've read all of these?' He jutted his chin in the direction of my books, carefully arranged by height and width. I shook my head. 'The top shelf is new stuff on the right, and stuff I feel like I really should read but haven't gotten around to reading on the left.' I moved close to him while I talked, and it was the first time I'd stood near him since he showed up.

I dipped my nose close to his neck and took a deep, long breath. He wore some kind of good-smelling guy cologne, something sharp and clean. But he also smelled like the outdoors and a little like sweat, which was sexy though I couldn't put my finger on why that was.

'Are you smelling me?' Jake glanced over his shoulder at me and grinned.

'I thought I was being pretty discreet about it. I guess I wasn't?'

'Nope.' His voice did that low and sexy thing. He reached out, carefully, like I was a wild animal that would bolt the minute he got too close. But I held dead still and let him gently take my arms and pull me closer. In fact, if I could have become a specialized Jake magnet I would have. Maybe I was, because he definitely seemed attracted to me. He moved his hands to my waist and pulled me in, and it was like we just clicked together.

The room receded; the colors, the music, all of it faded into the background. 'Are you going to kiss me?' I blabbed stupidly.

'I'm working up the nerve,' he said softly. His T-shirt was thin and faded, too. I could see the lines of his shoulders and pecs. His lips were dry, like he needed ChapStick. His skin was nice and smooth, tanned and clean.

I sighed. 'Your nerve is making me crazy. I'll just kiss you.'

And I did. Jake Kelly's mouth was hot and sweet. He took his time, pressing his lips to mine with steady pressure as if he were testing his ability to keep himself from giving in to anything wilder. I opened my lips slightly, and brushed my tongue over his mouth.

The next thing I knew, he was grabbing me hard under my butt and pushing me onto my new bed with the red poppies, and his mouth was hungry and quick on mine. We kissed and pulled back, kissed again and stopped to breathe. I could feel his long, hard body pressed on mine, and it felt so good, so exciting, I couldn't resist pulling his head down to mine again. His hands ran over my face, pressing into my hair. He pulled away and his fingertips traced my eyebrows and ran so lightly over my lips that they tickled. He touched my face like he was trying to memorize it with his hands.

I finally pulled him back to my mouth, kissed him deeply and ran my hands over his back and his ribs. His body was solid and warm against mine.

'Brenna, we have to stop.' I could feel, then, that he was hard and was pressing into me. 'I'm not used to going slow. I don't want to mess this up.'

It was shocking and exciting to hear him say that. Turning him on made me giddy, and it made me feel a kind of power I never really imagined I could hold over a guy.

'All right.' I pushed away from him, but he snatched me back and held me tight before I could get too far.

'Do you mind if I hold you?'

I relaxed against him and realized that my wish from the night before was being somewhat fulfilled. He was incredibly warm, and being in his arms meant that I was surrounded by him; his skin was all I could smell, I could hear his heart beat and his breath pull in and out, and I could see his face, so handsome it made me understand why there had been a small army of willing girls. There was very little not to like about Jake Kelly.

'I like this,' I said, and he snuggled closer to me in response. I felt a happiness like a thousand bubbles in a shaken soda threatening to burst out of me.

'So, I've been reading your book.' His breath tickled my ear.

'Which book is mine?' It was weird to have this semi-normal conversation wrapped in his arms. How were we ever going to be able to go back to just sitting across from each other in class?

'You know. *Lord of the Flies*.'

'Do you like it?' I looked at his silver-gray eyes. They were watching my lips. I smiled, and he mirrored my smile, then he looked up into my eyes, and I had to remind myself to breathe. In and out, one breath at a time.

'Yeah. It's a little dense, and the guy reading it on the book-on-tape thing is really slow, but I like the idea of the island as a microcosm.'

'My English teacher said it's supposed to be based on the world during World War II, or that's one interpretation.' I willed myself not to be surprised that Jake knew a word like 'microcosm'. Wasn't I the one always defending his intelligence?

'That makes sense in a scary way.' He ran his fingers along my hip and down the side of my thigh, then dragged them back up, over and over.

I moved my fingers over his features, the way he had with mine. I smoothed his eyebrows with my thumbs, brushed over his eyelashes, outlined his nose, and traced his lips.

'Did you like any of the girls you slept with?'

His eyes popped wide open. 'How did we get from *Lord of the Flies* to that?'

My hand was on his jaw. I pulled it away and picked at a loose thread on my bedspread instead. 'We didn't really. I just wanted to know. That's all.'

He swallowed hard, avoided eye contact, and nodded slightly, like he was about to face a firing squad. 'They weren't bad girls,' he said finally. 'They weren't sluts or whatever people would say. They were just looking for a good time the wrong way.'

'Because sex isn't a good time?'

He took my hand in his and linked our fingers together. 'No.' He shrugged his shoulders. 'Not when you don't care about the person.'

'Have you ever had sex with anyone you loved?' I tried to push away the sting of jealousy that poured through me.

'No.' Jake's eyes held mine. 'I can't wait for it to happen,' he said, his voice husky, the words almost whispered and a little shaky. 'I know it's going to happen one day, and it will make all the other times seem even more insignificant than they do now.'

It occurred to me that Jake really wanted to be right about this. Maybe sex hadn't been all it was cracked up to be for him. Maybe he was going to pin all his hopes for sex on his true love. Maybe he thought that I was his true love. Excitement and nerves clawed and twisted at my heart.

'Not that it wasn't fun.' In one sentence, he dashed my warm excitement. Fun? 'It just didn't mean anything,' he added.

'That doesn't seem possible.' I tried to pull my hand away from his, but he held tight.

'What do you mean?'

'If you were willing to do something that . . . I don't know . . . intimate with someone, wouldn't you have to feel something first?' I couldn't imagine that I would like any honest answer he gave, and I realized it was a tiny bit masochistic of me to ask.

'Sometimes it just happens. In the exact moment I guess it feels pretty good, but afterwards you just regret it completely, you know? And you think you won't do it again, but it's like you physically can't stop it.' He looked at me hard, willing me to understand.

I turned my eyes down, out of the direct line of his gaze. Wasn't that exactly what happened between me and Saxon? Given a few drinks, mood lighting and an available bed, I might have been in a heap of trouble with more regret than my already tortured soul could handle.

In the cold light of day the idea of taking my clothes off in front of someone, pressing against them, and not being freaked out by the wet, hard, messy aspects of it seemed crazy. But then so might falling into their arms and kissing them like crazy or sticking your tongue in their mouth. Yet I had done that with someone who I never had any intention of doing it with. Maybe it wasn't all that different.

His voice interrupted my thoughts. 'I know you can't really understand.'

'I might better than you think. Listen, I was with—'

Just then my cell phone buzzed and almost fell off my desktop. As I flipped it open, I thought about warning Jake to be quiet, but I could see from the panic in his eyes that he was ready to bolt through the window.

'Hey, sweetie,' Mom said, and my guts twisted.

'Hey, Mom!' I practically yelled, then wondered if she would hear something in my voice that let her know what I was up to. Paranoia flooded over me.

'Thorsten and I just got out of the movie. I'm going

to grab a Dairy Queen for him. You know Fa, he's always starving! Do you want something?'

My churning stomach settled down. Dairy Queen was a good fifteen minutes away from our house. 'Thanks, Mom, but I ate most of that pizza, and I'm stuffed.'

'OK. Love you, baby. See you soon.'

'Love you.' I clicked off.

'I should go.' Jake stood up like a shot. 'I don't want to get you in any trouble.'

I already hated the idea of him leaving. My bed even looked overly big and empty without him in it. I dragged my feet all the way to the front door, and then pulled him down on the steps next to me.

'Five minutes? Please?' I shamelessly bit my lip and made my eyes big and wide. It was the best sad face I could muster.

'If I get caught here, your parents will hate me even more than they're already going to.' But he sat next to me anyway and slid his arm around my waist.

'Why would they hate you?' I asked, even though I could think of a hundred reasons without thinking too hard. I leaned my head on his shoulder and closed my eyes against all the doubts and possible problems.

'If I were your parents, I wouldn't let you date

anyone. I'd keep you locked up in your room.' He pressed his lips to my hair.

'Why?' I tried not to concentrate too hard on his fingers, moving absently over my hip. This was also similar to something Saxon had said to me. It was strange how the two of them could be so different, but say so many similar things.

'Because you're smart and awesome and really beautiful,' he said, and my heart thumped all over the place. I turned to look into his eyes, darker in the twilight and hungry on my face. 'Just the things I'm thinking about you would get me killed if your parents knew.'

'What are you thinking?' I dared, nervous to know his secret thoughts about me.

Instead of answering, he kissed me, and his tongue licked and lips pressed at my mouth in a way that made little moans come out of my throat and answered some of the questions I had about his inner-most thoughts.

He ripped his mouth from mine with a groan. My hand flew to my lips, which felt puffy and stung from all the kissing. 'I'm going now.' His voice sounded a little choked. 'Can I call you tonight?'

'Yes.' I didn't want to let his hand go.

'Take care.'

I knew there was a lot more he wanted to say but didn't. He pressed his lips to mine one more time, and then, way too quickly, he was on his dirt bike and disappearing into the woods behind my house.

I went back to my room. Like my bed earlier, it felt strangely empty without him. I wondered if we were technically going out now. I was sure that Jake would say we were, but he hadn't actually asked.

I put my Kingsolver aside and dutifully took out my Golding. I read and took notes, trying to keep the smell and feel of Jake out of my mind, but it wasn't easy. It was like my entire brain was dying to think about him and nothing else. I wanted to do other things, but he kept cropping up in my head. I wondered if he'd gotten as far as I had in the book, what he thought of Jack's maniacal takeover, what he thought of my room, what he thought of kissing me.

I forced my mind back to Golding and took notes for another half an hour, before I heard the door open and Mom and Thorsten came in.

'Hey!' I hugged them both. 'What did you go see?' Even as they described the movie and laughed and hung their coats up, I kept expecting one of them to look over suddenly and say, *Where is he? We know you had a boy over, Bren.*

But, of course, they didn't. We hung out in the kitchen, and Mom made us tea.

I ran my fingers over the wood grain of the long table, my hand weaving back and forth over the swirling patterns and designs.

'I saw one of the members of the Rotary Club at Dairy Queen,' Thorsten said.

'What's the Rotary Club?' I sipped my sweet, milky tea.

Mom sat down by Thorsten, and I could tell by the way her eyes sparkled that it had something to do with me. Mom reserved a lot of her excitement for things concerning me.

'It's a group of community leaders who do social things,' Mom said. 'And they have this study abroad program!' Thorsten took a large envelope and slid it across to me. 'That's just the simple brochure,' Mom explained. 'He had some copies in his car. But we're on the mailing list to get the complete information.'

I opened the envelope and turned the pages of the glossy catalog, looked at the pictures of kids on ski slopes and swimming in rivers and wearing what looked like German lederhosen. 'This looks really cool,' I said, only lying a tiny bit. 'But I don't think I can take another year off high school.'

'They have a summer program.' Thorsten flipped

through and pointed to the summer program page for me. 'These are a little more like camps. The one in Ireland is a creative writing camp. There's one in Egypt that does archeology.'

Mom wrinkled her nose. 'I don't know about Egypt,' she said, making no attempt at political correctness. 'But wouldn't Ireland be amazing?'

They started to get me excited. 'There's a website. I'll check it out before I go to bed.'

We smiled and talked and laughed for a while, and when they were finally ready for bed, I went to my room too, clutching the envelope.

On the one hand I wanted to go so badly I was already packing my suitcase in my head. But on the other, a tiny little part of me wondered what I would miss if I left for a whole summer. There were a lot of normal teen things that I kind of wanted to do. Like go to beach parties. Or spend mind-blowing hours kissing my new boyfriend.

If that's what Jake was.

Or would be.

I checked out the website and read the testimonials, which ran the range from pure cheesiness to what sounded like honest life-changing experiences. It seemed like it would be pretty awesome.

I put my pajamas on, brushed my teeth, washed my

face, and tried to pop an enormous zit that was forming on my chin. Unfortunately it was just big and painful. I put a little cream on it – the kind that assures you that your zit will be gone in twenty-four hours, but never ever works, at least not on me – and tried unsuccessfully to relax. My brain refused to cooperate on that one.

I went back to Golding, now even more preoccupied, and forced myself through the required chapters and notes before I closed the book and put it in my bag. I looked at the Folly CD cover, trying to get inspiration, but it was pretty bland. Just the band name and a black background with green splatter. I listened to a few more of their songs, trying to get a feel for what I would put on a shirt if I did manage to design one.

And finally, my phone rang. I didn't want to admit how much I'd been waiting for it, but I had been. And it never crossed my mind to play games like waiting for it to ring a few times or keeping my voice even when I answered, because I didn't feel like I needed to hide anything from Jake or pretend with him.

'Jake!'

'That's a nice greeting.' I could hear his smile over the phone.

'I'm glad you came over today.' I listened to the

sound of metal jangling and hitting something. I imagined he was emptying the change out of his pockets and putting his keys down.

'Me too.'

'Did it take you long to get home?' I walked over to my window and put my hand against the freezing pane. I shivered when I imagined him riding through fields and woods on a night like tonight.

'No,' he said too quickly, then changed the subject. I knew he was lying to me, but I let it go. If I knew that it had taken forever and he'd been freezing the whole time, I'd have to tell him not to come again. And neither of us wanted that.

'So there's this movie theater in Newton.' He paused. 'They play, like, random older movies. So tomorrow they're going to play *Footloose* and *Dirty Dancing*,' he said with a groan.

And I squealed and got all girlishly excited. 'Jake! That's awesome!' I gushed. 'How did you know I love them?'

'Because you're a girl,' he pointed out. 'And because you have both *Dirty Dancing* and *More Dirty Dancing* soundtracks on your shelf.'

I felt a little embarrassed. 'I forgot about my CDs.' I had transferred most of them to my iPod, but some I kept for sentimental value.

'So, I'm too lame to be able to pick you up,' he said dryly, 'but I thought if your parents could drop you off, I could buy your ticket and popcorn and candy. If you want to?' He waited a second before adding a rushed, 'Or not.'

A date! My first date! 'No. I want to. I do. What time is it?' I danced around my room and silently screamed with excitement.

'The first movie starts at two o'clock.'

'I'll be there. Do you mind if I invite my friend Kelsie?' I fell back on the bed and clutched a throw pillow to my chest. Kelsie would love this.

'Kelsie Jordan?' he said, and I felt the clench in my stomach that I started to associate with finding out unexpected things about Jake.

'That's the one. Do you know her?' I held my breath and waited on the edge of a precipice for him to answer.

'I know who she is. Just from being around.' His voice didn't sound weird or upset. 'Bring her. It'll be fun.' I could tell from his tone he was mildly let down I'd crashed our date.

'It's just, if I ask my parents to randomly drop me off at a movie theater, they're going to want to know who I'm going with, and I don't want them to get all crazy if it's a date.' I stopped. 'It is a date, right?'

'Seriously, Brenna? I'm asking you to meet me in public to see two girlie dance movies. This is all about me trying to impress you.'

I pressed my hand over my mouth to stifle the insane giggles that threatened to overtake me. I had to take a deep breath before I could say calmly, 'Let me call Kelsie and check, and I'll call you back, OK?' I thought about it. 'Or are you beat? I know you worked all day, then came over here.'

'No, I'm not beat. And I definitely want you to call back. Even if it's late. I'll wait for you.'

We clicked off, and I dialed Kelsie's number with fingers shaking from pure excitement. It rang and rang and she finally picked up.

'Hey, girl!' Her cheery voice rang out in my ear. 'I tried your house today. Where were you?'

'Oh, we were busy all day getting stuff done in my room. I must not have heard the phone.' Maybe because I was locked in my room, wrapped around Jake Kelly?

'Oh, well, Newton is having this awesome movie thing, and a bunch of people are going.'

I laughed. 'That's so weird. That's what I was calling you about.' I examined my *Dirty Dancing* CDs, thankful for those few minutes of snooping that led to Jake asking me on a date.

'Are you going? Omigosh, you're going with your bad boy, aren't you?' Her squeal almost punctured my eardrum. 'I knew it! I called it!'

Even though I was hopping up and down with happiness, I managed to keep my voice calm and speak rationally to Kelsie. 'I'm going to meet him there, but I was hoping you would come too.'

'Well, I'll be there. Now that I know Jake will be taking you on a date, I'm going just to spy. Are you excited? Beyond excited? About to have a heart attack?'

'Yes! I have a lot to tell you, but I'm going to call Jake back and tell him we're good to go. I'll call you tomorrow?' I opened my closet and shuffled through my clothes, wondering what I should wear.

'Sounds good. Have a *really nice* conversation.' Kelsie dissolved into another fit of giggles.

'I will,' I said and couldn't help giggling right along with her.

I dialed Jake's number, and he picked up right away. 'Hey, Brenna.' His voice was slow and sleepy.

'Kelsie said a bunch of people are going. So, I'll meet you there?' I threw shirts and pants on my bed along with a few skirts and dresses. How dressy would this be? Should I dress as cute as possible or go understated?

When Jake spoke, his voice was measured and guarded. 'You don't have to go with me, you know. You can sit with your friends.'

'Maybe I want to go with you. And you can whisper all of Johnny's lines to me.' I plopped on my bed and wrapped my arms around my knees.

He laughed. 'Is that Patrick Swayze? Maybe if we were watching *Roadhouse* I could tell you all of his lines.' He cleared his throat. 'I know he says that no one puts Baby in a corner.'

I closed my eyes and soaked it all in. 'Ooh, that's the line! You sound tired.'

'I guess I am. I hate working a double on the weekend.' He yawned into the phone.

I thought about telling him about Saxon and my kiss to clear the air before our first date, but the timing seemed so off. And I just didn't want to talk about it. But there was something I wanted to get his opinion on.

'I wanted to tell you something. My parents found this summer study abroad thing where you go to another country and learn about something.' I held my breath and pressed my lips together, waiting.

He sounded more alert. 'Like being an exchange student?'

'Yes. But for the summer instead of the whole year.'

I closed my eyes and imagined us together all summer, maybe taking day trips to the beach, going out and getting Dairy Queen, snuggling at the movies. I half hoped he would be completely unsupportive and beg me to stay.

'Please tell me you're going to do it.'

Shock rippled through me. 'You want me to go?'

'No,' he said honestly. 'I miss you when you're half an hour away. I'll probably go psycho when you're across an ocean. But it sounds awesome, and I want you to do that kind of stuff. You're too smart to just rot in this little county. You need to get out there. It's good for you.'

'So now you know what's good for me?' I teased.

'I like to think so.' His voice was low and soft. I loved it. 'I wish I was there with you right now.'

'Me too,' I sighed. 'You need to get off of the phone. You need to get some sleep.'

'I can sleep in tomorrow,' he pointed out. 'You're right, though. We should both get some rest. Sweet dreams, Brenna.'

'You too,' I said.

He laughed low. 'There's no doubt about that.'

We clicked off, and it was a good thing I'd been up at the crack of dawn with Mom and Thorsten and worked all day, otherwise I would have been way too excited to sleep. I turned off the lights in my new room and stared at the paintings on my wall, which were eerie and strange in the moonlight. Before I knew it, I opened my eyes to the morning light that streamed in through my new curtains and it was time to get ready for my first date.

Chapter 7

In that foggy time between being asleep and awake, the first thing I thought about was Jake. I dreamed about kissing him. My sleeping mind was as preoccupied with him and his sexiness as my waking one. My dream was one long string of kissing and rolling around on my bed. I stretched and sighed, then got up to ask Mom if it would be OK to go to the movies. She said it was fine, she would drop me after Thorsten left for work, and part of me was disappointed by her easy answer. I almost wanted her to demand to know who was going and when and where, so I'd be forced to tell her that it was actually a date. But I knew that as much as I wanted to share, it was better to keep Jake to myself for now.

I went to the bathroom and showered, then took a long time drying my hair straight so it looked extra shiny. I put on my make-up and paid extra attention to my eyes. I thought they looked pretty sexy when I was done. I went to my room to pick an outfit, and realized I had a missed call. Jake!

I called him right back.

'Hey, gorgeous.' He sounded excited. 'I just wanted to call and say hello.'

'Hello,' I said and bit my lip to keep from cackling like a lunatic into the phone. 'Did you sleep in?'

'Yeah, a little. I can't really talk too long. My dad needs some help with stuff before this afternoon. But I can't wait to see you.'

'I can't wait to see you, either. Go help your dad.' I twirled around my room, so glad he couldn't see me acting like a maniac.

'See you soon,' he promised.

OK, we were dating. It had to be. You didn't call to check on someone every few hours and giggle on the phone and dream about them kissing you unless you were dating.

But he hadn't asked me to be his girlfriend. And I wasn't about to do any asking. I was all about being an independent woman, but there were lines I needed to draw pretty firmly when it came to dating. And I was not going to ask a boy to be my boyfriend. Period.

I went through all of my clothes three times and finally picked a black dress with a polo collar and a pink belt around the waist. I put on gray leggings and pink Converse low tops. I had a gray canvas peacoat with a flannel lining and a pink cashmere scarf and hat Mom bought me when she and Thorsten went on a trip to Paris.

Once I was dressed, I needed something productive to take up my time and keep me from pacing a hole in my bedroom floor. I did sketches for the Folly shirt, listening to their music in the background as I worked. I was starting to piece some things together I thought would look cool. I finally managed to lose track of the time, and before I knew it, Thorsten knocked on my door.

'I'm off to work, Brenna.'

I went over to him and kissed his cheek. 'Drive safe, Fa.'

'Have fun today,' he said and put a twenty in my hand. 'For the movie and snacks.'

'Thanks.' I gave him a quick hug.

When it was time to go, I grabbed my purse and coat, put on my hat and scarf, and went to get Mom.

'Ooh, honey, you look so cute,' she gushed as she grabbed the keys.

'Thanks.' I hoped Jake thought so.

At the theater, Mom kissed me and reminded me to have my cell on vibrate and call after the movie if I was going to get something to eat with my friends.

I wondered how long Jake would be allowed to stay out.

When I got out of the car and looked around, it wasn't Jake I noticed, but Saxon, leaned up against the wall, one leg bent behind him, smoking a cigarette. I saw Kelsie near him, and the guy Chris who's the lead singer in Folly. There were two other girls and a guy I didn't know.

Saxon looked over and our eyes met. He looked me up and down slowly, but he didn't greet me or call me over. I hated the warm flush that came over me as his eyes worked over my body, assessing. I wanted to erase my memory of Friday afternoon with him. I could tell from the way he looked at me that he was thinking about it.

Kelsie waved her hands over her head. 'Brenna! Over here!'

I waved at Mom, who smiled and pulled away, and I went to say hi to Kelsie, trying to avoid looking at Saxon while at the same time looking for Jake without being too obvious.

'Where is he?' She tugged on my dress. 'You look so adorable. I almost finished a necklace for you. It would go perfectly with that dress if you had a blue belt. Do you?'

'I don't know. Where he is,' I clarified. 'I do have a

blue belt. Thank you for the necklace.' My head was spinning. 'I didn't realize Saxon would be here. And Chris?'

'I know.' She dug her fingers into my arm. 'Saxon actually got everyone together.'

'Oh.' My mind immediately turned suspicious. I wondered if he had asked Kelsie to ask me. I could ask him if he had, but I definitely didn't want to.

'He'll be here.' Kelsie grabbed my arm and started to lead me to the group.

'It's OK,' I said, though it definitely was not OK. Where was he? What if he didn't show up?

And then he was right there. I didn't see him arrive, but once he was there, I didn't care about anything but pressing my lips to his. I was aware, somewhere in the back of my mind, that Saxon would see it, but I tried to push that thought away.

Jake looked slightly embarrassed when he saw the crowd. He pulled me over to the side before he kissed me. His kiss was hungry but quick, and not too indecent. I had a feeling Jake wasn't much of an exhibitionist and that was fine with me. Making out in the privacy of my room was one thing. Making out in front of a Newton movie theater was not cool.

'You look great.' He pulled back from me and let his

eyes wander from my head to my toes. 'I really like your dressy thing.'

'Thanks.' I pulled closer and kissed his nose. 'It's usually just called a dress.'

He laughed and pulled his hat off, running his hand over his shower-damp hair. 'You know what I mean. So these are your friends?' He threw a pointed look at the group clustered nearby, watching us without looking too obvious about it.

'Hey, Jake.' Kelsie waved and smiled. 'This is Chris, Amanda, Joey and Megan, and this is Saxon.'

Jake nodded and smiled politely until he saw Saxon. His mouth thinned into a hard line. 'Saxon.'

'Hey, Jake.' Saxon dragged on his cigarette and talked through the smoke that billowed out of his mouth. 'How's it going?'

'All right.' Jake pulled me closer to his side possessively.

They knew each other? The animosity between them crackled in the air. I gave Jake a questioning look, but he shook his head slightly, letting me know he couldn't talk about it there.

The weird vibes suffocated the group into an awkward silence, but neither of the guys looked ready to do more than glare.

'Maybe we should go and buy tickets,' I suggested.

'Good idea.' Kelsie raised her eyebrows at the huge group that had congregated at the ticket booth. 'It looks like the crazy fans are getting here.'

Sure enough, a gaggle of middle-aged women in handmade *No one puts Baby in the corner!* T-shirts jostled at the ticket window.

'I'll go get our tickets.' Jake squeezed my hand.

I took the twenty out of my purse. 'Here,' I offered.

'No.' He held his hands up and shook his head. 'This is a date, Brenna. I'm not letting you pay for anything.'

'But you have truck parts to buy.' I held the twenty out again. 'You worked hard for your money.'

'And I want to spend it on you, so let me.' He closed my hand over the bill and pushed it back toward me.

He walked over to get the tickets, and Saxon snaked into his place, his mouth close to my ear.

'So that's why you ran out of my car?' His cigarette was out, but he reeked of smoke. 'You're Jake Kelly's latest conquest. Have some self-respect, Brenna.'

Jake turned his head and scowled over at Saxon, obviously aggravated, but stuck in his place in line. Saxon gave him a cruel wave.

'I got out of your car because I was tired of your company. That's it, Saxon. And what I do or who I do it with is not your business.' I waved at Jake and he looked relieved.

Saxon reached out and tightened my unfurling scarf like he'd done the other day at school. 'You could do a hell of a lot better than Jake Kelly. I'm an asshole, but even I'm a better choice than he is.'

I could see Jake's body tense as he waited, switching from foot to foot impatiently.

I batted Saxon's hands away and threw my scarf ends over my shoulder. 'Jake's a great guy and I don't really want to talk about him with someone like you.' I narrowed my eyes and stepped away from him. 'Back off.'

'He's a walking STD, Blix.' He closed the space between us. 'The guy's slept with more girls than I've looked at. And he's an idiot. He can't even read.'

I was so done with him. 'Shut the hell up!' I hissed. Jake had paid for our tickets and was hurrying toward me. 'Just because he doesn't have a photographic memory doesn't make him less intelligent than you. In fact, he's ten times smarter and more interesting than you could be on your best day.'

He threw me an indulgent smile, like I was a toddler having a temper tantrum. 'It's your life.' He shrugged. When Jake was almost next to me, Saxon pulled me over and kissed me on the cheek, his eyes on Jake the whole time. I twisted away from him, and he winked at me. 'She's a real hellcat, right, Jake?'

'Come on, Brenna.' Jake linked hands with me and led me inside. He smelled so good and clean after the smoky, musky smell of Saxon. 'He's such an asshole,' Jake muttered. 'Was he bothering you?'

'No,' I lied. 'We just have classes together at school.'

Jake's mouth tightened. 'Oh. That's cool,' he said, even though it was evident it was anything but cool as far as he was concerned.

'We're not friends.' Even as the words were out of my mouth, I wondered why I said them. Even if Jake and I were dating, I wouldn't expect him to ask me to give up friendships just because he didn't like someone. Not that Saxon was someone I cared to keep a friendship with, but there was still the principle of it.

'He's just a lot of trouble.' He looked me in the eyes. 'And he's charming as hell. You don't even know he's screwed you over until he's done.' He shook his head. 'Never mind. You want some candy?'

I was glad for the change in subject. 'Yes. How about Raisinets?'

He made a face.

'What?' I jabbed him in the ribs with my elbow. 'You don't like Raisinets?'

'It's like fake candy. I always thought of it like

candy an adult would trick you into eating. Look, Brenna,' he said, his voice all high like a mad mother. 'It's not a raisin! It's yummy candy!'

I laughed, as much because I liked his silly joke as because I was glad we had moved past the weirdness with Saxon. 'Well, I love them.'

'Then you're getting them.' And suddenly, right in the line, he pulled me close and kissed me. 'I never thought I'd be so excited to go see, arguably, two of the dumbest movies in the world.'

I slapped him on the arm. 'These are cultural icons! These set the bar for all other dance movies!'

'Wow. I'm so glad,' he said drily. We were at the counter now, and the pimply girl selling refreshments didn't bat an eyelash in my direction. But she batted her eyelashes at Jake and asked if she could help him in a way that suggested she had more than scooping his popcorn in mind. 'Raisinets, Mike and Ikes, a large popcorn and a large . . . what do you want to drink?'

'Coke is great,' I said, and then saw all of the options. 'Oh, how about Cherry Coke? Do you like that?'

'Yeah, that's cool.' He never took his eyes off me. The girl behind the counter looked at me with daggers in hers. 'A Cherry Coke, please.' He finally looked her way and she smiled, then tossed me a look and went to get the drink.

'Does that happen a lot?' I asked after Jake paid a horrifying amount for our tiny candy boxes, tub of popcorn, and soda, and we moved away from the counter and the girl still throwing him longing looks.

'What?' He juggled everything in his arms while he tried to slide his wallet into his back pocket.

I took the popcorn and soda and tossed a kernel in my mouth to enjoy the perfect salty crunch that only movie theater popcorn possesses. 'Do girls fall all over you every time you go out?'

'What are you talking about?' he asked, genuinely puzzled.

'Jake, that girl would have hopped in your pocket and gone home with you if you looked her way. How could you not see that?' I offered him a piece of popcorn. He opened his mouth and I fed it to him, thrilled at the touch of his tongue on my fingertips.

'I don't know. She just seemed nice. To tell you the truth, I really didn't even notice her. Why would I be looking at any other girl here?' He put his arm around me.

'Very true. Very smart of you to mention it,' I said and gave him a quick buttery, salty kiss.

We found Kelsie and the group in the theater and tried to figure out how to sit all together. We moved back and forth along the row so everyone could find a seat. Somehow in the shuffle, Saxon just happened to wind up next to me. I tried not to care, but how could I not?

Jake looked completely pissed off, which was understandable, even though I didn't know their back-story. Saxon was so obnoxious, I could understand someone being irritated with him for no reason other than his being in the same room.

Jake put his arm around me and held me close as the lights dimmed and the movie began. I leaned my head on the hard, hot muscle of his shoulder. He was wearing a faded T-shirt and jeans with his boots and the same jacket. It occurred to me suddenly that Jake wasn't making any kind of fashion statement. He just didn't have many clothes.

I sneaked a sidelong glance at him as the movie flickered on the screen, panning across the rolling hills and sparkly lake of Kellerman's. He was always clean, but there was something about him that made me ache to help. He looked like he had enough – enough to eat, enough to wear – but nothing special. It was like no one had ever considered pampering him in any way. He had exactly what he needed and nothing more.

Suddenly I wanted to see where he lived. What was Christmas morning like at his house? Did someone make him a birthday cake? Had he ever been on a vacation? I had a feeling every answer would depress me. I squirmed a little when I thought about how much money he spent on this one date. He could have bought himself something nice. Or maybe his money didn't go on extras at all. Maybe a lot of it went on the basics. I had no idea what his dad did for work.

'What's up?' Jake whispered. 'Can't get comfortable?'

'These seats are so hard, aren't they?' I said, grasping gladly at the rope he threw for me.

'Here.' He moved the soda down to the floor so he could lift the armrest between us and press it back. 'Lean on me.'

I was able to drape myself across him and snuggle completely in his arms. I tucked my feet up on the seat and nestled against him. I was so comfortable physically I was able to calm down mentally.

Then I felt the oddest sensation. It was like someone was tracking a fingertip over my ankle. My ankles were bare since my leggings ended mid-calf and my socks were super short.

I hoped it was some kind of big crawly bug. I actually prayed that was the explanation.

Because if it wasn't, the only thing that could explain it would be that Saxon was deliberately touching me. I was torn. If I acknowledged it, Jake would be irritated at Saxon and Saxon would get the satisfaction of more drama. If I ignored it, Saxon might take it as a sign I wanted it or liked it. I pulled my legs up and away, but Saxon still managed to discreetly keep one fingertip gliding along the sensitive skin of my ankle.

I just concentrated on Jake. I made sure Saxon could see me bury myself in Jake's arms. At the particularly steamy parts, I leaned up and kissed him briefly. He smiled down at me, and I knew it had to be slightly nauseating to anyone without someone of their own to kiss and cuddle. When the awesome last dance/jump sequence flashed on the screen, I drew my foot back and kicked Saxon. Hard.

'Ow!' he yelped and looked at me with something between irritation and shock.

'I'm sorry, Saxon.' I kept my eyes wide and my expression serious. 'I had a leg cramp. I didn't notice you were so close.'

'No problem.' He looked at me with grudging respect.

When the credits rolled I said, 'Jake, I think we need to get a refill. Do you want to get one while I use the bathroom? I think there's going to be a line.'

'Sure,' he said, then turned and gave me a quick kiss that left me wanting more.

It was excellent anyway.

As soon as he was gone I grabbed Saxon by the hand and dragged him to the lobby. There was no point in making a scene in front of all of our friends, because he would love that.

'What do you think you're doing?' I hissed.

He looked at me for a long minute with his eyebrows raised, clearly enjoying the entire situation. 'You're going to march me into the lobby because my fingertip touched your ankle?' he asked, his voice cavalier.

'Don't do that.' I shook my head and pointed at him. 'Don't twist it so I sound ridiculous.'

'So what happened?' He reached out to put a piece of my hair behind my ear. I grabbed his hand, and held it, twisted out and away from my body.

'This.' I held his hand up high. 'You can't touch me like that, like we're together.' I gritted my teeth.

'I wasn't aware you were Jake's absolute property.' Saxon twisted and pulled his hand slowly so we were almost holding hands.

'I'm my own absolute property.' I pulled away from him. 'And I'm asking you to stop.'

'If touching your ankle does this to you,' he said, his body as close to mine as it could possibly be without actually touching me, 'imagine what we'd be like together.'

'You're an idiot.' I dropped his hand like it was a hot coal.

'Just a truth-speaker, baby.' He laughed at my back as I stalked to the bathroom.

Kelsie was in there. 'Hey, you!' She put on a coat of mascara and batted her eyelashes at her reflection in the mirror. 'How's your date?'

'Going good.' I was still shaky from my conversation with Saxon in the lobby. 'How's yours?'

'He's very cool.' She winked at me. 'Do you have the lipstick you're wearing with you?'

'Yeah, here you go.' I pulled it out of my purse and handed it to her.

'Thanks. It makes your lips look really soft, almost like you're not wearing lipstick at all.' She put it on carefully. 'How do I look?' She pursed her lips for me.

'Beautiful. I'm going to pee. You going back?'

'I'll wait for you if you want,' she offered. Her eyes crinkled in their usual friendly way.

'Thanks, but you go. Just tell Jake where I am if he looks frantic?'

'That's so cute.' She pinched my cheek. 'You guys are already like some old couple.'

I rolled my eyes. 'I know, we're so adorable it's nauseating.'

When Kelsie left, I thought about what I could do to

combat Saxon and realized that was probably exactly what he was counting on. Saxon lived for mind games, and his touching my ankle had nothing to do with actually touching me and everything to do with burrowing deep in my head where I couldn't get him out. I flushed and went to the sinks. I braced my hands on the cold white porcelain and looked at my reflection.

I was pretty. Especially with make-up and good hair and a cute outfit. But it wasn't my made-up eyes or my crazy style that had Saxon trying to tempt me with the tip of his finger on my ankle. My best guess was he liked me because I stood up to his bullshit. Maybe it was just novelty, or maybe it was compulsive. Because if I thought about being in a serious relationship with Saxon, I didn't see the mind games ending. In fact I thought it would be just the opposite. Every word he said, every action he took would be to trip me up, keep me on my toes. And I was positive he would get happiness from that, perverse or real.

Who wants to be constantly on her toes with her boyfriend?

I washed my hands and felt like splashing water on my face, but my mascara would never hold up.

I walked out of the bathroom and smashed into the wall of Jake's chest. My hands went up instinctively, and I could feel just how threadbare the fabric of his shirt was.

'Are you OK?' He cradled my face in his big hands. 'You were in there for a long time.'

I grinned at him because his panicked worry was just right, just what I wanted. And I realized he was what I wanted, and alone. 'I don't need Pepto, if that's what you're dancing around.'

His smile made his eyes crinkle up, and I loved it. 'You want to go in?'

'You know, I think they made a mistake putting *Dirty Dancing* first. How can you follow an act like that? I don't think *Footloose* is going to cut it.'

'What do you want to do?'

'I want to buy you some cheap Chinese food.' I gave him my best sexy wink. I'm not ashamed to admit I'd practiced it in front of the mirror. Not very ashamed, anyway.

'I can buy you dinner.' His offer was a tad defensive.

I knew I had to match his tone with an even more defensive one. 'I don't know why you won't let me pay my way,' I huffed. 'Are you going to be like this every time we go anywhere, 'cos I won't be coming in that case.' I raised one eyebrow at him, very slowly. And I knew he was completely taken aback.

'All right.' He rubbed the back of his neck, then shook his head and put an arm around my shoulders. 'Will your friends be worried about you?'

'I'll text Kelsie and tell her so they can meet us after if they want,' I said, and even as my thumb danced over the keys, I felt a slow burn of satisfaction when I imagined Saxon sitting in the theater, plotting. I wouldn't think of him even once for the next two hours. 'Done. Let's go.'

'Where is this place?' He zipped up his coat.

'Right around the corner.' I put on my scarf and hat.

'Wait a minute.' He slid his phone out of his pocket, held it up, and aimed at me. 'You look really cute. I'm going to take a picture of you. Smile.'

I did and he snapped the photo, then turned it so I could see.

'I do look pretty cute. Come to think of it, so do you.' I slid my phone on. 'Smile,' I ordered. He did, and the picture of him was perfect.

'Wow.' He studied the shot over my shoulder. 'That chip in my tooth is huge.'

'No it isn't.' I kissed his chin. 'It adds character.'

'Well, enjoy it while it lasts. Once I get a job with some dental coverage, I'm getting rid of all of this character.' We ran out of the lobby and were in the chilly afternoon before I could ask him why his dad didn't cover him dentally and when the last time he'd been to the dentist was.

I was coming to realize anything I thought I wanted to ask Jake, I probably didn't, both because I wouldn't like the answer and because he wouldn't want to talk about it with me.

We raced down the street. I liked the way the wind blew my hair back, and I had to swing my hand up to the top of my head to keep my hat from flying off. Jake's boots thumped on the pavement next to me, and if I could have taken those few seconds and folded them up to keep, I would have. They were pretty much as close to perfection as I've ever gotten in my life. It felt like I was running right on the line between being a little kid and being an adult. I felt free and happy and giddy, but also loved and wanted and wanting all at once. The air in our lungs made our hearts beat hard and fast and our skin turned pink with the cold.

It was over almost before it started. Suddenly we were over the line and nearer to being adults, and that had its own appeal.

The restaurant was dim and warmly romantic, complete with a bubbling mountain fountain model peppered with little porcelain pagodas and Chinese fishermen and -women all over it. Red paper lanterns with gold symbols and tassels hung from the ceiling. There were two walls of tiny booths and a few tables scattered in the middle of the room. A girl with shiny black hair and large yellow teeth took us to one of the booths and set menus in front of us.

Jake shrugged out of his coat, and I watched the way he moved out of his clothes with a particular interest that reflected deeper things I wanted and felt.

'Do you come here a lot?' He glanced around at the scrolls on the walls and the glossy menus.

'No. When I was younger we did. Thorsten thinks they serve cat meat.' I flipped open the menu and thought about which delicious meal I wanted, unworried about my stepfather's culinary prejudices.

'Thorsten?'

'My dad,' I said, not realizing I'd referred to Fa by his given name. That's just how I thought of him.

'Is he your real dad?' Jake moved the cutlery back and forth with his fingertips.

I was almost offended, but I reminded myself this was Jake asking me. There was no one who deserved to know more about me than he did. 'No. I've never met my real dad. Mom and Thorsten got together when I was in elementary school. He's awesome.' My words came out really clipped, even though I didn't mean for them to. Jake had poured his heart out to me two nights before; I could certainly fill him in on the basics without getting snippy.

'I bet he's cool. I mean, he picked you and your mom, right? Obviously smart.' He studied the menu with serious eyes.

'You've never met my mom,' I pointed out.

'I saw her today.' He never took his eyes off the menu.

'No.' I shook my head. 'You weren't there until after she dropped me off. You couldn't have seen her.'

He looked up from the menu and right at me. 'I was there.'

'But you didn't come out to meet me.' I felt a little burr of anger. 'I looked for you.'

'I was watching you.' His eyes were dark and serious.

'Why?'

'Because you're pretty.' He stated it like it was simple fact. It made me feel warm and tingly all over. 'Because I love the way you walk and how your hair is.'

'How it is?' I teased.

'Like long and always moving around. Like a wave. Or grass. Long grass. That doesn't sound flattering, not like I meant it to.' His face showed his frustration.

'I'm pretty flattered.' I blushed at the difficulty

of talking this honestly about things you don't usually talk about. 'I love when the wind blows the grass and it all ripples in a pattern. It's beautiful.'

'I'm sorry you have to take my weird compliments and try to make them sound normal.' He cleared his throat and pointed to the menu. 'Did you ever eat the spring rolls here?'

'I completely love your weird compliments.' I contemplated the menu, squinting a little as if I could make the tastiest thing pop out from the paper. 'The spring rolls here are the best. Let's get two combo platters.'

'All right.'

'We'll share. I want cream cheese wontons and sweet and sour chicken. What do you want?' I looked at Jake, and he looked uncomfortable, like he'd never ordered a plate of food from a restaurant. 'Do you want me to recommend something?'

'Just order for me.' He leaned across the table and spoke low, his eyes pleading.

The waitress came over, and I nodded to Jake. 'Hello,' I greeted her. 'We'll have two combo platters, please. I would like cream cheese wontons and sweet and sour chicken. The gentleman will have the spring rolls and beef and broccoli. And we'll both have Cokes. Thank you.'

187

Jakes body actually sagged with relief as she walked away from the table. 'Thank you. I get so freaked out at restaurants.'

'Really?' I was shocked to hear this confession. 'Don't you race dirt bikes? How could that be less scary than ordering food?'

'I've hardly ever been to a restaurant, but I got my first dirt bike when I was four.' He unrolled his napkin and balled up the paper napkin holder. 'So I guess it's just what I'm comfortable with.'

Mom and Thorsten took me out at least a few times a month, and I had eaten in some of the fanciest restaurants in the country; the ones that had extremely serious, trained waiters, professional runners for your food, and people whose only job was to refill your water.

'Well, next time we go out, you'll have to practice ordering.' I folded my hands on the table like I just made an executive business decision.

'So are you asking me on a second date?' Jake crossed his arms and leaned back, a huge smile on his face.

'Oh yeah.' I narrowed my eyes and gave him an evil grin. 'But just as a charity thing. You know, take a clueless guy out and teach him how to order food at a restaurant. You're practically community service for me.'

He laughed, and when the waitress set our glasses down, he blew the straw wrapper at me.

It was nice to eat with him, scooping things off his plate across the table and showing him how to hold the chopsticks I'd requested. I laughed every time they leaped out of his hands and flew across the table.

'I'd starve to death in China.' He picked up the thin pieces of wood for the thousandth time.

'C'mon, you're not so bad.' I watched him grab a piece of broccoli and open his mouth, only to have it slip out of the grasp of his sticks before he could get it in. I reached across the table and grabbed the piece tightly with my chopsticks, then lifted it helpfully to his mouth. He opened obligingly and ate.

'I might not starve if you were there to put things in my mouth every once in a while.' He wiped some soy sauce off the side of his mouth with a napkin.

'I'd do it for you. That's just how much I like you.' I pointed my chopsticks at him. 'You'd better be willing to do something for me in return.'

I saw a gleam in his eyes that made me realize he was thinking something completely different than what I meant. 'Oh, I think I'd be able to figure something out.'

'Maybe you can support us in China by being, like,

a male geisha,' I suggested and raised my eyebrows.

'What's a geisha?' His face was adorably suspicious.

'It's like an entertaining woman, and they're actually Japanese. You know, the ones who wear the white face paint and kimonos. They hang out with important men and sing and joke and play instruments.'

'But they're girls,' he said uncertainly.

'Yes,' I sighed. 'But they're supposed to be really attractive and people pay good money to have them around. That's why you'd be a good one. 'Cos you're a little bit of a man-whore.'

He laughed. 'Not anymore. Do geishas sleep with the guys?'

'No. I mean, they're not nuns, but they aren't expected to sleep with any clients unless they want to.' I placed the chopsticks neatly on the edge of my plate, empty except for a few grains of soy-sauce-soaked rice.

The waitress brought us the bill with two fortune cookies on top. I snapped it up, and knew I could afford it all with the tip because I had ordered everything. I put the twenty down and got up to leave.

'So what will you do while I'm a male geisha in

China?' Jake helped me into my coat and wrapped my scarf around my neck.

'I'll teach little Chinese kids to speak English.' I put my hat on my head and walked out the door he held for me.

'That doesn't really sound fair.' He put his hand on the small of my back, keeping me from the curb I was nowhere near.

'Look, you have to shake what your mama gave you, in every sense. You're the looks, so I'll have to be the brains. Or the muscle.' I closed my fist and popped my tiny bicep. Jake squeezed it appreciatively.

'I guess you could take a few thugs out with those.' He wrapped his arms around me and his body blocked the cutting wind.

We were just about to kiss again when I heard Kelsie's voice.

'Hey, Brenna! Jake! What happened? Did you feel OK?' The Chinese food place was right down the street from the theater, and we must have timed our meal perfectly with the end of the movie.

'Brenna felt dizzy. I thought she might need something to eat,' Jake covered for me.

'That was nice of you to watch out for Brenna,' Kelsie said, her voice overly sweet. I scowled at her. Her smile widened.

'No problem,' he mumbled.

'I know you guys ate, but we were going to head out and get something to eat at the diner. Do you guys want to come just to hang out?' I saw Chris and the other guy whose name I couldn't remember. Kelsie noticed me looking right away. 'Saxon and those two girls he dragged along left before the movie started. We thought they might have gone with you two, but I guess not.' She shrugged. 'You two in?'

'I can stay longer.' Jake looked at me.

'I told Mom we might head out to eat after the movie.' I was still reeling a little from the news of Saxon's exit. Did he see me and Jake leave? Did he have it planned from the start? Had I made a decision to outsmart Saxon only to get outsmarted?

I was more than a little disgusted. My point had been to *not* think of him at all and then gloat about it to his face.

We walked along the sidewalk toward the diner. The guys discussed the upcoming Folly gig.

'I listened to your album the other day,' I said to Chris. 'I thought it was really good.'

'Awesome.' He pointed at me. 'I hear you're a crazy artist.'

'Maybe. I heard you need some designs.' I felt a

swell of pride when I thought about myself as an artist. I liked it.

'Yeah, people have been asking for T-shirts at our shows. If you've even got a sketch or a digital image, we can get them screen printed, and we'd give you a cut of anything we make. Like royalties.' Chris pushed his glasses up onto the bridge of his nose, and I saw what attracted Kelsie to him. He was handsome in that lean, serious-faced, artistic way.

'I'll have something to you by the end of the week.' A job! I had an actual job that I was excited about.

'Cool.' He looked at me like he had confidence in my promise to deliver. 'I'll introduce you to the band at school.'

He responded to something Kelsie said, and I noticed Jake hanging back.

'You OK?' I took his hand in mine.

'Yeah.' He squeezed my hand. 'You're going to be famous soon, huh?'

'My design might be,' I said breezily. 'Are you already buckling under the pressure of being part of a celebrity couple?'

Whoops. The words were out of my mouth before I thought much about them. Honestly, it was just a funny thing to say. I looked at Jake, wondering what I should say now. We were at the diner, and I motioned for Kelsie to go in without us.

'Are you asking me to be your boyfriend, Brenna?' Jake's face was way too delighted for his own good.

'Nope.' I turned my nose up at him. 'I never ask guys out.'

'Really? Because I think you just asked me out.'

'No I did not. You misinterpreted. That happens a lot. My jokes are very highbrow.'

'Or just not that funny.'

I jabbed him with my elbow and he laughed.

And that's when I knew for sure we should be dating.

'I did not ask you out. But I would seriously think about not shooting you down if *you* asked *me*. Nicely.' I had to keep my pride.

He took both of my hands in his. 'Brenna Blixen will you be my girlfriend, please?' He held up one of my hands and kissed my knuckles smoothly. 'Pretty please. With sugar on top.'

'That was really nice.' I tried to keep my voice light and calm, but there was a knot in my throat. 'I'll do it.'

'Let's celebrate,' he suggested, his voice low and perfect. He pulled me close and kissed me, and his mouth felt extra warm and soft in the bitter autumn wind outside. We kept it relatively quick. We were on the sidewalk outside of a diner, for God's sake!

'I like a celebration kiss, but some celebration pie would be even better. But I'm broke.' I remembered too late that I had spent all my money.

'Good thing your new boyfriend is a high roller.' Jake's smile was so big and happy I was starting to forget what his expression looked like when he didn't have that big, goofy grin. We sat at the table with the others, and a young waitress in extremely tight pants hurried over as soon as she saw Jake sit.

'Can I help you?' She leaned over to better expose her already overexposed cleavage.

Jake looked right at me and winked. Then he took a deep breath and smiled at the waitress. 'The lady and I will each have a slice of apple pie à la mode.' He handed her the menus with that goofy grin still overwhelming his entire face.

Kelsie gave me a curious glance, but all I could do was mouth 'later' across the table. Under the glossy, black-speckled laminate table, Jake grabbed my hand and squeezed it hard. We ate our celebratory pie and joked with the others, and soon it was time to leave. I had to call Mom, even though I just wanted to stay with Jake all day. And all night, too, if I was honest about it.

But that wasn't possible, and I knew Mom would

have already been home most of today by herself. It was horrible to think about her eating all alone. So I told Jake I had to call her.

She sounded glad to hear from me, and she said she'd pick me up at the diner in fifteen minutes. Everyone else was slowly starting to trickle out and go home, too.

Jake sat in the diner lobby with me, facing the windows so I could see Mom's car when she pulled up. He put his arm around my shoulders.

'Awesome day.' He took a deep breath and looked very self-satisfied.

'It was pretty good.' I grabbed him and squeezed him hard. 'I'll see you tomorrow in school.'

'You're not calling me tonight?' He looked surprised.

'I'll call, but we can't talk too long because I have school tomorrow. And I have to call after Mom goes to bed. We watch shows on TV together and talk, and I can't miss out on that.' I wanted to, and felt ridden with guilt for even thinking that way. My mother had raised me for fifteen years; I had known Jake for less than a week. It wasn't a question of loyalty, because Mom would win hands down. It was just who I had a craving to be with. Guilty as it made me feel, that was definitely Jake.

'I wouldn't want you to.' Suddenly he moved away from me. 'Mom's here.' He kissed my cheek quickly. 'Get going.'

'How are you getting home?' I asked as I put my scarf and hat on.

'I'm getting a ride,' he said vaguely. 'Take care, Brenna. I'll talk to you later.'

I didn't like his answer, but that was nothing new. Jake was always giving me answers I didn't like, or I was always coming to conclusions about him that were probably right but made me sad.

'Take care.' I cupped his face and kissed him quickly on the lips before I hurried out to Mom's car. When I glanced back at the windows of the diner, they were so reflective I couldn't see anything but my own face staring back at me. That was good because it meant Mom hadn't seen Jake or his kiss, but it also meant I couldn't see Jake as we pulled away.

'Was it fun?' Mom asked after I slid in and buckled my seatbelt.

'Yeah. It was really cool to see the movies on the big screen.'

'Who went?' Mom asked.

'Kelsie and a bunch of kids from school she knows. We didn't get to talk too much because we were in a theater.' It was easier to lie to my mom if some of what I lied about was true.

'I'm glad you're hanging out with friends already.' Mom paused. 'Bren, I've been thinking about something and I wanted to run it by you.'

'OK.' I could tell she was nervous from the way she held tight to the steering wheel.

'I think I might like to take a job at the community college.' Mom glanced in the rearview mirror, then over at me.

'Mom, that's great!' Mom had gotten her Masters in Art History before we left for Denmark, and she had been working towards her PhD since then. 'Maybe you can work on finishing your thesis.'

'I thought that. The thing is, I would have to pick up a night class or two, and I hate for you to be alone until after nine on a school night.' Her perfect eyebrows pulled together on her forehead.

'Mom, it's fine,' I assured her. 'I'll have homework most nights anyway. And I've been thinking about joining track. I might not be around all that much.'

'But you still need me,' Mom said, and I felt a lump in my throat, because I knew she loved that aspect of our relationship.

'You're my mom.' I wanted to reassure her how much I loved her. 'I'll need you for ever. But I don't need you every minute. And you and I have cell phones. The community college is only twenty minutes away from our house. And I know all of the neighbors. You have to do this, Mom. You're such a great teacher, and the community college kids especially need really good teachers.'

Her forehead smoothed and her eyebrows returned to their rightful place like twin birds' wings over her blue-gray eyes. 'You're the best, Bren. How'd I get such an excellent kid?'

'Good genes?'

She reached across the center console and patted me on the knee. 'You got that right.'

We got home and I read some more Kingsolver, since I hadn't had a chance before. My room looked amazing. I was so impressed with how it had turned out, and having a really beautiful room made it much easier to hole up in there. Not that I needed any excuse. I'd loved being alone in my room since long before I'd had a boy to moon over. I popped open my laptop and transferred the picture of Jake from my phone to the computer, then ran it through my Photoshop program. I cleaned it up and made it black and white since the color was terrible. I hooked my laptop to my photo printer and printed it out.

Just looking at it made me feel light and bubbly. I

put it in my book as a bookmark, not wanting to leave it out in case Mom or Thorsten came in for something. There were a lot of reasons I didn't want to talk to them about Jake, but a really major one was I simply didn't know how they'd feel about me having a boyfriend at all. So I took the path of least resistance and didn't mention him.

Mom and I watched some detective show Mom was addicted to, but I could never follow it. Then she stretched and yawned and told me she had a good book to read and was heading to bed.

'Love you.' She kissed me. I told her I loved her too, and waited a minute before I switched off the TV and put the plates in the dishwasher. Then I went to my room, trying not to hurry too much because I wanted to savor this time before I called him. It was almost torturous. I washed my face, brushed my teeth, and got into my pajamas. Then I sat on my bed, staring at my phone until I couldn't wait one more second.

'Brenna.' His voice sounded sleepy already.

'Hey, Jake.' I snuggled down in my bed. 'How are you?'

'Pretty great. I got this amazing girl to agree to date me today.'

'Really? Was she super desperate?' I teased.

'Oh yeah. She couldn't keep her hands off me

during the whole date. Poor thing. I think she's obsessed.'

I liked the fact that we could joke about being together. I was dreading the idea that it might get too serious or too sappy. I really didn't know anything about dating or having a boyfriend. Every single thing was new for me. 'You sound tired, Jake.'

'Not too tired to talk to you,' he said and yawned.

'I think you're too tired to be awake at all.' I flipped open my book and traced the picture of him smiling at me in black and white.

'You took too long to call me,' he accused, his voice sweet.

'I wanted to savor it,' I said quietly, now embarrassed.

'You're pretty seriously adorable.' The need for sleep made him suddenly open up.

'You're quite deliciously irresistible yourself,' I whispered. 'Bedtime, Jake.'

'Tell me you can't live without me,' he insisted.

'I'm having trouble taking a breath unless I'm looking at your picture.'

I lied, but it wasn't a huge lie.

'You have a picture of me?' he asked, surprised.

'The one from today. From the movie theater lobby.'

'The one with my big ol' chipped tooth?' His voice was slurred with drowsiness.

'That's the one.'

'You like that picture?' He sounded astonished.

'You look good.'

'Brenna.' My name was a sigh on his lips. 'How do you see good when you see me?'

'Because you are good,' I said simply. 'And that's it. Goodnight, Jake.'

'If I'm good, you're a thousand times better than the best,' he said sleepily.

'Goodnight, Jake,' I repeated, thinking about his head on a pillow, the phone loose in his hand.

'Goodnight, Brenna. I'll be there tomorrow.'

'OK. Me too. Sleep.' I clicked my phone off.

Chapter 8

And just like that, my world slowly started to spin around Jake Kelly. He was my boyfriend, but more than I'd ever thought a boyfriend could be. Because it wasn't all about being physical, even though I loved that aspect, and Jake was always respectful of my lack of experience and my wariness to go further, to the places he'd been so many times without really thinking about it much at all. School centered around looking forward to Jake and avoiding Saxon.

After the weekend at the movies, Saxon was completely quiet and cold to me in school. We didn't walk to class together anymore, and the only reason I still sat at his lunch table was that it was too awkward to try to find other friends to sit with. Kelsie and I didn't have the same lunch period, and since most of the kids had already clumped together in their strangely unbreakable clans as soon as the year began, they weren't very willing to change.

The best part of my day was just after lunch when I got on my bike and headed to Tech, even though the weather was increasingly colder and the wind bit angrily through all of my layers. I pushed my feet against the pedals, willing my body closer to Jake. Unlike Saxon, Jake was someone I could work with easily. I loved when the two of us sat across from each other in companionable silence, grinning whenever our eyes met across the rough shop tables. Sometimes he would catch my leg under the table with the top of his boot and rub the rounded top of the toe along the bottom of my calf, up and down. He never looked at me when he did it, which made it even more adorable. I liked the feel of his slightly hard boot sliding up and down the soft curve of my leg.

He walked me out to my bike one freezing Thursday afternoon. 'It's cold.' His teeth chattered a little.

'It's not bad once you get going.' I tied my scarf firmly around my mouth and nose and pulled my hat down over my ears.

'You look like a snowman.' He reached out to tuck loose hairs back under my hat.

I knew he was worried about me, but that seemed so ridiculous. He was the one with the threadbare coat and holey hat. His boots were scuffed and the laces were fraying, and the denim of his pants was so worn it felt silky. I had no idea how he got to work or home, and I had no idea what his house was like once he got home. I didn't know where he slept or if he even had his own room. Or bed. For all I knew he might be camped on his couch. Or worse.

I blinked those thoughts away, forcing a laugh at his joke. I was glad he couldn't see much of my face with my entire anti-cold outfit on. 'This snowman had better get going before Mama Snowman brings out the icy fury.'

'I can't believe your mom is still cool with you riding to school,' Jake stalled.

I sighed. 'C'mon, not you, too. I like it. It makes me feel very independent.'

'This winter is one of the coldest we've had in years, Brenna. You should hear the Zinga brothers bitching about the crops that got destroyed by the frost. I can't wait until I can drive you home.' He squinted at the sky. 'It looks like snow. It smells like it, too.' He gave me a worried look.

'Mom forbids cycling in the snow. If it snows tomorrow, I'll take the bus,' I promised.

'It's going to snow now,' he said, his legs spread over the front wheel of my bike, his hands gripping the handlebars. 'Go home now.' He pulled the scarf down and kissed me, lightly at first, then with a little more hunger.

I leaned into him, trying to find the balance between quietly savoring the kiss and pressing in, tapping into the rush of feelings I had to keep bound inside. If I let go, went where my body begged me to, it was like a switch tripped in Jake's head, and he backed off entirely. I had to play it just right, leading him in and making him forget what we were doing.

We were tangled around the cold metal frame of my bike, our arms, and chests, and lips pressed together urgently, his tongue sliding sweet and quick over mine. Then I shivered.

Just the tiniest imaginable shiver.

'Get going,' Jake barked. He pulled away and left me panting for more of him. Even as I sulked and snapped back that he wasn't my keeper, I checked him out from under my eyelashes.

I knew why every girl we ever came within ten feet of pressed her breasts into his face and batted her eyelashes like she was having a facial spasm. He was the perfect mixture of pure angelic good boy and hot dangerous bad boy. He was sweet and well-mannered and romantic, but there was an edge to him that made me bristle and swoon at the same time. Swoon, just like Scarlett O'Hara. It was like I could imagine him carrying an old lady's groceries to her car, but I could also picture him in a fist fight. And I wasn't sure which image intrigued me more.

Sick, sick, sick. But I couldn't lie about him. I felt my chest get hot and tight every time I thought of him. I was falling head over heels in love with Jake Kelly, and the feeling was better than anything I'd ever felt before.

'Bye,' I snapped, narrowed my eyes at him, and then I pretended I was going to pedal away even as I waited for the pull of his hand on my bike.

'Can't let you go angry.' He pulled my bike back, just like I knew he would. Then he kissed my lips again gently. He fixed my scarf over my mouth and nose. 'Brenna, you know you're crazy, right?' His smile was so wide it crinkled his eyes; eyes as gray as the sky before the snow.

'I thought that was part of what drove you to me.' I couldn't resist him for even a minute. When Jake turned on his charm, I was defenseless.

'I want you to be safe.' He rubbed his red, chapped hand over my mittened one. 'Look where you're going and don't make any stops.'

'I'm not an idiot, Jake,' I said through my scarf.

'I never said that,' Jake returned calmly. 'Even pretty, smart girls can get caught in storms. Go.'

I dropped my hands from the bike and let it balance between my legs, drew him into a hard hug, and darted away. I didn't like to look back, because I knew exactly where Jake would be standing, watching me race away from him as he stood there, shivering until I was out of sight. Jake was right about the weather. As soon as I crested the hill beyond the school, snowflakes started to flurry and swirl. I felt a prickle of irritation. It wasn't even winter yet. New Jersey was always cold, but this was just crazy. It was like even the weather was conspiring to keep me from riding to school.

I rode as hard I could and kept my eyes on the road. I was just past Frankford when a car rumbled too close to my side. I didn't even have to look to know who it was.

I waved a hand to my side, flagging him away, but he crept dangerously close, refusing to back off. Finally I had to stop or risk being run into a deep, leaf-filled ditch on the side of the road.

I smacked my hand hard on the warm bonnet of his car in frustration, and Saxon gave me an amused grin from the interior. His passenger window was open and the smoke from his cigarette mixed with the swirling snowflakes; a weird combination of clean and cold with the smoldering, dirty fumes.

'I'll give you a ride.' It wasn't a suggestion. As usual. Typical Saxon.

'No thanks. It's getting worse, so why don't you stop trying to drive me off of the road and let me get home?'

He took a long drag on his cigarette then flicked the filter out the window, the cherry burning bright orange for a few seconds before it went out. I made a face. There was nothing I hated more than seeing the ground littered with cigarette butts.

'Mommy is going to be pissed off.' He gestured with one hand. 'Get in.'

'My mother will be extra pissed off if I pull up in your car. I'm not allowed to drive with idiots.' I got back on my bike.

I heard Saxon make a noise between a yell and a snarl of frustration before he opened the driver's door, got out, and closed it with a bang. I was on my way, but the road was slick from the settling snow and one of my tires wobbled and slipped from under me. Saxon caught up with me easily and grabbed my bike at the same time that I slammed my feet off the pedals and onto the pavement.

'You're going to get yourself killed.' He held the handlebars in a vice-like grip, the opposite of Jake's gentle hold. 'Get in the car.' He saw my stony expression and his eyes softened in a way I didn't completely trust. 'I won't put the moves on you, Blix. If I let you get killed, who would I have left to irritate the crap out of me?'

I hated to admit how handsome he looked, how attracted I was to him, despite my best efforts to resist.

The snow was falling more rapidly now, coating the swerved tracks from my bike, and then erasing them completely. It was dangerous. Mom would be frantic.

'Fine.' I picked my bike up. 'Pop your trunk.'

He ignored my request, yanked the bike out of my hands and jerked his head towards the passenger door. 'Get in.'

As I slid in, I could see that he had already popped the trunk. He was so sure I would jump in the car with him. I don't know what made me angrier: his arrogance or the fact that I'd done exactly what he expected.

I had my arms crossed over my chest when he got in, refusing to warm my cold hands by the vents that blew such inviting hot air in my direction.

'Call your mom.'

I didn't want to just do what he said, but I didn't have much of a choice. If I didn't call her first, she would be driving to get me or sending out the National Guard. My mom had a way of frightening men in positions of authority, and I just prayed she hadn't already called the cops. I punched the number into my cell.

She picked up on the second ring. 'Brenna! Where are you?' Her voice was pure panic.

'I'm fine, Mom. One of my classmates offered me a ride home because of the weather.'

'Thank God.' In my mind I could see her putting a shaky hand over her heart. 'Just drive slowly. Don't rush. And tell her thank you.'

'Uh, I will.' I chose to ignore the pronoun confusion. 'Love you.'

Saxon smirked while my mother told me she loved me.

'Tell her I love her, too,' he said in a stage whisper.

I gripped my phone in my hand. 'Tell her yourself when you get to my house,' I dared him. He shut up.

We rode for a little while in silence. I tried to make mine a pointed, obvious silence, but Saxon refused to acknowledge there was anything weird about my lack of conversation. He seemed perfectly comfortable with the whole thing.

'Pretty crazy weather, eh, Blix?' I couldn't believe he was bringing up something as mundane as the weather when there were such intense emotions flying around between us.

'It sucks.' Mom would say I was being petulant. So what if I sounded like a priss? That's how I felt.

'I think it was fate.' He leaned back in his seat. He looked good, and I knew he knew it. His jet-black hair was a little too long and messy. His eyes were dark and knowing, and his shirt and pants were obviously too light for the weather, but he didn't even have a goosebump. And even though I really didn't want to notice it, it was hard to ignore how his sculpted muscles showed through his Sex Pistols T-shirt and his ripped-up pinstriped suit pants.

'I don't think fate had anything to do with it. This is just you creeping around where you knew I'd be passing,' I said a little too firmly. I had a huge superstitious streak so I usually believe in fate. But I didn't want to in this instance.

'I think you're a liar. Don't be so glum, Blix. It's not cheating to take a ride. Even if it is from me.'

'Jake wouldn't care,' I said hotly, all the hotter about it because I was secretly a little nervous that he *would* care, and also a little annoyed I was even thinking that way.

Saxon shrugged. 'I thought you would be more concerned, now that your Jake's girl.'

'Like I said before,' I snapped, 'I'm my own girl. No one else's.' No matter how much I liked Jake, I would never think of myself as belonging to him.

'So how about Folly?' Saxon made a stab at neutral conversation. 'I heard you gave them some designs that were pretty awesome.' And then he brought it right back into uncomfortable territory. 'You and me should go to the gig next Saturday.'

'No thanks,' I said automatically.

His smile curled over his face like smoke curling from a burning cigarette. 'You aren't remotely interested in how your design will sell?'

I was. And I liked Folly. I managed to ignore the fact that Saxon had made the Folly mix for me and I had spent a few nights listening to it. 'I'm not saying I won't go. I just don't want to go with you.'

Saxon leaned over and upped the heating until every dial was set to maximum. I started to sweat in my seat. 'Well, however you get there, I'll be there, too, so it will technically be a date.'

I balked at his words and resisted the urge to throw my coat off. 'That makes absolutely no sense.'

'Really?' he challenged. 'I'm asking you to meet me at the Folly concert. If you're there on Saturday, you accepted my date request.'

I glanced at the speedometer and saw he was hardly doing fifteen miles an hour. This ride would never end. 'I'll go with Jake.' I unknotted my scarf, dragged my hat off, and put my mittens in my lap, and I was still sweltering. I didn't know what was more uncomfortable: the extreme heat of the car's interior or the slow, hot burn of rage that was spreading through me in response to Saxon's ridiculous games.

'Isn't the motocross race at the Valley next Saturday?' he taunted.

My ears burned. I had forgotten! Jake hadn't said anything about it for days. I'd already told him I would go. I wanted to go. How was I going to fit everything in?

Now I was aggravated, and Saxon was purposefully crawling along even more slowly. I knew there was no way he'd normally drive this slowly even in a blizzard. He just wanted to torture me.

'Can we talk about something else?' I growled. I hated his arrogant smile and how he knew exactly which buttons to push to rile me.

'Sure,' Saxon drawled. 'What would you like to talk about, Brenna?' The way he said my name was warm and slow, and it coiled down low in my gut.

'Are you on the soccer team this fall?' I asked, my voice falsely bright.

'Yeah.' He shot me a smile. 'I'm a forward.'

'Like on the soccer team?' He didn't seem like a

joiner, let alone one of the most important members of the soccer team.

'Like on the soccer team. So are you doing any sports? Cheerleading?' He suggested with a laugh. 'Kidding,' he added, and I smiled despite my best attempt to scowl at him.

'I was thinking about track,' I admitted.

'You should. You run like Gump.'

I rolled my eyes. 'Yeah, I know. I've heard you and your friends chanting for me.'

'You're inspiring, Blix.' His tone wasn't joking anymore. He looked at me with this expression of naked appreciation, and he didn't try to hide it. He clearly wanted me to see it.

'And I'm sure you make all of the girls burn with desire when you're on the field.' I shrugged out of my jacket, finally completely broken under the heat torture. 'At first I didn't think soccer forward fitted you, but it actually makes perfect sense. You're the center of attention, calling all of the shots and having everyone worship you. Perfect.'

'Are you calling me a diva?' Saxon grabbed a pack of Tic Tacs from the assorted wrappers, empty cigarette packets and crumpled papers scattered on the dashboard and offered them to me.

'I call 'em like I see 'em.' I accepted his tiny orange

peace offering. 'I would have been home ten minutes ago if I'd ridden my bike.'

'Or you would have been dead. Bikes aren't made for snowstorms.' He held out his hand so I could shake Tic Tacs in his palm. 'You're kind of obnoxious.'

'Glad you think so.' I flipped the vents down and pointed the hot air at my feet. 'Let's not be friends.'

'Friends,' he scoffed as he tossed the candies into his mouth. 'We're so similar, we should make an alliance. The two most obnoxious people on earth would be a true force to be reckoned with.'

'We are not alike.' I really wanted to mean it.

He drove with one hand on the steering wheel, his head turned to look at me. 'Why do you think we drive each other crazy? Why do you think there's that certain something in the air whenever we're around each other? We're alike. We attract each other.' His voice was low and smoky in my ears.

I shook my head. 'No.'

'It doesn't matter what you say. It is what it is.' He lifted his hand from the steering wheel in a huge shrug. 'Can't help it. Trust me, I don't like it any more than you do. I'm just not as good at lying to myself as you are.'

'I don't lie to myself,' I lied.

We both laughed, and I realized two things at

once. The first was that we were pulling into my driveway. The second was that I felt upset for some reason. Some part of me wanted more time with Saxon – the same Saxon who insisted he was just like me when we were worlds apart.

I had my hand on the door handle before he'd even pulled to a complete stop. 'Thanks.'

He killed the engine and reached for his door.

'No.' I shook my head for emphasis.

'Yes.' He got out and headed to my side of the car, then opened my door. I felt a red flush creep up my face.

I hated having him on my own turf. Being a smartass with Saxon in class or his car was one thing. Now I was home, with the mother I loved, and I wasn't sure how to act around him again. It also made me a little mad he was going to meet my mom and be an official guest before Jake got the chance. This was Jake's spot, not Saxon's, and that fact annoyed me.

I marched to the house, Saxon at my side, wheeling the bike, and Mom's telltale curtain-fluttering sent my heart into overdrive. There was no script for this between me and my mother. Usually I would have asked permission to bring anyone over. I wasn't used to being cavalier with my mom, and I was nervous about facing her disappointment. I was nervous she would interpret Saxon as something other than what he was. And I was most nervous she would approve of him, or possibly even like him and link us together in her head, in that place that already belonged to Jake, even if she didn't realize it yet.

The snow coated my driveway and hid the shiny pieces of quartz gravel that usually made a bumpy white track down the drive. I took Saxon through the garage entrance and walked straight into my mother's open arms.

'No more bike.' She shook me by my shoulders gently before she hugged me hard. She turned to Saxon. Her look wasn't exactly welcoming, but she wasn't kicking him out either. 'Thank you for driving Brenna home. We don't usually allow her to ride with teenagers, but I understand this was an exceptional situation.'

I gloated at Saxon. I loved my mom's crisp, scary voice. She could put any boy in his place, even if his eyes were black as sin and his smile made it feel like someone had grabbed a fistful of your stomach and was squeezing hard.

'I understand, Mrs Blixen.' The voice that tumbled out of his mouth was modulated and humble. 'I'm glad I could help Brenna out. Her friends have been worried about her cycling home with the weather so unpredictable.'

I wanted to snort at his nonsense, but my mother's look of approval made my throat stick. Saxon did *not* just charm my mother!

'Well, I appreciate your worry. We've felt it too.' She gave me another shake. 'I'd love to ask you to stay . . .'

'Saxon Maclean, ma'am.' He stuck his hand out.

She shook it and looked disgustingly charmed. We'd love to have you stay, Saxon, but this weather will only get worse, and it's going to be unsafe to drive soon. Do you need to use our phone to tell your parents that you're on the way home?'

Saxon had parents? It seemed unthinkable.

'No, thank you,' said Impeccably Mannered Saxon. 'I have a cell phone. It was so nice meting you, Mrs Blixen.'

'Same here.' Mom seemed to revel in his thickly-laid-on crap. 'I hope you can make it over for dinner sometime when the weather's a little less freakish.'

'I'd love that.' He turned to me and gave me a sweet, friendly smile, while his eyes danced with devilish triumph. 'I'll see you in school tomorrow, Brenna. I might need to call you later for help with AP government.' He looked at my mom, his eyes as innocent as two freshly picked blackberries. 'Brenna has a real brain for government, and she's one of the youngest in the class.'

I wanted to gag. Mom preened like a proud mama peacock. 'Well, she'll be home if you need help. She is very bright.'

'I think I know where she gets her brains from.' He smiled and winked. He actually winked! 'Goodnight, ladies.'

'Drive safely!' Mom called as he left, looking all agog. I had to suppress a groan.

She went to her favorite crack in the curtains like a friendly sentinel. 'He seems very sweet. And very gentlemanly.'

'Mmmhmm,' I murmured noncommittally.

'And he's definitely got eyes for you, Bren,' Mom went on. Her eyes followed his sleek black car as it backed out of the driveway. 'He's really good looking. Almost too good looking. Is he your boyfriend?' Her voice was just on the edge of being nervous.

'No.' I paused. 'We're just friends. I think he has a thing for Kelsie.' It wasn't completely a lie. He had had a thing for Kelsie.

Mom wrinkled her nose. 'I don't think so. Kelsie is sweet, don't get me wrong. But she can't hold a candle to you, honey.'

I gave Mom a weak smile and tried to think of some way out of this completely awkward conversation. 'So, did you hear from the college?'

'I did!' she exclaimed. 'I have a night class every Tuesday and Thursday, but everything else is during the day.'

'That's awesome, Mom.' I moved toward her to give her a hug. 'Are you teaching something you like?'

She squeezed me hard then shrugged, flicking the curtain back with a jerk of her hand. 'Art History 105 and 106. It's nice to look at the whole timeline of art again. No complaints here.' She smiled at me, her blue-gray eyes crinkling prettily around the edges.

'I'm so happy for you.' We watched the snow fall outside the windows in fat, beautiful flakes. 'Do you think we'll have a snow day tomorrow?'

'You never know. I just can't believe we're getting this much snow and it's still only the beginning of October! I can't remember winter starting this early in years. Listen, I know you don't like it much, but you're going to have to start taking the bus, Bren.'

'I'll be home really late, though.' I bit my lip as my bike privileges slipped away before my eyes. I was positive I'd be able to ride right up to the beginning of December, but this freaky weather had ruined my best-laid plans.

'Why?'

'Tech drops off here after they loop Sussex and

Vernon. I'm going to be on the bus for over an hour and a half.'

'What? That can't be the only option!'

'That's what it said in my information pack.' I pointed to the packet on top of the fridge that Mom had glanced through before school started. I was usually pretty good about filling her in on everything she needed to know, so Mom didn't drive herself crazy reading every letter from the administration.

'I can't believe that's the only option,' Mom repeated as she flipped through everything with an angry shuffle. She found a phone number, but no one was there when she called it. 'Well, I know I don't usually allow this, but that Saxon boy can take you back and forth. Just back and forth to school. He seems very responsible. Though he smelled like smoke. Does he smoke?'

I felt my panic subside. There was nothing Mom hated more than a smoker. 'Yes. I had to tell him to put out his cigarette before he picked me up.'

'Well, as long as he never does it when you're in the car, we'll have to make do.'

Then Mom went on getting ready for dinner like it was any other night and she hadn't just broken a half dozen of her own firmly set rules in allowing me to ride back and forth to school in Saxon Maclean's black shark of a car.

I opened and shut my mouth a few times and tried to come up with a logical argument, but I couldn't will myself to argue for a bus ride that would eat up close to two hours of every afternoon, not to mention how much earlier I was going to have to get up in the mornings to get to school on time. It would take about ten minutes to drive to school and back. Saxon couldn't get under my skin if I didn't let him.

Yeah, right.

I went to my room after we'd eaten dinner and watched some television together. I excused myself by saying something vague about a lot of homework, but I tried Jake's number as soon as I was behind my closed door. It went to his voicemail. I knew he was at work, probably doing something mundane and labor intensive in this horrible freezing snowstorm. I realized if I called him just to complain and confess, I would make his work day suck even more than it probably already has. I couldn't do that to him.

But I needed to talk to someone. Kelsie had wrapped her life completely around Chris, to the point where it was hard to talk to her about anything else, but that was actually OK with me. When Kelsie was paying attention, she was very perceptive, and there was way too much going on that I'd rather not have her know about.

Before I could think much more, my phone rang. I didn't recognize the number that popped up, but something told me it was him.

'Hello?' My irritation grew when I heard the voice I'd anticipated.

'Blix, I really need help with that chapter on jury duty. I'm really confused.' Saxon chuckled softly. 'Don't be mad.'

'You're a dirty liar.' I punched a pillow a few times, and then flopped back on my bed. 'My mom thinks you're some sweet friend of mine.' I kicked my backpack off the bed and onto the floor with one thrust of my leg. 'You can't just barge into my life like that.'

'I wasn't barging.' His voice was all sweet coercion. 'Listen, some girls would consider what I'm doing a modern form of chivalry. I truly do have your best interests at heart. If you'd got run off the road, and I didn't do anything to stop it . . .' He let his voice trail off expectantly.

'You'll have no one to harass?' I put in edgily. 'I just don't want to play your games.'

'What games?' His voice sounded a little surprised. But I knew Saxon well enough to know that the surprise could just be a part of his game. Ugh!

'I know you don't have any actual interest in

my health and well being—' I started, but he inter-rupted me.

'Look, that's a load of crap.' Saxon was usually good about never letting anything ruffle him, but he definitely sounded ruffled now. 'I don't know why, and trust me, I wish I did know just so I could some-how stop it, but I can't put you out of my mind. I know you're doing your thing with Jake for whatever reason, but that doesn't mean I can just switch off what I feel. And that doesn't mean I want to see you ride that piece-of-shit bike in a snowstorm.'

'It's a great bike.' But my voice fell flat. I tried my best to absorb what he'd just said. 'You could date anyone you wanted,' I said after a few long seconds.

'I know that.' His voice ground out irritably. 'Don't you think I know that?'

'Why don't you?' I got up and looked out the window, staring into the vicious tangle of snowflakes that swirled outside my window. I worried about Jake working and getting home in this mess.

'Don't you feel it for Jake?' he asked, his voice barbed. 'Or are you just another conquest? You seemed pretty damn self-righteous about the whole thing a few days ago. Is that all gone?'

'No. I care about Jake. It's not about physical stuff.

I mean, it's not only about that.' My face got hot just talking about it. I couldn't stop myself. I knew I should just end the conversation as soon as possible, but something about Saxon's honest, raw voice kept me on. I leaned my overheated face on the frosty glass of my bedroom window.

'I . . . Jesus Christ,' he muttered, then took a deep breath. 'I care about you. I can't even believe I'm saying this.'

'How can you care about me?' I was desperate to undo what he had just said. My breath made a fogged patch on the glass.

The line was so quiet, I checked to make sure we were still connected. After another few seconds, his voice came through, crackling with frustration. 'How can I not? It was first-sight crap. I want you out of my system, and I'm still hoping that's going to be the key, though I doubt it more and more every day I'm around you.'

'This doesn't seem like a head game,' I ventured cautiously. I traced a heart in the circle of condensation with my fingertip.

He snorted. 'You guessed it, Blix. This is all part of my elaborate plan to be crowned prom king. C'mon. You think I like this? You think I haven't tried to ignore you? You think I wouldn't like to roll around with

Karen Tanner? It just isn't happening. And it's because of you.'

'Karen Tanner?' I asked dumbly, picking the safest group of words in his confession. I pressed my palm to the window and blotted the heart out.

'Head cheerleader.' He took a deep breath and blew it all out in one long rush. 'Hot and into me. But I can't get serious with her. I can't get you out of my damn head. It sucks.'

'I'm with Jake.' I clutched the phone so hard my hand shook.

'I know that. I'm not begging for you to dump him. I'm just explaining why I keep creeping around like some sad old pervert.'

That made me laugh. 'I guess it would suck,' I conceded.

'Yeah.' His voice was hard.

We sat for a minute, and the quiet tempted us to say all those things that we weren't really ready or able to say. Finally I broke through the swirl of unsaid emotions with a watered-down version of a few things I'd been thinking. 'Let's just be friends. Maybe you're so used to getting girls to like you romantically that you think that's what you want from me.' Where was this coming from? Probably mostly from the fact that he had softened me up with his embarrassing confessions. And maybe there was an attraction; not the intense kind I felt for Jake, but an attraction, nonetheless.

'I think it's a fairly shitty idea, but let's try it. At this point, I'm willing to go along with anything.'

'Karen Tanner will be rolling around with you before you know it,' I promised. 'There's nothing particularly awesome about me, Saxon. Once I'm not so unattainable you'll back off.'

'I hope so. Look, let's go to Jake's thing together and then we'll all go to Folly. As friends.' He added an extra sneer to the last word, just for good measure.

I didn't want to touch that offer with a ten-foot pole. 'You and Jake aren't really friends, though. Won't it be weird?'

'I'm sure he needs a ride there anyway. His old man isn't going to bother to take him. There's some un-resolved stuff between me and Jake. Maybe it's time to resolve it.'

'What is it that makes you hate each other?' It had bothered me since the movies, but I couldn't get a thing out of Jake. Bringing up Saxon's name practically guaranteed to put him in a foul mood.

'Mostly stuff we never said, misunderstood stuff. Nothing serious. Nothing I can't smooth over.' The words were all cocky bravado. I heard a hint of uncertainty underneath them. As strangely attractive as Saxon could be when he was arrogant and swaggering, this weirdly human version was even more interesting. It was as if Saxon was peeling back a layer and letting me see something real that he didn't show to anyone else. I loved the sense that I shared some kind of secret with him.

'I still don't think he's going to be into you taking me to see him.' I tread carefully around his invitation. 'I'm not really willing to upset him before a big race. It's important to him.'

'Maybe you should talk to him about it,' Saxon challenged.

That's exactly what it was. A pure challenge. He knew I was uncomfortable about it, and he wanted to call my bluff on my *I'm nobody's girl but my own* rant.

'I will.' I realized just how easy it was for Saxon to manipulate me into doing what he wanted. It was not a pleasant realization. 'I need to call him soon anyway. We have other things to talk about.' I just wanted the conversation with Saxon to be over. He made me think way too much, and it was unnerving. Talking to him wasn't comfortable, even if it was exciting. I got off the phone with him as quickly as I could, but I could hear the laughter in his voice as we hung up. He knew exactly what he was doing, and he was enjoying it.

I called Jake's number, even though I knew he'd probably just walked through the door from work that minute. I didn't like calling before he had time to shower or relax for a few minutes. It seemed somehow desperate. But today I made an exception. And typical Jake, he didn't seem upset to hear from me at all.

'Hey, Brenna! You called me early.'

'Sorry.' I felt the sinking in my heart. How was I going to put this to him? Saxon had snared me in an old trap; if I didn't ask and just told Saxon no, he would assume, correctly, that I'd chickened out. If I did ask . . . well, that was its own distinct craziness.

'Don't be sorry. I love hearing from you. Call any time you want to.'

'Thanks,' I said. Then, awkwardly, I added, 'So I don't have a lot of details about your race. What's up with it?'

It was like I opened the floodgates. Jake talked faster than I'd ever heard him talk before. He said he'd been preparing in his free time, this race was a huge deal, and he was really excited I would be able to be there to see him. That it meant so much to him that I would be there to support him.

And that's when I had to drop the bomb on him.

'So, how are you getting there?' I closed my eyes and winced at his frustrated silence.

He finally said the obvious. 'You need a ride.' He wasn't offering because he couldn't. I'd never met anyone so worried about the fact that he couldn't drive.

'Not exactly.' I twisted the corner of my bedspread. 'I have a ride. Kind of.'

He waited with typical Jake-like patience.

'With Saxon.' Even as the words left my mouth, I wondered if I should have mentioned it. Mom could still veto the whole thing; but this afternoon's insanity gave me the feeling it was unlikely. She had really taken a strange liking to Saxon. That and her desire to see me go out with friends more would probably push her toward saying yes. How weird to be upset that my mom was most likely going to give me permission to go hang out all day Saturday with two different boys.

Jake exhaled in one long, irritated whoosh of air. But he didn't say anything.

'Say something.' I really didn't know what I wanted him to say. I didn't want him to be annoyed, but I could understand why he might be. I knew it would be strange to expect him to be cool with the whole thing, but it was also important for me to understand what was going on between him and Saxon.

And then he said something so un-Jake-like it shocked the words right out of my mouth.

'I'd rather you didn't come see me than show up with Saxon.'

I hadn't expected him to go that far, and I felt hot boils of anger pop and sizzle right below the surface of my skin.

I finally managed to string a few words together. 'You don't want me to come if I get a ride from Saxon?' I clarified, fighting hard to keep my voice controlled. Because in a few more sentences, all of that control would be gone, and I knew it.

'That's right.' His voice was granite hard.

That edge set me off. 'I don't know what the big secret is, but it's getting ridiculous. Just tell me!'

'It's not important.' He'd never spoken so sharply before. 'Look, do what you want, Brenna. I can't tell you what to do.'

I felt that annoying, cloying heat in my throat that let me know I was very close to crying.

'It *is* important.' My voice wobbled, to my complete humiliation. 'We're arguing about it, Jake, so I guess it's pretty important. What is it?'

He let out a groan, and just then I heard a light knock on my door. 'I have to call you back.' I slid the phone off and looked intently at the mounds of paper and books piled on my bed so it would look like I had been busy plowing through homework.

'I'm going to turn in for the night.' Mom walked in and kissed my head.

'Love you, Mom.' I fought hard to keep my voice and expression normal. Just the trying raised her Mom-Alert.

'What's the matter, Bren?' Her eyes searched my face.

'Just a lot of school work,' I lied.

'Is it too much? I think you should reconsider going to two high schools. It takes a lot out of you. I know you enjoy what you're doing at technical school, but let's face it, you're going to go to college, honey. You need to focus on academic subjects.' Mom sat on the bed and smoothed my hair away from my face. I leaned my cheek into her hand and loved the super soft brush of her palm on my skin.

'It's not that. I think it's just an adjustment.' That word had power. It gave me time and leeway.

'Well, keep what I said in mind. High school is supposed to be fun. I don't like the way you're always worrying lately.'

'Lately?' I asked, surprised.

'I've just noticed you seem a little distracted.' She smiled at me like she understood, but she couldn't possibly. What Mom was seeing was the Jake effect.

'It's still a little weird being the new girl.' I hated lying to Mom, but omission was OK in a twisted way.

'You'll get to relax tomorrow anyway. Snow day.' Mom beamed.

'Already?' They usually waited until early morning to call something like that.

'They just flashed it on the news before I came to say goodnight. I think it's probably because they don't have the resources together for an October storm. It's freaky weather we're having.' She squeezed me close. 'You're going to be spoiled with all these three-day weekends.'

'I don't think I'll ever have it any better than an entire year off,' I said.

'Good point. Now, I'm going to bed. Tomorrow we can have a cocoa and candles date.' She kissed me again and left.

I held my phone in my hand, thinking about how nice things had been last year. Mom and I had been able to relax and tour Denmark a little. Thorsten had been happy to be home again. I had been a little lonely, but happy, too.

That life already felt really far away. I was sad that it was gone, even though I knew there was no going back to it. What I had now, with Jake, had changed my very definition of happiness. If I had never met him, it might have been different. But now that I had, it was unthinkable that I might not know him anymore or be close to him. And that's what made me dial his number again, even though I had been close to crying when we'd hung up before.

'Brenna?' His voice sounded weird and tight like mine. I couldn't imagine him crying, but I'd never heard his voice sound that way before.

'I had to go. My mom needed to talk to me.'

'Did you talk about how to get rid of loser boy-friends?' He sounded a little sad for himself.

That was irritating.

'No. Believe it or not, I have more things to talk about than you, Jake.' It felt good to shoot him down a little, even if the only reason I didn't talk to Mom about Jake was because I was scared out of my mind for her to know about him and what he meant to me.

'I'm sorry, Brenna,' he said in a rush. 'I'm sorry I got so pissed off before, and I'm sorry I assumed your world revolves around me. This is a freaking mess.'

'Yep.' I let my mouth pop around the word. Now that he was taking the blame for our fight, I was fully prepared to let him accept it all. If he would just tell me what was up with him and Saxon, I wouldn't have to play guessing games with him.

'So, how do I fix it?' His voice was worn and tired.

I felt a tiny pinprick of pity for him, even though I didn't want to. I think it was because I knew Jake was sweet and caring and good; I knew he was in Saxon's web as much as I was. So I went easy on him. 'You have to be more understanding. Just because I take a ride with Saxon doesn't mean he's my boyfriend, or even my friend. I want to go see you, but I haven't told my mom about us yet, so it's kind of weird getting a ride.'

That last fact sat heavy between us.

'Oh,' Jake said flatly. 'Are you going to tell her?'

'I want to.' We both knew it was a weak response.

'Do you think she wouldn't approve of me?'

No. I knew she wouldn't. Even if, by some miracle, she really liked Jake, she was still against my having a boyfriend at all. And the problem would be, once she knew I was with someone, she would start watching me more. If I was sad, she'd blame him; if I was angry, she'd blame him. I just knew that's how it would be with my mother. Her love was incredible, but also a little claustrophobic.

But I didn't even have the energy to explain all that to Jake. 'My mom doesn't want me to date.' I left it at that.

'Oh.' He sounded a little relieved. 'So she would hate any guy?'

I thought about her gaga behavior with Saxon. 'Yes,' I lied.

He laughed softly. 'Am I crazy for feeling like that makes it a little better?'

'No.' I grabbed the book with his picture in it and flipped it open to his smile.

'Are we OK, Brenna? If I screwed this up . . .' He didn't say anything else, but I could hear the strain in his voice.

'You haven't,' I promised. 'When you're ready, you can tell me about Saxon. Once I know, it will make things easier. I know it will.'

Jake sighed. 'That's the thing with Saxon though.' There was a bitter ring to his words. 'I'll tell you the story, but I can't really explain what exactly I have such a problem with. He can complicate things in a way no one else can.'

'I think I might understand better than you think,' I said, remembering Saxon's fingertip on my ankle.

'Remember I told you I was drinking a lot that one summer?'

'Yes.'

'Well, I stopped once before I stopped for good. I had been with a girl, and she thought we were going to go out, and she got really upset when I told her that wasn't going to happen. She was all right, you know? I just didn't want to date her.'

I felt my heart thud irregularly. 'OK.'

'So I decided to stop because I realized I was hurting people I hardly even knew. Saxon was my best friend. Had been for years. He was the one who got the alcohol from his older cousin. When I said I wanted to stop, he called me a pussy, said I got soft over some slutty girl. Anyway, I wound up at a party and he was there. I told myself I wouldn't drink, then I decided I'd just have one or two.' He was breathing hard.

'You don't have to tell me.' A big part of me wanted him to stop, but I also wanted to know the truth, even if it was going to hurt. But I was in way over my head, and I had the distinct feeling I would drown in all of it.

'I *do* have to.' His voice shook hard. 'Man, I should have just done this in one clip.' He stopped and took a ragged breath. 'That night, Saxon was there, and I couldn't stop drinking. He wasn't doing anything I could put my finger on, but it was like I wanted to show him that I wasn't a lightweight, or that I could control myself even if I was drinking. It sounds so damn stupid now. But I got really, really drunk. That's the night my tooth got chipped and I woke up in someone's bed and my shoes were gone. The girl told me Saxon had punched me in the mouth and broken my tooth. She told me he took my shoes and told her to take me to her house or he'd kill me.'

'Why?' I was a little sad I wasn't more shocked.

'I have no idea. I swear. I never talked to him again. I never answered his calls, I never went to another party. And I never drank after that night.'

'Jake.' I sighed.

'Yeah, I know. I hate a guy because I got drunk and he might have stolen my shoes and broken my tooth. It sounds ridiculous.'

'No, it doesn't.' I fell back on my bed and stared at the ceiling without seeing it at all. 'Saxon has a way about him; he's tricky.'

We sat in silence, both of us thinking about how Saxon had managed to make us feel something we didn't want to feel or do something we didn't want to do.

'He likes you, Bren.' Jake's voice was barely audible. 'Oh God, he's done this a hundred times with a hundred girls, but I never cared about any of them until now.'

'You think I'd leave you to go out with Saxon?' I asked, my voice a little high with rage.

Finally, Jake laughed a little. 'Well, when you get all bent out of shape like that it gives me hope that you won't.'

'I don't like Saxon, Jake.' I debated telling him about Saxon's annoying presence, about the kiss, about the ride. But, in the end, I felt like enough had been confessed. Or maybe I was just plain chicken.

'He has a way of growing on people,' Jake warned.

'Like a fungus,' I griped. He laughed again.

'So, what are we going to do about Saturday?'

'Don't get pissed off, but—' I started.

'Brenna,' he said, his voice a little cracked. 'I'm never pissed off at you. I've been really unfair so far, and you've been nothing but awesome to me. Don't hold back. I promise you, I won't get pissed off at anything you have to say.'

'Saxon is kind of fishing for something. We should let him see we're stronger than that. He seemed like he genuinely missed hanging out with you. Why don't we let him see we can be together around him and it will be on our terms?'

As I said it, I felt a red WARNING sign flash in my head. Saxon was the king of head games; Jake and I were rank amateurs. Messing with him was only asking for trouble.

Despite those reasons, I wanted to do this. And I

wasn't about to admit to myself the reasons why.

'I don't love the idea of you being alone with him.' I could tell he was moody by the clipped way the words fell out of his mouth.

'Why don't we ask Saxon to pick you up first?' I suggested. 'Then you can both come and get me, and we'll all go to Vernon.'

'That's a lot of driving for him,' Jake said uncertainly.

'Are you worried about his gas mileage?' I laughed.

'Do you think he'll agree?' Jake asked, not laughing.

'Yes, I do.'

It took him a few seconds. 'OK. It's a deal.' He was quiet again. 'Do you mind if we talk about something else?'

'I would love it.'

'I wish I could see you right now.'

'I know exactly how you feel.' I wriggled against my pillows.

'What are you wearing?' His voice twined deep and low in my ears.

I felt a rash of goosebumps prickle over my skin. 'A blue tank top and black underwear.'

He let a long breath crush out of his lungs. 'It's snowing outside, Brenna,' he scolded, his voice a little shaky.

'My mom keeps the heat on really high.' I ran my hand over the skin that peeked out in the gap between my tank and my underwear, and I wished it was Jake's hand instead. 'So what are you wearing?'

'Just my boxers.' It was like I could feel his blush right through the phone.

'Jake Kelly, it's snowing,' I scolded back. I wondered what he looked like in just his boxers. I'm sure that was the point of this whole game. We were supposed to wonder what the other would look like, feel like. I had never actually seen his chest and stomach, but I knew he would be ripped because I had felt his muscles through his old shirts.

'I don't have pajamas or anything. If I had them I might wear them. This house lets so much wind in, you'd think you were outside.'

I felt the familiar sadness for Jake that bobbed up whenever I thought too much about where he lived or what his life was like outside of school. 'Are you cold?'

'Nah. I've got blankets. It would help if I had you here.'

'How was work today?' I didn't exactly want to get away from our topic, but it was making my head spin and my heart race, and I didn't know how to deal with it.

'Crappy and cold. My hands feel like they're going to fall off.'

'Don't you wear gloves?' I remembered how red and chapped his hands were when he walked me out after school this afternoon.

'You can't for everything. I drove the tractor today, and it's hard to grip the steering wheel and the gear lever with gloves on. I'm just bitching, though, Brenna. Work was all right because this is the week that I get the big paycheck.' His voice glowed with pride.

'What's the big paycheck?' His enthusiasm was contagious, as usual, and I found myself free-falling into the excitement with him.

'It's the one that will fix my truck. I think it'll get the motor going, and once that happens, I'm ready for my license.'

I laughed, because he sounded like such a happy little kid. 'You can't wait to get your license, huh?'

'Of course I can't wait. I mean, I was always excited, but now that I have you, I really can't wait.' I could hear the smile in his slow, deep voice.

'Why do I change things?' I had a good idea what the answer would be, but that didn't mean I didn't want to hear it from him.

'Because I'm going to be able to drive you home. I won't be so worried about you getting back and forth to school. And I'm going to take you on real dates. Like dates where I pick you up and drive you somewhere nice.' His voice mapped out so many delicious possible ways we could spend more time alone together.

'Jake, you know my parents aren't really OK with me dating yet.' I was looking forward to Jake driving too, but I was also nervous about it. I imagined sitting close to him, listening to mixes I made just for him, parking and kissing. But I also imagined having to tell Mom and Thorsten that I was dating Jake and begging permission for him to come pick me up.

'You have an entire month to get them ready for it.' Jake sounded determined. Then his voice softened. 'I couldn't stop thinking about you today.' I heard springs squeak at his end, like he'd turned over on the bed.

'Really? Why's that?' I turned over on my stomach.

'I don't really know. I was harvesting pumpkins in the snow, and I couldn't keep my mind on work.'

'Do you mean to tell me even pumpkins in the snow couldn't take your attention away from me?' I teased.

He laughed. 'Smartass. I mean I couldn't keep my mind on work. I was thinking about how much I wanted to kiss you again. And I was worried as hell about you getting home.'

'It was fine,' I lied quickly.

'It will all be different soon,' he promised. 'Then I'll come pick your cute little butt up and kiss you senseless in my truck.'

I felt a warm tingling. 'You've got a one-track mind.'

'I like you for more than the physical stuff, Bren,' he said, suddenly all serious.

'No, not me.' I felt a tickle of pure giddiness. 'The truck.'

'Well, she's a great truck.'

'Ugh,' I groaned. 'You're referring to your truck as "she".'

'You would too if you could see how pretty she is.' The note of wistfulness in his voice was half endearing, half completely frustrating.

'This conversation is too romantic for me, with all of the pumpkin and truck love. I'm going to bed.' I smiled and cozied down, ready for sweet Jake dreams.

'Not yet,' he said, his voice low again. 'I was trying to tell you, before you interrupted, that I couldn't get you out of my mind all day.'

'Are you complaining again?'

'Not at all. I'm telling you I really care about you. I worry about you all the time. And I like you. I like talking to you on the phone. I never wanted to talk on the phone to anybody before. And I like looking at you working in class. I like reading the same books as you. I just feel like we're going to be great together.'

There was a lump in my throat. 'Thanks, Jake.' My voice quivered. 'I feel the same. I feel like we're so good together.'

'I agree. And now that I got that off my chest, I've got a sexy girlfriend wearing almost nothing to go dream about until I get to see her in school tomorrow.'

'Oh, we don't have school tomorrow, Jake. Snow day,' I said, remembering the news Mom had delivered.

He groaned. 'I can't believe I'm saying this, but that sucks. All right, this is scary.'

'What's that?' I asked, and I couldn't stop smiling. I heard him get up, and a few seconds later he opened the fridge, popped a can, and drank. 'Are you drinking soda?'

'Yeah.' He laughed. 'That's all Dad buys. You sound so shocked.'

'It's the middle of the night, Jake. That's so not good for you.' I felt a little gross just thinking about chugging a soda before bed.

'Well, I'm not used to all this talking.' He paused and I heard him take a long drink and swallow. 'I need to keep hydrated. And I'm in shock that I feel so sad about a snow day.'

'Are you missing me already?'

'Don't joke about it. I really am.'

'I miss you, too.' I ran my hands along the wide, empty bed. I was suddenly so tired I couldn't keep my eyes open. 'Wow, I'm tired.'

'Sleep, then. Sweet dreams, Brenna.'

'You, too,' I said through a long yawn. 'I'll see you soon.'

And then I thought I heard something, but maybe it was sleep deprivation. Maybe it was the stress of all Jake had dropped on me in one night. But it could have been real.

I thought I heard Jake say, 'I love you.'

Chapter 9

The next morning, the sun was shining bright against the snow, which was already melting. The weather had changed completely again, leaving a chilly, soggy day that was getting warmer by the minute.

'Hey, sweetie.' Mom peeked in my room. 'I got my office assignment today and was going to run down for a bit and set up. I know it's early, but the other adjunct will be there, and I can get some serious work done. Will you be OK on your own?'

I rubbed my eyes and blinked. 'Of course. Go! Get set up. Do you need help?'

'Maybe later next week,' Mom mused. 'But no, honey, not today. Are you sure you'll be OK all day alone?'

'Mom!' I groaned. 'I love you, but you worry too much. I'm just going to veg and watch TV and read my new book. I have my cell on.' I held it up for her to see.

She kissed my face and told me to lock the doors and keep the phone by me, then left. I went to the kitchen and watched out the window as her car pulled backward down the driveway. I was glad she had her job, but there was something lonely about it, too. I had been with her every single day last year, just the two of us and Thorsten. Now we were both getting on with our own separate lives, and something in me ached for the time we had before, even as I reached out for Jake. And maybe Saxon.

I pushed boys out of my mind for a while. I made my porridge and ate, then flipped on the television. After about fifteen minutes, I turned it off again. How could people get addicted to this crap? There was absolutely nothing good on.

I took a long shower and got dressed, then straightened my room. I was just thinking about calling Jake when I heard the mechanical whine that had scared me before. I checked my make-up in the mirror, then pulled open the front door and burst into Jake's waiting arms.

'Jake!' I cried and pressed my mouth to his. He wrapped his arms around me and kissed back, opening his mouth and deepening the kiss like he was hungry for the taste of my mouth.

'It's so good to see you, babe.' He was a little

breathless when he pulled away. 'Are your parents around?'

'No.' I felt a little bit of guilt at how happy that made me feel. 'Come in. I mean, do you want to?'

'Seriously?' He grabbed my hand and followed me into the house.

I dragged him to my bedroom and we tumbled on the bed I'd just made. I was lying flat on my back and he was propped on his side, just looking down at me.

'Hi,' I said, and felt shy suddenly.

'Hey.' He smiled, and I put a finger on his eyetooth, then pulled away. He traced a finger down my nose. 'You're so beautiful.'

I swallowed hard. 'You too.' He laughed. 'Or handsome.'

'Whatever.' He shrugged. 'As long as you like what you see, I'm gonna consider myself lucky.' Then he lowered his head and kissed me softly on my lips. I stretched toward him for more, but he pulled back and kissed me on my cheek, then my jaw, then my ear, then my neck, then my collarbone. He stopped at the little dip between my collarbones. He was breathing pretty fast.

'Is it hard to be with me?' I felt nervous about what to do next, how far to go.

'No,' he said too quickly.

'I mean, is it hard to kiss and fool around, even if you know it won't lead to sex?'

'No.' He shook his head so hard his hair fell into his eyes. 'I want to take things slowly with you.'

'You haven't asked what *I* want.' I looked him right in his light gray eyes.

'Don't do that, Bren,' he whispered, pressing his forehead down on my shoulder.

'Do what?'

'Tempt me,' he said in a strangled voice that was muffled by my shirt.

'I'm not trying to.' I immediately felt like a tease.

'I know.' He looked back up at me. 'It's just easy to do more than you mean to. I don't want to do that to you. But tell me what you do want.' He closed his eyes and set his mouth in a hard line.

It was funny to see him so serious. It wasn't like I was going to ask him anything crazy. 'I want to see you . . .' I started, then felt myself blush. 'I want to see you with your shirt off.'

He looked relieved. He jumped back off my bed and kicked his boots off. Then he lifted the hem of his shirt a little, showing me a glimpse of flat, hard stomach. To my complete shame, I felt my mouth start to water.

'Looking good.' I sat up on my elbows.

Jake shook his hips jerkily in what I imagined he thought was a sexy dance. I laughed so hard I could hardly draw breath.

'Are you ready for this?' He pointed at me and raised his eyebrows.

'I was born ready.' I wiggled on the bed.

He turned so his back was to me and took his shirt off in that weird way guys do it: he pulled the back collar and yanked it over his head.

His back was nice, firm and bulgy with muscles. His shoulders and biceps were also bunched and powerful looking. When he turned, his face was bright red, but I can't say I looked at it too long. His pecs were hard flat planes of muscle, and his stomach was ridged and defined all the way down.

'Ooh,' I sighed. 'You have a real six-pack.'

He smiled and crawled onto the bed, his strong arms boxed around me. I reached my hand up and moved it along his newly revealed body. He closed his eyes. I didn't. Hello, I had the world's hottest boyfriend! There was no way I wasn't going to take a good long look.

I slid my palms along his ridged skin, bumping all the way down to the line of his boxers. It was a little strange to touch him so intimately, but the truth was, I'd thought about doing this a thousand times. If there was one word going through my mind, it was *finally*. His hips were narrow and a little bony. I could see them at the edge of his pants, which he wore a bit too low. I dipped my fingers under the band of his boxers to the skin just above the region where I knew I shouldn't go. He sucked his breath in through his teeth, and I ran my fingers under the elastic, in the front and back. I wasn't going to go any further, and it didn't look like I needed to. I could tell that he was completely hard.

When I pulled my hands away, he let his body settle on top of mine and kissed me deeply, hungrily. I moaned into his mouth and felt my own sound tumble into his body.

He pulled away and steadied himself. He was pressed against me, and it felt good. I liked the fact that he was turned on, and I liked that it was because of me.

His hands slid up my shirt, to just under where my bra ended. His fingers felt so hot on my stomach and rib cage that I was surprised they didn't singe my skin. One thumb, then the other traced the skin just beneath my underwire.

'Is this OK?' he asked vaguely, but I knew exactly what he wanted, and since I wanted it, too, I nodded.

His hands pressed up under the cups of my bra,

and the contrast of our skin made me gasp. His hands were rough, hard and scratchy. The skin of my breasts was very soft. His hands pulled against them firmly, squeezed and pressed. I couldn't believe how good it felt. He kissed my neck and the space behind my ears. I lifted my hips and rubbed against his thigh, pressing myself to him. He increased the pressure and speed of his sure fingers, and his lips traced down along my neck and to my collarbone.

I was warm and wet from it, and wriggling against him. His hands continued to move over my skin and my breath came out in short pants that made me want to grind my hips against him with more force. When I felt his calloused fingers on my nipples, there was a sudden shuddering between my legs. It felt like it radiated out, filling me with a warm, shaky heat. My body went stiff, and I pressed hard to him and moaned a little. Jake pressed his mouth over mine and kissed me fiercely again.

He closed his eyes and pulled his hands from under my shirt slowly, as if he were using all of the strength in his body to do it.

He rolled off me, so we were lying next to one another.

Jake stared at the ceiling, breathing heavily. 'Did you come?'

'I don't know.' I was surprised he noticed what I thought was a very slight tremor in my body. 'How would I know for sure?'

He laughed and reached for my hand. When he found it he squeezed hard. 'It's different for guys. I mean, I know when it happens for me.'

'It felt really good.' My voice sounded completely dreamy in my own ears.

'Very glad I could help.' I looked at his profile, the funny crooked smile and his messy hair, and I kissed his ear.

'Did you come?' I put my mouth close to his ear.

'No.' He turned to look at me. 'I don't need to.'

'I think you might want to reconsider that.' I looked right at his pants where he was obviously still hard.

'I'll take care of it later.'

'Is there, um . . . is there something I could do?' And I did want to. When my fingers were almost where they shouldn't have been, I'd wanted to go further. I was curious about his body, and I wanted a little of the power I knew would come when I touched him. I had been thinking about him, dreaming about him, and I wanted to touch him, plain and simple.

'Brenna.' He groaned and slung an arm over his eyes. 'Don't do this to me.'

'Do what? I want to help.' I brushed my lips over

his cheekbone and his forearm, the one covering his eyes.

'Are you sure?' he asked, his voice choked.

'Of course. I want you to be happy.'

He took my hand and guided it down his pants, and left it where I had stopped before. He undid the button of his jeans and unzipped the zipper. He dipped his hand under the band of his boxers and pushed them down, exposing his penis.

I tried not to look too shocked, but it was the first time I had ever seen one close up. I couldn't judge very accurately, but it looked big to me. It was surprisingly pink. I ran my hand lightly over it and he shuddered a little. I was surprised it was so hard but also really smooth and soft, and warm.

'What do you like?' I asked.

He still had one hand over his eyes. I couldn't tell if he felt embarrassed, or if he was just overwhelmed. 'I use lotion,' he said, and I could see him blush. 'And I just . . . uh, rub it.'

I hopped off my bed and got a tube of hand lotion. I squirted some in my hand and wrapped my fingers around it uncertainly. I rubbed up and down.

'Like this?' I asked.

He put his hand over mine and squeezed more than I would have thought would be comfortable. He helped me set a rhythm and after a few seconds, he removed his hand. It was just me, touching Jake in the most intimate way in the quiet of my room. I watched his face, and saw his mouth was hanging open slightly. He had moved his hands to his sides, and his fingers were balled into fists around the covers. His eyes were screwed tightly shut, and it almost looked like he was in pain. Soon he was jerking his hips up slightly, and I moved faster, when he suddenly half sat up and knocked my hand away, covering the tip of his penis quickly. He fell back and moaned, his hand still over his groin.

'Brenna.' He shook his head and smiled.

I felt a strange sense of pride and uncertainty when we did something new together for the first time.

'Do you need a tissue or something?' I asked, returning his smile. He turned red and nodded.

I went to the bathroom and grabbed a box from the closet, planning to keep it under my bed. I didn't even want to think about why I did that instead of just grabbing a handful, because that would be admitting my complete deviant transformation. I stopped in front of the mirror and took a quick inventory.

Sometimes when I was a little kid, I'd look at my own reflection on my birthday and really expect to see a change I would notice. I felt that way now, looking at myself after being with Jake. It was the same old me, but I expected something to look new or weird or changed. But it was just the same old Brenna.

I handed Jake the box and he mumbled a thank you, cleaned up and threw them in my wastebasket, then pulled his shirt back on.

He seemed suddenly sullen and quiet.

'Jake, is something wrong?' I was surprised he wasn't happier.

'No.' He sat on the edge of my bed. 'I just feel a little bad. Did I go too fast for you?'

'It's more than I've done before,' I admitted. I sat next to him and put my arm around his waist, kissing his neck. 'If I didn't want to do it, I would have told you so. Do you believe me?'

'Yeah.' He smiled crookedly. 'You're pretty direct. You're actually really direct.' His voice changed, like he was shocked by my 'directness'.

'Is that bad?' I felt just a little offended.

'No. Not at all. Just, before, I was always in control, if I can even say that. I was always drunk. And as far as I know, so was the girl.'

'So, was this the first time you've fooled around sober?' That was a crazy thought.

'Yeah.' He put his arms around me and dragged me onto his lap. 'But, more important, it's the first time

I've ever done that with you. Everything's going to be really different with you.'

'Because I'm so direct?' I narrowed my eyes at him. But I also felt a little rush of happiness. Because I wanted it to be better with me.

He laughed. 'I meant it as a compliment. Was it really . . . um, was it really the first time?'

'Yes! Was I terrible?' I wasn't being humble; I really thought it was pretty awkward.

'No,' he said solemnly, shaking his head. 'Not at all. I've never been so turned on in my life.'

I kissed him and soon we were back to lying on the bed, kissing and holding. Now that he had come he wasn't being as aggressive, but I liked it both ways.

I was kind of surprised I'd liked it so much. When Jake first told me about how he fooled around with so many girls, I thought it might be cheap or disappointing. I think the difference was I really cared about Jake, so instead of the whole thing being awkward, it felt freeing and safe and good. Really good.

He just held me, and I was breathing the smell of him in when he sat up in a panic.

'What time is it, Bren?' He grabbed around for his boots.

I checked my bedside clock. 'Three-thirty. Why?'

'Damn it, I've got to leave.' He pulled his boots on. 'I still have work today.'

It was on the tip of my tongue to ask him to skip work, but I decided against it. Much as I wanted him around, I knew his job was really important to him, and he needed the money.

I walked him out the door and stood by while he put on his jacket and hat. The sun was already low, and it was getting colder by the minute. I shivered a little, and Jake pulled me into his arms and kissed me.

'Go inside, Brenna. I don't want you to be cold.' He rubbed his hands up and down my arms.

'OK.' But I couldn't uproot myself from the spot right in front of him.

He kissed me again. 'I'm so glad I got to see you. And I had a really good time.'

'If there are no snowstorms, I'll see you tomorrow.' I kissed him.

'Are we going to talk tonight?'

'Yeah, we will. Call me when you're showered and in bed after work.'

I hated catching him before he took some time to clean up and eat. I knew he would never turn down my phone call, which was sweet but so impractical.

'I will.' He looked like he wanted to say something else. I thought about the last words he might have said on the phone the night before. My heart was so full of feeling for him, it felt like it might burst out of my chest. I knew the words he wanted to say were the same ones I wanted to say. I was feeling brave, so I put my hands on his neck and pulled him close to me. 'I love you, Jake,' I said. I meant it with every beat of my heart.

His eyes went wide and for a minute he was perfectly still, just looking at me. Then he untied his tongue. 'I love you, Brenna,' he said shakily, then leaned in and kissed me hard again.

The next instant he was on his dirt bike and flying through the wooded space behind our house, heading to Zinga's and away from me for now. I went back into my room and lay on the bed where he and I had just been and wallowed in the sad emptiness of it.

The rest of the day went by quickly. I felt a little bit like I was in a daze. Mom called to tell me she had her office almost set up and was going to pick up Chinese food. I was glad to have her company at home, but I also felt an incredible sense of guilt when I thought about having Jake over. I cleaned up in the living room and kitchen, and even vacuumed and mopped the floors as a kind of self-imposed penance.

When my phone rang, I should have realized it was too early to be Jake, but I was keyed up and ready to hear his voice again. It made me a little happy that my heart sank at Saxon's voice.

'Hey, Blix. We on for next Saturday?'

'I have to check with my mom,' I said honestly.

He sniggered. 'Didn't have the guts to talk to Jake?'

'Jake's cool with it.' I was fully aware that I was seriously stretching the truth. 'He was wondering if you could go get him first – you know, to help load up his bike and all that.'

The line was quiet for a while, then Saxon's voice came over again, hot and deep. 'Help with his bike, huh? Have you taken a look at Jake lately? He's pretty ripped. I think he just wants to make sure there's no Brenna and Saxon alone time. Am I right?'

'I thought you wanted us to be friends. Why are you always looking for reasons to screw everything up?' The fact that Jake and I had shared what we did made me feel like I had a protective shell that Saxon couldn't break through.

'Cool it.' Saxon sounded upset, and I felt a thrill of triumph. Maybe he didn't hold all of the cards after all. Maybe I could play this game just as well as he could. 'I'll be at Jake's Saturday morning to take him to the race. Do you want me to help with Mom? Maybe I can ask her for you?'

I felt my anger bubble up, but I forced it back down.

'Don't worry about it.' Maybe the shell wasn't quite as thick as I would have liked. 'By the way,' I said suddenly. 'Monday's forecast is sunny and warm. Don't come pick me up.'

'Your mom and I had a deal.' His voice was sharp.

'My mom won't want me driving with you if the weather is nice. She harped on about your smoking after you left,' I lied. 'I mean, I know my mom seems super sweet, but she's just really old-fashioned about things.'

I could hear Saxon struggling on the line, trying to see through what I said and judge whether it was crap or not. But Saxon wasn't me. Seeing through crap was *my* specialty. Dishing crap was his.

'I didn't check the weather,' he finally said.

'Wow, it would be pretty pathetic of you to stoop to checking the weather every day. How about I just call you when I feel up for a ride?' I couldn't help gloating a little at how effectively I had turned the tables on him.

He chuckled. 'You're deceptively good, Blix. Just the perfect amount of bitch to be sexy.'

I felt my ears go hot. 'Whatever, Saxon. I'll see you in class on Monday.' I threw my phone on my bed.

Mom and I chatted during dinner, and she turned in early, not even watching her favorite cop show. I guess it had been a long day for her. I went to my bedroom and did a little extra homework on Golding. I also read ahead for American government. I wanted to make sure I kept up with Saxon. I hated to give him the cocky satisfaction of doing better in class than I did. I also wanted to work on a special Folly shirt for Kelsie. I had come up with a design using a picture of Chris and her I had snapped a few days before. Mostly my reason for entering dork mode was to keep myself out of hussy mode. If my brain wasn't bogged down with English boys gone crazy and Minnesota voting patterns, I would have been thinking about Jake Kelly and how good it felt to put my hands all over him today.

The rest of the weekend and Monday consisted of me talking to Jake whenever I had the chance and avoiding Saxon. By the time Tuesday had rolled around, Saxon hadn't said a word about the race on Saturday, and I was hoping he wouldn't. But there were three more days before Saturday, and that could be an impossibly long time. When the phone finally rang that night, my heart thudded with pure happiness.

'Hello!'

'Brenna.' Jake's voice simmered in my ears. 'How was your day after school?'

'I missed you. But I cleaned the house and did homework. How about you?'

'Just work. It was cold as hell, and I couldn't stop thinking about you.' I heard a zipper in the background.

'Are you taking off your jacket?'

'Yeah. How did you hear that?'

'Jake, you should take a shower and get ready for bed. Why didn't you do that before you called me?' I didn't like to think he was still freezing and achy. 'What about dinner?'

'I'm standing in my kitchen cooking right now.' I could hear him doing things in the background. I heard his keys hit the countertop and the cabinets bang open. I could hear the sharp clatter of the dishes he took out of the cabinet. 'That's so cute.'

'What?' I demanded.

'Your little bossy temper tantrums.' I heard a pan clang. 'No one's given a crap what I do in a long time.'

'What's for dinner?' My heart squeezed like it had been pressed into a vice thinking of Jake alone with no one to keep him company.

'Hot dogs and beans. And a soda.'

'You're going to die,' I gagged. 'That's the most disgusting dinner imaginable.'

'It's my Tuesday dinner.' I heard him rip a package open.

'Every Tuesday?'

'Yep.' I heard a loud sizzle. 'Monday is eggs, Wednesday is sandwich day, Thursday is pasta, and Friday is TV dinner night. Every week for as long as I can remember.'

'Are you serious?' It was so disgusting and sad.

'Yeah. I'm in charge of food shopping. My dad just drops me off with some cash and comes back to pick me up. I know exactly how much I can buy with the money he leaves me. And it's all stuff I can make pretty easily.'

'What about weekends?' I couldn't imagine eating such a limited amount of food. What about fruit and vegetables? Fresh breads? Cheeses? Desserts?

'We go out to Arby's sometimes. Or I just find something. I used to eat at friends' houses.' I could hear him eating. It must have been hot, because he was doing the inverted blow.

'I feel bad for you.' I tried to make my voice light, but my joke was too close to the truth. I really did feel sad when I thought about his pathetic dinners.

He laughed. 'I won't say no if you want to come over and spoil me with your cooking. But don't feel bad. It's not totally unhealthy. It keeps me full, and it's easy to make. And it hasn't killed me yet.'

I couldn't put my finger on exactly what bothered me about it. Maybe it was just how lonely and monotonous it was. My dinners were always at least eaten with Mom. I realized company was probably the exact reason Jake had chosen to call me while he ate instead of after.

'Maybe you could add some salads in once in a while. And switch to juice or water sometimes,' I recommended.

'I'll do it if you think it's a good idea,' he said easily. 'But I don't really want to talk about what food I eat.'

I lay back on my bed and breathed deeply. I imagined I could still smell his scent lingering on the bedclothes. 'So, what do you want to talk about?' I asked while I nuzzled into the pillows.

'You and me. I had a good time when we hung out Friday.' There was that feeling when he ended the last sentence that made me think he was going to slap a big 'but' on. I waited, but he didn't.

'Me too.' I sighed.

'But it can't happen again for a while,' he said firmly.

So there was a *but*.

'It was great. But it was too risky. You're not experienced, and you don't know what you're asking for.

I've never felt so out of control. I don't trust myself with you.'

'So now you know what I want and don't want?' I found both my hands knotting into fists.

'No!' he said, too fast. 'Well, maybe. I just know more about it in general.'

'Know more about drunk, awful sex,' I argued, striking low and mean because I was so mad, I was beyond being reasonable. 'I liked being with you. I didn't feel pressured, and I definitely don't regret what happened.' I felt like a gigantic weight landed in the center of my chest. 'I don't think I'm cool with you calling the shots.' I knew my voice sounded a little wavery, but I didn't care. I needed to make my point.

'What we said when I left . . .' he said, trying a new tack.

'That we loved each other, Jake. That's what we said.' Now I was getting pissed off. Here he was, telling me the limits of our relationship, and he wasn't even brave enough to say the word *love*.

'Right. That.' He stumbled around it awkwardly. 'I meant it. I do. I love you. And I don't want this to be like the other times.'

I rubbed my fingers over my eyes. 'Jake, I thought you told me every other time has been a one-night stand with some girl you barely cared about.'

'Yeah.' I could hear the frustration in his voice.

'Then it doesn't really have anything to do with sex, does it?' I argued logically. 'It's about caring for the person.'

How could he argue with that?

'You don't understand, Brenna,' he said patiently. 'You're really new to this.'

In my head, I opened my mouth and screamed into the phone. In real life, I couldn't wake my mother.

'This is so stupid. You're lumping me with those other girls you used to date. This is unfair.' I sounded childish, and I couldn't care less.

'Brenna, I just want to protect you. Things went a lot further and faster than I expected them to today. We should just be careful.' He spoke with an authority that I didn't want to respect, even though I knew he technically had more experience and understood more.

'Fine.' It wasn't fine. It was far from fine. It was a nasty, messy, tangled knot that only got more snarled the more I thought about it.

'Are you OK?'

I'd said *fine*. Didn't he know *fine* was the word that always meant, *no, not even close to fine*? Usually I was more direct. Isn't that what Jake told me about myself just a few hours ago? But he wasn't listening to reason. It was funny that he kept trying to pin it on me when he was the one with regrets.

'You regret what we did.' The full reality of it dawned on me the minute the words popped out of my mouth, and it made my heart ache to imagine that he felt the opposite of what I felt.

'Just that we went so fast.' He took a deep breath.

'We didn't have sex!' I cried.

'There aren't many more steps between what we did and sex,' he said knowingly.

'I'm not an idiot, Jake!' I was on the brink of tears. What happened was wonderful, amazing. It was nothing to be ashamed of or to regret. 'If I decide to have sex, I will. And if I decide not to have sex, I won't.'

'You're not ready to make those choices,' he said, his voice still annoyingly calm.

'I am too!' I practically yelled. 'I am ready to choose, and I certainly don't need you to decide for me.'

'Brenna, I didn't mean to make you upset.'

'Yeah, OK. I have to get to sleep. I'll see you to-morrow.' My throat burned and I closed my eyes tight in an attempt to stop the tears that clawed behind my lids from falling.

'Wait—'

I clicked the phone off.

I squeezed the phone in my hand and shook it. How could he be so pigheaded? How could he feel like this was something he could decide for me? I lay on the bed, but I knew it would be a long time before I fell asleep.

I tossed and turned, looked at my phone and ran my fingers over the screen, ready to dial his number six different times. Every time, I stopped myself. We would just wind up having the same roundabout conversation and get nowhere.

Finally I closed my eyes and counted my breaths. I counted to ten on my inhale and ten on my exhale. I kept doing it until I fell fast asleep.

Chapter 10

The next morning I dressed extra cute. I straightened my hair and trimmed my fringe a little. I put on dramatic make-up and wore a tight V-neck tunic T-shirt I had designed, and my favorite jeans with Converse sneakers. I opened the window of my room and stuck my head out. It was cool, but not cold.

'Morning, Mom!' I called when I heard her pottering around.

'Hey, Bren.' She smiled when I stepped into the kitchen. 'Porridge is on the table. Did you sleep OK?'

'Yeah, thanks. I read online that the weather is supposed to stay pretty nice. Is it OK if I take my bike? I told Saxon I'd only call if you didn't think it was a good idea.'

She sighed, a long-suffering sigh. 'Go ahead.' She shook her head. 'But I have my school computer set up to get the forecasts, so don't think you're going to be on that thing if it's supposed to be nasty out.'

'I promise I won't.' I kissed her and headed to school.

It made my heart skip to feel my blood racing and the air rushing into my lungs and back out. I thought about Jake and how patronizing he had been when we last spoke. I thought about Saxon trying to force me to ride with him. Screw them both!

I whipped into Frankford's front area and ran to English. Mr Dawes was handing out a quiz. Everyone groaned and mumbled.

'Honors English,' Mr Dawes droned. 'It means I'm not your babysitter. If I tell you to read through chapter ten by Tuesday, I think it's more than fair to quiz you on the reading on Wednesday.'

A whiny girl raised her hand and asked what to do if we had left the book at school.

'Then, Ms Henson, you would be unprepared, wouldn't you? Here's some advice: take your book home. Every day.' An evil smile curled over his face and the girl huffed.

Devon muttered under his breath. I glared at his back, but decided not to engage with him. Devon didn't need a broken nose because my boyfriend was an idiot. I finished the test, double-checked the answers and turned it over on the desk. Mr Dawes saw that I had finished and motioned for me to bring it up. He graded it while I stood there, then did that crazy, embarrassing thing teachers sometimes do.

'Class!' he called. Every other student looked up with bleary eyes and vicious mutters. 'Ms Blixen has completed her quiz and made a perfect one hundred. Consider your average ruined.' He laughed cruelly, and I slunk back to my seat and opened the book to read a little more. If the class was going to hate me, at least I could get the best grades and truly earn their loathing.

Mr Dawes collected the papers and put some notes on the board. He finished grading the quizzes while we wrote down the notes. Then he handed the quizzes back, and put even more notes on the board. We copied until another teacher poked his head in, and Mr Dawes went out to talk to him.

Devon Conner turned around in his seat and looked at me. 'I got a seventy-five,' he announced.

'What are you talking about?' I flipped the pages of my book with my thumb.

'The quiz.' Devon pointed to my paper 'You got a hundred.'

'What's with you?' I snarled. 'I'm smart, Conner. Accept it. And get over the fact that I do Share Time. Obviously, lots of smart people do it. Why does it amaze you so much?'

'I was going to say that you probably have a lot more work to do since you have your normal classes here and all your work at Tech, but you still got a hundred.' He stared at me with wide, unblinking eyes.

'Oh,' I said, because what else could you say in the face of such social awkwardness? 'Well, study more. I study a lot. And I've read the book before.'

'Don't you think it's kind of boring?' His shoulders relaxed very slightly.

I rolled my eyes. 'It's kind of dense, but that doesn't mean it's boring. I mean, a bunch of boys going crazy and killing each other on an island? Not exactly boring.'

He nodded. 'We have a group project on this at the end of the unit.' He gave me an expectant look.

'OK?'

'Will you be in my group?' he blurted.

I wanted to say something mean and blow him off, but there was something weirdly likeable about Devon Conner. Maybe it was just his directness. He reminded me a little of me. 'Sure. Just don't think I'm going to be doing all the work, partner. I don't get Cs.'

'Thanks.' He looked at me with his small eyes, blinked nervously a few times, then turned around and went back to reading. I noticed he was about three chapters behind. That made his C a fairly decent grade; it also warned me I might not have such an easy time reining in Devon Conner.

Saxon looked up when I walked into government and stared at me as I sat down. We were setting up a telephone polling survey we would have to carry out later. 'You all have cell phones!' Sanotoni barked. 'We'll call on Friday. The team with the most responses wins.'

'What do we win?' asked shrew-faced Lynn.

'A trip to the polling booth next week,' Sanotoni answered. 'All-day pass out of class.'

I was going to raise my hand and ask about my schedule. I didn't want to win if it meant missing Tech. It would also be a day alone with Saxon, which was a bad idea no matter what I might secretly want. In the end, I decided the simplest thing was to make sure I didn't win. It would be easy enough; I just wouldn't be that good a caller.

'Hey, buddy.' Saxon looked me up and down.

'What are you looking at?' I snapped.

He gave me a slow, calculating smile. 'You look hot when you're riled, Blix. Come. Sit. Learn.'

He was writing! He actually had a pen in his hand and was working.

'What are you doing?' I couldn't tear my eyes away from the pen clasped in his hand. Had I ever seen

Saxon willingly hold a pen during class? I couldn't recall a single instance.

His black eyes danced with evil mischief when he looked my way. 'I'm winning a date with you. Granted, it's the frigging lamest date on earth, but I'm winning it anyway.'

'The poll?' I asked dumbly.

'I saw your face when Sanotoni announced it. You're going to throw our chances,' he guessed. 'But I'm going to use my many, many skills to win.'

'We're only a two-person group,' I pointed out. 'You drove Lynn off the first day.'

'That nag will have the most hang-ups in the class,' he said with absolute conviction. He looked over at her and shook his head. 'She would have brought us down. Of course, I might not be right about you.' He looked up at me again and smiled, a gleaming, wolfish grin.

'What do you mean?' I asked narrowly, clicking my pen so fast it was like my thumb was having a spasm.

'You're a sneaky one, Blix.' He put one hand over my clicking hand and squeezed. 'I can't wrap my head around you. Even if you want to throw this, you might not be able to. A date with me might be more than you can resist.'

'Saxon, first of all it wouldn't be a date.' I tried to pull my hand out of his grasp, but he held tight. I relaxed my hand and he released his hold, finger by finger. I shook my hand out and glared at him. 'Secondly, I don't have time to screw around at the polling booth. Third, I have no interest in sharing any more time with you than I have to.'

'Liar,' he muttered under his breath.

I gritted my teeth and went to work. The thing was, I was so busy being mad at Jake that I wasn't sharp enough to deal with Saxon. By the end of the period, Saxon and I had completed writing out our polling survey and got Sanotoni's stamp of approval.

He clapped us both on the back. 'Look at these mighty brains!' he said, his rough laughter punctuating his words. 'Rule change. Any team finished by tomorrow gets Thursday and Friday to call.'

Our classmates looked at us with steely glares. Every single hair on my neck prickled in anticipation. This was war.

'Great,' I said under my breath to Saxon. 'Now we have an entire battalion of brilliant geeks out for our blood.'

'They have drive, but they have no charisma.' He put his hands behind his head and leaned on the back two legs of his chair. 'We'll take this by a landslide.' Then he let the chair drop hard.

The bell rang, we filed into the corridor, and Saxon

threw an arm around my shoulder. It was the kind of simple, friendly gesture that people exchange all of the time. When they're friends. But Saxon and I weren't. My blood ran hot as I felt the long length of his body against mine. I could smell the musky clean scent of his deodorant, my face bumped against his solid shoulder. Something in me prickled and squirmed.

He looked down at me, nestled in the crook of his arm, and pulled me closer against him with one rough jerk, turning my body so we were face to face. Now both of his arms were linked around my shoulders. His mouth was a few inches away from mine. I could smell him: cigarettes and orange Tic Tacs.

'I have to go.' I tried to pull back out of his embrace, but he held me closer, and I could feel the lean muscles of his arms at my back.

'Don't.' His voice was velvety and rich in my ears. It was an invitation I almost wanted to accept. Almost.

'I have to.' My eyes met his, and I could see his pupils dilate, making his eyes look completely, endlessly black. 'Let me go.'

'Skip art.' His eyes smoldered like hot coals. He pulled me a little closer.

'No.' I snapped out of his spell. I pushed at him with both hands, and his body was solid muscle under my palms. 'No, Saxon. Go.'

He shrugged, but there was a gleam of anger that flashed in his eyes. 'Fine, Blix. I'm gone.'

I saw him stalk down the corridor and grab the arm of Karen Tanner. He smiled and whispered something to her. She smiled back and practically rubbed herself against him. He didn't even look around before he went out of the side doors, dragging Karen behind.

I went into the craft class and sat by Kelsie and Chris. My head was spinning, and I hoped they'd be so wrapped up in each other they wouldn't notice if I sat quietly, lost in my own thoughts. No such luck.

'Brenna! Brenna!' Kelsie waved her hand in front of my face. 'Are you OK?'

'Fine.' I fished for some semblance of a smile that would convince them. 'I think the long weekend just threw my sleep patterns off.'

'Are you sure that's it?' She leaned away from Chris to give us a chance for private confession. I nodded. She gave me a long look, then reached into her school bag. 'Well, I have something that might wake you up. We just got the Folly T-shirts this morning!' She shook one out so I could see it.

'Wow,' I breathed. It was very cool to see my design one a T-shirt and to know that, soon, a whole lot of people would be wearing it. My final design was a silhouette of all four band-members surrounding an exploding 'Folly'. I had outlined each figure in neon colors, and the entire effect was bright, but also edgy. 'It's cool, right?' I asked.

Kelsie nodded and waved to the shirt as if to say, 'See for yourself!'

'Oh.' I leaned over, excited. 'I forgot. I made you a special one at home.'

I pulled it out of my bag. It was Kelsie and Chris in profile with an exploding heart behind them and tiny 'Folly's with hearts for the Os.

'Oh my God.' Kelsie squealed and did a quick, energetic dance. 'This is so cool! Chris, look at this!'

'Bren, that's rad,' Chris said. 'Seriously. Do you have the design lying around? This would be an awesome shirt for the Folly fans who are a little ... softer.'

Kelsie glared a little, but Chris kissed her forehead quickly, and she smiled at him.

'Yeah, I have it saved on my memory stick.' I fished around in my bag and handed it to him. 'It's under "Folly Hearts".'

'Love it.' Chris jumped up to go to an open lab computer in the corner of the room. 'Thanks, Bren.' He ruffled my hair as he walked by.

'Chris is so nice,' I said as Kelsie watched him walk across the room, and I knew that look of love on her face. It was the exact look I saw in the mirror when I was thinking about Jake.

'Yeah.' Kelsie sighed. 'He asked me out last year, but I turned him down.'

'Really?' They seemed so well-suited, it was odd to think Kelsie ever had a reason to say no to him.

'I just didn't want to date right then.' She shrugged, her dozens of silver bracelets clattering together when she threw her hands up. 'And he seemed really intense, like he'd want to be boyfriend and girlfriend right away. I thought it would be more fun to date around.'

'Was it?' I asked, curious. 'Dating around' was what Mom always encouraged.

'Yes and no.' Kelsie wound her dark hair into a makeshift bun and stuck two colored pencils in it. 'It was fun to go on dates, but the guys who want to date around aren't usually interested in conversation and art and music, if you know what I mean.' She raised her eyebrows.

'I hear you.' Kelsie went back to her pottery project and I tangled with my sad macramé mess for a few minutes. 'Kelsie?'

'Yeah?' She was concentrating on her clay.

'How much do you and Chris, um, fool around?' I closed my eyes a little as I waited for the answer to my brazen question.

Kelsie stopped working, but she didn't look like she was going to faint or anything. 'We haven't had sex.'

'Oh.' I bit my lip.

'We've done other stuff.' Kelsie wiped some clay off her hands with a rag and folded them in front of her.

'Is there . . . do you guys ever disagree about how far is too far?' I looked down at my ugly, badly knotted macramé effort. It felt a little like I was looking at the mess Jake and I had made of our relationship.

'Chris isn't a virgin, so there's that. He's not pressuring. Not now anyway. But sometimes I want to go further because I'm curious. But it's such a big step, and I want to make sure I'm doing it with someone I really care about, not just out of curiosity.' She bit her bottom lip thoughtfully. 'Why is Ms Sexy Mama Blixen asking these questions?'

'Jake and I were fooling around the other day. And I felt really good about it. Then we talked on the phone, and he basically said he didn't feel comfortable with it because he didn't want it to end up like all the other times.' I shoved the knotted strings across the table and rubbed my temples in an attempt to squash the headache that was slowly throbbing to life.

'What did you say?' Kelsie leaned toward me, her eyes shiny with interest.

'I told him he had no right to tell me how far I should go with my body and that he didn't run the relationship. Then I hung up on him.' I offered her a sheepish half-smile.

Kelsie crowed, obviously delighted with me. 'Holy crap! Bren, you are so awesome! That's exactly what I would have said if I'd had half your guts. Good for you! The fact that Jake has all of this baggage sucks, but he has to deal with it. Not dump it on you.'

'He never called back.' I bit my lip and tried not to think about the fact that our little fight might have tangled into a knot that would be impossible to undo.

'Jake seems really nervous with you, Brenna.' Kelsie rubbed a piece of clay between her fingertips slowly. 'You know his mom died when he was really young?'

'Yeah. How did you know?' My senses prickled.

'Jake used to be . . . with one of Chris's cousins. She said he was always super emotional about his mom, and the big fight he had with Saxon was over her.'

'What happened?' I believed Jake when he told me his version of the night, and it made sense that if he had been as drunk as he said, he wouldn't have remembered many details.

'She didn't say. Just that it was about Jake's mom. Anyway, he's probably got issues. Like with women.' I looked at her curiously. 'With women leaving him.' She gave me a look and nodded her head.

'Oh.' I felt deflated, like all the strength suddenly seeped out of me. 'So I was probably overly harsh to him?'

'No. Just because he has stuff he's dealing with doesn't mean you should become some kind of door-mat. I'm proud you spoke up for yourself.' She put one clay-crusted hand on mine and patted. 'If Jake really cares about you as much as he says he does, he'll think about what you had to say.'

I nodded. Before I knew it, class was over and I was headed for PE. I was surprised to see Saxon on the soccer field after his abrupt departure with Karen Tanner, but there he was, hooting and calling when-ever I finished a lap like all was fine between us. Coach Dunn tried to corner me to ask about track, but I managed to slip away from her. I sat quietly through lunch, brooding.

'What's up, Blix?' Saxon threw a chip at me. 'There's still food on your plate. What's wrong with you?'

I had been mulling over everything that had happened since Jake first told me about his big break-down. I looked at Saxon, his black eyes laughing, his mouth twisted in a self-confident smile, and I felt a burning hatred for him.

'What did you say to Jake that last night you two hung out?' I asked suddenly.

The entire table went dead quiet. Saxon stood and grabbed me under the elbow, then marched me out of the lunchroom, past the teachers on duty.

'She said she feels like she's going to puke!' he called, and we were given a wide berth. He brought me outside, next to the bike rack. It was warmer than it had been, but still too cold to stand outside without a jacket on. 'What the hell was that about?' he shouted in my face.

I shivered, but I didn't want him to see me shake, so I clenched my teeth and held my body rigid. 'I just want to know what you said to Jake. The night you broke his tooth.' I crossed my arms over my chest.

'I didn't say a thing!' he yelled, then ran a hand through his hair. Saxon had lost all his cool. He wasn't even trying to act like he was keeping it together.

'Liar!' I yelled back at him, my lips trembling in the cold, and my voice echoed in the chilly air. 'You're a liar,' I repeated, more calmly.

He looked at me and licked his lips, opened his mouth and closed it. 'I didn't say a thing Jake didn't already know. I was just warning him.' His eyes begged me to believe him.

'About what?' The wind whipped my hair across my face and threw me off balance, closer to Saxon than I wanted to be.

'About ending up like his dad.' Saxon gritted his teeth.

'You mean the drinking?' I remembered Jake telling me about his father's drinking and how it didn't stop him from getting into it. But I thought Saxon was the one who got him started?

'That,' he growled. 'And the stupid girls.' He grabbed his hair with his fists in obvious frustration and let go with a grunt. He looked completely wild and predatory, different than I'd ever seen him.

'What do you mean?' My face got hot just thinking about all the other girls.

'I told you, Jake slept with every girl who looked at him and smiled. That kid seriously couldn't keep it in his pants. And he was drinking all of the time. Sleeping with girls who were looking for someone just like him.' He looked at me coldly, searching my face to see if I was going to respond to what he said.

'I know this stuff.' I was glad I had the cold to blame all my shaking on. 'Jake told me everything he remembers.'

Saxon snorted. 'Well, that's not everything, trust me, Blix. That night, there was a girl there. No good. She was looking to get pregnant. She wanted to hook Jake.'

'How do you know?' I tried hard not to look too shocked. Pregnant? Who would want to get pregnant in high school? Had it happened?

He shook his head. 'You wouldn't get it. You come from a whole different world. She wanted to make sure Jake stuck around. He'd slept with her before, but didn't even remember her name. She was talking about it. How she'd tried poking holes in the condom with another guy. Whatever, she was a skank.'

'What does this have to do with Jake's mom?' My head was spinning so hard I wanted to sit down or lean against something. But there was nothing near me except for Saxon, and I wasn't about to lean on him.

'His mom was the worst mom imaginable.' Saxon practically spit. 'She was more interested in who she could get in the sack than taking care of Jake. Once, she got drunk and told Jake's dad that she didn't even know if Jake was his.'

'Oh my God.' Was that why Jake and his dad had such a tense relationship?

'Anyway, her dying was the best thing that could

have happened to Jake. And it was like, as soon as he was old enough to make some decisions on his own, he started to put the worst elements of her back into his life. Like some kind of miserable-ass tribute to the worst mother on earth.' Saxon shook his head and ground his teeth. 'And that night, I told Jake he was about to sleep with a no-good whore like his mother.'

'Saxon!' I cried. It didn't matter what your background or how cool you might be, no one could cross the mother line. I could only imagine Jake's fury when Saxon said that about his mother. His mother who had died so young. 'It doesn't matter what his mom did. She was still his mom, and you had no right saying anything about her.'

'Bullshit!' Saxon yelled, pointing a finger so close to my face I backed up. His breathing was heavy and his eyes were bright and furious. 'No one cared about that kid the way I did! No one! He was like a brother to me, and I wasn't about to watch him ruin his life!'

'What did you do?' I closed my eyes, waiting for his answer. I had the distinct feeling I wouldn't like what I heard.

'I punched him in the face, tried to knock his ass out.' Saxon's voice was rough. 'But he's tougher than he looks. I just wound up chipping his tooth. So I asked one of my friends to let him sleep with her and stole his shoes so he couldn't leave on foot.' He looked at my face. 'Not "sleep with" like that, Blix. He was out of it anyway. When he woke up, I let him blame it all on me – the whole night, the drinking, his whorishness. I'm glad I did, too. He stopped hanging out with those losers, me included. He hasn't had a drink since. He got a job, stopped screwing up in school. It's everything I ever wanted for him.' Saxon hung his head. 'It's the best thing for him.'

'But you had to give him up.' I felt tremors that had nothing at all to do with the temperature. I wanted to wrap my arms around Saxon, because I knew the pain and loss that overwhelmed him was completely real. And no one understood better than I did what it was like to care about Jake and worry if he's OK.

'Yeah.' Saxon stared at the tops of his shoes. 'But if I hadn't, who knows what stupid shit he would have gotten himself into? I can't talk; I exposed him to most of it. So there was no way he'd listen to me.'

'You miss him.' The realization hit me like a bolt of lightning. 'You don't *hate* Jake at all. You *miss* him.'

'We were friends since before pre-school. So, yeah, I miss him. But it's easier this way. I wouldn't trade it for anything.' He looked at me and grabbed my shoulders. 'Don't screw with this, Blix. I'd like it if he didn't out-and-out hate my guts, but I don't want him to know the whole story. You're the only one who knows, so I know whose ass to kick if it gets back to him.'

But he didn't hold me like he wanted to kick my ass. He rubbed his thumbs on my shoulders. Then he pulled me against him and pressed his forehead to mine.

'We can't do this, Saxon.' I could feel the pain radiating off him in waves, and I wanted to still it for him. I wanted to hold him tight and tell him it would be OK. But if I did that, nothing would be OK again.

'I know.' His hands pressed harder, until they bit into my shoulders, but I didn't tell him to stop. 'You're the best thing that's ever happened to Jake. You're so damn good for him.'

'I really care about him,' I said, my breathing heavy. I could smell Saxon, and it was a musky, sharp smell that turned me on even though I didn't want it to.

'You'd be . . . you'd be so good for me, too, Brenna. Being with you, it would be a total game changer.' His voice was so low I almost couldn't hear him. 'I've given up Jake. Now I have to give you up too?'

'We can be friends.' I closed my eyes so I wouldn't see the disappointment on his face.

I knew he wanted to kiss me. I knew he wanted to do more than that.

'I don't want to be your goddamn friend,' he said, pronouncing each word carefully.

'That's all there is for us,' I said, then pushed away hard and broke his hold on me. I didn't have my jacket or my backpack, but I needed to get out of there. I saw my bike and bolted over to it.

'Brenna, don't be an idiot! Brenna! You don't even have a coat on! Brenna!' Saxon screamed. I heard a long, loud stream of swear words, but it faded fast, as I leaped on the bike and pulled away.

I pedaled like a maniac, trying to keep myself from getting too cold. The faster and harder I pumped, the better I felt. I made it to Tech in no time. I was early, but not by much. I slammed into the school and ran to the cafeteria. I walked in and looked around at the students crowded at tables eating and joking. Jake sat apart from a group of kids, his arms crossed and his face sullen. He seemed to sense I was looking at him. His head snapped up and he kicked his chair back, got up and strode over to me fast.

'Brenna, you're freezing.' He pulled his thermal off, popped it over my head, and rubbed his hands up and down over my arms. He had one of his threadbare T-shirts on underneath. 'What are you doing here so early?'

And then I was crying, my face on his chest. Jake

put his arm around me and walked me out of the crowded cafeteria, where we were drawing way too much attention. He led me into a deserted stairwell and frantically pressed my hair back and shushed me. 'What's wrong, Brenna? Don't cry, baby. What's wrong?'

'I'm sorry!' I wailed. 'I didn't want to mess things up with you!'

He pulled me into his arms and ran a hand from the crown of my head down my back. 'Are you crazy? *I* messed things up. Don't cry, shh.' He kissed me quickly, warmly. 'Don't cry, babe. I'm sorry. I shouldn't have gotten all self-righteous on you. If you want to strip on a pole . . . well, I'll stand guard with a gun, but I'll support you. You haven't made a fraction of the mistakes I've made. I'm the one with a screwed-up perspective.'

'That's not true,' I said, though it was in a lot of ways. 'But I have to tell you something, and I don't know how.'

'Just tell me.' His face looked so trusting. 'Just tell me. There's nothing I would be mad about. I promise.'

I laughed shortly. 'You can't promise that, Jake. You can't predict how you'll react.'

'Nothing you say is going to make me pissed off, OK?' He brushed his thumbs under my eyes, pushing away stray tears.

'Saxon and I . . .' I started, unsure exactly what to say.

Then I saw Jake's eyes harden with a deep hate, much deeper than I'd anticipated. His hands on my arms tightened.

'Jake, ow! My arms.'

'Sorry. I'm so sorry.' He rubbed them, his eyes frantic. 'What about you and Saxon?' His words were razor sharp.

'He and I are in class together,' I began lamely. 'And he told me you two were good friends.' Why did I back down again? I should tell him the whole truth!

'I told you that.' The crazy gleam left his eye, and there he was again. It was such a relief to see his face looking so tender, I decided partial truth was the best I could manage.

'But I think he wants to be friendly again. He wants you and him to get along. I think.' I wanted to tell him more. I wanted to pour my heart and soul out to him, but there was too much at stake, too much to lose.

'Why were you so upset about that?' Jake dipped his head to look at me.

'Because . . .' I was standing right on the line of truth and lies. I didn't want to have Saxon come between me and Jake, but telling Jake might blow everything up. He needed to make peace with Saxon.

'Because I don't think Saxon likes me very much. And I think that's standing in the way of him reaching out to you.'

He looked at me for a long minute, and I expected him to see through the lie and walk away. Instead he smiled. I looked at his adorable chipped tooth and thought of Saxon's fist making it. 'You're so wrong.' Jake laughed. 'Saxon likes you. A lot. A whole lot more than makes me comfortable, actually. I can see it in the way he looks at you. He's not used to not getting what he wants. But you're mine.' And the glint was back, this time not as maniacal, but still pretty damn unsettling.

'Maybe we can just come to a truce?' I begged.

'Whatever makes you happy,' Jake said with an easy smile. 'C'mon out here. I've got a big surprise for you.'

We left the school and went to the parking lot. Jake led me to a big blue truck with massive tires, chipped paint, a crack in the windshield, and a huge bench seat. I looked at it for a long minute, then remembered where I had seen it. It was one of the few pictures on Jake's Facebook page.

'Your truck? How did you get it here?'

'I became a full-time worker at Zinga's last week.' He pulled his wallet out of his back pocket and slid out a small plastic card. I took it from his hand and saw his photo, looking uncharacteristically stern.

'This is a license,' I said stupidly.

'A farmer's license,' he explained. 'They only give it out if you can prove you work full-time on a farm or your family operates one. That's why I had to run in early on Friday. I wanted . . .' He ran a hand through his hair shyly. 'I wanted to pick you up this morning, but I knew you were probably pretty pissed off with me.'

'Jake,' I breathed, and threw my arms around him. 'I'm so happy for you. You've been dying for your license!'

'I know.' He smiled that big dopey grin I loved. 'It's less than a month to my birthday, but I'm glad I got it a little earlier.' He pressed me up against the passenger side door. 'I know you aren't a bad girl . . .' His voice rumbled low in my ears. 'But didn't you say something about skipping school once in a while?'

'Are you asking me to skip with you, Jake Kelly?' He smelled like clean soap, mint, sweat: Jake. I loved it. I couldn't resist him. Just as easily as I'd pushed Saxon away, I pulled Jake in. 'I think I will.'

'Where's your coat?' Jake pulled me around to the passenger's side.

'I left it at school.'

Jake looked at me questioningly, but he didn't press. 'Well, let's go and get it.' He helped me into the truck and got in on the driver's side. It was sexy watching him drive. Jake was the kind of guy who was born to drive. We pulled around the school and he parked, hopped out, and threw my bike in the back. Then we drove to Frankford and Jake walked in with me. He handed me a hall pass.

'Where did you get this?' I stared at the little green pass.

'All county high schools use the same ones.' He smiled sheepishly. 'I swiped mine from the front office at the beginning of the year.'

I shook my head and filled one out for each of us. We shouldn't have worried about it. The corridors were empty. We headed down the back corridor to my locker and were ready to leave two minutes later, when a familiar voice broke through our self-enforced quiet.

'Hey, Jake.' Saxon leaned lazily against the wall. His eyes flicked to me. 'Blix.'

It was like he'd appeared out of nowhere. Jake threw him a stony look.

'We were just going, Saxon.' I shoved my arms into my jacket and grabbed my backpack from Jake's hands. Jake had that weird Jekyll and Hyde gleam in his eye.

'Wait. I've got something to say to Saxon first.' Jake stomped close to him. 'Stay away from Brenna, you lying bastard.'

Saxon didn't even cringe, and Jake looked big and fierce.

'I'm pretty sure Brenna can determine who she wants to be around for herself, Jake. Or don't you trust her?' He looked at me, his smile menacing and gorgeous. 'I mean, you two are always honest with each other, right? No lies. No half-truths.'

'Shut your damn mouth!' Jake yelled and slammed Saxon up against the lockers. 'You always had that ability, didn't you?' He was right in Saxon's face, and Saxon traded his lazy look for a predatory snarl. It was impossible to tell who was more furious. 'You could turn any situation in your favor. You could make anyone swallow your bullshit and believe it was the truth. Not me, not anymore.'

'You don't know anything,' Saxon spat, shoving Jake back. All of his cool completely evaporated and was replaced by a boiling swell of emotions. 'I watched your back, brother. I kept you out of trouble.' He shoved Jake again.

'You introduced me to every stupid thing I ever did,' Jake growled, grabbing a fistful of Saxon's shirt and shaking him hard. 'I should have lost you years ago. You're a parasite.' Jake opened his hands and let Saxon go.

After a few heavy breaths, Saxon's cocky smile came back out. He straightened his shirt and shook the hair out of his eyes, then ran a look from my head to my toes that made a blush burn on my skin. 'Whatever. But don't think you're going to tell me who to like or not. And we'll let the lady decide in the end. Best man wins?'

His look was all swaggering arrogance. I was torn between fear that he'd tell Jake the secrets we had shared and the urge to do it myself. I hated that he knew he had a stacked deck. Jake was furious, his fists balled.

'Come on, Jake,' I willed him. 'If a teacher finds us, we're all screwed. Let's go now.'

'I'll call you later, Brenna.' Saxon grinned and blew me a kiss.

Jake was at him in a split second, his fist flying through the air and straight into Saxon's jaw. I heard the thick thud of skin and bone colliding.

'Jake!' I cried.

Just then a teacher appeared at the end of the hall. 'What's going on down there?'

Saxon stood up woozily and moved his jaw back and forth a few times. 'Nothing. I was just headed to calculus.' He pointed up. Before he walked away, he spat a tooth on the floor.

'You two, get a move on!' the teacher snapped, looking absently at our passes. I bent down and grabbed the tooth before he noticed it. We ducked into the stairwell, waited a minute, then slid out the side doors while no one was looking.

Jake and I ran back to the truck. He still opened my door, though I would have preferred for him to step on it and rush a little.

'Have you been talking to Saxon?' Jake asked, his voice cold.

I sighed. It was truth time. 'I want to tell you—'

Jake cut in. 'Never mind, Brenna. That's exactly what Saxon would want. Me to doubt you.' He shook his head. 'That prick. He knows what he's doing five moves ahead of everyone else. Don't even acknowledge I just asked you anything.'

I clamped my mouth shut and held it shut. What else was I supposed to do?

'You hit him really hard,' I said softly.

'I'm sorry, Bren.' He leaned his forehead on the steering wheel and shook his head from side to side. 'I dropped my basket. I know it. Are you all right?'

'Sort of.' I felt tears prick my eyes. 'I've never seen

you just lose it like that.' I opened my fist. Saxon's shiny white tooth was in my hand.

'Saxon's tooth.' Jake swallowed so hard I could see his Adam's apple jump.

'That was pretty biblical of you, Jake.' We both looked at the white calcified piece of Saxon.

'A tooth for a tooth. Holy crap.' Jake shook his head. 'I guess I should just let it go with Saxon now. I'm sorry you're in his classes. I'm sure I've made this a shitstorm for you.' He pulled out and drove slowly, focused on the road and all the thoughts I'm sure were running through his head.

I unclipped my seatbelt, slid to the middle, buckled the lap belt, and leaned against Jake's shoulder. He felt good and solid under my cheek. I dropped the tooth into the rusted ashtray.

'Don't worry. It will be fine.' I hoped it would be. I debated telling Jake about the government project, but I didn't know if I should. I didn't know if maybe I should just bury it with all of my other Saxon secrets. It was hard to know.

We drove for a while and finally pulled into a local state park viewpoint. The lot was completely empty. Below us was the spread of trees, gold and red and orange in the afternoon sun. Jake turned the engine off and grabbed an old blanket from the back. He took my seatbelt off and made me lie down, my head nestled against the muscles of his thighs. He ran his hand along the lines of my face.

'My race is in a few days,' he said in the quiet of the cab.

'Are you excited?' I tilted my head to look up at his face.

'Yeah,' he said, but his voice was a little dull for Jake. 'I don't really know if I'm ready.'

'Maybe you should practice. Is that how it works?' I rubbed my hand under his shirt, along the hot, soft skin of his stomach.

'Yeah.' He laughed, but it was muted. 'But I don't have a lot of time now. I'm bumped to full time at Zinga's. Just getting the day off for the race was a big deal.'

'So, no weekends together for a while?' My heart sank a little.

'Sorry, Bren. But now at least I can drive you back and forth to school.' His palm scratched along my cheek, and I pushed my face against it.

'Jake, I can't take rides back and forth with you.'

'Why?' His voice was clipped, because he knew the answer.

I sighed. 'Mom will not be cool with it. And you'll

be going out of your way. It's too much time added on to your day.'

His hand stopped for a few seconds, then he started rubbing my head. 'You were pretty pissed off with me when I said I didn't want to go further, uh, physically.'

'Yeah.' I felt a deep hussy blush. 'Sorry.'

'You are not.' He looked down at me with a wide grin. 'It's OK, you don't need to be. I should have been more sensitive about your feelings, and I wasn't.'

I sat up on one elbow and craned my neck to look at him. 'This isn't an apology, is it?'

He shook his head and said, 'Nope. It's a point. If I'm going to try to respect your wishes even though it makes me uncomfortable, shouldn't you do the same for me?'

'So you want me to be cool with you getting a lot less sleep and spending a fortune in gas?' I crossed my arms, annoyed.

'Yeah, Bren. And I'll try to be cool about you throwing yourself at me.'

I slapped him on the arm, and he laughed. I sat up and twisted myself around so I was facing him, and then nestled myself on his lap, my legs on either side of him and my knees pressed on the worn seat. The steering wheel was close at my back, so I was squashed against Jake.

'I'll let you pick me up tomorrow.' I ran my finger down his nose and to his lips, then pressed on them to keep him quiet. 'But you have to wait at the end of the road for me. I'm not going to have this fight with Mom. And I promise I will ask her if you can pick me up on Saturday.'

He kissed my finger. 'Thank you.'

'Don't thank me,' I warned. 'It's a trade.'

He closed his gray eyes and groaned. 'What do you want?'

'A lot of guys would be happy to have such a shameless girlfriend,' I balked.

'Well, I'm not one of them,' he growled. 'We don't have to rush things. There's plenty of time.'

And behind his caution for me, I could see a caution for himself. It had never really occurred to me how nervous this all might make him.

'Are you nervous?' Way to go, super-direct Brenna.

'Maybe I am,' he said, his smile a little embarrassed. 'When you're drunk, you always have this feeling like you're the man. But maybe I'm not the man, you know? Maybe it was all an illusion.' His hands moved up and down on my back, rubbing in wide circles through my hair and shirt.

'I don't have a lot of experience, but I think you're better than your hype,' I said honestly.

He kissed me softly. 'Thanks. I want to be good for you.'

'You are.' I pressed against him.

'But?' he asked, his voice husky.

'You could always improve. With practice.' I leaned my head to kiss him. My hair fell forward and brushed his face. His hands moved up my back and slipped up my neck then under my hair. He cradled my head, kissing me softly and surely.

He pulled back. 'What do you want, shameless hussy?' He kissed my nose.

'What I did for you,' I demanded, trying to keep my voice from wavering. Because, of course, I was nervous.

He kissed me harder then, rubbed his hands over me, moved them under my shirt and beneath my bra. I pressed against him and his kissing got erratic, his lips rubbing my face, cheeks, and neck. He moved his head down and pulled my shirt up. He looked at me, his eyes worried with questions. I nodded.

He pulled my shirt over my head, unsnapped my bra without fumbling and pulled me closer on his lap in the chilly afternoon light. His hands were on my back. He rubbed up and down slowly and made my skin a rash of goosebumps.

He looked at my body for a long time. His hand

shook when he brought it up to my breast, his fingers gentle on my skin. I felt a shiver erupt over my skin where he touched me, and where I wished he would. Without looking away, Jake reached for the blanket and draped it over my shoulders. I saw him swallow hard before he moved his head down and kissed me on my breastbone. He leaned his forehead against me, and I felt his breath warm on my skin. Then he was kissing, kissing all over, and it felt really good. I leaned into him, and just when I thought it couldn't feel any better, he opened his mouth and sucked on my nipple. I could feel it get wet and hot between my legs. His hands cupped my breasts and his mouth licked and kissed me, then sucked hard, and once in a while he pulled away and groaned. He was hard.

I rubbed my body against his, not completely sure what I was doing, but just going on what made me feel good, then better.

His mouth still on my breasts, Jake slid his hand down and undid the button on my jeans, then slid the zipper down. He moved his big, rough-skinned hand down, into my panties. My eyes opened wide when I felt his fingers slide against me. He pushed them in deep, where I was completely wet, and then slid them out and rubbed against where I felt most sensitive. He pulled his mouth away from my breasts and watched me closely. His fingers moved around, sometimes feeling uncomfortable, sometimes feeling so good, it made me close my eyes and pant a little. He took his cues from me, repeating whatever made me squirm and grab hard at his arms. Soon he had set up a rhythm, and I felt like his hand was some kind of key, unlocking something I had always wanted to feel, but hadn't known how to get at. And then there was the feeling I had on Friday, but this time it shook my whole body. It felt like every muscle in me clenched hard, then relaxed and melted. I cried out and threw myself against him.

He pulled his hand away, and I lay against him, breathing heavily.

'Are you all right?' he asked into my hair.

'I think I came.' My body felt like I had just stepped out of a warm bath or plunged down a log flume or eaten the most amazing piece of chocolate cake with whipped cream, or maybe all of those at once and better. It was weird and awesome all at the same time.

He laughed. 'Yeah. I could tell.'

I laughed too. 'I love you, Jake.'

'I love you, too.' He kissed my mouth, then found my bra and held it up, at a total loss for what to do with it. 'Um, I have no idea how this goes on.'

I laughed and shrugged it over my shoulders, then

reached around my back and snapped the clasp back in. 'You're an old pro at taking them off, aren't you?'

'I can't believe you put it back on that fast.' His hands turned my shoulders so he could look at the closed clasp.

'I wear one every day, Jake. When you first wear one, most girls put it on backward, then move it around.'

'But you're a pro now.' He ran one finger under my strap.

'I've had boobs for about four years.' I cupped my pink-polka-dot-bra-covered ones in my hands. 'They're not much, but I like them.'

'They're really nice,' Jake said, a blush on his face. He smiled at my laughter. 'Seriously, they're the most perfect boobs I've ever seen.'

I laughed giddily as Jake pulled my shirt back over my head. I loved him, and it felt so good. My body felt new, the way it had after a few months in Denmark with a different diet and exercise, but this change had been almost instant. I felt like me, but better.

'You're still hard.' I kissed his neck.

'No way.' He lifted me off of his lap and sat me back on the seat. 'It doesn't always have to be about me.'

I rolled my eyes. 'You're just chicken.'

'Because you're such a temptress?' he said softly,

his hand on my cheek. 'God, you're so pretty, Brenna.'

And it was definitely the perfect thing to say. Because I melted right there and stopped arguing with him, and we kissed for a long time. In fact we kissed for so long, I lost track of time entirely.

'What time is it, do you think?' I blinked in the warm, low sun.

He checked his cell phone. 'Wow. Time to go. Now.'

We rearranged ourselves into normal sitting positions. Jake turned the key and the engine purred with a loud rumble. He started to pull out of the parking spot, then looked over at me. 'Where do you need to go?'

'Wait a minute.' I pulled out my phone and dialed my mom. 'Hey, Mom.' I wondered if her mom radar would be up. I wondered if she'd know I spent the afternoon letting a boy kiss my breasts instead of going to class.

'Hey, baby,' she said absently. 'I'm headed to the office to get some things in order. Class starts Monday.'

'Oh, you should go and get ready. I was just going to say I think I might go for cross country after all. They have tryouts this afternoon.'

'Good, honey. I'm glad you're getting into a sport. I think you'll enjoy it.'

'I hope so.' I stopped. There was so much I should tell her, so much I felt uncomfortable keeping from my mother, the woman I loved and respected more than anyone. But there was a rift between us now that would never close. She and I would never be as close as we had been, and as sad as it made me, I knew it was all just a part of growing up and letting go. 'Anyway, I'll take the late bus probably. But I'll have my phone on.'

'I can come pick you up, honey. I don't have to stay late here if you need me.' Mom's voice was sweet and pleasant on the line.

'Don't worry about it tonight, Mom. I don't really know the schedule, so I can't even tell you a time yet. But I might need a ride once I know how things work.'

Mom sighed. 'All right, sweetie.'

'What's wrong, Mom?'

'Nothing,' she said, her voice high and tight. 'Sometimes I just wish you were a little girl again and we spent all day together.'

I blinked against the scratch of tears. 'Mom, I love you. You know that.'

'I do,' she said, and I could hear her smile. 'I love you, Brenna.'

'Let's do something on Sunday.' I really wanted to spend some time with her, just the two of us together.

'That would be really nice, baby.'

We said our goodbyes and I slumped back in the seat. Jake looked over at me expectantly.

'You all right?'

'Just feeling sad. I miss hanging out with my mom like I used to. But it's stupid. I mean, I'm happy with how everything is now. I'm just being stupid.' I took two quick swipes at my eyes with the backs of my hands to sop up the tears.

'It's not stupid at all. I know how much your family means to you, and I'm sorry you guys haven't been able to spend as much time together as before. That sucks.' He looked ahead to give me time to dry my tears in peace.

'I'm going to Frankford,' I said, needing to change the subject. 'I'm trying out for cross country.'

He looked over at me and smiled. 'So you decided? You're definitely trying out?'

'Yeah. I'm good at distance running. Anyway, with you and Mom and Thorsten working all the time, I need to do something to keep myself busy.'

'Sounds good.' Jake slid me a look that was all sexy mischief. 'Do you wear those really short shorts?'

I remembered Saxon asking the same question and rolled my eyes. 'No! This isn't the 1970s. At least, I hope not.' I realized that I'd never seen the official

311

school cross-country kit, I didn't know what it looked like.

We pulled up at Frankford, and Jake said, 'I'm at work until seven. I know you'll get out earlier, but if you need a ride, call me.'

I leaned over and kissed him. 'Thanks for today. I really liked skipping with you.'

'I really liked it too.' He held my hand for a second.

Eventually he let go and I got out and went around for my bike.

'Don't.' Jake leaned out the window and waved me on. 'I'll drop it by your house on my way to work.'

'Thanks!' I watched him pull away, happy we had been able to spend the day together and nervous to face Coach Dunn. I wasn't even sure what day exactly tryouts were. I hoped I hadn't had Jake drop me off for nothing.

I really did want to run. If I wasn't going to be riding into school, I needed to do something to keep my body in shape, and running seemed like a good, mindless alternative. Before I went in, I checked my pocket.

I had Saxon's tooth in it. Somehow, I hadn't been able to leave it in Jake's ashtray. Saxon had definitely provoked the punch, but I had a feeling that had been his intention. Like, if Jake got a good shot in, maybe Saxon could feel like the score was settled.

I headed toward the gym, unsure where to go or what to do. Coach Dunn found me immediately.

'Blixen!' she yelled. 'Get on your practice clothes and stretch. Make sure you do a full set; I don't need you pulling anything. Then get running.'

'Am I in time for tryouts?'

She looked at me for a minute. 'Let's say you tried out in class. You're on the team. We practice every day after school until five. Think you can handle it?' She put her hands on her hips, her legs wide apart. For all of her rough, muscled, sporty looks, she had this amazing golden blonde, shiny hair that looked fabulous and soft no matter how hard she tried to plaster it to her head.

'Yes.' I pointed to the locker room and jogged toward it. 'I'll go change!' I called over my shoulder.

I changed into my practice clothes in the empty locker room. When I got out to the track, there were people everywhere, running laps, doing sets of push-ups, running relays. The soccer team were out there bashing soccer balls off their heads and knees and chests and into each other and grunting, and in the middle of it all was Saxon. As I went through my stretches, I wondered if he still felt woozy from getting punched in the jaw.

I decided ignoring him was probably the best thing I could do. I put my iPod in, pulled up my hood and started running. Soon I was breathing in a quick rhythm and everything around me faded. I thought about Jake on my bed, in his truck, on the phone, in class. My heart pounded to the thoughts of him, and soon I had to stop running and panted, hunched over, on the edge of the track.

'What's up, Blixen?' Coach Dunn called.

'Out . . . of . . . breath.' I spluttered.

She power-walked over to me and squatted down so she could watch my wheezes. 'You need to try double clutching.' I shook my head and gasped in an attempt to tell her I didn't understand. 'Double clutch. Two breaths in, one out. Two in, one out. It will keep you from hyperventilating on the track.' She clapped me on the back. 'Get to it!'

I stumbled to my feet while my muscles were still warm and propelled myself forward. Two breaths in, one out.

My thoughts wandered back to Jake, but this time I checked my breathing before things got too crazy. Two breaths in, one out. I managed to get on pace and let my body fly, while my brain focused on my boyfriend.

But that was euphoric thinking, and it was like my brain could only handle so much of that before guilty thoughts crept in. I started to think about my mom, how I was lying to her, sneaking around and hiding things. We had been so close a few weeks ago, there was no one in the world I could confide in more, and now we were so far apart. I felt an anvil of guilt on my chest about Sunday, because even though I knew I'd have so much fun with her, I also knew I'd be thinking about Jake the entire time and wanting to be with him.

He was like some insane addiction. I craved him, and the more I had of him, the worse the cravings got.

After my brain hammered out all of my guilt, it brought me back to my love/hate obsession: Saxon Maclean. I thought about Jake's fierce insistence that Saxon was just playing one big head game, but my heart couldn't believe that. Not entirely. He had opened up to me. He had done things that made no sense, which was not unusual for Saxon, but some of the senseless things had done nothing to benefit him. Why would he bother?

When he talked about Jake and how everything had fallen apart, he wasn't acting. I knew that for sure. Even Saxon wasn't that good. He had let himself be Jake's fall guy. Even today. He could have come out and told Jake about our kiss, the rides home, but he just played on Jake's hatred and let him take another swing. If Jake was going to feel any anger, it was at Saxon, not me.

Why would he do that unless he really cared about Jake?

I was lost in the tangle of it. I was nervous about the calls and the ridiculous government date. I had never seen Saxon so determined. If he still had it in his head to win this thing, he would. I hoped Saxon would let me go now, but I didn't think it was likely.

Finally, I was broken out of my reverie by Coach Dunn waving her arms at me.

I yanked my ear buds out. 'Sorry, Coach.' I breathed heavily.

'Good job, Blixen.' She scowled and shook her head. I thought for a minute she was being sarcastic. 'Really good time. You're improving a little with every run.' She clapped me on the shoulder. 'See you tomorrow.'

I jogged into the locker room and changed. I didn't feel like showering anywhere other than my comfy home bathroom with all of my good shampoos and soaps. Besides, I hated putting my feet down any-where really grimy and gross, like the concrete of a high-school shower stall. I was on my way out and wondering how long the late bus would take when I ran into Saxon.

Chapter 11

Actually I crashed into him. He caught me around the waist, and I stood in his arms for a few seconds, until my head cleared and I backed away, breaking the circle we made together.

'Jesus, watch where you're going, Blix.' He shook me a little. 'C'mon. I've been waiting.'

'For me?' I was confused. 'I can't, Saxon. I have to catch the late bus.'

'You're not riding the shitty late bus. C'mon.'

He didn't look at me, just walked. And because I had a million things to clear up with him, because I had his tooth in my pocket, because I wanted to let him know that I understood the good under all his cocky pretend-bad, because I knew he loved Jake as much as I did, I followed. Down the long hallway with gold-tiled walls, down the crumbling stone steps to the lower parking lot, and right up to his big black car, I followed Saxon. He got in and pushed my door open, and I got in next to him. We sat for a moment; Saxon didn't start up the engine.

'I watched you run.' He lit a cigarette and drew in deeply. He exhaled in one long breath.

'I didn't watch you.' I waved the smoke away from my face and he switched hands.

'I know.' He took another drag and blew it away from me.

'How's your tooth?' Or the hole in his head where his tooth was before Jake smashed it out. But I didn't think he'd appreciate specifics.

'Gone. I have one bitch of a headache.' He leaned his head back on his seat and took a long drag. 'He needed to do that.'

'Not really.' I thought I understood why Saxon did what he did, but I wanted to hear it from him, if that was possible.

'More importantly,' he said, taking another drag, '*I* needed him to do it to me.'

'You could tell him the truth.' I knew Saxon and Jake would never be friends again, but some kind of peace had to be better than all this.

'So could you,' he bit back, reminding me that there were many circles of truth when it came to me and Saxon and Jake.

We sat in silence for a few minutes. He smoked the

entire cigarette faster than I'd ever seen anyone smoke one before.

'I might.' If I wasn't such a wimp, I already would have. How had it all gotten so tangled so fast?

'You know it's not about truth or lies.' He lit up another one. 'It's about Jake's perception. You and I have one more thing in common now.'

'What's that?' I gripped the sides of the leather seats.

'We're both protecting Jake.' He pressed his thumb hard between his eyes.

'Come here.' I motioned with my hands.

'Where?' I could tell from the way he squinted his eyes that he was in a lot of pain.

'On my lap.' I didn't like saying it out loud, because it made it sound tawdry, when it was really just my best attempt at a peace offering. And hopefully an end to all the head games.

'We need to get in the back for that, Blix.' Saxon tried to sound sexy, but the pain made him grimace through it.

'Not for that.' He pretended to pout, and I gave my best glare. 'I'll rub your head.'

His eyebrows pulled low. 'All right.' I knew he was evaluating my angle, the reason for my sudden concern, but he didn't seem able to come up with anything. He flicked his cigarette out of the window, right under a 'No Smoking' sign, and nodded towards the back.

We both got out and into the back of the car. He stretched across the long backseat, his head cradled on my lap. I pushed his shiny black hair back off his forehead. He pressed his head harder onto my thighs and made a low humming noise, like a purr. I thought about the first day I met him and how he reminded me of a jungle cat.

I rubbed his temples, up into his hair, down the sides of his face and all around his eyes. He breathed low and deep, almost like he had fallen asleep. His face relaxed, all of the muscles finally slack. He was beautiful. He had it all: great skin, great bones, great hair. He was just bad enough to be interesting, he was brilliant, he was funny. A soccer forward, AP student, resident badass, and the love of my life's personal martyr.

I pulled away, but his hands reached up and caught me around the wrists. He still had his eyes closed. He ran his fingers up and down my forearms.

'Please, Brenna,' he said in a voice so unlike Saxon's usual voice that I could hardly believe it was him speaking. 'Don't stop yet.'

My hands shook when I put them back on his head,

smoothing his hair back and running my fingers through it. I traced his features, ran my hands over the skin of his face and along the column of his neck. It wasn't until he shifted, and I saw exactly what my touch was doing to his lower regions, that I pulled back.

'I have to get home, Saxon.' My voice shattered the tension in the air.

'Right.' He sat up and climbed into the driver's seat while I squirmed into the passenger's.

We drove out of the now-empty parking lot and along the winding roads to my house.

'Are you going to tell Jake?' The minute I got back in the front of the car, I wondered if I had just dug myself into a deeper hole than I could get back out of.

'What? That you rubbed my head? It isn't exactly a lurid story, Blix.' His voice was hollow, like he was saying the words and playing the game because he knew he had to, not because he really wanted to.

'All of it. The kiss, the rides, the phone calls. All of it.'

'I'd like to have something just between you and me, Brenna,' he said finally. 'Jake and you are what you are. If I have to take your head rubs and rides home like some dog begging for pathetic scraps under the table, I guess that's what I'll live with. But they'll be *my* pathetic scraps.'

'If you told him—'

'You would both hate me. It's not like I'd win your hand at the end of it anyway.'

I felt a shiver go through me at the thought of being Saxon's girlfriend. It was mostly disturbing and not all that appealing; but it was also kind of fascinating.

'I saw you leave with Karen Tanner the other day.' I hoped it led somewhere, but knew if that were true the last half-hour would never have happened.

'She gave me head, Blix.' His voice snapped at me like he hoped I would be shocked and disgusted. 'It was good enough. She's nice enough. I think she's into a senior guy on the team, though. I was just someone to pass some time with.'

'Oh.' I tried hard not to be prudishly shocked at the thought of a girl going that far with someone she had no intention of being with more permanently.

'I tend to be someone to pass the time with.' It was a little self-pitying, but mostly just true, and we both knew it, so neither one of us said anything more on the topic.

We were in my driveway. Mom wasn't home yet.

'Thank you for the ride.'

'Thank you for the head rub.' He turned to me, his lazy, frightening smile back and more dangerously gorgeous than ever with a tiny, bloody gap in the back where Jake had knocked his tooth out. 'I have other parts that could use a rub. You've got great hands, Blix.'

I rolled my eyes at him, not even bothering to get worked up over that. I opened the car door and went to get out. Saxon grabbed my hand.

'Invite me in.' I could see something desperate in his eyes. He was only half kidding.

'No.' I shook my head for emphasis.

'We don't have to tell anyone. I promise you'll like it.'

I didn't feel offended or mad or anything like that. Most of all, I felt tired. And sad. That Saxon had to fall for me of all people. That he and Jake couldn't be friends. That he was brave and good and smart, but so completely screwed up. That even at his most vulnerable, I knew in my heart he was somehow damaged and could really hurt me.

No matter how dangerous he was, I was drawn to him. I couldn't stay away from him.

'No, Saxon.' I leaned back into the car and kissed him on the side of his mouth. 'Go home now.'

He clenched his jaw hard and as soon as the door shut, he peeled out of my driveway so fast he kicked up dust and gravel.

By the time Mom got home, I could hardly keep my eyes open. She came into my room and sat on the edge of my bed. 'You look beat, Bren.'

'Yeah. Practice kicked my butt.' I stretched, and my muscles screamed in protest.

'You made the team?' She brushed my hair back with her fingers.

'I didn't even have to try out. Coach Dunn said she could just use my class runs as my tryout. It wore me out, but I think I'm going to love it.'

'Congratulations, sweetheart. Tell me your meet schedule. Thorsten and I want to see you run.' She worked her fingers through a knot in my hair.

'Mom?'

'Yeah, honey?'

'Saturday there's this race.' I didn't know how to tell her.

'Do your friends have plans to go?' she helped.

'Yeah. There's a motocross race early in the day, and then this band called Folly is going to have a show later that night. I actually designed a T-shirt that they're going to sell there.'

'That sounds fun, sweetie. You're a real teenager now, with all these exciting plans. No more Saturdays home playing in your room,' Mom said, and her eyes were a tiny bit sad.

'Oh, Mom.' My voice was scratchy with tears I almost couldn't hold back.

'Ignore me.' She waved a hand in front of her face and blinked hard. 'I'm happy for you. I guess I just had last year to pretend you were a little girl again, so I didn't have to face how grown-up you're getting. Tell me about Saturday,' she insisted.

If telling her about general plans made her so sad, what would she say when I brought up Jake? 'My friend is the one riding the dirt bike. He offered to pick me up on his way. If you don't like the idea, it's OK.'

Mom sighed. 'Bren, I really don't want you driving with all these teenagers.'

'It's OK. I could get dropped off.' I had to make it there for Jake, and I wasn't about to take any chances.

She looked at me hard. 'Let me meet him on Saturday. I need to see if he's responsible. But I don't like it.'

I grabbed her hand. 'I don't like it when you don't like it,' I told her. It was the truth.

'That's what makes you such a great kid.' She shook her head. 'And that's why I don't like to say no when I know something's important to you.'

'Thanks, Mom. Seriously, I appreciate this.'

She squeezed my hand then got up to leave. At the doorway, she turned. 'Bren?'

'Yeah, Mom?'

'Is he a boyfriend?'

I was so tired of lying. So guilty. And I trusted my mother, no matter what. 'Yes,' I said. 'He's great. And I really want you to meet him.'

She pressed her lips together like she was trying to keep from crying. 'OK. I love you, sweetheart.'

When she left my room, I had nothing better to do than stare at my ceiling. Kids were always bitching about how terrible their parents were, grounding them, screaming at them, being suspicious. But I had awesome, loving parents who cared about me, and every time I lied or made them sad, I felt a crush of guilt that turned everything sour.

My cell finally rang. I was so tired, I could barely fumble for it. I picked it up and yawned.

'Brenna?' Jake laughed.

'Hey, you,' I said. 'How was work?'

'Hell of a lot better since I didn't have to freeze my ass off riding my dirt bike back and forth.'

'Isn't that illegal, Jake?' I asked sleepily.

'Only if you get caught.' I could hear his smile. 'Thanks for playing hooky with me.'

'I'd say "anytime", but you might convince me to never go back.' I laughed a need-to-sleep laugh.

'You're adorable when you're tired. Go to sleep.'

'Not yet,' I babbled. 'I have to tell you something.'

'What is it?' I could hear his can of soda pop.

'I told Mom. I told her about you today. And she wants to meet you. Saturday.' I yawned.

'Cool,' he said, his voice a little nervous. 'Did it go OK?'

'She almost cried. Like I told you, Jake, she's sad about the idea of me dating, not the idea of me dating you.' My pillow felt deliciously comfortable.

'I'm really glad. Thank you for telling her. I put your bike in the garage. You guys should really lock it.'

'Thanks. Thorsten's Danish. He never thinks about locking doors.'

'I'll meet you at the end of your road tomorrow morning. What time do you head in?' He sounded really excited.

'Usually seven thirty.' I snuggled under my duvet. 'Jake, you don't have to.'

'I'm just psyched to get to see you every morning, Brenna.' I could hear him eating.

'Sandwich day?'

'Tuna and pickles. I love you, babe. Get some rest.'

'I love you, Jake Kelly,' I said dreamily as I let the phone drop on my bed and fell into an instant, deep sleep.

Chapter 12

The next morning I woke up super early, probably because I fell asleep before eight o'clock. I had time to shower, blow-dry my hair, put on a lot of make-up. Change three times. By the time Mom was at the table with my porridge, I'd already been up for almost two hours.

'You look good, sweetie.' Mom kissed my head and sipped her coffee as I wolfed down my breakfast, nervous about the upcoming day.

'Oh, look, Mom.' I lifted up the black-and-white striped ballet-neck sweater I loved and showed her my Folly T-shirt, the one with Kelsie and Chris and the hearts.

'Bren, this is so beautiful.' She leaned close to look at the design elements. 'The font is perfect. I love your color contrast.' Her eyes glowed with pride, and she grabbed my face in her hands, squeezing my cheeks between her thumb and fingers. 'I love you, my talented girl.'

I smiled, my cheeks still squashed. 'Luff you, too.'

She released me and I headed out, knowing she would watch me ride down our driveway and onto the street. It made me feel bad and sneaky for agreeing to ride in with Jake. Maybe I should just ask her. I would, I decided, after Saturday. There was enough to worry about up until then.

Down the road from my house I saw Jake's blue truck parked up. I rode over and he got out and threw my bike and helmet in the back.

'Hey, beautiful.' He leaned over to kiss me, and it was still so shockingly good and exciting it sent shivers through me. I hoped kissing him never got boring. 'Did you eat?'

'Yeah,' I said, still recovering from the feel of his lips on mine. 'I always eat breakfast.'

'I figured,' he said with a smile. 'But I picked this up anyway, so maybe you can just eat it later.' He handed me a bag with an orange juice and a bagel with cream cheese.

'Mmm. I just felt my appetite come back. Thanks, Jake. That was really sweet.'

He was so happy to be driving, it was ridiculous. Jake was always a happy guy, but in the space of one day he had gone from pretty happy to goofily, fantastically, colossally happy.

'I'm kind of freaked out to meet your mom,' Jake confessed suddenly. 'But I'm also glad. That you told her. I know it was hard for you.'

I chewed carefully. 'It's not about you, Jake.' I hoped what I was telling him was accurate. My mother was going to grill him a little, and I figured Jake would probably have all the wrong answers. But I didn't want to coach him at all. I was becoming pretty averse to lies. I wanted to tell Jake the truth about everything, but I just couldn't do it. And now the lies were a tangled web, a constant hissing threat in the back of my brain. I didn't want any more of that.

'I hope it isn't. I have a nice shirt.'

I smiled. 'Aren't you going to be racing a dirt bike?'

'Yeah, but I can change in the truck.' He glanced at me, his eyes almost hidden under his baseball cap. 'I want to make a good impression. You think it would be too much?'

'A shirt with buttons?' I teased. 'I think my mom will be able to handle it.'

'Smartass.' He grinned and threw his arm around my shoulders. 'Maybe I should do Share Time,' he said as we pulled into the school parking lot. He took my hand in his lightly.

'You could, Jake.' I tried not to get too excited. I couldn't imagine his Tech academic courses were any challenge. 'You're in district. I could help you with your homework.'

'I'll look into it for next year.' He smiled shyly. 'Do you think I'd be in any of your classes?'

I knew Jake was smart, but I couldn't see him in AP government or honors English. I had completed my math requirements overseas. I was decent at math, but bored by it, so I figured it would be better to get them done. I was also a little ahead in science, but would be back in physics next year.

'Maybe. I might have some senior classes next year. I have a weird schedule because I home-schooled last year, but I'll tell you what I'm taking next year when I decide.'

'So that's why you have classes with Saxon this year?' Jake asked suddenly.

'One class. The class is mostly juniors,' I said carefully. Saxon was still a super-sensitive topic between us. 'But I'm not totally a sophomore. I'm like a sophomore and a half.'

'So you're in some junior classes?'

'Just government. With Saxon. Same as we do in Tech.' I grabbed his cap off his head and brushed the hair that fell into his eyes back. 'You need a haircut.'

'You want to stop talking about this?'

'I want to stop talking.' I slid over to his side of the truck. The interior was cavernous, so I had to drag my butt over a good two feet to be near him. I pulled his face down to mine and kissed him long and hard. I had my hands at his shoulders. I loved how they felt – big and muscular. He ran his hands down my back and grabbed me hard around the waist. He jerked me toward him, and soon we were fairly tangled around each other. I loved the taste of him. I loved the feel of his mouth against mine. I just loved Jake Kelly.

Finally I pulled away. 'Gotta go. We've got a group project on *Lord of the Flies* today.'

'I finished the book!' Jake said and ran a hand through his already mussed hair. 'Holy shit, they were some frigging messed-up kids!'

'I know!' I cried. 'I hated that one who was Jack's henchman. He was so creepy.'

'Stick-sharpened-at-both-ends boy?' Jake grinned. 'What a little freak.'

'How'd you like the ending?' I leaned back for a better look at his face.

His forehead creased as he thought it over. 'I didn't see it coming. I thought it was just going to be Armageddon. But I guess the end Golding wrote was more depressing than that.'

I looked at him for a long minute. 'You thought it

was more depressing than Armageddon?' I asked, curious how he could have come to that conclusion.

'Yeah.' His eyes were serious. 'Because it was just the truth. You know, no big war to blame it on or anything. Just the sad load of bullshit they all swallowed because ... I guess because Jack made a world for them where bullshit was all there was.' His smile was edged with sadness, and his chipped tooth glinted in the morning light.

I shook my head.

'What?' He looked sheepish.

'Don't pull that humble act with me. You know you just dissected Golding like an honors English student. I want you to seriously think about Share Time, Jake. I need someone smart to debate with in English class.' My head was spinning. I had underestimated Jake's English skills by a mile. I kissed him and put his cap back on his head. 'See you after lunch!'

'Brenna! Um, do you want me to get you before lunch? We could eat together. If you want.'

It would mean not eating lunch with Saxon and his friends anymore. I wasn't sure how I felt about that. But eating with Jake was appealing enough to tempt me.

'I'm not really supposed to leave.'

He flashed me an eager smile. 'Who's gonna know, Brenna? Come to the dark side.'

'You're a bad influence.' I leaned in and kissed him again. 'I'll wait right here for you. Don't be late. They have parking-lot monitors.'

'I'm never late.' He put his foot down and the truck roared out of the school toward Tech, and I walked into Frankford.

Saxon was waiting in the lobby. He walked next to me, not saying anything for a while, then, 'Jake's driving.' There was so much more to that statement than the obvious.

Saxon's ability to drive me had been a gold ticket he held over my head.

'It's a farmer's license,' I explained. 'He'll be able to get his real license in a month.'

'You don't need a ride to his race,' Saxon said, his brows knitted.

'No.' I bit my lip. 'It's better this way, Saxon.'

His laugh was coarse and rough. 'Yeah, better for you, Blix.'

'And you.' I put a hand on his arm. 'Come on, Saxon, this isn't real. You and me, this is all a game, isn't it? Why don't we just stop?'

'I can't.' He grabbed me and pulled me into an alcove off the corridor. We were tucked into a small, dark space together. His eyes were on me, gleaming with anger. 'It's not just a damn game. Whatever it is that I feel for you is more real than anything I've ever felt before.'

'Because you can't have me,' I insisted, my voice high. 'Because I'm with Jake. It's just your testosterone, Saxon. And maybe your ego, too.'

'That's a load of bullshit. I thought you were good at seeing through that.'

I could see the veins standing out in his neck, could smell the smoky, musky guy smell of him. I knew what his mouth tasted like, knew what it felt like to have his arms around me. I knew he had a strange loyalty that was admirable. I knew he would take a punch in the mouth as penance for hurting his friend. I knew so much about him, and then again, I didn't know him at all.

And I realized he was going to kiss me. When we kissed the last time, Jake and I hadn't been together officially. The only way I could forgive that time was because of a huge technicality. Now, there was nothing like that looming over us. If he kissed me, it would be cheating pure and simple, and I would have no choice but to tell him.

And if I had to tell Jake that, it would all come out. That couldn't happen. Not yet.

I turned my head so his lips grazed my cheek.

'You want to. Don't be such a coward.' His breath was hot on my ear.

But I kept my face turned away. He looked at me for a few seconds, his chest heaving with his excited breath.

He put his mouth close to my ear. 'You're a coward. This is bullshit.' He pushed off the wall and stalked away, and I sank down against the door of the student planning offices and sat for a few moments, until the shaking stopped.

I walked to class slowly, realizing I would be late, but not caring. When I walked through the door a few seconds after the bell, I saw the entire class buzzing with activity. Only one person sat completely alone, looking like a deer in headlights.

Devon Conner.

My partner.

Everyone else had teamed up in pairs or groups, but Devon sat alone, staring blankly at his assignment page. Mr Dawes read the newspaper at his desk. He was the kind of teacher who wouldn't give a crap if Devon didn't wind up in a group. When it came to classroom social politics, Dawes's leadership style mirrored Jack's in *Lord of the Flies*: kill or be killed.

I walked in and grabbed the closest empty desk to Devon's. He looked at me with naked relief on his face.

'I thought you were absent.' He sank against his

seat and rubbed a hand over his forehead.

'I'm not.' I took out my book and notebook and clicked my pen. 'What's the assignment?'

Devon grabbed the paper and scanned it. 'We have to break Frankford down into the island. We need to talk about how different cliques represent different people or groups.' He looked up and his small eyes searched my face. 'I don't think you would fit anyone on the island.'

I glanced up from my notebook. 'What do you mean?'

'You're not psychotically cruel, like Jack, or you wouldn't have agreed to be my partner.' Devon doodled small squares on the edge of his notebook. 'You're not a goody-goody like Ralph because you go to Tech and date Saxon Maclean.'

'I don't date Saxon,' I interrupted. He raised his bushy eyebrows at me. 'I don't,' I repeated.

'That's weird. I saw him put a guy in a headlock for saying you were hot after German yesterday.' Devon scribbled over the squares on his paper.

I know my face flushed red. 'We're . . . not dating,' I said finally.

'Anyway, you aren't a goody-goody. You aren't pathetic like Piggy. That's what people like me represent.'

'You aren't pathetic,' I said without much conviction. I just felt pity when I said it. Which was pretty pathetic.

'Yeah, I am. I know I'm weird. I always have been, socially. I just can't figure it all out. Like Piggy. Or Simon. Maybe I'm like a combination of them.'

I cringed – the two who were totally bullied throughout the entire book.

'You aren't like Sam and Eric because there's no one you're that close to. You aren't that popular. And you're not Roger.'

'If you meet someone like Roger, run the other way fast,' I said. He smiled at me. It was an awkward, nervous smile, but it was still a smile. 'You'll know him. He'll have a stick sharpened at both ends.'

He laughed out loud, a kind of donkey bray mixed with a wheeze, which made me laugh too.

'So I think we should do whatever we agree on first.' Devon took out a fresh, non-doodled piece of paper. 'What about Piggy and Simon?'

'Don't lump them,' I warned and took out my own paper. 'Piggy is thoughtful and believes in leadership. Simon is more of a free spirit, and he's the only one who communicates directly with the Beast.'

Devon and I broke the school down, agreeing on groups and assigning. We gave Piggy to the Righteous

Whiners/Social Misfits, those aggravating kids in your AP class who remind the teacher there was supposed to be a pop quiz when everyone else was praying the teacher forgot. Simon, we decided, was the Achieving Pothead group: still socially present, but nervous, panicky and prone to seeing more than was there. Sam and Eric were the Jocks and their groupies, happy together, likeable, not many real thoughts of their own. Ralph was the Moral Intellectuals, those do-gooder achievers who aced every test and worried over the fate of everyone in the world. Roger was the Quiet Rage group, the ones who loved horror flicks, made lists of people they wanted to kill and were gleeful about torture and little else.

That left Jack.

'Jack is Saxon, your not-boyfriend.' Devon wrote Saxon's name next to Jack before we had even discussed it.

'Hey, Devon, I think that's a little bit of a leap.' I tapped my pen on his book.

Devon looked at me with his eyebrows raised. 'You think that's a leap? He's arrogant, right?' I nodded. 'Kind of charming? Kind of inspiring? Kind of evil? Kind of manipulative?' I was nodding so much I felt like a jack-in-the-box.

'But that's just a list of some of his traits,' I argued

lamely. Why was it bothering me so much? It was an English assignment. Didn't I just want it done with? Wasn't it better to just let Devon fill in whatever and finish?

'Well, there's also the core of Saxon.' Devon put his pencil down and looked at me. He was bright and likeable. I wondered why he had become the Piggy of the class. Why was he such a loner?

'What do you think the core of Saxon is?' I was suddenly interested in knowing Devon better.

'That he can take a totally normal situation and twist it into whatever he wants. That's what Saxon's all about.' Devon picked his pencil back up and started to write again. 'Oh, we need a code name. Dawes said we could use the person for description's sake, but not to use any real names.'

'OK.' I wasn't really listening to Devon. Was Saxon's mind-gaming that obvious? 'Devon?'

'Yeah?' He looked up from his scribbled notes.

'Is this all stuff you just noticed about Saxon?'

'Well, yes, but not really.' I raised my eyebrows, demanding an explanation. 'He got the kids in middle school to gang up on me and exclude me.'

'What did he do?' I wanted to know so badly, but I had a feeling the answer wouldn't really surprise me.

'It sounds so stupid.' Devon shook his head and

shrugged. 'He just said, "fag" every time he walked by me. Every single time. Always. Even if there was a teacher right by us. He never laughed or said anything else. But it made me into a misfit, and then everyone else just decided to hate me.'

'That sucks.' I imagined the horror Devon must have gone through day in and day out, battling a master of manipulation.

'Yeah, I know it sounds dumb. Don't ask how it worked. That's Saxon's magic. He can create total havoc with hardly any effort.' Devon drummed his pencil on the desk frantically.

'Like Armageddon.' I echoed Jake's words from that morning. I looked at Devon: smart, sensible, friendly Devon. How was he still a misfit? 'But didn't Saxon stop?'

'Oh yeah.' Devon drummed his pencil with more force. 'One day instead of saying "fag", he just completely ignored me. I never really knew why he started. He's never even talked to me since, like, seventh grade. But whatever he did stuck like a curse.'

'Devon.' I grabbed his hand and the pencil fell from his fingers. He looked up at me with panic all over his face. 'He's just full of shit. His bullshit can't define your life.'

He looked at my hand on his and smiled. 'But it's

already defined my life. Don't look so upset. It's not so bad.'

He was different now, comfortable with me. A few days before he had a wild rabbit look to him and he blurted out stupid things I knew now were just nerves. He was still under Saxon's curse, even if everyone else had forgotten.

'Do you hang out?' I knew I was venturing into dangerous territory.

'Nope, and I like it like that.' His jaw tightened at the lie.

'There's a concert on Saturday. A bunch of us are going.' I made sure my voice was casual.

'Folly?' He avoided looking directly at me, but I could see he was interested.

'Yeah. You want to go? My boyfriend can pick you up.' I felt like any wrong word would send him running in the opposite direction.

He looked at me, not quite trusting me. 'I don't know.'

I shrugged. 'It's no big deal. You have a cell?' He nodded. 'Here.' I wrote my number on a piece of paper. 'This is my number. You can call if you feel like it. Oh, and have this.' I pulled out one of the Folly shirts I had designed and gave it to him. I planned to give them all to Chris for future sales, but it seemed like a decent good-faith gift to let Devon know I wasn't inviting him out to get a bucket of pig's blood dumped on him like some twisted replay of *Carrie*. 'I designed it for the show, but it's the first, so no one else has one yet.'

He held the shirt out and stared. 'What if I don't go?'

'It's a T-shirt, Devon. You could always just wear it to school.' I went back to writing, even though my mind was pulling in a thousand different directions.

'I'll think about it.' Devon said it like he was doing me some big favor. 'And, um, thanks.'

I smiled at him, and we didn't say anything else for the rest of class, both of us pretty lost in thought.

By the time the bell rang, we were further along than any other group. Thankfully, Mr Dawes didn't feel it necessary to announce that fact to the whole class. Devon and I walked quietly to my government class.

'I have government now.' I pointed to the door. 'Where are you headed?'

'Biology.' He looked intently at a poster for fall drama auditions on the wall.

'That's on the other side of the school. Devon, you don't have to walk with me.'

'I like the company.' He tore his eyes away from the poster and smiled.

I smiled back. 'Cool. Think about Saturday. It's supposed to be pretty fun.'

He nodded, then gave me an awkward wave and turned the other way. I went into government, where Saxon moodily tapped his foot, cell phone in one hand, call sheet in front of him. He barely looked at me when I walked in.

'Do you remember Devon Conner?' My words clicked out of my mouth with undisguised fury.

He stopped tapping his foot. 'Who are you, the Ghost of Christmas Past? Lay off today, Blix. I'm in no mood.'

'Do you?' I pressed, ignoring his comment.

'What part of "not in the mood" causes you confusion?' He met my eyes and tried to stare me down; I wasn't about to let him win this one. He gave up and shook his head with disgust. 'He was some dork I went to middle school with. I haven't talked to him in years.'

'Did you organize your classmates to exclude him?'

He looked at me with narrowed eyes. 'Yeah, then I burned a cross on his front lawn. Could you calm down the melodrama? I was, like, twelve the last time I had him in a class. Whatever I did to him, I'm not apologizing for it now.' He went back to tapping his foot.

Sanotoni came in and barked a laugh when he saw the cell phones out. He rubbed his hands together. 'Looking good, young pollsters. Let's get started.' He checked his watch. 'On the hour. OK, go!'

Thumbs worked overtime, and for the next forty-five minutes there was the endless chaos of phone dialing and dozens of low conversations going on simultaneously. Saxon was polite, direct and fast. He flew through half of our list in no time. He got snagged by a few talkers, but managed to get himself out without being rude. I planned on taking my time, but once I got someone on the phone, the thrill of competition crept over me and I couldn't help but do my best. When the final bell rang, Saxon and I were in the lead, with thirty completed surveys between us.

'We go again tomorrow. Dismissed,' Sanotoni said.

'Don't win this,' I begged Saxon in the corridor. 'It's just going to make problems.'

He laughed me off. 'Don't try to direct me. I'm not Jake. And try not to be a chicken shit when we win. It's a day out of here. Plus,' he said, and he moved his mouth close to my ear, 'you know you want to spend the day, just the two of us. Now you don't have to lie to Jakey. Tell him it's for school. Don't go into detail. Wouldn't want to confuse him.'

Saxon turned and stalked away, pushing past the

flow of traffic just to be an asshole. I was left with nothing to yell at his back: no angry retorts, no clever comeback. I slunk into craft class and grumbled through my macramé mess, ran so hard in PE I could hardly breathe when it was over, and stomped past Saxon on my way out to Jake's truck.

He was leaned against the passenger door, and as soon as he saw me, he opened the door and helped me in. *That*, I thought to myself, was the difference between dating someone like Saxon and dating some-one like Jake. Jake had basic manners. Jake was thoughtful and kind. Jake wasn't wreaking personal Armageddon on the lives of innocent dorks for fun.

Maybe he had slept with half the female population of Sussex County. I honestly couldn't care less. He loved me, he was good to me, and when I thought about him it felt like my heart was in bloom.

He smiled at me from the driver's side. 'I'm loving that I get to see you for lunch.' He pulled me over to the middle and threw his arm around my shoulder. I leaned my head against him and breathed in his smell.

We pulled up at Tech and he led me into the lunchroom. He felt me hold back a little bit.

'What's wrong, Bren?'

'I just . . . I don't know anyone here, I guess.' It

was that raw, jangly first-day-of-school feeling all over again, but I was already a month in.

'I do, though.' He rubbed his thumb over my knuckles. 'C'mon. You can meet my friends here.'

We went to a round table, the one I had seen Jake at the day before. 'Hey, guys,' he said. 'Brenna, this is Lou, Jesse, Ellen, Aaron, and Chloe.'

They all smiled friendly smiles and waved.

'This is the famous Brenna?' Lou asked. His lean face was friendly. 'We've heard a lot about you. A lot. Like never-endingly a lot.'

Everyone laughed.

'Shut up,' Jake mumbled, flicking a Dorito from Ellen's bag at Lou. They laughed again.

'All good stuff, though,' Lou added.

'Good to know,' I said and smiled at them all.

Jake led me to the cafeteria line. The selection was different than Frankford's, not better or worse, just different. I loaded my tray up.

'Is it OK here?' Jake stacked two yogurts on my tray with anxious fingers.

'It's good.' I squeezed his hand while I balanced my tray with one hand.

When we got to the checkout cashier, Jake paid for the both of us.

'I don't want you doing that.' I put my wallet back in my pocket with a frown.

'You're my girlfriend. I want to pay for you. I know you think I'm really poor, but I do work full time. Doubles on the weekend and three evening shifts a week, at least until I turn seventeen and can get my full license. Then I'll cut back.'

'I don't think you're really poor,' I said, even though I did. 'I just get money from my parents for lunch. What will I do with it all?'

He grabbed my tray, put all of my food on his, and slid the empty tray under the shared one. 'You mean you can't think of anything to do with extra money?'

I shrugged. I hadn't been shopping, except for my room, since I was in Denmark. 'Fine. I'll spend it on something else.' I thought about what I could get Jake for his birthday; would he be offended if I bought him new clothes? Money was a testy issue for him.

Back at the table, Jake touched my arm and thigh every so often to check on me. I realized part of the reason he wanted me to eat lunch with him was to show me off a little. He bragged about me to his friends, which made me blush and them laugh. It was weird to watch him talk about me. It was like eavesdropping on his thoughts, or reading his journal. If Jake kept a journal. It was flattering.

The rest of the day flowed smoothly. Our projects were almost ready to submit. We had created a set of business cards for our fictitious companies, and they wound up coming out better than I expected. Jake's work was a little more conventional, but he was meticulous and put a lot of thought in. My stuff was more creative. I was happy taking risks and playing around with ideas that were new or different. Our teacher was impressed.

'You two should do the next partner project together,' she said as she flipped through our portfolios. 'You both have excellent designs, and you have polar-opposite strengths. You'd do well together.'

Jake and I nodded respectfully, but under the table, he rubbed my leg.

'I guess we're pretty good together,' he whispered against my ear later in the corridor.

'Is that what she said? I thought she said you could learn a lot from me.'

He kissed me against his locker, pressing into me in a way he didn't often do in public. I hung on and kissed him back, pushing away everything I had done or left undone. I finally had a little bit of a grasp on the weight of Jake's regrets.

Friday was the longest day of my life. Saxon said nothing to me. He didn't catch me in the corridor, didn't walk by me, didn't talk to me. I was glad that day's government was the second calling session. We didn't have to speak to each other at all.

We won. Of course. Neither one of us spoke about the win or the day we would have to spend together the next week.

Devon decided to go to the concert. He was getting dropped off, but I told him the time and we planned to text when he got there, so we could meet up. He bit his lip nervously all through English. When we walked down the corridor together afterward, I caught sight of Chris and Kelsie and purposefully stopped to talk to them. I introduced Devon and mentioned the gig. Chris was all excited when Devon mentioned that his favorite Folly song was 'Slow Dog'.

'I wrote that song!' Chris exclaimed. I had never seen him that excited. 'You are my personal favorite fan, Devon.'

Kelsie punched his arm. 'What about me?'

'You are my personal favorite person,' he clarified.

We laughed, and Devon stopped chewing on his lip.

Kelsie gave me a necklace, one of her beaded ones made from blue glass. 'It's the same color as your eyes.'

I hugged her. 'It's beautiful. You're going to be famous someday.'

'Then that makes two of us.'

When it was time for track, I ran hard and long. Coach Dunn was ecstatic, which she showed me by thumping me on the back a few times until I felt like I might hack a lung. I had taken the late bus home on Thursday, and it had only been about half an hour. Friday, Mom picked me up.

'How was your class last night? I wasn't up when you got in.'

'Just some rotund stone fertility goddesses.' She smiled at me. 'Are you up for movies and ice cream? It looks like this group of students is going to drive me to consume Ben and Jerry's at least three times a week.'

'I'd love that.'

So Mom and I got some Chunky Monkey and Cherry Garcia and rented *My Big Fat Greek Wedding* and *The Birdcage*, two of our all-time favorites. We snuggled on the couch and laughed and ate our totally non-nutritious dinner, and it felt like old times again.

I knew Jake wouldn't call until late. He had to work extra hours to make up for taking Saturday off. Then he had to make sure his bike was in good working order, and then he was going to do a few laps on a course near his house.

By the time the movies were done, Mom could hardly keep her eyes open.

'Um, Mom?'

'Yeah, honey.' She took our bowls to the kitchen while I turned off the TV.

'My friend . . .' I took a deep breath and stood next to her in the kitchen. 'My boyfriend, Jake, is coming tomorrow. I just didn't know if you remembered.'

She turned and looked at me, my pretty mom with her blue-gray eyes and her good cheekbones that I didn't inherit. She tucked a piece of light hair behind her ear and blinked a few times. That was tears. I felt my throat tighten.

'Mom.' I took the bowls out of her hands and put them on the counter. 'We don't have to do this. If you don't feel comfortable, you and Thorsten could give me a ride.'

'No.' She put her hands on my shoulders. 'You're a good kid, Bren. I want to meet this Jake. If you like him, he must be something special.'

And now I had to bring in my backup, to make my mother feel better and spread the good kid thing on thick.

'I filled out that application for the Rotary Club study abroad. I emailed it last night, while you were at work.'

'Oh, baby.' Mom sighed and hugged me close. 'You are going to have such a great time.'

'Well, they have to accept me first. There might be a lot of applicants. It's possible I won't get in.'

Mom snorted at that. Then she smiled at me and said the words that made us both crack up. 'Brenna, sweetheart, who can hold a candle to you? You're *world traveled*.'

In my room that night, I laid out different outfits. I wanted to look cute, but stay warm. And I didn't want to wear something too dressy. Jake was riding a dirt bike, after all. But I wanted to look good, because I guessed we would head to the Folly concert without coming back to my house to change.

I finally settled on a pair of skinny jeans and a custom-made Folly shirt. It was the one with Kelsie and Chris on it, but I had printed it on a long-sleeved black V-neck T-shirt, so it was slightly different than the ones at the concert would be. I would wear my hair long and straight, and I decided to pull out the navy-blue, lace-up leather boots I got in Sweden because they were technically outdoor boots even if they were gorgeous and finely detailed, and I would be tramping through the mud in them. I laid Kelsie's necklace out, impressed by my friend's incredible talent.

Before bed, I trimmed my fringe. It was a little scary the first time I ever attempted it, but I like it to be right above my eyebrows, and if I didn't trim it myself, I'd have to go to the salon every two weeks. I had watched a few YouTube videos and read two online articles; it's shocking how much information there is online about cutting your own fringe. And I did a good job. More importantly, cutting it took my mind off all the emotions that tumbled through me about the next day.

Finally, there was nothing else I could do to stall. And just when I was getting desperate, the phone rang.

'Jake,' I said automatically, but it wasn't Jake.

'Brenna,' the voice on the other end slurred.

'Saxon?' My head spun. Why was he calling so late? I could hear music and laughing and yells in the background. 'Where are you?'

'Partying.' His voice was heavy and angry around the word. 'I want you.'

'Enough,' I hissed. 'I'm with Jake, I love him. I don't love you.'

He laughed a hard sound. 'I don't love you either.' He had obviously been drinking. 'I just *want* you.'

'I'm hanging up now.' I was irritated I hadn't checked the number before I dived for the phone.

'What if I change my mind about telling Jake?' he threatened.

I thought about how brave Jake had been, telling me about the things he had done that made him so ashamed. I'd listened, and Jake thanked me for not judging. But I had been full of shit.

I'd judged him. I'd looked down my nose at him, while I did the same and worse. When Jake had slept with those girls, he hadn't had anyone to care about. He hadn't had me.

But I had Jake. And I was gutless. I was letting things go too far with Saxon. I was letting my fascination with someone totally warped ruin the best thing I had ever had with anyone.

'Tell him.' There was no fear when I said it. I even laughed at him. 'But I know you won't. If you don't have it to hold over my head, you won't have any power over me, will you? You're counting on Jake being so pissed off with me that he breaks up. You're counting on me running to you.'

'Jake will be pissed off,' Saxon slurred. 'And I will be here.'

'You've always underestimated Jake.' I shook my head. 'So have I. We're the stupid ones. Because Jake is stronger and braver and more honest than either one of us. I've been scared to tell him, but that's because

I've been expecting him to react the way I would.'

Saxon laughed right back at me. 'He will, Bren. Jake's only human, no matter how much you want to make him into a damn saint. He's going to do what any human guy would do. He's going to dump you.' The last words came out in a sneer.

'No, he won't.' I refused to let Saxon burrow in my head. This was his favorite game, and I had to keep that in perspective.

His voice was dark and mean. 'Try it. And when it all falls apart, I'll be here. Waiting for you. 'Cos you and me, we're the same kind of people. We don't deserve anybody but each other.'

I clicked the phone off and chucked it on the bed. I hated that I was letting him do this to me. I hated that he made me doubt Jake.

But I did doubt. How could I not? I had betrayed Jake's trust, and I was honest enough to know that even if Saxon and I hadn't technically done anything to constitute cheating, I had crossed a line that I wasn't comfortable with. If Jake had done the same things with another girl that I'd done with Saxon, I would have been heartbroken.

I had used Jake's past against him. I had let him feel guilty for what he had done, and I had used it to justify my own shady conduct.

I realized I had to make a decision for myself. I had to be as brave as Jake had been.

When the phone rang again, I picked up and felt my throat close like I was going to cry.

'Hello? Brenna?' It was Jake's voice. 'Brenna, are you there?' He sounded worried, a little wild.

'Jake.' The tears started. 'I need to talk to you.'

'Go ahead, baby,' he said softly. 'I'm right here.'

'I don't think I can do it over the phone. I have to tell you . . . I have to tell you some things I'm not . . . I don't . . .' By now I was crying so hard, I wasn't making any sense.

'Calm down. I'll be there in ten minutes.' The phone clicked off, and I paced my room for the ten longest minutes of my life. Just when I was in control enough to call Jake back and tell him not to worry, I heard a light knock on my window.

I lifted it open, and Jake was there, mud smudged on his face and clothes. He looked panicked. 'I got here as soon as I could. Did something happen? Tell me what's wrong.'

'Where's your truck?' I glanced out the window.

'I parked down the street, off on the side. No one will see it.' He shivered a little.

'Do you want to come in?' I decided to tell him

everything, but not hanging out the window in the freezing night air.

'I'm covered in mud. Your room is so clean.'

'Leave your clothes under the window, behind the azaleas.'

'The what?' Jake asked, his voice a few feet away.

'The bushes.' I heard him scurry around, and then he hoisted himself as quietly as he could into my bedroom window wearing just his boxers, his shoulders hunched and his body shaking with cold. I ran and grabbed a towel from the bathroom, then wiped him off and led him to my bed. We stood together at the side.

'Are you sure?' His look told me he wouldn't blame me one bit if I sent him back into the frigid night.

I nodded, even as every fear and nerve in my body screamed at me, telling me this was risky and stupid and would not end well. Thorsten could stick his head in to check on me, Mom could get up and need to see me. But the risks didn't outweigh the benefits for me.

I pulled the covers back, got into my bed and held my arms out. Jake climbed in next to me, his skin clammy and cold against mine. I wrapped my arms around him, and pulled his body close, cocooning him with my warmth. I ran my fingers through his hair, pressing it back off his face.

'What's wrong, baby?' he asked. 'Why are you so sad?'

I realized then that my eyes stung. Wet sloppy tears trailed down my face. Jake put his hand up to my cheeks and wiped them away as they fell.

'I've lied to you.' I said the words slowly, so he wouldn't miss them.

He waited for me to go on, his gray eyes trusting. The only light in my room was from my iPod dock, so there was a blue glow and nothing else.

'Tell me. It's no good keeping it in.'

I realized he was wise for how young we were. He was kind and understanding, and I had completely underestimated him. The tears ran faster, and I had this choking sense of fear. I was so afraid I would tell him and I would see those eyes change. I didn't know how I would be able to stand it if I saw anger and, worse, disappointment. What if he didn't want to be with me? What if he was so mad he got up and left and that was it? I cried a little harder, and the tears turned into choking sobs.

'Brenna.' He smoothed my hair back with big, rough hands. 'I'm here for you. Whatever it is, I won't be mad at you.'

'You . . . you can't say that. You can't . . . you can't know that.' I was having a hard time breathing.

'Shh,' he whispered against my ear. 'Don't worry. I do know that. I love you. I can't be mad at you.'

So I grabbed onto his words and took them at face value. I put my hands over my face because I didn't have the guts to look at him while I confessed, and I started at the beginning, the day I met Saxon. I didn't leave anything out. I didn't smooth over anything. I told him what I felt and thought. A heavy blanket of shame crept over me. I was so wrapped up in my story, I couldn't pay any attention to Jake's reactions. The last thing I told him about was Saxon's call, just before his. I heard him suck his breath in, but he didn't say a word.

When I was done, there was just silence in the room, deafening and complete silence. I peeled my hands back from my eyes and looked at him in the dim light, holding my breath against my worst fears.

'Jake?' My voice wobbled.

'Yeah?' I heard his voice crack a little. I couldn't see his face clearly, and I was relieved because I really didn't want to see him crying.

'Do you want to break up?' I could hear how pathetic and scared my voice was, but I didn't care. 'Because I don't blame you if you do.'

'No.' He laughed sadly around what were

definitely tears. 'I, uh, just know how you must feel knowing I was with other people.'

'But you weren't since we were together.' Even though he couldn't see my face, I hid it behind my hands in the dark, ashamed of how out of control things had gotten. 'You should be so pissed off with me right now.'

'I am a little, but I also understand better than you think. And, no, I haven't been with anyone else since I met you.' I reached out to touch him. My hand strayed up past his chest and I felt the rapid beat of his heart. 'But I fell for you really hard, Bren.'

'I fell for you hard, too. I'm not blaming this on Saxon, but there were a lot of weird situations that I didn't know how to handle. I messed up, Jake, and he kind of took advantage. He thought I wouldn't have the guts to tell you, and he kept threatening me with it.'

I felt Jake go rigid. 'That asshole. Don't ever think you can't tell me anything. I swear to God, I will never turn my back on you. No matter what.'

'I got pulled into his bullshit. That's all there is to say, I guess. I thought I was smarter than him, but he's tricky.' I took a deep breath, because this was the hardest thing for me to admit to Jake. 'I also . . . underestimated you, Jake. I didn't think I could tell you the truth. And I looked down on you when you told me about all the stuff you'd done with other girls. I thought you didn't have any self-control, but the whole time, I was doing the same thing. And I wasn't drunk.'

He pulled me close to him. Our faces were just inches apart. 'I love you. And I'm glad you trusted me to tell me. I can't say I'm happy about this, but I don't want you to ever feel like you have to lie or not tell me something.'

I pressed my mouth to his, suddenly needing to kiss him and feel him against me. Being in my bed with him, under my covers, it felt like we were the only two people who existed on earth. I forgot about everyone else, forgot about Saxon completely, and even forgot Mom and Thorsten. It was just me and Jake in our own little world.

'It feels so good, being here with you.' His voice was husky and deep. He kissed me again, slowly. 'You're really warm.' He sighed and kissed my neck.

'You are too. You are now.' I wrapped my arms around him.

'I don't want to leave you,' he said, his voice torn.

'Stay for a little bit,' I begged.

I felt him try to get up, but I held on to him. I kissed him and touched him, even though he told me not to.

Soon our hands were all over each other, our lips were all over each other, and the thought of him leaving was enough to make me feel like I couldn't breathe. We kept our voices muffled and let our hands move slowly. He didn't stop me when I moved my hand under his boxers, and when he finished, he laid me on my back, his hands making me squirm and press against him until my body broke into a thousand pieces, and I moaned at the incredible perfection of it. We fell asleep with our faces close, tucked against each other like two puzzle pieces.

Chapter 13

When I opened my eyes, the sky outside my window was gray-pink with dawn. Jake was up and creeping out of the window.

'Were you leaving without saying goodbye?'

He started at my voice, then came back to sit next to me. 'Yeah. It took me fifteen minutes to scare myself enough to get out of bed. I am not getting caught sneaking out of your window the day I'm supposed to meet your mom.' He leaned toward me and kissed me softly. The bed was still warm where he had been. 'I'm getting a little addicted to you. It's hard to leave you.'

'You need to go back to sleep when you get home.' I traced his face with my fingers. 'Your race is today.'

'Screw the race.' He grinned and kissed my nose. 'Last night was the best night of my life. So far.' He ran his hand over my hair and kissed me again.

'When will you be back?' I held him tight against me.

'You'll hardly even know I was gone. The race is at ten, so I'll be here by nine, if that's OK.' He went to the window and looked down at the muddy clothes. 'Just to prepare you, I am going to cry like a baby when I have to put those on.'

'I don't think I have anything that would fit you. I could grab something of Thorsten's,' I said, getting out of the warm bed and following him over.

'No way. Too risky.' He jumped out the window. He shook his delicious, muscled limbs and put his clothes on, jumping up and down with cold. 'I'll see you in a few hours. I love you, Bren.'

'I love you, Jake.' I leaned out the window and kissed him, trying not to get choked up as he moved away from me.

It wasn't even possible to think about going to sleep again, but I wanted to be ready for the day, so I made myself at least lie down and breathe deeply – in twice and out once, my chest rising and falling – until I dozed. When I woke up with a start, it was eight o'clock. I had an hour to get ready.

I made my bed, and it seemed impossible Jake had been there with me the night before. I felt so good and light after telling him everything. Saxon wasn't hanging a sword over our heads anymore, and I finally felt like I could breathe easier. I was still a little ashamed I had doubted Jake's commitment to me.

I showered and got ready, taking extra long because I was freaking out about the day, and I preferred to focus on getting my mascara on without any clumps than imagining what would happen when Jake and Saxon and I all wound up in one place together later that night.

Before I knew it I heard the familiar rumble of Jake's truck and the crunch of his tires on the gravel of our driveway. My heart raced and I gripped the washbasin for a few seconds, trying to work up the courage to go out and meet him.

I heard Mom open the door. I heard Jake's low voice, and I heard her say, 'Thank you, Jake. That was so thoughtful of you.'

I crept out of the bathroom like the coward I was, and saw Jake had handed my mom a bunch of flowers. He had on a blue shirt that brought out shades of blue in his usually gray eyes. His hair was brushed down and gelled. It seemed like he had worked really hard to get a certain look, but I wasn't sure what it was. Maybe 'responsible boy who won't break your daughter's heart'.

Thorsten came down the stairs and shook Jake's hand. I was so relieved Fa was here today. His cool Scandinavian calm tended to offset Mom's natural crazy neuroticism. Jake stood awkwardly when I came down the hall.

All three of them looked at me at once. Thorsten looked happy and kind, as usual, Mom looked like she was trying really hard not to cry, and Jake smiled so wide it looked like it had to hurt.

It was Jake who moved forward first, then stopped. He seemed to sense my mother's territorial vibe.

'Wow. You look really pretty, Brenna.' Jake fumbled with one of the buttons on his shirt.

My mom gave him an assessing look. 'She does, doesn't she?'

'You're going to need to keep away from the track. It's way too muddy.' Jake looked a little worried.

'Is it dangerous, Jake?' my mother asked.

'No, ma'am, not for Brenna. Sometimes the riders wipe out, but we're in a gated track.'

'I see you drove.' My mother gave Jake a long, piercing look that I'm pretty sure most interrogators would kill to master. 'Have you been driving long?'

'Yes, ma'am. I've worked on a farm since I was about fourteen, and I drove their tractor the first day. After a few months, they let me drive the work trucks, too. I never speed,' he added hastily.

'You work on a farm?' Thorsten asked. He grew up

on a farm, so he had this agricultural camaraderie thing. 'Where do you work?'

'Zinga's, sir.' He looked at me, just a really quick flick of his eyes, but I could see he was nervous.

'I love their apple tarts!' Thorsten said enthusiastically.

It broke the tension. Everyone laughed.

'Fa loves to eat anything,' I said.

'I should be very fat.' Thorsten patted his stomach. 'I have to walk everywhere, or I'll get a big gut.'

Mom laughed. 'Well, you kids should get going. Brenna, do you have your cell phone on?'

'Of course.' I took her into my arms and held her very tight. 'I love you so much. Thank you.'

'Well, he's very polite,' she whispered as I held her. 'And he certainly is very good looking.' Louder, she said, 'Wear your seatbelts at all times, no exceptions. Give me a call when you get to your concert and when you get out. I don't care how late it is.'

We agreed, I hugged her and kissed Fa, and grabbed Jake's hand. If it was possible, I felt even lighter than I did after I'd talked to Jake the night before. As Jake opened my door and I climbed into the old truck, I saw the familiar flick of the curtain, and it made my heart glow with toasty warmth.

Jake pulled out very slowly and carefully. He

probably overdid it, but I imagined Mom would appreciate his effort to impress her with his caution. 'Wow. Your mom is scary.' Jake undid the top button on his shirt and took a deep breath.

'I thought she was being nice.' I felt the defensive prickle that I always felt when someone said something not completely complimentary about my mom.

'I didn't say she wasn't nice. I said she was scary.' He looked a little pale. 'She stared at me the whole time like she was trying to decide if she should punch me in the face or let me go out with you.'

I laughed. 'You're exaggerating. She told me she thinks you're hot.'

He looked over at me, his eyes dancing. 'No way!'

'When she hugged me.' I reached over and tousled his perfectly gelled hair a little.

'Wow.' He shook his head.

'What?'

'Your mom's like this super-scary, super-hot professor. I guess I'm just really flattered.' He raised his eyebrows at me. 'Do you think I'm hot?'

'I do.' I leaned against his shoulder. 'Especially in that shirt. I love all those buttons.'

We laughed easily. It was nice to be able to be so comfortable with him. I thought after we slept in the same bed, there might be some awkwardness, but there was nothing like that. He kept one hand on the steering wheel and shrugged out of his shirt. He was wearing a worn T-shirt underneath.

'I'm a little nervous about the race,' he admitted.

'Don't be. You'll do great,' I said, though, of course, I had no idea at all.

'I don't usually mind screwing up, but I don't love the idea of doing it in front of you.' He tapped his hands nervously on the steering wheel. 'Just don't go home with the winner instead of me.' He wanted it to be a joke, but he couldn't bring himself to laugh at it.

'Don't be insane. Like I'd even be interested in anyone else? Anyway, maybe you'll win,' I suggested. 'I can't even tell if there's a real chance that you will. You're always so pessimistic about yourself, I don't know if I should believe you.'

'We'll find out soon enough.' He changed gear and drummed on his steering wheel faster, not able to settle down at all.

When we pulled up, there were hundreds of other cars already there. I felt my jaw drop. I guess I had been expecting a couple of dozen people and a little dirt track. This was huge. The track was enormous, and there were already really little kids flying around it. Kids who looked small enough to be in kindergarten.

Jake looked over at them and grinned. 'I was that age when I won my first race.'

I remembered he had told me he was four when he started riding. 'Do you win a lot?'

He laughed and rubbed his neck. 'A lot for an amateur.' He reached into his backseat, pulled out a long-sleeved motocross shirt, and put it on. He got back in the truck to put on his pants, then boots and knee and elbow pads. When he stood and turned, his helmet tucked under his arm, I felt a girlie thrill. He looked very sporty and tough.

In the back of the truck, under a tarp, was his dirt bike. It was bigger than I expected, and very clean.

'Did you wash it for the race?' I pulled a finger along the shiny metal of the fender.

'Of course.' He looked at me in shock when I laughed. 'What's so funny?'

'Jake, you washed your *dirt* bike the day of a big *dirt*-track race? You don't think it's funny?' The more I thought about it, the more it made me giggle, then full out laugh.

Jake just sighed. 'You,' he said, and kissed me between giggles, 'just don't understand.'

He parked near one of the ramps that were set up in the area, hopped into the back and pushed his bike down. He set the helmet on the bike, and then we walked to a tent where people were waiting with clipboards and number placards.

The sound was intense. There was the constant whine of a dozen bikes racing at the same time coupled with the cheers of the crowds and the droning announcements from four big loudspeakers.

'Jake Kelly.' Jake smiled at the older woman checking people in.

'Jake! How nice to see you! I hope you win the big one this year.' She smiled and handed him two large number seventy-eights for his bike and his shirt.

'Thanks,' he said shyly and we moved on.

'So, are you some hot shot in the world of dirt-bike racing?' I asked as he attempted to pin the number on his shirt. I brushed his hands aside and pinned it for him, making sure it wasn't crooked.

'In the world of Sussex County amateur dirt-bike racing I'm like a demi-god.' He winked at me.

Just then a gaggle of girls called his name. When he looked up, one of them took a picture of him with her phone, and they giggled and ran.

'Oh no.' I put my hands on his big, broad shoulders. 'This is going to be one big Jake Kelly love-fest, isn't it?'

'I hope it's one big Jake Kelly win-fest.' He tugged me closer and leaned to whisper in my ear, 'I'd prefer a private Jake Kelly love-fest later on, if you know what I mean.'

He was just about to kiss me, when a bunch of guys wearing the same kind of motocross outfits came over to us.

'Hey, Jake,' said a guy with slicked black hair and crooked teeth. 'Ready to lose?'

'If I'm racing you, it isn't really a worry.' He put his arm around me tight.

I noticed every guy in the group looked at me a little hungrily.

'Who's your girl, Jake?' the crooked-toothed guy asked.

'Guys, this is Brenna. I'm not introducing them,' he said cheerfully to me. 'They're mostly idiots, and you don't really need to know anyone here but me.'

The guys hooted. 'He's just scared you'll realize there's something better than the old village dirt bike,' Crooked Teeth said, half joking, half nasty.

I smiled dumbly because I didn't really know what to say. The tone was a little meaner than I was comfortable with. The guys moved on quickly, most of them looking back to whistle or cat-call.

'That was weird,' I said.

Jake reached for my hand, put it to his lips, and kissed my knuckles. 'They're scumbags. Listen, don't talk to any of them while I'm racing, OK?' His eyes had that strange, maniacal gleam that only bubbled up when he got seriously angry.

I felt my face go hot. 'I know I'm not really in any position to be offended that you just said that, but c'mon, Jake.'

'I'm not worried about you.' He kissed me softly. 'They're like damn dogs. Give them any encouragement, and you won't be able to get the hell away from them.'

'When is your race?' I asked.

'Twenty minutes. But I get a few minutes to run the course between races. I'll take you over to the stands, OK? You want a soda or some food?' There were little vendor huts set up all over. The track had turned into a little city with food and clothing vendors, portaloos, repair stations, and sponsor huts.

I was a little hungry, but I didn't want Jake to miss out on any practice time. 'I'd rather get something with you after you race.'

'All right.' He squinted a little in the sun and smiled. 'I'm glad you're here. No one's really come to see me race before.'

'Never?' I couldn't believe his dad never wanted to be by his side when he raced.

He hesitated. 'Mom of course, before she died. And

Saxon, back when we were friends. He used to race, actually.'

'Oh,' I said. He shifted uncomfortably, and I switched tack. 'I'm glad I'm here, too.'

'Good.' His smile was a little more guarded. We walked to the stands. He came as far as he could go with his bike, then directed me to sit where he could see me.

'It's important.' He held me by the elbows. 'I want to be able to see you, OK?'

'I get it. Wait.' I took my camera out of my purse. 'Stand next to your bike.' He did and gave a cocky smile. I snapped the picture and kissed him again. 'Have fun and be careful.'

He laughed. 'Love you!'

'Love you, too!' I called. When I turned to go into the stands, I saw it was dirt-bike-groupie central. There were girls all over, talking on cell phones, reading magazines, watching the track, chatting and laughing. I sat just on the perimeter. No one talked to me, but I was fine just watching.

'Hey!' called a girl with really white blonde hair and a top that looked exactly like a corset. I thought it might just be a frilly tube top, but when I looked closer it was definitely a corset. Like a Victoria's Secret black-and-red lace corset that's usually worn under clothing or just in the bedroom. But this girl had it on as a top, with tight jeans. I was a little shocked. 'You Jake Kelly's girlfriend?' She laughed behind her hand and some of the other hoochie-looking girls laughed along.

'Yeah,' I said. 'I am.'

'Well, enjoy it while it lasts.' She snapped her gum loudly. 'He goes through them pretty quick.' She made a nasty face at me. I was being taunted by a corset-wearing, gum-cracking hoe with straw for hair.

'Thanks,' I said with a big, fake smile, then opened my eyes really wide. 'I think one of the girls just got out.' I pointed to her chest.

She pressed both hands over her scantily covered boobs and looked down frantically. I had already turned back to the race, but I did hear her call 'bitch' in my direction. I sighed. It would be nice if everyone here wasn't a leering idiot or a backstabbing hooker-wannabe.

To top it off, I had no idea how the race worked. I didn't know how many laps they did, I didn't know what the classes were, and I didn't know what the different divisions meant. Honestly, I never imagined it would be this complicated.

Just as that thought went through my head, I noticed the girls turn into a giggling, preening pack of hyenas. There had to be a guy coming over.

There sure was.

'Saxon!' My heart leaped into my throat.

Not this, not now, not when Jake was so nervous and excited.

He had a cardboard box balanced on one hand. He wore dark aviator sunglasses and his usual tight thermal top and worn jeans with a studded belt.

'Hey, Blix.' He walked up to me.

I was practically deafened by all the hissing coming from the rejected hussies.

'You need to leave.' I put my hands up and shook my head.

He ignored me and sat down by my side. He looked pale, his lips were dry, cracked, and busted in two places, and a long bruise purpled his cheek. 'I brought something. A peace offering.'

'What happened to your face?' It looked painful.

'Forget it. Here.' He pushed the box in my direction.

Hot dogs all the way and icy Cokes. Salted fries with . . . 'Is that vinegar on the fries?' I asked eagerly. What was I thinking? This was Saxon, the guy who had almost ruined what I had with Jake.

'Yeah.' He put the box in my lap. 'I had a feeling you'd be the kind of girl who liked her fries doused in something gross.'

It was . . . nice. He looked like he felt guilty. But I had fallen hard and deep into his bullshit before. I wasn't that stupid.

'Thanks, but I'm not hungry,' I said over my growling stomach. 'You just need to leave.' I picked the box up and passed it back to him.

'I need to talk to Jake. I need to apologize.' Saxon looked in my direction, but I couldn't see his eyes behind his mirrored sunglasses.

'Not now. I'm sitting where he can see me. He's about to race. If he sees you, you're going to throw him off.'

Saxon shoved the carton of food on my lap again. He was looking at Jake, who had already seen him and stalked over.

'I told him,' I whispered in Saxon's ear before Jake got close enough to notice. I still cared about Saxon too much to throw him to the wolves completely.

'What happened to keeping some things between you and me?' he growled through his teeth.

'There wasn't enough room for everyone. I had to throw you overboard.'

He smiled painfully around his split lip. 'Like I said: hottest at your bitchy best. Score one, Brenna.'

Jake was at the stands by now, his eyes bulging with rage.

'You come for more dental work, Saxon?' He hoisted himself over the gate and into the stands.

Saxon held up his hands. 'Down, killer. I'm here to say that I am a huge asshole. And I'm sorry. I'm sorry for the shit with Brenna. I'm sorry for what I said about your mom. That's it. I'm just sorry.'

'Fine.' Jake shrugged and pointed out of the stands. 'Now get the hell out of here and stay away from her.'

I felt a tad like a piece of meat, but also, somehow, touched. I didn't exactly like that Jake had reduced me to a single pronoun, but I also knew his anger came from an urge to defend me and prove his trust in me.

'I thought I'd stick around for the race,' Saxon said. 'For old times' sake.'

Jake and I looked at each other for a long minute.

'Did you get Brenna food?' He looked at the box I held. I felt like I should put it down or drop it.

'Yeah. I didn't think she would realize how long it could take.' Saxon smiled a little at Jake.

Jake sneered back, then looked directly at me. 'Eat, Bren. I'll be racing in another ten minutes, OK?'

I laid the box on the bench next to me and put my arms around him. 'You can trust me, Jake,' I whispered.

'I know that,' he whispered back. Then he kissed

me, extra long for Saxon's benefit. He jumped the gate and headed back to the track.

The pack of girls behind me was practically clawing and hissing.

Saxon gave them a glance that was pure disgust. A few of them got up and moved further down the bleachers.

'So you two laid it all out?' He picked up a fry, looked at it, slightly nauseated, and put it back.

I felt less guilty eating his food once I realized how much it grossed him out. Based on his phone conversation from the previous night, I could safely assume he had a major hangover.

'Jake already bared his guts. I was the one who had to quit taking the chicken-shit way out.' I chowed down on one of the hotdogs. Saxon looked a little green, which only convinced me to eat with more relish. Pun intended.

'What did you tell him?' Saxon looked straight ahead, probably to avoid the sickeningly good smell of chili sauce and onion.

'I told him every little thing, Saxon,' I admitted. 'Every look and conversation and kiss, and even what I felt.'

'What *did* you feel?' He leaned back in the stands and gave me a long look.

'That you were intriguing. That you were at least worth my friendship.' I drank from one of the cups of Coke. Even though there were two, Saxon took the one I was drinking out of my hands and drank from it. I knew exactly why he did it, but I had no idea how I felt about it.

'You're using the past tense, Blix. Can I assume that means you don't find me intriguing or friendship-worthy anymore?'

'No.' I put the half-eaten hotdog down in the box. 'I should have used the present tense. You are those things for someone. Just not me. And more important than all your good qualities put together is your one main bad quality.'

'Enlighten me.' He shook the cup, took a sip, and crunched some ice between his teeth.

'You're toxic.' It sounded awful and nasty, but it was the honest truth. 'You poison good things, and I don't think you even do it on purpose.'

'You don't think so?' He was mocking me, but there was a strain in his voice.

'I hope you don't. Because otherwise you're a total sociopath.' I could see the guys on the bikes lining up. I squinted and was pretty sure I could see Jake. The announcer was a mumbler. I couldn't fathom why anyone would put someone so inarticulate in charge of announcing important things to an audience this big.

'He's the fifth in from the outside.' Saxon leaned forward, watching.

'I thought that was him. So is it one lap?'

Saxon laughed. 'No. It's twenty.'

'Oh. What's he doing?' I watched Jake fiddle with his bike. Was it safe?

'Nervous habit. He's making sure his fuel switch is on.'

'But aren't they all on?' There was a dull roar coming from the gate.

'They'll run for a minute or two if they're switched off. No one wants to be the dipshit who loses the starting advantage because his fuel switch is off. He's waving at you.' Saxon's voice was bland around his last words.

But I had seen Jake's wave before Saxon mentioned it. I already stood on the bench, waving back like an idiot. 'Go Jake! Good luck!' I screamed.

Saxon pulled me gently back down. 'All right, Blix. The enthusiasm is admirable, but he can't hear you.'

'He knows,' I said confidently. I chewed on some vinegar fries. 'You used to race?'

'Yeah.' Saxon winced and rubbed his temples. 'But I got tired of the humiliation of getting my ass handed to me by Jake every time we competed. So I just stopped racing and started going to cheer him on. And make bets on him.'

'You bet money on Jake?' I had no idea there even were bets made on these races.

'Always have.' Saxon leaned forward again. 'He's a sure thing on the track. I have close to a grand riding on this race.'

I felt dangerously close to choking on the fry I was in the process of swallowing. 'A thousand dollars?'

'Every one of these hot shots thinks he's gonna come out the dark horse. Not with Jake Kelly on the track. He should go pro.'

The flag dropped and the bikes roared out of the gate. Jake was a few feet in front of every other bike.

'That's my boy.' Saxon's slow smile widened. 'Got his lead early on, and he'll keep it.'

I stood with my hand over my mouth, willing Jake to go faster and keep ahead of everyone else.

'Sit back and relax for a few laps,' Saxon advised. He leaned his head back and groaned. 'I guess I'm out of the loop for head rubs?'

'Yeah.' I only took my eyes off Jake for a second. 'You really are.'

He laughed. 'You're a stone bitch. I mean that in the most complimentary way possible.'

We watched Jake race around the track. He flew over a jump a few laps in and took both hands off his handlebars.

'Jake! You idiot! Jake!' I yelled.

I think Saxon had been napping. He sat up and his glasses slid off of his nose. 'What's wrong?' he asked sleepily.

'Jake's just being stupid.' I looked closely. He was holding on again. 'He did some kind of stunt.'

'What kind of stunt?' Saxon yawned.

'He took his hand off the handlebars while he was jumping,' I said hotly.

Saxon let out a short, harsh laugh. 'Calm down. He was changing the film on his goggles.'

'What?'

'The goggles he's wearing. They probably have a good inch of mud on them. So he's peeling the film off so he can see.' He chuckled again. 'Don't worry. Jake loves to win. He won't do any stunts.'

'Oh.' I felt incredibly dumb. 'I don't really know much about dirt-bike racing, I guess.'

'Motocross,' Saxon corrected. 'That's what it's called. Didn't you two talk about this before his race?'

I felt a wave of embarrassment when I thought about what we had done so often instead of talking about dirt bikes. Or talking at all.

Instead of answering Saxon, I took a sip of Coke and watched Jake. He was really fast. It was exciting to watch, but a little scary too. It was also really nerve-racking. I didn't want him to crash and burn, and I couldn't take my eyes off the race because I was afraid that was exactly what would happen the minute I looked away.

'You guys going to the Folly gig tonight?' Saxon rubbed his temples hard, and I could only imagine the pain that was pounding through his head.

'Yeah. My T-shirts are going to be selling tonight.' I was proud of that. I'd worked hard on them.

'Well, I'll make sure I buy one. I like putting my money toward any good charity.'

'Do you have to work hard at being an asshole, or does it just come naturally?' I asked cheerfully.

He grinned at me and took his sunglasses off.

'Saxon!' I kept half an eye on the race and tried to look at his face at the same time. 'Seriously. What happened to your eye? And, you know, the rest of your face?'

'I started out being my natural asshole self. Then I worked on it for a few minutes. And this is what I got.' He slid the glasses back on and winced.

'Who did it?' I felt a surge of anger. I couldn't help it. Saxon might be a deranged lunatic, but I couldn't help feeling like he was something damaged that needed my protection.

'Some senior who wasn't particularly happy I was making out with his girlfriend.'

'Was she someone special?' I hoped she was for a lot of reasons.

'Yeah, Bren. I proposed to her right after she let me feel her up in someone's parents' bathroom at a house party. It was magical.'

'Whatever,' I muttered, and turned my full attention back to Jake's race. If Saxon wanted to purposefully stick his face in front of angry fists, that was his deal.

I made it a point to move far away from Saxon. I got my camera and took a bunch of pictures of Jake. Thorsten had bought me a really high-speed camera the Christmas we were in Denmark. One of the features was supposed to be that it took really great action shots. It was how I got the one of Mom rocking out to 'Yellow Submarine'. But I'd never had the chance to try it out on an actual sport. I was happy with the results so far, and I was already trying to figure out how they would look silk-screen printed.

'These are the last two circuits,' Saxon said, sitting up. 'Come on.'

We left our seats and went to stand by the guard

rails, where the bikes flew by so quickly and so close we could feel the heat of the engines.

We watched for a minute, and Saxon pointed to the tower where they waved a white flag. 'We're coming to the last lap. He still has the lead, but that bastard on the yellow bike is right on his ass.' And then Saxon did something that shocked me. 'Come on, Jake!' he screamed. 'Don't be a pussy! Watch your turns!'

'I thought he couldn't hear you.' I had never seen Saxon get so worked up and excited.

'He knows.' He looked straight into my eyes. Then he turned back to the track. 'Win this bitch, Jake! Come on, Jake!'

I screamed along with Saxon. Jake took the first turn wide and the yellow bike inched up behind him. I put my hands to my mouth and pressed, nervous for him. At the next jump, Jake gunned it and he flew past the others. I knew it must be risky from the way the front of his bike wobbled.

'Oh God, don't be stupid, Jake,' Saxon said low.

'What's he doing?' I felt a wave of panic overtake me.

'He's taking the jump way too fast so he can make up for lost time. But if he doesn't land just right, he's going to crash and burn.' Saxon gripped the guard rail, his knuckles white. 'He's going to get himself killed.'

He was genuinely worried about Jake. I put my hand on his, and he looked up at me and smiled a little.

'Don't worry, Blix,' he said, changing his tune a little when he saw my anxious face. 'Jake will make the landing. Watch.' He sounded more hopeful than sure.

The bike was on the descent, and when it landed there was a shock of rubber and metal on dirt. My breath caught in my lungs as the bike skidded across the lanes. It looked like there was no way Jake could stop the inevitable tilt toward complete wipeout.

The stands were unusually quiet as everyone watched. Despite the laws of gravity, despite all reason, Jake righted the bike and raced ahead. He rounded the final turn and the checkered flag went down. The other bikes sped in behind him.

Jake won the race.

Saxon looked at me and held his arms up, screaming in triumph. He grabbed me and lifted me up, shaking me and screaming with happiness. He dropped me back with a thud and screamed again.

They announced Jake's name as the winner. He rode to the stands and hopped off his bike, yanked his helmet off, jumped the rail and grabbed me, covered in mud and sweat. I didn't care.

'You won!' I grabbed his face in my hands.

'I did,' he grinned. 'You were right here for me.'

Then he kissed me. His arms were around me and the roar of the crowds was behind us. I could feel his excitement from the win, and it was like I could taste the adrenaline on his tongue. He held me for a few more seconds, kissed me again, then jumped back down to get his bike.

Saxon grabbed my hand. 'Come on. He'll need help with his bike.'

We went to the truck. Jake was collecting his prize – a check for a hundred dollars, Saxon explained.

'He could make a lot more. He could be a pro, no question.' Saxon pulled out a cigarette.

'Does he want to?' I asked.

'I don't know anything about what Jake wants anymore.' Saxon's mouth was set in a line. Jake hadn't even acknowledged him when he jumped into the stands. I realized it had probably hurt Saxon.

I scanned the crowds for Jake. 'Why are you here, Saxon?'

'I had a grand riding on this.' He took a long drag.

I put a hand on his elbow. 'Why did you bet on him?'

'I told you, he's a sure thing,' he growled. He didn't shrug my hand off, but from the way he stared,

I got the message that I was playing with fire, and I let it drop to my side.

I didn't say anything else to him. Jake came over a few minutes later. He was breathing hard, and he looked exhausted.

'Let me help.' Saxon stubbed his cigarette out under his boot sole.

Jake didn't look like he had the energy to protest. His hair was plastered to his head with sweat, his shoulders sagged, and his eyes were red rimmed.

He and Saxon pushed the bike back up the dirt ramp and into the bed of the truck.

'Good job, man,' Saxon said.

Jake squinted at him. 'Thanks.'

They stood in awkward silence.

'I'll see you guys around.' Saxon turned on his heel and stalked off, hands in his pockets.

I watched Saxon walk away while Jake kept his eyes on his bike. 'He bet on you.'

He swung his head to look at me. 'He seriously put down a bet?'

'A thousand dollars. Or he won a thousand dollars. Maybe you should bet on yourself sometime,' I suggested.

Jake looked at me hard. 'He told you that?'

'Yeah, when we were in the stands. He explained

about the race. I didn't realize how much I didn't know.' I looked at his face, trying to gauge if he was angry. He just looked tired.

'Do you mind going to my place so I can shower?' he asked finally, ignoring the whole issue.

'No problem.' I pulled him to me and kissed him again. 'I'm really proud of you. You did great out there.'

'Thanks.' He wrapped me in a bone-crushing hug for a few long seconds.

We drove to his house, Jake singing along to the classic rock station at the top of his lungs. I laughed hard and joined him.

I was totally curious to see his house. We pulled into The Lake and drove for a few minutes, winding down a few different roads until we came to a neat white house. It was clean and maintained, but it was boring. There was no landscaping, no decoration. Just a little white box.

He parked and came around to open my door.

'Am I going to meet your dad?' I asked.

He shook his head. 'He bowls all day Saturday, then watches ESPN with the guys all night.' He went to the back of the truck and got the bike out, rolled it to a small shed with a lock, and came back to join me.

'He went bowling instead of going to your race?' I linked my hand in Jake's.

His eyes looked hot and angry, and I wished I had kept my big mouth shut for once.

'Yeah.' He opened his front door and led me in. We stood in a small, depressingly plain living room. The walls were stark white. The carpet was brown. There were two old LazyBoy recliners and a plaid couch. I followed Jake to the kitchen, white with dark cabinets and a dingy yellow laminate countertop.

There was a small dining alcove with a dark wood table and four straight-back chairs.

'You want something to drink?' Jake asked. 'All we have is soda.'

'I drink soda sometimes.' I smiled and looked around, taking in all the boring nothing of Jake's house. 'I'll have one.'

The drink was the store brand, but I wasn't brand picky when it came to soda. It all tasted like sweet bubbles to me. He led me to his bedroom.

There was a single bed with a dark-blue cover. There was a scratched desk with a lamp and a plain chair. A dresser in the corner supported a fairly old TV and a banged-up PS3. A few motocross posters were tacked neatly on the wall, and Jake had printed the picture of me at the movie theater and taped it right next to his bed.

'I know.' He smiled apologetically. 'It's pretty boring.'

'It is,' I agreed. 'We could redo it sometime, if you wanted. If your dad was cool with it.'

He shrugged. 'I just sleep in here. My father never comes in, so it wouldn't matter to him either way.' I sat on his bed and he sat next to me. Then he pulled me back and we bounced against the mattress and laughed. He started to kiss me, but I, for once, held back. 'What's wrong?' he asked.

'I'm sorry. You're getting dirt all over me.' The dirt on his gear was drying and crumbling.

'I'll fix that.' He jumped off the bed and stripped off his clothes, right down to his boxers.

'You're pretty comfortable getting undressed in front of me.' I had a hard time taking my eyes off him.

'You're always figuring out some way to get me out of my clothes,' he accused. He put his stuff neatly in the hamper and smelled his own armpit.

'Jake!' I yelled. 'That's gross.'

'What?' he balked. 'I stink. I was doing it out of consideration for you.' He pounced on me and pinned me to the bed. 'I was just going to tell you I need to get in the shower before I overpower you with my pit stink. I'm a pretty nice boyfriend, aren't I?'

I pretended to gag. 'I can't think. You smell too disgusting.'

He kissed me all over my face, and I giggled because his good mood was contagious. He jumped up and headed out the room. 'Five minutes. Try not to get in any trouble.'

The minute I heard the shower come on, I started to conduct a thorough search of his room, and I didn't feel the least bit guilty about it. It was my right as Jake's girlfriend to spy.

It was fairly disappointing.

His closet was disgustingly tidy. He had barely any clothes, and they were all clean, hung up and neat. The drawers of his desk held fairly normal things: a Swiss army knife, thumbtacks, scissors, a razor knife, a ruler, some glue and rubber cement. Next to his bed was a small nightstand. I was not surprised to find a bottle of lotion and a box of tissues. There was one little box under his bed. That was the only thing that made me feel at all guilty, but I looked in it anyway.

It had some Boy Scout patches, an old Spider-Man action figure, a little first-place MiniMotocross ribbon, and some pictures. They were mostly Polaroids, and mostly blurry. One was a woman with long brown hair wearing a tube top and big sunglasses. She was smiling and there was a baby on her lap. He looked like he could be Jake, but I couldn't be sure. Babies mostly looked the same to me. There were a few more pictures of little Jake, some really cute school pictures and a Halloween picture where he was dressed as Dracula. There was one where Jake was probably six or seven. A dark-eyed boy with spiky black hair had his arm around him. Saxon?

In the bottom of the box there was a little folded note. When I opened it up, I felt a warm, sweet heat flow through me. It was the note we'd written in class, the one where he invited me to the race. He had kept it tucked in the box where he kept all his most valuable possessions. I ran my fingers over the creased edges.

I heard Jake come out of the bathroom and shoved the box back under the bed, then sat very still on his mattress, wearing my best innocent face.

'Were you snooping?' Jake asked, a good-natured smile on his face.

I opened my mouth to deny it, then shut it. No more lying.

'Just a little. I was curious.'

'That's OK.' He waved his hand at the room. 'Sorry I don't have much to snoop through.'

'It was fun, anyway.' I leaned back on my elbows.

He had his towel wrapped around his waist and nothing else on. His eyes looked me over hungrily. 'I saw you in the stands the whole time.' He came to sit next to me on the bed.

His skin was still warm and damp, and it smelled so good, with that soapy-shower scent clinging to it. The gel had been washed out of his hair, so it fell messily, almost in his gray eyes. I caught a whiff of mint from his toothpaste, and when he smiled, that twisted eyetooth made my heart thud.

'I watched you the whole time. And I was brave. There were many scantily clad girls who were not happy to know you were taken.'

He pulled me over and kissed me. 'Definitely taken,' he said, his voice deep. He kissed me until I was lying back, my hands on his nearly naked body, running over the relaxed muscles. He was already hard.

'I know where your lotion is,' I whispered.

He laughed. 'Shameless hussy,' he said and kissed me again.

I took over then, and when I had satisfied him, he returned the favor, and then we lay in each other's arms, staring at his too-white ceiling, talking and giggling and making out for so long, I forgot about the time.

'It's kind of weird that I'm still completely dressed and you're completely naked,' I said in the comfortable silence.

'That's the kind of manipulative girl you are. Somehow you always convince me to get naked, whether I want to or not.' He kissed my nose. 'But, speaking of my nudity, I need to get dressed if we're going to get to the gig on time.'

I sat up to watch him. His body was so muscled and lean he could have been a Greek statue. I had never watched a guy get dressed before. He didn't even have to look at his clothes. Everything he owned was bland, and it all matched everything else. He could pull the first shirt off the first hanger and it matched every pair of pants he owned. He had two pairs of work boots. One pair was dirty with a frayed pair of laces. The other pair was dirtier with masking tape on the toe. He chose the dirty pair.

His socks had holes in them and his boxers were threadbare.

'Jake,' I suggested. 'Maybe you should use your prize money to buy some socks without holes.'

Jake shook his head. 'Can't. If I buy my own socks, my dad has nothing to get me for Christmas.'

'Like in your stocking?' I felt a little babyish, but I wanted to know. I was spoiled, being an only child, and my stocking was always stuffed full of magazines, make-up, candy and funny gag gifts. I also got a ton of stuff under the tree, all thoughtful, wonderful gifts Mom and Thorsten had picked up and stored away all year long.

'No, under the tree. I always get two bags of socks, a flashlight and fifty dollars.' Jake said it matter-of-factly.

'That's all you get?' I tried to wrap my head around such boring, repetitive gifts. 'Every year?'

'Yeah. It's kind of weird that I get a flashlight every year, since they last. My father buys really good-quality flashlights.' Jake opened his closet door and pointed to the top shelf. There was a collection of flashlights, all black and industrial looking.

'That's so thoughtless and depressing,' I griped, disliking Jake's father even more.

'I do get fifty bucks, Bren,' he pointed out. 'So I can go buy myself something I like. Don't feel bad for me.' He put his arm around me. 'We have a tree and Dad buys turkey TV dinners. We even watch *It's a Wonderful Life* together. I get to do Christmas stuff.'

I shook my head. Jake's entire home life seemed so bland and miserable. How could someone so creative and passionate and loving have sprung to life in this soulless place? It didn't seem possible. 'It just seems . . .'

'Depressing?' he finished. 'Only if you're expecting something else. It's not. I promise, it's all right.'

It was just one of the many topics concerning Jake that it was better to avoid. It seemed to bother me more than it bothered him, so why argue about it? I forced myself to let it go. 'Hey, I got you something for tonight.' I was happy to change the subject completely. His worn T-shirt made me remember. I grabbed my purse and pulled out a rolled shirt. 'It's one of the designs they're selling tonight, but I did some extra stuff to it.'

'Thanks, babe.' He put it on right away. 'What do you think?'

'Sexy.' It was a good fit. I had never seen him in anything but the boring neutrals, the nice blue shirt (which was the fanciest clothing in his wardrobe), and his motocross outfit.

We got preoccupied with kissing for a while, and I almost didn't want to leave. Despite the general sterility of his house, it was the most alone and relaxed we'd been able to be together. But he was intent that we get to the Folly gig early.

'It's your big night, Bren.' He pushed up off the bed and crooked his finger at me.

'It's actually Folly's big night,' I pointed out, still sprawled lazily, my head nestled in his pillows.

'Made even bigger by the fact that everyone will be wearing your T-shirts and it will be super cool. So let's go.'

I groaned as he pulled me up off the bed, and laughed when he threw me over his shoulder. It looks thrilling in the movies, but it's actually pretty uncomfortable.

'Ow!' I whined. 'Your bony shoulder is digging into my gut.'

'Then you should have gotten your lazy ass up,' Jake said, still bumping me along, out the door and up the driveway. He flipped me into his arms like a baby and put me down in the truck. 'Oof. I'm glad I lift my dirt bike so much. You're heavier than you look.'

I jabbed his arm. 'You're just weak. Maybe you should do a sport. You're becoming a big lazy driver.'

'I don't have time for sports.' He pulled my seatbelt across my lap and clipped the buckle. 'Unless you consider pumpkin-chucking a sport.'

'How did I wind up with such a hick for a boyfriend?' I griped happily. Jake laughed as he started the engine and we passed a few minutes with the only sound the constantly changing radio station, since I couldn't find anything I liked. When Jake spoke next, he brought up what I knew had been bothering him all day.

'So, did Saxon bug you at the track?' His mouth was a tight, hard line.

'No.' I thought about Saxon walking away from the track after waiting for Jake to acknowledge him somehow. 'Jake, I know he's been crazy, but he really does care about you.'

'You're getting sucked in again, Bren,' Jake warned. 'Don't fall for his shit. How many times does he have to screw you over before you believe that it really is all an act?'

I nodded. 'You're right,' I said, even though I didn't think that at all. 'It's just, he was really concerned about you at the race.'

'He was probably praying I broke my neck on every jump so he could steal you away from me and have his wicked way with you.' He looked at me and wiggled his eyebrows like an evil villain in a bad play.

'Whatever,' I sighed. 'I was there. I saw him.'

'Saw him putting on a convincing concerned-friend act. Trust me, he doesn't give a shit about me. He was the one who gave me my first cigarette when I was ten.'

'You smoked?'

'Yeah, like a chimney, right up till I stopped hanging out with Saxon. He poured me my first shot, hooked me up with the first older girl I was . . . uh . . .

with.' He blushed a little. 'Just because he's interested in hanging around you to get close to me doesn't mean he really gives a crap, OK? He's sneaky, but you're smart. Don't let him trip you up.'

Jake had been so understanding the night before after my humiliating confession, I felt I had to drop it, even if I thought there was something that just didn't make sense.

The Folly concert was being held at a local bar called the Red Pony. It was a pretty sad bar, but it had a stage and it was available. By the time Jake and I pulled up, there was already a nearly full parking lot.

And everywhere you looked, people were wearing my T-shirts!

I saw Kelsie working a table with a set of cardboard boxes marked 'S', 'M', 'L' and 'XL'. I dragged Jake with me and we looked at the piles of my designs.

'That's cool.' Jake picked one up and held it in front of him. 'What do you think?'

'I think you're already wearing that shirt, you adorable fool,' I said cheerfully.

He kissed me. 'You are both an entrepreneur and a sweet, sweet woman.'

'That's me.' I kissed him back.

'Brenna, these are selling like crazy!' Kelsie called. 'We only have five medium shirts left!'

'How many did we start with?' I ran my hand over the piles of T-shirts that were being snatched up right in front of my eyes.

'Seventy!' she called back.

Wow! Kelsie was busy, so Jake and I made our way to the Red Pony's entrance when my cell beeped. I checked the text and held Jake up. 'It's my friend Devon.' We went to the parking lot where Devon was getting dropped off by his mother, who was still yelling cautions after him as he walked towards us. I waved, and she stopped yelling, then waved back. Maybe it relaxed her, because she pulled out and left.

'Hey, Devon!' I gave him a quick, awkward hug. 'How are you?'

'Good.' His smile was a little strained.

'This is Jake, my boyfriend,' I introduced.

'Hey, man.' Jake stuck his hand out. They shook.

'Wow, Brenna, everyone's got one of your T-shirts on.' Devon craned his neck and looked around.

'Cool, right?' Jake squeezed me around the waist. 'Do you guys want to go in?'

'Let me call Mom first.' Devon's crazy mother had reminded me of my own sweet, sane one waiting back at home. I called and told her about the shirts, and she was excited for me and told me to have fun and call later. I fully appreciated my mother's coolness, especially after I witnessed Devon's mom's relative insanity.

We headed to the door, paid our five dollars, got our red wristbands and headed in. If you were old enough to drink, you got a green wristband, but Folly's fan base was relatively young, so those were few and far between. In the handful of minutes I left Jake to go and get Kelsie, who had just been relieved from sales duty, a pretty brunette with a green wristband was flirting outrageously with him.

Kelsie shook her head. 'Jake is one serious girl magnet.' Jake was pointedly ignoring the girl and trying to talk to Devon. 'Is that Devon Conner?' Kelsie asked.

'Yeah.' I watched them talk, and it looked like Devon was loosening up. Maybe. A little.

'He's such a nice guy. He helped me with my algebra worksheet the other day in lunch,' she said.

'Yeah, he's cool.' I smiled when I heard Devon's donkey bray of a laugh and saw Jake join in laughing with him.

'Chris is so excited,' she gushed. 'Ooh, you're wearing my necklace! It goes perfectly with your eyes. You look so cute!'

'You, too,' I said. 'Hey, Jake had a big race today, and he won.'

'Motocross?' Kelsie looked at me with surprise.

'Yeah. It was actually really fun to watch. I didn't think I'd like it as much as I did.'

'Was it the Vernon Valley Amateur?' Kelsie asked. 'Did Jake win a set there?'

'Yeah. You know it?' Kelsie's eyes were wide. I really wished I knew more about racing. 'He was amazing. Is it a big deal?'

'I think so. My little brother said it's the biggest in the northeast. I don't think it's big money or anything, but it's super-competitive.'

I was impressed all over again. 'He's full of surprises.' The group of girls around him was growing. 'I think I have to go before he gets mauled.'

I made my way back to Jake and Devon. Devon was talking to a group of kids from Frankford, and Jake looked relieved when he saw me.

'Brenna!' The girls around him scowled and moved aside.

'I was talking to Kelsie.' I elbowed past his admirers and slid next to him. 'She said your race was a pretty big thing. Like entire northeast big.'

He smiled. 'Maybe a little.'

'You could have explained a little more about it to me.' I narrowed my eyes at him.

'You're never interested in talking when I have you alone,' he said and kissed me quiet.

'Jake!' It was a whiny voice. And there was corset girl. Was she impervious to New Jersey's cold autumn chill? Her deep tan was also strangely at odds with the rest of the pasty-looking crowd. 'I saw your win,' she said, ignoring me. 'That was a pretty incredible jump in the last leg.'

'Thanks, Shayla.' Jake pushed me forward a little, like he wanted to make sure she couldn't possibly miss me. Or like he was using me as his personal anti-groupie shield. 'I really want you to meet my girl-friend, Brenna.'

'Hey,' she said to me with a little eye-roll, then immediately looked back at Jake. 'So, are you heading to Digman's for the next set? I guess it's a little point-less since you already placed at Vernon, but it's going to be fun and everyone's excited to see you race again. Me especially.'

Jake shrugged. 'Brenna and I will talk about it. Good seeing you, Shay.' And he moved me toward the stage. 'Sorry. Just a girl from my distant past who never seems to go away.'

'It's all right.' I put on my best tolerant face. 'Sussex County must be pretty full of girls from your past.' I smiled for him and he relaxed a little.

That moment, Folly came out on the stage. The crowd went crazy, stomping, cheering and calling out.

The lead guitarist leaned over the microphone. He had a blue Mohawk and enough facial piercings to set off a metal detector from five feet away. 'Hey, guys. We're Folly, and we just want to say thank you for everyone who came to support us tonight.' The crowd screamed and cheered. 'And we see a lot of Folly T-shirts out there. We want to give a special shout out to Brenna Blixen. Brenna, are you here?'

'Right here!' Jake yelled and pointed to me.

Folly's lead guitarist smiled a devilish smile. 'She is hot,' he said to Chris, and there were hoots and whistles from the crowd. 'Thanks for the designs. We sold out, but there will be more at our next show at The Lodge in Vernon next month. All right, let's get this started. We're dedicating this one to our man Devon, a true appreciator of music.' They started to play the opening strains of 'Slow Dog', and the cheers almost drowned out the beginning of the song.

I had never been to a gig before, and it was amazing how alive and electric it felt. There were so many people crammed in a space that wasn't designed to be so packed. A lot of the people sang along to the chorus, shouting the lyrics and dancing to the music.

Jake wrapped his arms around me and leaned close to my ear.

'So, the guitar guy likes you,' he said.

407

I turned toward him, wrapped my arms around his waist and squeezed. 'You and I are both hot commodities in Sussex County, I guess.'

'In a few years, you and me, we'll be out of here for good. Just the two of us, no groupies, no Mohawked rockers.' He kissed me again, and I felt a shock at his words.

Of course, they were probably just words that he said to add to my joke. Was he really thinking that far into the future? If I went for the realist's perspective, I had known Jake for only a month. That seemed the most shocking fact of all. Was it possible that just a few weeks ago I had lived an entirely Jake-free existence? My heart ached at the thought. He felt like he had always been somewhere in my life, waiting.

I turned back toward the stage and leaned on Jake. I moved my head to the side and breathed the smell of him in. I loved him. I loved Jake Kelly so much it made my heart thump. I stood in his arms through the first set, then Folly broke for an intermission. Jake offered to get me a soda, and I saw some guys come over and start talking to him. I was so busy spying on Jake, I didn't notice that someone else had approached. Saxon grabbed my arm and pulled me towards the door.

'C'mon,' he said over his shoulder.

'No way, Saxon. No!' I dragged my feet. 'Jake will be looking for me.'

'Five minutes,' Saxon pleaded.

Against my better judgment, I followed him into the cold night. 'What do you want?' I still felt drawn to him. Even though he had abused my trust and Jake's, there was something good at his core that made me want to give him another second chance, every single time I saw him.

'I have a confession, Brenna.' He ran his hands through his hair over and over and breathed hard. I looked at his bruised, scarred face. 'I have never told anyone this, but I need to tell someone. I need to get this off my chest, finally. I need to tell you.' He stopped and grabbed my arm again, leading me even further away from the din of the Red Pony.

'Saxon, what is it?' I shivered. He moved to pull me into his arms, but I backed away quickly. He kicked at the stones on the drive, grunting with frustration.

'I don't know why everything has to be so fucked up.' He ran his hands through his hair again until it stuck up at slightly crazy angles. 'I fucked up with Jake, I can't leave you alone, and now I'm going to tell you this.'

I backed away again. 'Don't tell me.' My voice was smaller than I wanted it to be. 'Whatever it is, I don't need to know.'

'I have to. It's more than I can stand.' He walked over to me and grabbed my shoulders hard. 'When I see the look on your face when you see me, I want to break something, Brenna. But you might understand this whole shitty situation better if you just know this one thing.'

I wanted to bolt, but there was something in his black eyes that was desperate. He fumbled in his back pocket and pulled out his old leather wallet. He took out a faded, frayed-edged picture and handed it to me wordlessly.

It was the spiky-haired boy from Jake's Polaroid. So that *was* Saxon. There was a woman with his black hair and eyes and his wicked-sexy smile. And there was a man.

Who looked exactly like Jake would look in a few years.

The lights and sounds and cold of the night all faded away. Jake's father was in a family picture with Saxon? Had there been an affair? What did this mean?

'Who is in this picture?' I traced my finger over the three faces lightly.

'You tell me,' he ordered, his voice hard.

'The kid is you,' I identified. He nodded. 'The woman is your mother?' He nodded again. 'The man is Jake's father?'

Saxon's eyes were pain ravaged. He just shook his head. 'Not exactly.'

I breathed a sigh of relief. 'Who is he? Jake's uncle?'

Saxon let out a shaky breath. 'That asshole in the picture is *my* father, Brenna. And he had an affair with Jake's mother. Jake doesn't know.'

I held the picture tighter. 'The man who Jake lives with is not his father?'

'No.' Saxon shoved his hands into his pockets. 'My father got Jake's mom pregnant and she married someone else, and pretended that the baby was that guy's.'

'That means you and Jake . . .'

'Are half-brothers.' Saxon finished my sentence and hung his head. 'I've known for years. I swear I tried to be a good brother to him. My father never acknowledged him. When he split, he told me to look out for Jake. I just wound up screwing it up, though.'

I looked at Saxon, not sure what to say. It explained the undefined thing I saw when Saxon looked at Jake. It was love.

'Are you going to tell Jake?' I looked down at the picture again.

Saxon shook his head. 'No. I'm telling you. That's it. And I don't really want you telling Jake. This stays between us.'

'No.' I put my foot down. 'No more me and you, Saxon. You need to tell Jake. You're brothers. He needs to know. From you.'

'Why? So he has more people to hate for letting him down. If I'm just his friend, it doesn't have to rip him up that I suck. But if I'm his brother? And the guy who's raising him, he's a cold robot, but he's around, buying Jake a damn flashlight every Christmas. What about a father who wouldn't even acknowledge him? It's better if I keep it between you and me, Brenna.'

'But why me?' I searched his face, his deep black eyes brimming with sadness. 'Why not just keep it to yourself?'

'Because I know you'll understand.' He put his hand out for the picture, but when I offered it, he grabbed my hand instead. He ran his fingers along my skin and closed his eyes while he took a deep breath. He stuffed the picture back in his wallet, hidden from view once more. 'I know you see the good in me, even when no one else does. And that's damn rare. If Jake wasn't my brother, I'd do everything I could to win you from him. But I've screwed him enough. He deserves you. I know you two are good for each other.' Saxon tilted his head back and exhaled a long breath of air. 'That doesn't mean I can accept you hating me. I knew you could see that I cared about him, but you didn't understand my motives. I just want you to know I'm not a complete fuck-up.'

He pulled me close and I let him. His eyes were completely black and deep and bright with despair. 'Let me hold you. Just for a minute, Brenna, let me feel like a fucking human.'

I put my arms around him and let him crush me, the air squeezed out of my body by his grip. He rubbed his face on my hair, breathed it in and groaned a little before he broke his hold and held his hands up like he was surrendering. 'Go,' he said gruffly. 'Go back to him.'

He started to walk away. 'Saxon!' He turned. 'Where are you going?'

'I need to think.' Then his wicked smile was back. 'But I'm not very good at that. So I'll probably end up drunk and brawling. Just keep your fingers crossed that I get laid, too.'

I held up my hand, middle finger twisted over my index finger.

'You know I love you best when you're a bitch, Brenna.' He slid into his car and peeled away without a backward glance.

I watched until the dust died down. I didn't even notice Jake behind me.

'Jesus, Bren! You scared the hell out of me!' His eyes

were worried. He took off his baseball cap and ran a hand through his hair. 'Tell me before you leave, OK? I'm not even going to tell you what was going through my head.'

I threw myself into Jake's arms and held him tight. 'I'm sorry. I'm really sorry.'

'It's all right, Bren.' He tilted my face and kissed me softly. 'What were you doing out here?'

I looked at his gray eyes, his crooked eyetooth, his kind smile, and I loved him just the way he was. I didn't know if I'd be able to keep something so big from him forever, but for this night, I just wanted to be with him and enjoy the moment.

'Just thinking,' I lied.

'What about?'

'How today was such a huge day for both of us. So much has happened so fast, it's just a lot to take in.' That was true. I was glad to see that he smiled, looking relieved at my confession.

'We're good together, Bren.' He looked into my eyes. 'I think it's just going to get better.'

'It will,' I said, with so much authority I nearly convinced myself.

Epilogue

I woke up the morning of October 11th way earlier than I should have. Mostly because Jake was stretched across my bed, his leg draped over my mine heavily. I ran my fingers through his hair, newly cut in preparation for my birthday celebration. Thorsten was taking us all into the city for lunch at a famous Chinese restaurant, and then we were going to the Met, since Mom and I had been dying to go since we got back to the States and Jake had never been. Jake had parked down the road and sneaked in to sleep with me, just as a treat, just for my birthday. He had to leave early so he could get home and get ready to drive back before my parents came in to wake me.

'Wake up, Jake,' I whispered.

He cracked one eye open. 'Hey, pretty girl.' He pulled me into his arms and kissed me all over my face and neck.

'You've got to go. It's dawn.'

'Happy birthday,' he stalled.

'Thanks.' I put my hand over his face, spread my fingers and looked at his features from behind the bars I created. He kissed my palm and fingers, then leaned over the bed and grabbed his jeans.

'Good.' Even though it wasn't really good, part of me felt relieved. He had to leave before he got caught. 'No more fooling around . . .'

He came back up with a tiny wrapped box. Even the paper was great – bright pink with tiny gold stars all over it. There was a miniature gold bow on the top.

'Jake! You didn't have to.'

'Just open it.' He kissed the tip of my nose.

I ripped the paper away and took the lid off the box. I removed the cotton wool, and sitting there was a silver cursive 'B' pendant on a black ribbon with three teardrop pearls hanging off it.

'Remember that book about Anne Boleyn we read? Well, you read and I listened to?' he asked eagerly. 'This is the necklace she had in the movie.'

'You got me an Anne Boleyn necklace?' I asked, not exactly sure how I felt about it. 'She, uh, got her head chopped off, Jake.'

'Yeah, I know. But she was badass and smart and sexy, so I thought we could just forget the whole beheading and focus on the good stuff. And your first and last name start with "B".'

Just the fact that he had put that much thought into it made it awesome even if I would think about being beheaded every time I wore it. 'Thank you, Jake.' I wrapped my arms around him. 'It's so beautiful and literary, and historically feminist. I love it!'

He picked up the ribbon and tied it around my neck. I got out of bed and looked at it in the mirror in my room and instantly loved it. Maybe I would think about going after what I wanted and being kickass when I wore it instead of beheadings after all.

'I'm glad you like it.' He grinned. 'I'm sorry, baby, but I have to leave now.'

He pulled on his jeans and his boots, grabbed his shirt and pulled it over his head, and threw on his jacket.

'I can't wait for today. Don't be nervous.' I grabbed him around the hips.

'I'll wear my blue shirt,' he promised.

'I love you.' I kissed him hard. 'I love you, love you.'

He laughed. 'I love you, Bren. I'll be back in four hours.'

He jumped out the window and went running. I stuck my head out and watched him. I was about to snuggle back into my warm, if empty, bed, when I saw a package wrapped in brown paper on the windowsill. I smiled. Jake must have left something else.

I pulled the package in and unwrapped it. It was a hardcover copy of *Sense and Sensibility* by Jane Austen. I'd read *Pride and Prejudice* after *Lord of the Flies* and fell head over heels for Austen, but hadn't had a chance to read *Sense and Sensibility* yet. I flipped it open, but the inscription was in a precise, neat script that wasn't Jake's. I knew exactly whose it was.

Blix,
It's the great underestimated Austen. I like it because the people who should end up together do, romance be damned. Willoughby's a douchebag, but he truly loves Marianne right to the bottom of his sucky black soul. Doesn't matter. Austen knows that you end up with the person who makes sense, not the asshole.
Stick to Austen's plan.
Happy birthday.
Love,
Saxon

My heart pumped and my head spun. I had to double clutch, two breaths in, one out, two in, one out.

Without really thinking about it, I sat on the bed and opened the book. I was reading when Mom and Thorsten burst in, hours later, to wish me a happy birthday.

'Brenna!' Mom rushed to the bed. 'Why are you crying sweetheart?'

'Just a book,' I sobbed.

Mom tilted her head and looked at the cover. '*Sense and Sensibility?* Honey, it's a romance. I don't remember anything sad in the book.'

'I'm not done yet.' I wiped my tears away, embarrassed now. 'Mom, why doesn't Willoughby end up with Marianne?'

'It will ruin the book, honey.' Mom stared at me with wide eyes.

'Please.' I grabbed her arm.

She sat on the bed and swept my hair back off my neck, kissing me softly. 'He makes her believe he has serious intentions for her, then gets forced to choose to be poor with her or marry a woman he doesn't love for money. He marries the one he doesn't love.'

'So he was just a huge jerk?' I said, calming down.

'Yes.' Mom tilts her head and considers her answer. 'But he did honestly love Marianne; he just chose the person who was right for him realistically and let her marry the person who was right for her. He realized that being in love wasn't all there was. He had to face certain realities.' Mom sighed. 'I wrote a great paper my junior year about that book.' She looked dreamy.

'I'm sorry I was so weird.' I rubbed my eyes and gave them a watery smile.

'That's OK, baby. When you're ready, Thorsten is making his famous waffles.' She kissed my forehead and left. I heard her talking about 'Brenna's emotions when she has her period . . .' as she walked down the hall with Fa.

I would have to finish the book later and figure it out for myself. I closed it with a snap. There was a big difference between fiction and real life. I could cry all I wanted over Austen, but thinking about the reality of my upcoming day made me smile despite all of the bullshit.

Acknowledgements

First and foremost, I want to thank my strong, smart, fierce mother. Her maniacal faith in my ability to do absolutely anything is sometimes overwhelming and always encouraging; especially when I start, I get the urge to curl into fetal position and eat massive amounts of comfort pudding. I give her all the love and respect in the world.

And thanks to my baby sister, Katie, who never pulled a single punch in her young, mean life. Especially the day she ripped that 'Do you want to be a writer?' leaflet from an Avon novel back when we were in high school, raised her perfect eyebrow, and stuffed the page in my hand with a single, fateful remark: 'You could write a better book than this, so you should.'

I want to thank my brothers Jack and Zachary for supporting me even if they act like books will burn them if they hold them for too long. Thank you to my 'baby' sisters Jessica, Jillian, and Jamie, who make me laugh and remind me of what it was like to grow up in NJ. Thanks to my dad, who constantly calls and updates me on any book/writing/publishing news he hears on NPR. I'd like to thank my grandparents for calling me and nagging me to get my work out there or just generally encouraging me so I could make some money and stop mooching off them. But also, of course, because they love me and think I'm a decent writer. Thank you to all my family who have cheered me on and believed in me, no matter how obnoxiously lost in my own fictional world I've been. I want to thank those friends who inspired the friendships in this book and still warm my cockles (Ronan, Jessie, Kimmy, Liz, Jesse, Aaron, Ellen, Lou, Fran, Frank, Chloe, Elisa, Lauren, Biffy, Holly, Jen K . . .)

An unimaginably huge debt of thanks goes out to the long line of teachers who loved and nourished my voracious little reader-mind: Mr Post, Mrs Schroth, Mr Flynn, Mrs White, Ms Mattil, Ms Hassenplug, Mr Bauer. Every single one of you swept me up in reading and inspired me to write more. Or less, if I was being too longwinded. Thank you for your red pens, your passion for words, and your patience with my sometimes irritating exuberance.

I could not have done this without my best friend

and amazing beta reader/editor, Alexa Offenhauer Thompson. She untangled my crazy sentences, updated my 'nineties-era fashion nightmares, and rooted for the book with her entire, brilliant heart from day one. A huge thanks also goes out to the hugely talented YA authors Caryn Caldwell and Angie Stanton for being so sweet but firm as critiquers, Tamar Goetke for reluctantly embracing her inner teen and being my meanest beta, and Brittany Hansen for her uncontrolled squeals of girlish delight. I tucked them in my head for ear cleanings and to give me happy courage when I just wanted to sink into a bottomless pit and stop this writing madness.

Huge, professional-but-enthusiastic kisses to the Dystel and Goderich team! Every single interaction I have with them makes me thankful for the day I got Jane's exciting call all the way from lovely New York City. Thank you, Lauren, for calling when she probably just wanted to shoot a quick email, because she is amazing and always knocks it out of the park with her empathy, encouragement, and professionalism.

Enormous international thanks to the amazing crew at Random House UK! The day I opened the email from Lauren Buckland was the beginning of a journey so cool, I still want to pinch myself every day. From cover designers to editors to agents, every single person has made this one of the most amazing experiences of my life. Thank you to Carmen McCullough, who's always happy to ogle new covers and email me a million times a day when I'm full of questions . . . her patience and humor have been a daily joy.

Thank you to my band of wild naked ewoks. May we put on our monocles and ride our unicorns into the sunset holding hands, no matter how dangerous an idea that may seem. You ladies have cheered me on, encouraged me, advised me, and been the net that let me close my eyes and leap over and over again into a thousand scary new challenges, and I hope you know how covered in slobbery kisses each one of you will be every time I see your lovely faces (which I know will be more and more often in the coming years).

Thank you to Steph. You had my heart in your hands when you compared Brenna to Jessica Darling, and your friendship has been a crème brûlée buffet that gets more delicious every passing second. I don't even try to resist with you.

Last, but never least, thank you to my girl, Amelia, who I hope grows up crazier and more amazing than any girl I could imagine in any book . . . but not too fast. And a big, wet, sloppy thank you to my husband, Frank, my love, my best friend, and the coolest guy

I've ever known. His awesomeness has inspired some great fictional romance.

And a huge thank you to my readers, bloggers, book enthusiasts, reviewers, and word junkies! This world would be a cold and dreary place without your little notes of encouragement, emails, screams for the next book, and general total awesomeness on every conceivable level. I hope Brenna, Jake and Saxon meant as much to you as they do to me.

Turn up the heat with Liz Reinhardt . . .

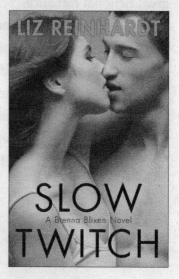

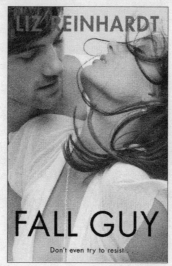